The Martian Epic

The Martian Epic

The Titans of the Heavens
The Agony of the Earth

by
Octave Joncquel & Théo Varlet

Translated by
Brian Stableford

A Black Coat Press Book

ISBN 978-1-934543-41-2. First Printing. August 2008. Published by Black Coat Press, an imprint of Hollywood Comics.com, LLC, P.O. Box 17270, Encino, CA 91416. All rights reserved. Except for review purposes, no part of this book may be reproduced or transmitted in any form or by any means, electronic or mechanical, including photocopying, recording, or by any information storage and retrieval system, without permission in writing from the publisher. The stories and characters depicted in this novel are entirely fictional. Printed in the United States of America.

Introduction

The work here translated as *The Martian Epic, L'épopée martienne*, was originally published in Amiens in two volumes, as *Les Titans du ciel* and *L'agonie de la Terre*, in 1921 and 1922, by Edgar Malfère. The published versions were the work of Théo Varlet, an author already well-known for his poetry, literary criticism and translations from English, who had previously published short fiction but was making his first excursion into the novel. The works appeared as a collaboration, however, with Varlet's name in second place because they were based on two previously-written manuscripts by Octave Joncquel, "*Les derniers Titans*" and "*La fin des mondes.*"

Little is known about Joncquel, although an article signed "Alfu" appended to a 1996 reprint of the portmanteau *Epic* reproduces a colorful description of him recorded by Jean Garel in the *Bulletin de la Societé Jules Verne* in 1983, which represents him as a well-known "character" in Amiens. Garel describes Joncquel as a "Bohemian," tall and strong, but also child-like, who dressed strangely and earned a living of sorts by doing odd jobs, especially working as a sandwich-board man. He appears, however, to have been a knowledgeable man and a voracious reader; he thought very highly of Jules Verne, who had once been Amiens' most famous citizen. Indeed, he may well have relocated to Amiens in honor of Verne, having been a Picard by birth. He seems to have been an enthusiastic lover of the entire genre founded by Verne, which would later be called "science fiction;" his Bohemian affectations extended to writing numerous novels, most, if not all, of a bold sciencefictional stripe, for which he sought in vain for a publisher for many years.

When Edgar Malfère first set up shop in Amiens, in 1920, Joncquel gave him all his manuscripts, approximately 15 in number, for consideration. Malfère declared them unpublishable, but not uninteresting; he volunteered to look for someone who might be able to knock them into shape. Malfère then gave one of the manuscripts to Théo Varlet, with whom he had previously worked on other projects, and whose short story collection *La Bella Venere* [the name is that of a boat] (1920) had been one of the first books he issued after moving to Amiens. Varlet was then resident in the small southern coastal town of Cassis, but he took annual summer holidays in the village of Saint-Valery, on the Somme estuary, not far from Amiens; it was probably there that he began work on the collaborative project.

Whether Joncquel knew Varlet is unclear, but they had both been born in the same region and might conceivably have been old acquaintances. The London Library's copies of *Les Titans du ciel* and *L'agonie de la terre* are both inscribed—to the writer Edmund Gosse—and both inscriptions are signed "Octave

Joncquel and Théo Varlet," but the entire signature is rendered in the same hand, which must be Varlet's. (The first inscription reads "Hommage à Monsieur Edmund Gosse, en souvenir de feu *La Plume*, ce livre parti de Wells" [A tribute to Edmund Gosse, in memory of the late *La Plume*, this book based on Wells]. *La Plume* was a short-lived periodical and publishing imprint, operated by Colette's husband "Willy," to which Varlet and Gosse had both contributed. The London Library, unusually, has a run of *La Plume*, which was presumably also donated by Gosse.)

The arrangement between Malfère, Joncquel and Varlet lasted long enough for the former to publish both parts of the *Martian Epic* and for Varlet to complete an adaptation of a third Joncquel manuscript, "*La terre océane*" [*The Ocean-Covered World*], but at that point, it broke down. Alfu suggests that the cause of the breakdown was that Varlet spent his 1922 summer holiday in Saint-Valery working on a text with another author, André Blandin, in preference to revising one of Joncquel's, and that Joncquel took extreme offense, but I do not know what the evidence is that supports this interpretation of events. What is on record, however—carefully summarized, in detail, by Alfu—is that Joncquel initiated a lawsuit against Malfère, on the grounds that Malfère had made an oral agreement with him to pay him a royalty of five per cent (half the conventional amount) on copies of the books that were sold, which the publisher had failed to honor. Joncquel claimed that this had ruined his "literary career" and demanded damages of 30,000 francs, as well as the royalties he was allegedly owed.

Malfère, who had copyrighted the two published volumes in his own name, presumably having paid Varlet a fixed fee for the revision work, defended the case on the grounds that what Théo Varlet had done with the manuscripts Joncquel had provided, was to write entirely new texts recycling the fundamental ideas, while retaining hardly any of Joncquel's actual text—so that, in effect, Varlet, not Joncquel, was the actual author of the two published books.

Perhaps unsurprisingly, given the relative social status of the two men, the court sided with Malfère. Joncquel lost the case, and it was he who was ordered to pay damages to Malfère, to the modest but doubtless deeply wounding extent of 500 francs. Malfère was, however, forbidden to publish the third volume already completed by Varlet, or to proceed with a fourth, "*La guerre des microbes*" [*War of the Microbes*], whose manuscript had also been forwarded to Varlet. These, along with all Joncquel's other manuscripts, were returned to their author, and nothing more was heard of any of them. What became of them—and, for that matter, of Joncquel—remains unknown. This loss must be regarded as unfortunate; however inept Joncquel might have been as a writer, he certainly seems to have possessed an imagination that was somewhat ahead of his time.

As a typical science fiction fan, long before there was any such thing, Joncquel presumably believed, passionately and perhaps justifiably, that the essence of such fiction is the ideas it deploys, and that matters of narrative method and literary style are secondary issues of no great significance. He presumably went to his grave believing that he had been cruelly ripped off, and that it was his ideas, rather than Varlet's literary polish, that rendered the *Martian Epic* interesting. There is, of course, no way for modern readers to assess the relative contributions of the two writers, but it seems likely, given that the narrator, Léon Rudeaux, is so obviously a stand-in for Varlet,[1] that the latter was introduced, along with his "love interest," by Varlet to make a text that might have started out as a conspicuously distanced imaginary history far more intimate and more readable. The second volume, into much of whose action Rudeaux is very awkwardly intruded, although that does not inhibit his narrative's dogged self-obsession, does read as if the intrusion might have been a daring improvisation.

Alfu notes that Malfère stated in court that Varlet had thoroughly altered the plots and modified the sequence of events of both published volumes, specifically observing that Varlet had only taken "a single amusing scene" from "*La fin des mondes*" in compiling *L'agonie de la Terre*. As well as the narrator, Varlet probably contributed the anti-Soviet rhetoric, and certainly added some of the settings—including his home-town of Cassis, with which Joncquel can hardly have been familiar. There are, however, several significant elements in the portmanteau text with which Joncquel and Varlet must have been equally familiar, and in which both must have been keenly interested, including its rapt fascination with astronomical science, its extrapolation and theorization of the pattern of contemporary technological development, its intricate relationship to previous scientific romance, and its complex attitude to war. In these respects, the books are surely a true collaboration, reflective of an authentic and productive meeting of minds.

Given that Joncquel handed over some 15 manuscripts to Malfère in 1920, we cannot be entirely sure when "*Les derniers Titans*" and "*La fin des mondes*" were written. It is possible that they might have been penned closer to the date of the text that inspired them—H. G. Wells' *The War of the Worlds* (1898)— than to the date of their eventual publication, but that seems unlikely. No matter how carefully one strips the narrative flesh back to its bones, however, the two stories told in the portmanteau novel seem to be very obviously, and quite painfully, based on the recent experience of the Great War of 1914-18, which had not yet acquired the name of World War I. Indeed, there is a sense in which the imaginary history of the two volumes can be seen as a repeated echo of that war, attempting to dramatize, in no uncertain terms, the nowadays-oft-quoted dictum that "those who fail to learn from history are condemned to repeat it, first as tragedy and then as farce."

---

[1] Varlet's own first name was Léon and the pun linking "Varlet" to "Rudeaux" is obvious in both French and English.

It is not impossible that Joncquel already had the requisite attitude of mind before 1914, given that one of the authors whose work he seems to have admired was Albert Robida, the pacifist author of the parodic illustrated future history *La guerre au Vingtième siècle* (1883; text tr. as "*War in the Twentieth Century*"), but the likelihood is that the two published volumes were based on the most recent, and least Vernian, of Joncquel's abundant stock of manuscripts. At any rate, the *Martian Epic* is, in its most fundamental essence, a "Martial Epic," its epic dimension echoing as well as subverting the central concern of all epics of warfare, from the *Iliad* onwards. All such works, arguably, depict brutish men striving to sustain the absurd pretense that there is something noble and moral in human warfare, which makes it worthier than a mere egomaniac preference for behaving like rabid dogs, but Joncquel and Varlet attempt to take that principle to its ultimate extreme, as well as breaking it down by cynical analysis, and certainly achieve a success of sorts.

In this respect, there is no doubt that *Les Titans du ciel* and *L'agonie de la Terre* were the product of the deep disenchantment that was the immediate emotional aftermath of World War I. They are saturated with the awful shock of that war, and the moral desperation that it engendered. Whatever the initial internal dynamic of Joncquel's manuscripts might have been, the thrust of Varlet's reconstituted narrative is a gradual but implacable movement towards the absurd and the surreal; a bitterly inexorable transformation of clinical descriptions of destruction into sarcastic black comedy, groping towards extremes that imaginative fiction, even in France, had not attained or even attempted, before.

Although there is nothing quite like the *Martian Epic* in the Wellsian fiction that was written in Britain, Varlet's text does have some clear and definite affinities with two near-contemporary apocalyptic romances, Edward Shanks' *The People of the Ruins* (1920) and Cicely Hamilton's *Theodore Savage* (1922; revised for US publication as *Lest Ye Die*). Both of those novels partake of the same dumbfounded cynicism and the same resentful nihilism, although they retain a typically British dignity that prevents them from embracing the typically French surrealism and black comedy of the absurd that comes quite naturally to Varlet, as it presumably had to Joncquel.

There are also parallels to be drawn between English and French reactions to the war in terms of an urgent revival of interest in spiritualism, to which literary men were particularly vulnerable—especially if they had lost sons in the war. H. Rider Haggard, Arthur Conan Doyle and Rudyard Kipling were three high-profile victims to hopeful spiritualistic delusion, all of whom incorporated such delusions, fervently and poignantly, into their post-war fiction. In France, however, the relationship between "*spiritisme*" and speculative fiction had much deeper roots and a much more robust supportive tradition, with which Joncquel and Varlet were both familiar, at least via the works of Camille Flammarion and his more recent successors.

The French literary tradition in question is far more elaborate than the tradition of Spiritualism itself, regarding the mere fact of survival after death as trivial and being more concerned with the manner in which afterlives might be organized into some kind of cosmic plan. In particular, French speculative fiction in this vein became fascinated with the notion of "cosmic palingenesis:" the idea of serial reincarnation on different worlds. The notion had first been mooted by the 2nd century Christian apologist Origen, but his insistence on "the plurality of worlds" became unorthodox when it was opposed by St Augustine and was out of fashion for more than 1000 years, until it was revived in the wake of the Copernican Revolution, which reduced the Earth to the status of one planet in a solar family, which then numbered six (or seven, if the Moon was included as a "world").

The idea of cosmic palingenesis was strongly revived, in a specific form that was reproduced in many subsequent French scientific romances, by the astronomer Christian Huygens, in his posthumously-published *Kosmotheoros* (1698; tr. as *Cosmotheoros*), which was rapidly translated into French. A minor literary boom began some 70 years later with the publication of Marie-Anne Roumier's *Voyages de Mylord Céton dans les sept planètes* [*Milord Seaton's Voyages to the Seven Planets*] (1765) and Louis-Sébastien Mercier's "*Nouvelles de la lune*" (1768 in *Songes et visions philosophiques*; tr. as "*News from the Moon*" in the Black Coat Press anthology of that title), assisted by Charles Bonnet's philosophical tract *Palingénésie philosophique* [*The Philosophy of Palingenesis*] (1769).

Other works in this same vein include Nicolas Restif de la Bretonne's *Les posthumes* (written 1788; published 1802), the dialogues making up Camille Flammarion's *Lumen* (1866-1869), Flammarion's best-selling *Uranie* (1889; tr. as *Urania*) and the first winner of the Prix Goncourt—published by Willy under the *La Plume* imprint—*Force ennemie* [*Hostile Force*] (1903) by John-Antoine Nau (Eugène Torquet). Joncquel and Varlet were probably familiar with the entire sequence at second hand, because of the elaborate summary of it provided in Flammarion's *Les mondes imaginaires et les mondes reels* [*Real and Imaginary Worlds*] (1862), which had been revised for a new edition in 1905. Varlet and Joncquel may well have differed somewhat in their attitudes to the fundamental thesis of cosmic palingenesis—Joncquel's second title suggests that he must have been responsible for the notion of the Solar System as a sunwardly-oriented cosmic scale, which comes under threat by virtue of the Martian Mechanists' vulgarization of their own religious creed, while Varlet must have been the author of the sequence describing the more expansive cosmic voyage undertaken by Léon and Raymonde as disincarnate souls—but they certainly seem to have been singing from the same hymn-sheet.

This is, of course, this aspect of the *Martian Epic* that is bound to seem most alien to modern English and American readers, but it is worth noting that it does crop up in English fiction as well, in such novels as Mortimer Collins'

Transmigration (1874), which features a series of incarnations, one of which takes place on Mars. That particular notion was further popularized by Theodore Flournoy's *From India to the Planet Mars* (1900), a report by a psychologist of accounts of past lives "experienced" by a medium, which included an incarnation on Mars. Joncquel and Varlet were not the last writers to use the notion productively in French scientific romance; Varlet's friend, J. H. Rosny aîné (Justin Henri Boëx)—one of the judges who had awarded the Goncourt to Nau—was to develop it in all seriousness in *Les autres vies, les autres mondes* [*Other Lives, Other Worlds*] (1924) and provided a literary dramatization of it in his own Martian fantasy, *Les navigateurs de l'infini* [*Navigators of Infinity*] (1925).

It is not only as an anti-war story that the *Martian Epic* echoes the work of Albert Robida; the story also carries forward another significant tradition of French imaginative fiction with which Robida had involved himself. The tradition in question had been initiated by Léon Gozlan in *Les émotions de Polydore Marasquin* (1856; tr. as *The Emotions of Polydore Marasquin, A Man among the Monkeys* and *Monkey Island*); Robida carried it forward in spectacular style in the first part of his parodic homage to Jules Verne, *Voyages très extraordinaire de Saturnin Farandoul dans les 5 ou 6 parties du monde et dans tous les pays connus et même inconnus de M. Jules Verne* [*The Most Extraordinary Voyages of Saturnin Farandoul in the 5 or 6 Continents, in all the lands known, and even unknown, to Jules Verne*] (1879; first part tr. as "*The Monkey King*" in the Black Coat Press anthology *News from the Moon*). This deeply sarcastic, manifestly absurd and incipiently surreal tradition involves the use of various real and imaginary species of monkeys, especially anthropoid apes, to conduct a sarcastically satirical investigation of the relationship between human beings and the residues of their animal ancestry. Although *L'agonie de la Terre* is not as witty or as focused as its predecessors, in this regard, it certainly takes the tradition forward into new and interesting territory, by virtue of what must surely be a close combination of Joncquel's and Varlet's efforts.

Other works of French scientific romance echoed in the *Martian Epic* include Gustave Le Rouge's two-part Martian adventure comprising *Le prisonnier de Mars* and *La guerre des vampires* (1908-1909; tr. in a Black Coat Press edition as *The Vampires of Mars*). The description of the native Martians—represented in the *Martian Epic*'s plot by the Magi—as winged creatures, who are explicitly likened to bats on several occasions, strongly recalls Le Rouge's Erloor, while the second-volume invasion of psychic vampires is more faintly reminiscent of the invasion sub-plot in Le Rouge's second volume. It is, however, quite likely that Varlet had not read Le Rouge (although Joncquel probably had) and that the echoes retained in the final text were carefully muted. Both men, however, are very likely to have read Guy de Maupassant's brief "*L'Homme de Mars*" (1888; tr. in *News from the Moon* as "*Martian Mankind*"), which similarly features winged Martians and offers a supposedly-rational argument for the likelihood that humanoid inhabitants of Mars might have wings.

Another writer with whom Varlet was undoubtedly familiar and Joncquel may also have read was Claude Farrère (Charles Bargone); Varlet loved Farrère's book of drug stories *Fumée d'opium* (1904; tr. as *Black Opium*)—the self-based protagonist of his story "Messaline" declares that he has "Farrère in his soul"—and had presumable read some of the short metaphysical fantasies later collected in *Où? [Where?]* (1923). The Farrère book whose imagery and sentiments are most likely have influenced the writing of *L'agonie de la Terre* is *Les condamnés à mort* (1920; tr. as *Useless Hands*), a hymn of hate against the inexorable pragmatism and ultimately-brutalizing effects of excessive automation, whose rhetoric is echoed in Varlet's complaints about Martian "*machinisme*" (Mechanization). The groundwork for this rhetoric must, however, have been laid in Joncquel's original texts.

It is these undoubtedly-collaborative aspects of the portmanteau *Martian Epic* that make it highly distinctive as a work of imaginative fiction, and ensure its continued interest to modern science fiction enthusiasts, but it is also worth noting the distinctive variety of philosophical introspection displayed within it, which is probably due almost entirely to Varlet. Especially in its later stages—notwithstanding the blatant artificiality of the author's attempts to spice those stages liberally with conventional melodrama—the "epic" has a deeply personal flavor, which sometimes approaches the stream-of-consciousness effect of "automatic writing" more closely than any of the late *romans feuilletons* beloved by the surrealists. Although it is arguable that Varlet's fondness for verb-less sentences and for continual shifts from past to present tense do not work entirely to the advantage of the novel's coherency or readability, they certainly allow what had probably started out, in Joncquel's version, as a conspicuously distanced narrative, to acquire an intense intimacy.

This intimacy becomes particularly obvious, and markedly odd, at points when the story has manifestly lost all contact with rational plausibility—which it is always rather prone to do. There is a sense which the entire work is so dreamlike that it begs to be treated as a nightmare, progressing unsteadily from horror to absurdity, but it never dissolves to the point at which its protagonist becomes uninvolved, or to the point at which the reader can no longer take his involvement seriously. In that respect, as in those already cited, the work is rather remarkable—and in order for the reader to appreciate that aspect more fully, it is worth going into a little more detail regarding the identity and career of its progenitor, Théo Varlet.

Léon Louis Etienne Théodore Varlet was born on March 12, 1878, in the city of Lille in Northern France. His father was a lawyer, but the wider family was unusually well-off, by virtue of having property and business interests in Russia, and he grew up feeling that there was no particular need for him to make

11

a living. He decided, instead—following in the footsteps of many other fashionably disenchanted sons of the newly-prosperous bourgeoisie—to dedicate himself to a literary vocation. He published poetry and criticism in a wide range of literary periodicals—and, like almost every other person of similar inclination, founded one himself, in collaboration with two friends.

Varlet published four collections of poetry before the outbreak of the Great War, beginning with *Heures et rêves* [*Hours and Dreams*] in 1898. Although he arrived on the scene too late to participate in the Decadent Movement, Charles Baudelaire was one of the more obvious influences on his work, and seems to have served as a powerful role-model in other ways; Varlet cultivated a quasi-Baudelairean reputation as a resolutely determined non-conformist, embracing a fervent pacifism that won him an easy isolation and a certain notoriety when war eventually broke out. He made a particular point of attempting to follow up Baudelaire's "research" in the use of drugs to attain "artificial paradises," reporting extensively on his own experiments with hashish, opium and—most dangerously—ether. In *Au paradis du haschisch; suite à Baudelaire* (1930), he catalogued more than 100 such experiments conducted between 1908 and 1914, including illusory out-of-body experiences that took him into remote regions of outer space and illusions of existing in another person's body—both of which experiences are reproduced in the plot of *L'agonie de la Terre.*

Given Malfère's claim that only one "amusing incident" survived into *L'agonie de la Terre* from "*La fin des mondes,*" it can probably be taken for granted that Varlet's involvement with the entire text of the *Martian Epic* became increasingly more intense as he gradually abandoned the distanced narrative he had been given—which is probably rendered more or les straightforwardly in Chapter I of *Les Titans du ciel*—and that his transfiguration relied increasingly heavily on his own experience of "altered states of consciousness." Although it not only the acknowledged hallucinatory sequences of *Les Titans du ciel* that contribute a striking phantasmagoric feel to that part of the story, there is a sense in which *L'agonie de la Terre* is quite distinct in its narrative method, and can be read in its entirety as a "drug novel."

In spite of Varlet's non-combatant status, the war contrived to ruin him anyway, by making the Russian Revolution possible. The family fortune, which had provided his living expenses while he made little or no money as a writer, went up in smoke, and—like many other initially-vocational writers before him—he was confronted by the necessity of making a living from his pen. Novel writing was, however, something of a last resort; he had to be persuaded into it, and never achieved any conspicuous success in commercial terms. For the remainder of his life, his primary source of income was translation work; from the outset, he made a particular specialty of Robert Louis Stevenson, translating the great majority of the Scot's works of fiction, but he was also the French translator of John Buchan's *The Thirty-Nine Steps,* J. K. Jerome's *Three Men in a Boat* and many other popular works, including novels by Herman Melville,

Rudyard Kipling, Hilaire Belloc and Pearl S. Buck. One thing he never seems to have involved himself with is the translation of British scientific romance, but that was probably not a matter of policy. The decade following the end of the Great War, when Varlet was busiest, was a very thin time for scientific romance; little of note was published and almost none of it was translated into French. By the time the British genre became prolific again, in the 1930s, Varlet had been forced to slow down because of ill health.

The only volume of prose that Varlet published in advance of the *Martian Epic* was the Malfère collection of short fiction, *La Bella Venere*, some of whose contents were recycled in the later and better-known collection *Le dernier satyre* [*The Last Satyr*] (1922). His collaboration with André Blandin, which Octave Joncquel allegedly saw as a betrayal, was a timeslip romance, *La belle Valence* [*Valencia the Beautiful*] (1923). He subsequently published three solo novels, including two scientific romances, the Vernian *Le roc d'or* [*The Golden Rock*] (1927) and the ambitious apocalyptic fantasy *La grande panne* [*The Great Breakdown*] (1930). A further scientific romance, *Aurore Lescure, pilote d'astronef* [*Aurore Lescure, Spaceship Pilot*] was issued posthumously in 1940. He died in Cassis, where he had been based for the greater part of his adult life, on October 6, 1938.

Many aspects of Varlet's own experience are echoed in the *Martian Epic*: his holidays in Saint-Valery, his ambiguous attitude to his native city of Lille, his affection for Cassis and the nearby city of Marseilles, and—perhaps most of all—his fascination for astronomy. Although he undoubtedly knew and respected Flammarion's works, he had a particular fondness for the popular astronomy books written by Abbé Théophile Moreux (1867-1954), the director of an observatory at Bourges, and himself the author of a science fiction novel, *Le Miroir sombre* [*The Dark Mirror*] (1911), and paid homage to his mentor by giving him a thinly-disguised part in the *Martian Epic* as the director of the Mont Blanc Observatory, Abbé Romeux, who eventually becomes the political and spiritual leader of the Last Men.

Although the fall-out of Octave Joncquel's lawsuit prevented the *Martian Epic* from being reprinted, as most of Varlet's subsequent novels were, during his own lifetime, the Amiens-based firm Encrage eventually reissued it, rather handsomely, as the first volume of a projected series, entitled *Oeuvres Romanesques I* (1996)—although no others have appeared as yet. The volume includes a number of essays on the *Martian Epic*, and Varlet's work in general, including the one by Alfu previously quoted, which summarizes what is known of Octave Joncquel's life, and a painstaking analysis of the text and its context by Michel Meurger, "*Les Martiens sont là*" [*The Martians Are Here*]. Meurger wonders in one section of his essay whether the *Martian Epic* might qualify as a *roman à clef*; as well as identifying the model of Romeux as Moreux and emphasizing Varlet's personal reasons for wanting to portray Bolsheviks in the worst possible light, he suggests that Léon Rudeaux's other mentor, Ladislas Wronsky, might have been based on the Polish mystic Josef-Maria Wronski (1776-1853), who is known to have influenced Baudelaire. This seems unlikely, however, and it is more probable that Wronsky, along with Gideon Botram, was inherited from Joncquel's original text. Meurger does not attempt to find a model for the other characters who might conceivably be drawn from life: the ruthlessly pragmatic medical practitioner from Lille, Doctor Goulliard, who is ever-ready to do the "dirty work" for which Abbé Romeux is too squeamish while the Last Men are fighting for survival. Whether it qualifies as a *roman à clef* or not, though, there is no doubt that Varlet threw himself into his work of revision wholeheartedly, and that the published volumes would have been very different had Joncquel's manuscripts been turned over to a more orthodox editor.

This translation has been made from the Encrage edition of 1996, but I have compared that text with the London Library's first editions, and it seems to be identical, save for the omission of the synoptic account of the plot of *Les Titans du ciel* that precedes the first edition of *L'agonie de la Terre* (which I have similarly omitted, for the same reason—that it is unnecessary in an omnibus edition).

The task of translation was not straightforward, but I have attempted to reproduce the net effect of the stylistic flourishes and tics of Varlet's narrative style—the verb-less sentences, the tense shifts, the fondness for *argot*, the inordinately long-winded sentences, and so on—without becoming so stubbornly literal in the replication of grammar and punctuation as to make the text too difficult to read in English. Any work of antique science fiction is bound to cause problems in terms of obsolete and mistaken science, improvised terminology and neologisms; I have tried to resist the inevitable temptation to correct even minor scientific errors, although I have footnoted some of the more egregious mistakes, and I have also tried to resist the similar temptation to translate invented terms in such a way that they seem more prophetic than they are. I have taken a slight liberty in translating *"foudroyant"* as "blaster," as a translator working in 1921-22 would have been unlikely have done, without the example of pulp science fiction cliché to suggest the term, but I have tried to play fair with respect to the various kinds of aircraft and spacecraft described, stubbornly translating *"obus"* as "shell," as it would certainly have been translated in 1922, even when "missile" or "spaceship" would have been warranted by the context, and leaving *"volvite"* alone rather than construing it as "jet" or "rocket-ship." (Varlet has trouble with the volvites himself, initially describing them as a type of *"rotatif"* [helicopter] even though their main distinguishing feature is their lack of rotor blades.)

Brian Stableford

BOOK ONE

THE TITANS OF THE HEAVENS

*"At any rate, whether we expect another invasion or not,
our views of the human future must be greatly modified by these events.
We have learned now that we cannot regard this planet as being fenced in
and a secure abiding-place for Man; we can never anticipate
the unseen good or evil that may come upon us suddenly out of space."*
H. G. Wells
The War of the Worlds

Part One: The Season of the Torpedoes

I. Before the Opposition of Mars in 1978

The Great War, in which the greater number of the civilized nations hurled themselves upon one another at the beginning of the 20th century, had been the last.

One invention, anticipated for some time, combined with the initiative of a few bold intellectuals and men of action, accomplished what the spectacle of death and vain devastation, the declamations of pacifists and the reasoning of economists, had been unable to do. The savage and ferocious instincts that had marked humankind since the legendary Cain with the stigmata of its animal origins, and had hindered the development of intelligence incessantly with its periodic explosions, constraining humans to organize mass murder instead of devoting themselves to the peaceful conquest of the planet, were conclusively strangled and reduced to impotence.

The solution of the "problem of war" was, so to speak, a two-step process. In the beginning, what was known as "universal disarmament" remained utopian, insofar as it was supposed that it had to emerge from mutual good will. The sudden attack in 1932 by the allied Japanese and Chinese, which had militarized 20 years before—the famous "yellow peril" about which the incredulous Europeans joked until the very last minute—almost overwhelmed the West, which had scarcely recovered from its previous war, but the Great Discovery, perfected in the most absolute secrecy by a committee of men who combined scientific genius with the noblest plans for the future of humanity, thwarted the invasion and, at the same time, struck the first mortal blow against militarism.

Controlled at a distance by telemechanical waves, hundreds of "deflagrators"—silent helicopters working in relays—flew over the Asian hordes by night, bathing them in high-frequency electromagnetic radiation. Under that influence, powerful sparks sprang forth in every direction from metal objects. Cartridges exploded spontaneously in their cases, girdling soldiers on the march with fatal fire, and shells exploded in their boxes in every ammunition dump, arsenal and munitions factory. In a few hours, like Sennacherib's army mowed down by the Archangel's flaming sword, the soldiers of the Nipponese and Celestial Empires were strewn in millions upon the plains of Siberia. Europe was saved, without suffering any other losses than a German advance-guard that had already arrived in proximity to the invaders, whose munitions had been subjected, without any differentiation, to the effects of the incendiary waves.

Emboldened by this success and the unique possibilities that it offered, the government of France—or, rather, the CSP (Committee for Science and Progress), whose members had the frightened politicians at their mercy—faithful to the immortal principles of 1789, immediately revived the old idea of general disarmament and, in the name of definitive peace, proposed *urbi et orbi* the immediate creation of a United State of Europe under the nominal presidency of His Highness the Prince of Monaco. The ultimatum, supported by the tacit threat of the teledeflagrators, was accepted at once. All the munitions of every country were transported to remote regions, the areas surrounding the depots was evacuated, and, on a given day, the fatal helicopters circulated silently, under the sole control of directive antennae, along all the meridians and parallels of Europe, which resounded for several hours with millions of explosions of every magnitude.

The United States of Europe was founded once and for all. Gradually, the ex-nations learned to consider themselves as members of the same human fraternity, having no more interest in going to war with one another than the people of the Bouches-du-Rhône against those of the Pas-de-Calais or Londoners against Glaswegians.

It is true that the bellicose instinct occasionally reared up its ugly head, in the beginning. Attenuated by the suppression of firearms, on the powers of which it had supported itself like a millionaire on the virtue of his banknotes, such instinct was nevertheless profoundly anchored in the depths of human nature. Under various pretexts of rivalry, sporadic skirmishes took place—and, since airborne patrols of deflagrators circulated on a regular basis, prohibiting the use of cannons, rifles or revolvers, people fell upon one another with swords, pikes, lances, bows and arrows, as in ancient times.

The CSP, however, soon contrived to suppress these whims, and, by the same token, reduced the scourge of war conclusively. As soon as the news of these disturbances reached the central government, the aerodrome at La Turbie sent a helicopter which descended from the sky above the combatants and hovered a few meters above the ground. A Senegalese leaned out of the cockpit, armed with no other apparent weapon than a sort of white baton, like the ones carried by traffic police, but terminating in a small parabolic reflector. After three instructions had been ignored, he pointed his mysterious staff at the most persistent combatants; a long jet sprang forth and, with a dazzling explosion, those it touched fell where they stood, not so much blown apart as volatilized without the least residue, utterly annihilated.

No resistance was possible. Whether or not they were hypnotized—as some people claimed—these black gendarmes were as devoted to their masters as the famous Assassins once were to the Old Man of the Mountain. Rather than give up the secret of their "blasters," they would blow them up by means of a special trigger, together with themselves and their assistants.

Besides, the submission imposed by this sort of scientific dictatorship was not too hard to bear. The CSP was soon transformed into the Paris-based Terrestrial Directorate. By virtue of the forced incorporation of every country into the United States of the World, it only used its police for the purpose of maintaining the order and peace necessary for the integral development of humankind. The terrible "blasters" themselves were merely the first application of a new principle, whose generalization soon permitted the replacement of coal, oil and other combustibles, saving the enormous human effort employed in their extraction. In effect, the means had been discovered of releasing at will, in a matter of seconds, all the powerful intra-atomic energy embodied in radium. It was anticipated that the same "activator" might be applied to other, less scarce, metals, allowing their energetic produce to be industrialized.

While people waited for this limitless source of energy to make the social problems disappear, their acuity was much diminished. After a few political—or, rather, economic—experiments, stable and definitive peace bore its fruits. Humankind, in its entirety, thus protected against its violent instincts, experienced unprecedented well-being and prosperity, to such a degree that the last survivors of the period preceding the Great War of 1914-18, ever ready to talk up those distant days as a kind of lost paradise, ended up admitting the superiority of the contemporary era.

The perfection of mechanical technology and the limitation of the birthrate—finally admitted as the natural consequence of a civilization that had arrived at its apogee—had reduced the duration of the working day to three hours, offering people more leisure time. Numerous public festivals channeled the need of the masses for external entertainment, while their moral aspirations were satisfied by the practical obligations of the various official religions—which, in Europe, now included Theosophy and Buddhism. A new elite, which replaced the old ruling classes, devoted itself to the noble joys of scientific curiosity, passionately conducting research organized by the Terrestrial Directorate. That institution, positing as axiomatic that the pursuit of truth is an essential duty of the human species, dedicated the disposable resources of its global budget to works of pure and disinterested science. Previously subject to the demands of practical utility, and funded in a derisory fashion while its adepts—considered as harmless lunatics—were left to die of starvation, speculative science was now triumphant; progress, directed towards ever-loftier horizons, marched at an ever-accelerating pace.

Gigantic laboratories, furnished with equipment whose excessive cost had previously inhibited their construction, were given to researchers intoxicated with the sublime joy of exploring the secrets of nature. Astronomy benefited especially from this unprecedented largesse; new optical instruments far in advance of the telescopes of yesteryear, which had been privately funded by the likes of Lick and Carnegie, scrutinized the sidereal depths.

The problem of the plurality of habitable worlds was taken up again—a problem that had once had its martyrs, such as Giordano Bruno, burned at the stake for having proclaimed that the Earth was not the only world in Creation on which thinking beings lived, and which had caused so much ink to flow while there was no practicable means of resolving it. The idea, boldly expressed in the 19th century, of sending fiery signals to our brothers in space was finally realized, and every night, across the extents of the Sahara, immense geometrical designs solicited the attention of extraterrestrial observers. At the same time, extremely powerful TSF [2] waves, beamed by the Equatorial Alternators, bombarded our neighboring planets, Mars and Venus, incessantly.

The result of these sublime efforts to secure interplanetary brotherhood was not long in coming, but the first success, obtained at the beginning of 1975, amazed the cultured world. The paradoxical news was hardly believable: the response came from Jupiter! Jupiter, the sparkling jewel of terrestrial nights; Jupiter, the giant of the Solar System, eleven times greater in diameter than our modest globe; Jupiter, enthroned, escorted in its majestic orbit by its nine satellites, five times more distant from the Sun than Earth; Jupiter, finally, which orthodox science had hitherto deemed uninhabitable because of its enormous mass, which must have prevented it from cooling for much longer, conserving in its bosom the temperature of a scarcely-extinguished Sun. But the fact was there, soon confirmed and undeniable; in the round black shadow that the largest of the Jovian satellites, Ganymede, projected on its mother planet as it passed in front of her, enigmatic moving lights first observed a long time before were resolved by the magnification of the most powerful telescopes—Mont Blanc and Gaurisankar—into distinct luminous lines, which eventually reproduced, one by one, the geometrical signals from the terrestrial Sahara!

There was no more doubt. The solitude in which the indifferent material blocks of ancient astronomy floated was no more. Intelligent beings were living up there, among the abysms of the Heavens, the bounds of which had been gradually extended by the bold investigations of science. The vertiginous infinite Space that had replaced the naïve firmament of the Ancients, whose crystalline spheres were secured by golden nails, no longer intimidated the imagination with its limitless void. Humankind was done with the sensation of being lost in the bosom of unfathomable gulfs, a unique and isolated spectator of the incomprehensible mystery of the universe, shivering in the loneliness of its infinitesimal globe! Life and intelligence were no longer reserved to one sole planet, among the smaller members of the Solar System. Minds analogous to ours populated, at the very least, the giant Jupiter!

---

[2] TSF stands for *"télégraphie sans fil"* [wireless telegraphy]. As the equivalent English acronym is not used, it seemed sensible to leave the French formula in place.

A wave of sacred enthusiasm ran through all the thinking brains of Earth. Public ceremonies were organized, and thanks were offered in the temples of every religion, for the fact that other humans existed, who undoubtedly praised the glory of a Creator, and were now susceptible, thanks to the new means of communication, of being introduced to the knowledge of the one true God, if they did not have it already.

It was not only members of the scientific elite, but the masses ordinarily inattentive to the progress of pure knowledge, who followed the development of the experiment passionately. A feverish curiosity held minds in suspense during the long months that passed before a satisfactory conventional language was established, so that an exchange of ideas could take place in consequence between the two planets—or, rather, between the planet Earth and the Jovian satellite Ganymede, from which the signals described on Jupiter's sea of cloud in the moon's shadow were emitted.

The task was arduous and complicated, to be sure, but Champollion had succeeded in deciphering the hieroglyphics of a race that had vanished 2000 years before. In the present instance, the most lucid and ingenious brains of two life-bearing planets were devoting all their energy to the solution of the problem.

After ten months, intelligible conversation was established, and revelations were arriving from outer space, for which—for the first time since the origin of man—news of the Earth was sent in exchange. Every morning, the newspapers reproduced a "Message from Jupiter," and cinemas projected filmed images of Jovian life that telescopes had initially picked up on the dark screen of Ganymede's shadow... but the specialist works published on this subject are too numerous and widely-circulated for there to be any need to continue.

The most powerful impression was, perhaps, created by the news that the human population of Jupiter had very close affinities with the human population of Earth, even in the matter of physical constitution. Savants with preconceived ideas were astonished, but an explanation was soon forthcoming from the Jovians themselves, whose wisdom had proved to be superior to ours from the first. The kinship of the planets, all similarly emitted from the primitive Sun—or, rather, the primal Nebula—implied an analogical evolution on their surfaces of the identical seeds of life, or *cosmozoons*, incessantly brought to each heavenly body by the millions of aeroliths that are strewn through space in every direction—seeds that only develop to provide the root stocks of the entire series of vegetable and animal species in narrowly-defined circumstances, in particular under the influence of certain rays formerly projected by the Sun but absent today from its impoverished light.[3]

---

[3] This thesis regarding the necessary similarity of life-forms on the various planets of the solar system was proposed by Christian Huygens in *Kosmotheoros* (1698); Joncquel and Varlet probably had read the summary of that text in

At any rate, the intelligent race on Jupiter, having appeared much sooner than its Earthly equivalent, possesses not only a very extensive scientific knowledge but a perfect dominion of its mental faculties over animal instincts. According to the Jovians, this is due to the particular nature of their individual longevity, which—in the course of years that are almost equal to 12 terrestrial years, each comprised of 10,455 days of 10 hours—permits them to acquire at an early age the experience and the equilibrium that are, in us, the prerogative of decrepit old age.

War has been unknown for thousands of years on this sagacious world, whose inhabitants, their needs satisfied in moderation, live for the joys of study and contemplation. Their practical industry seems to be quite limited in its development, but they have taken pure science and certain of its applications to a point of marvelous perfection. These include the domain of optics, for astronomy is there considered to be the highest of the sciences.

It is true that the atmosphere of the planet, frequently charged with opaque clouds, is unpropitious for the exercise of their preferred science—and perhaps that initial difficulty made them all the more determined to pursue it. At that time, the greater number of the sedentary inhabitants of certain equatorial zones never saw the solar disc, and, for the very best of reasons, had no knowledge of the marvelous spectacle of the stellar firmament. A long time ago, however, the Jovians learned how to communicate with their satellites. The five smaller ones, which were uninhabited, served as places of exile for rare degenerates, while a peaceful and fraternal alliance was established with the inhabitants of the four larger ones; observatories were established on one of them, Ganymede. Minuscule as it is by comparison with the immense planet, that world is quite sufficient to accommodate all the Jovian astronomers with ease, since its diameter is greater than that of the planet Mercury. Vehicles powered by "solar batteries" still permit mere amateurs to go there, in order to contemplate the marvels of the Heavens from the ideally pure atmosphere of the satellite.

The description of their telescopes, whose details the Jovians did not attempt to conceal, took up numerous and laborious transmission sessions. Faithful to its rules of conduct, however, the Terrestrial Directorate kept the core of these revelations to itself. Only the general principle was divulged, and people were amazed to learn that the Jovian telescopes, which were only a little larger than those at Mont Blanc and Gaurisankar, nevertheless permitted the attainment of limitless magnification. Indeed, their images, instead of only being magnified by a system based on an ocular mirror, were also subjected, by means of special relays, to an "amplification" analogous to that which the terrestrial microphone imposes on sonic vibrations. This was so successful that, not only had the luminous signals in the Sahara been perceived immediately, but the life of the Ter-

---

Camille Flammarion's *Les mondes imaginaires et les mondes réels* (1864; revised ed. 1905).

rans had been studied for centuries with troubled solicitude, much as a biologist might track a colony of microbes in the focal field of an ultramicroscope. The luminous signals projected from Ganymede on the screen of its shadow had not, therefore, been created at hazard, but specifically to attract the Terrans' attention.

Now, it seems that the members of the planetary family are steeped in a sort of spiritual atmosphere analogous to that which reigns in the bosom of terrestrial civilization. It seems that the manifestations of the Spirit follow a strictly parallel course on the surfaces of the Daughters of the Sun. In addition to material communications, there are "interplanetary ideas"—much as there are ideas "in the air" here, thanks to which an invention emerges, when its time has come, in a host of brains at the same time, in various parts of the world. A preliminary proof of this hypothesis had just been given to us by the simultaneity of efforts made by Earth and Jupiter to establish intellectual communication. A startling confirmation soon arrived to convince us of its exactitude.

The detailed description of Jovian television technology had scarcely finished when the receptive antennae of the interplanetary TSF, mute until then in spite of daily appeals, were suddenly activated. Clear and precise signals arrived, in the dots and dashes of a conventional alphabet of the Morse genre, instituted by agreement with Jupiter. It was believed at first that this was a new mode of communication that the giant planet was bringing into play, at the instigation of Earth, to supplement the optical signals.[4] On the first day, the news, published in that form, did not excite much curiosity—but after several hours, there could be no more doubt, and the provenance of the "cosmograms," duly received and verified, was confirmed. It was necessary to yield to the evidence. The planet Mars had, in its turn, joined the circuit.

With marvelous sagacity, the Martians, ideally placed between the two planets to decipher their communications simultaneously, had succeeded in discovering the conventional key. With an immediate mastery—at the first attempt, without any fumbling—they had transposed the luminous language into TSF. Without a doubt, they had perceived the Hertzian signals radiated from the Earth into space at the outset, but had omitted to reply to them for some reason or other. Perhaps their transmission apparatus was not yet ready, or perhaps…

---

[4] Varlet inserts a footnote here: "The optical exchange of signals did, in fact, become precarious during Jupiter's conjunctions, which is to say, when the orbits of Jupiter and Earth placed them on opposite sides of the Sun, as much by virtue of the distance involved—six times greater than that at opposition, when the Sun, the Earth and Jupiter were aligned—as by virtue of the radiance of the central star. TSF apparatus had therefore been established by Jupiter, according to designs transmitted to it by Earth, but the apparatus did not function in the correct manner before the second week of the Martian torpedoes.

When these questions were posed, though, Mars refrained from answering. From the very first messages, it was understood on Earth that this was not a matter of the noble exchanges of ideas to which the sagacious planet Jupiter had accustomed us. Clear and curt questions, positive and technical, unfurled on the tapes of the receptive apparatus, and were then published, causing the public to reflect, divided between their naïve admiration for such imperious precision and their disgust for the dry and arid character of the messages. What was the exact population of the Earth? The greatest aggregations of population? What force was exerted by the most powerful lifting apparatus? Where were there ores of...? (After elaborate explanations, it was understood that the question related to radium.) And then, pell-mell, as if at hazard: Explosives? The most powerful means of destruction? Exact thickness of the Earth's crust? Composition of the atmosphere? The precise concentration of argon, in particular? Climate? Temperature? Salinity of the seas? Etc, etc...

In brief, questions seemingly representative of an aimless curiosity, which the public soon found repellent, but which flattered the vanity of terrestrial savants happy to demonstrate to their brothers in space the level to which their knowledge had already risen. The Terrestrial Directorate itself, on this occasion, lifted its embargo concerning certain secret formulas. What danger could these Martians, orbiting 50 million kilometers away, pose? They would never be able to do us any harm or inhibit the forward march of Progress and Civilization?

Oh, nobly trusting Earth, as naïve as some *nouveau riche* counting his gold coins in front of thieves—how soon and how cruelly you were disabused!

Now that the catastrophe has happened, and bitter experience has revealed the true character of the inhabitants of Mars to us, I think with respectful admiration about the intuition of our distant ancestors, who were certainly ignorant of astronomy, but were situated in mysterious proximity to the profound heart of Nature, in which their souls could read a language that the subsequent development of rational thought caused us to forget.

Mars, whose name has always been associated with carnage since the distant epoch when our first forefathers fought to the death on the icy slopes of Pamir to conquer the fertile plains; Mars, whose occult influence alone seemed to drive men mad; Mars, symbol of war and devastation; Mars, savage and pitiless god, presiding over discord and violent death—thus consecrated by an infallible prescience of the threat that the red planet would bring down from the heights of Heaven upon the Earth and the human race!

And, more recently, at the dawn of the 20th century, that other seer, worthy of being placed in the rank of prophets inspired by the universal Spirit, for whom the future and the past were contained in an eternal present—that simple English man of letters who was perhaps enabled by the impending approach of the event to interpret similar presentiments, made precise and concrete, in a visionary document. He had seen, through the mists of the future, the monstrous invasion to which we, the last terrestrial humans, would be witness less than a century later! But his novelist's brain, distorting the horrors to come in order to please an optimistic public, had softened the terrible denouement, and, imbued with the scientific theories of his own day, had attributed a fantastic cephalopodan anatomy to the Martians...

Oh, if we had only been able to remember his book during those first Martian communications, not as an imaginary fantasy but as an augural *Mene, Mene, Tekel upharsin!*—what an irreparable disaster we would have been spared by a modicum of suspicion and foresight!

But the gods blind those they wish to destroy, and, after happening upon the secret of Jovian television as it was transmitted, Mars was benevolently instructed by the Earth as to the most precious discoveries of our science—including the principle of the radium "blasters," which was delivered to them by an unpardonable sin of the Directorate.

II. The Martian Menace

Those weeks of civilized tranquility still seem peculiarly clear to me now, despite the abominable adventures that I have undergone since—along with all our human brothers, without exception—even though the period of my life that preceded that calamitous era generally seems as strange to my present self as the troubling reminiscence of some previous life. Tracked by death, hardened to misfortune and the brutal assassination of my own finest hopes and those of humankind, my contemporary soul, crystallized by desperate stoicism into a block of black diamond, remembers with melancholy pity the naïve trust of yesteryear and the sweetness of life in those days.

In the wake of some excessive mental toil, I had decided to take a premature vacation in Saint Valéry, in the relaxing and restorative region of the Somme estuary. Even in those culminating days of civilization, the little town conserved its immutable appearance and its late 19th century customs. Savoring that restfulness with delight, I spent my days perfecting my knowledge of botany—drawn until then from textbooks—by empirical study. I spent long hours absorbed in the examination of plants collected from the hedgerows, the woods and the fields. I learned to dismantle flowers piece by piece—petals, sepals, stamens, pistil—and to distinguish, in the infinite variety of formal combinations and the manifest numbers of these elementary organs, the characteristics of families, genres and species.

My herbarium increased every day with numerous specimens. The placid joys of the collector seemed to me to be supplementary, however. I was impassioned primarily by the sentiment that these detailed explorations of vegetable tissues developed within me: an intellectual penetration of the secrets of life, a subtle communion with the essential heart of nature, which gave my contemplation of the landscape a profundity that my simple visual delectation in colors and forms had never given me. I perceived, dimly, my true place in nature. I plunged sensuously into the depths of the uninterrupted flux of life, which worked assiduously upon the surface of the planet, unfolding its progressive phases from the most infinitesimal moss to the sequence of mammals, as far as humankind, under the impulse of the universal Soul.

From that pantheistic point of view, the civilization—"forced," like a hot-house plant—that pulsed beyond the horizon in great cities seemed infinitely distant to me. The rumble of electric trains passing in the distance in the depths of the valley, coming from London or Paris, the drone of a few antique aircraft in the sky or the quieter flight of ultramodern helicopters, inspired me to a smile of disdainful pity. What good was all that haste, that all that mad, hectic activity? How was the simple and easy life I was leading in that obscure village, in the midst of its coarse and cordial population of fishermen, less desirable than that of the Parisian whirlwind? Did the intensive civilization of the great cities do anything for the great majority of men but exasperate the conflict of the vulgar instincts, and show up in stark relief the deadly effects of our animal descent—the true and ineradicable "original sin"?

And, as I looked at the setting Sun, whose crimson disk striped by horizontal bands of mist reminded me of Jupiter as seen through a telescope, I envied the lot of the Jovian sages who had been able to ally progress with the moderation of desire, to use the discoveries of science discerningly, in order to put them at the service of their noble curiosity, and adopt the search for truth as the goal of their species instead of the illusory and troublesome satisfactions of wealth and well-being....

I scarcely paid any heed to the newspapers, and had become so accustomed to the interplanetary reports that it took me several hours to digest the importance of the enigmatic bulletin of June 22, 1978:

Mars has stopped replying to our transmissions. Is this silence due to an equipment malfunction, or should we see it in correlation with this new signal received from Jupiter: A projectile or bolide has been launched from Mars, headed in the approximate direction of the Sun?

I had just picked a superb *Chrysanthemum sagetum* when the threat hidden in that ambiguous sentence suddenly emerged into my consciousness. The Sun? But the red planet was almost in opposition, since it was presently passing through the constellation Scorpio and shining in the sky for the greater part of the night. A trajectory traced from its surface towards the Sun had to pass close to the Earth, perhaps intercepting it! It was our planet, rather than the central star, that the Martians had selected as a target!

In a flash, the whole of the English writer's prophetic novel came back to me. The time had come when the Martians, finding it untenable to remain on their minuscule planet, frozen, dehydrated and partially stripped of its atmosphere, had resolved to "relocate," and were putting the resources of their industry to work on that basis. And look how many of the secrets of the Jovians and Terrans had been revealed to them, with inconceivable naivety! What a hopeful abode, what a veritable paradise, the Earth must seem to them, less ancient and closer to the Sun, with its rich atmosphere, oceans and seas covering three-fifths of its surface. It offered conditions similar to their own, in terms of a day and night of almost equal duration to those on Mars, with seasons similarly accentuated—distributed, it is true, over a much shorter annual period, but whose more rapid alternation could only have a stimulant and renovating effect on Martian organisms.

Despite all these reflections, which unfolded automatically within me—as they must have done, that day, in the majority of readers endowed with any astronomical knowledge—and having re-read the printed passage, I could not believe it. Was that due to the state of nervous exhaustion from which I was convalescing, or to the empery of nature, which always had the effect of distancing me from human preoccupations? Or was it the rebellion of my survival instinct, which prevented me from believing that the threat was real, rejecting the monstrous possibility?

The last reason was undoubtedly the true one, for the indifference was almost universal. Public attention was then concentrated on the exploits of the famous Patagonian boxer Quiensabe, and his match with the Japanese champion Matsu, which was to take place in a few days time at the Timbuktu Olympic games. The alarmist reflections published by two or three daily newspapers on the subject of the extraterrestrial menace passed almost unnoticed. The hypothesis that it was a scare story, put forward by the majority of the papers, seemed to be confirmed, in the following days, by the absolute silence of interplanetary communications—which had, in fact, been suppressed by government censorship. Personally, lost in the joys of the neophyte botanist, I silenced my rational dread and tried to set aside my obscure presentiments of an impending catastrophe.

I was roused from this semi-somnolence by a visit I received from my old friend Sylvain Leduc, to whom I had just written, thinking that he was still in Le Bourget. My letter had reached him at the experimental airfield at Le Crotoy, where he was the chief test-pilot, and he had made haste to cross the bay of the Somme, in the course of testing a turbine-driven helicopter,[5] to shake me by the hand. He told me some grave news, unknown to the public, which he had received from his wife Gabrielle, an interpreter of the Jovian signals at the central Office of Terrestrial and Interplanetary Communications, in Mont-Valérien. Not only had the launch of a Martian projectile towards the Sun—and the Earth!—been confirmed, but subsequent messages had announced that further launches had taken place on a daily basis, in the same direction. With fraternal anxiety, the Jovian astronomers were following the progress of these machines, whose point of impact they were endeavoring to determine in advance. That of the first seemed to be in western Europe.

It transpired, moreover, that the secret was ill-kept by the translators of interplanetary communications, and the rumor had spread—in the big cities, though not, so far as I knew, to Saint-Valéry—that the "Martian missile" would fall on French territory. It was to avoid a panic that, on the day after my conversation with Sylvain Leduc—on July 7—the newspapers were authorized to publish the results of the Jovian observations. The trajectory of the so-called "celestial messenger" (and there was mention of only one) had been conclusively established; it would intercept the Earth's orbit and strike its surface obliquely

---

[5] As will become apparent, Varlet's hypothetical *rotatifs* [helicopters] have two propulsion systems, the principal rotor blades supplying vertical lift while other "propulsive engines" provide horizontal momentum. At least some of these other engines have propellers, like the aircraft with which Joncquel and Varlet were familiar, but these more advanced types might be more akin to jet engines.

33.8 seconds after 5:58 on the morning of July 8. The point of impact, with a possible margin of error of a kilometer, would be the site of Nancy.

The evacuation of the city and its suburbs, begun the previous day, would be completed that evening. All measures had been taken for the immediate destruction of the projectile and its occupants, if they manifested any bellicose intentions. A cordon of teledetonators was surrounding the threatened area, and batteries of long-range blasters were aimed at the probable point of descent. The inhabitants of other regions of France—and, *a fortiori*, of Europe—had, therefore, no reason to be anxious. The same government that had repelled the Asian invasion and put an end to the scourge of terrestrial warfare would also be able to avert the Martian peril and deprive the invaders of any chance of renewing their criminal attempt.

These official assurances must have set the minds of the general public—whose opinions doubtless resembled those I heard voiced in the Café des Pilotes in Saint-Valéry's harbor—completely at rest. While playing cards, the regulars commiserated hypocritically with the poor people of Nancy, obliged to leave their homes—they would doubtless be generously compensated at the taxpayers' expense, worse luck!—but their faces were smiling jubilantly as they told themselves that they were quite safe here, and that there was not the slightest risk of their being splashed, or having a window smashed by stray shrapnel.

The ferocious egotism of these numbskulls revolted me; I hurried out of the café to parade my muted disquiet and melancholy reflections along the deserted dike—but, contrary to my habit, I found solitude hard to bear. I would gladly have shared my reflections with a friend, felt myself surrounded by the presence of numerous human brothers, or mingled in a crowd, using the sight of a great city to defend myself against the menace from outer space, whose nature my imagination could not specify but which overwhelmed me with ever-more-sinister presentiments. If it had not been so late in the day, I would have gone to Le Crotoy to see my friend Sylvain.

The sunset distracted me somewhat from my anguish, with the spectacle of its melancholy serenity.

At the very edge of the dike, where I stood thoughtfully among white and pink clover, yellow bird's-foot trefoils and various graminaceous plants, their stalks swaying in the cool evening breeze and overhanging the bronzed depths of the Somme. The stream glowed red in the fading sunlight, already deformed by refraction, beneath a sky steeped in nacreous pinks and pastel blues. Chirping birds filled the wooded parts of the old cliff, beyond spreading groynes interspersed with grey mud-banks carpeted with saltwort and Artemisia. A red-brown cow lowed periodically in the vast peace of the quiet evening, which extended over the grey and glossy sands of the bay, streaked with sinuous puddles of the rising tide, bordered by the low dunes of Saint-Quentin, the familiar silhouette of Le Crotoy and a long blue-hazed fringe of poplars. A flock of seagulls went by, screeching. At the junction of the two arms of the river, the water splashed against the prow of a punt in which a man was sitting, carelessly fishing with a line—as if there had never been a planet Mars in the Heavens, and no projectiles launched by its treacherous inhabitants were heading towards the Earth, charged with a nameless menace, compared with which the invasions of Attila and Tamerlane were nothing but idyllic and amusing children's games!

For my own part, though, I felt horribly certain that I was contemplating Nature, within the ancient and traditional security of humankind's reign on Earth, for the last time!

III. The Death of Paris

It was impossible for me to sleep that night. Haunted by the most somber presentiments regarding the Martian attack, I only closed my eyes to see a series of images of disaster, as clear and sharp as illustrations printed in histories of the most calamitous wars and the prophetic visions of the English novelist. The cylinder fallen from the sky in the London suburb, the Heat Ray, the "tripod" war-machines devastating several English counties, the hideous invaders succumbing after a matter of days to the microbes of their new domicile... Would we escape so lightly? I dared not believe it.

I lost myself in wondering what motives had impelled the Martians to that abrupt attack, instead of requesting permission to establish themselves peacefully in some region of our world. Humankind would not have refused a refuge to those sidereal brothers forced to leave their native planet by cold and the rarefaction of its atmosphere and water—in brief, by the destiny that was reserved for us, in a more-or-less distant future! With a bitter laugh, though, I divined that the utopian ideal of Charity had no currency on Mars, which must be populated by beings of a uniquely positivist intelligence, ferociously utilitarian, who would gladly have massacred all the inhabitants of the Solar System in order to lodge their race in a more comfortable abode. And I thought about the noble and sympathetic Jovians, who would have preferred to die, to the very last member of their race, rather than perpetrate a deliberate injustice...

I abandoned all thought of sleep. My eyes wandered, via the open widow, over the liquid expanse of the moonlit bay, where the tide as beginning to ebb. In the North, the luminous beams of the lighthouses at Berck and Le Touquet swung back and forth on the horizon, and the searchlights of Le Crotoy illuminated the passage of the moving silhouettes of helicopters. As dawn broke, solitude became suddenly unbearable; I got up, dressed myself, and set off across the sands towards the airfield.

It was 5:45 a.m. when I arrived. My friend Sylvain, already up and about, was not in the least surprised to see me. He was almost expecting me, sure that I must be feeling the same anxiety and need for reassuring company that he felt himself. In his flying-suit, accompanied by three mechanics, he was working on his new machine, powered by a reactive turbine. It was, he affirmed, much superior to the helicopters currently occupying the hangars aligned as far as the eye could see on both sides of the aerodrome.

The camp's main clock chimed six.

"There it is! Nancy's fate must be sealed!" joked the youngest of the grease-monkeys.

"Do you think it's clever to joke at a time like this, idiot!" Leduc spat at him. "You'd be laughing on the other side of your face if you were there!"

"Unless, by chance, Ganymede was mistaken, and…" I did not finish. Releasing an inarticulate cry, the young jester extended an index finger, whose direction our gazes followed, immediately magnetized. A long streak of red flame slanted across the sky to the south, and sank, like a falling star, but visible in broad daylight, slowly beyond the horizon.

Dumbfounded, we had not moved a muscle when a prolonged whistling sound, descending in frequency, reached us in its turn. Only then did our exclamations of horror escape.

Leduc took his forehead in both hands. "Headed for Paris!" he murmured. "Who knows… My poor Gaby, at Mont-Valérien… Oh, the filthy brutes!" He suddenly shoved his aides. "Get a move on, you lot! Get ready for take-off... No, good God, not the new kite—my old crate, the number two. At the double! If I'm not in the air in three minutes from now, watch in hand, I'll report you for disobeying an order!"

The three men ran to the hangar towards which he was pointing.

A sudden inspiration overwhelmed me: a furious desire to see for myself the unknown spectacle, suspicion of whose awfulness was twisting my guts. Oh, if Leduc left without me, I would go mad on the spot! But he must have read my thought in my eyes, for I had no need to speak. He dragged me by the elbow to his wardrobe.

"You're coming, of course, Léon? Quickly, put on this suit…n Now the helmet… Good, that'll do!"

The helicopter's motor was already purring. Leduc helped me into the cockpit, which was entirely composed of a material of glass-like transparency, took his place beside me in the pilot's seat, closed the hermetically-sealed door, connected the telephone wires to our helmets and put the machine into gear. The supportive rotor-blades accelerated their rotation, becoming no more than a circulatory phantom… then the propulsive engines… I felt myself plastered to the padded seat by the rapid ascent.

Through the transparent floor—with a singular sensation of insecurity—I saw the farms, the cattle, the trees, the verdant countryside, the sands of the bay, the houses of Saint-Valéry and the bright ribbon of the Somme diminishing vertiginously within my field of view. Despite the noise of the engine, the tumult of the rotor-blades and the rush of the air cut through at top speed, the voice of Leduc—hunched over his controls and his indicative gauges—resonated in my microphones as a clear whisper: "I'm switching on the oxygen; we'll go up to 8000 meters, so that we can go faster. We'll be over Paris in 35 minutes. There's Abbeville, slightly to port…"

Anguish was eating me up. Despite the evident rapidity of our flight, the journey seemed to last for hours. Amiens, miniaturized by distance, allowed me to see through binoculars a crowd of carelessly swarming humans, dotting the streets and squares around the cathedral; the trams, visible by virtue of their white roofs, seemed motionless.

There was a zone of cloud beyond; the Sun only appeared at intervals...

Smoking factories: Creil...

Suddenly, a cry vibrated in my helmet: "Paris is on fire! It's fallen on Paris!"

Directly in front of us, on the emergent horizon, a pall of bizarrely reddened smoke was ascending into the azure sky. From moment to moment, it grew larger, assuming an increasing importance in the panorama. I could soon make out with the naked eye the suburban towns and part of the capital: the Right Bank, strewn with secondary fires. The great curtain of smoke, shot through with red flames, visible in spite of the bright sunlight, seemed to be following the sinuous course of the Seine as it extended into the distance towards the west.

The Eiffel Tower was invisible, but our altitude permitted us to make out the giant antennae of Mont-Valérien beyond the disaster zone.

"Your wife is safe, in any case," I said to my friend, dazedly.

"Don't be stupid! She doesn't live up there on the Mont. She lives at No. 7, Rue Dupleix, on the far side of the river, near the Champ de Mars."

I made no effort to find words to reassure him. The curtain of red smoke, or fire, that was blocking our view, following the exact course of the Seine, might have engulfed the entire Left Bank! In any case, the Right Bank, whose provincial houses were arrayed beneath our feet, seemed to have been peppered by incendiary shells. Twenty or 30 plumes of that uncanny red smoke were scattered between the monuments—which were now easily recognizable, because we were arriving, at reduced speed, over La Chapelle. The Ourcq canal and the Bassin de la Villette were also giving off that tumultuous red effervescence. On might have thought it a firework display in broad daylight... yes, fireworks were alight everywhere: at the Gare du Nord, at the Arts et Métiers, in Les Halles, beside the Opéra, around the Arc and the Etoile—everywhere, as far as the scarlet barrier of the Seine. Yes, the Seine itself was transformed into a river of fire!

A sublime and horrible spectacle: the capital of France and the United States of the Worlds, Paris, the brain of the world, had been condemned to destruction by our brothers from Outer Space! But how had the Martian torpedo been able to produce this gigantic conflagration?

I felt my reason vacillate in the face of the unexpected disaster. I could not tear my eyes away from it. A few hundred meters beneath our feet, the scintillating gold of the cupola of the Basilica of Montmartre was visible, still intact, a vain aegis—but beyond it, below the square form of the Butte, a crater seemed to be agape, vomiting a veritable eruption of viscous red-tinted vapor, which ran in the manner of a liquid, overflowing into the Boulevard Rochechouart, where we could see people desperately fleeing the all-devouring tide in every direction.

In the Place de la Trinité, I believe, at the corner of the Rue Saint-Lazare, a squadron of firemen gathered around their pump were directing powerful jets at the forefront of a torrent of red gas that as slowly spilling out of the Rue de Londres. By means of some inexplicable phenomenon, however, an enormous flame—whose hiss we could hear through the walls of the cockpit—sprang forth on contact with the water and leapt up tumultuously to the level of the uppermost floors of the neighboring buildings, in which fires immediately broke out.

We were still going forwards, through—heading straight for the Rue Dupleix, as Leduc shouted to me—and the roaring curtain of flame, above which we would have to pass, hypnotized us. The waves of burning naphtha which, it was said, spread everywhere at Baku, on the Caspian Sea, surely could not have presented a more frightful grandeur than was offered by the Seine transformed in its course downstream into a flaming Phlegethon, nourished by four or five subsidiary streams of red gas. One of them, in the Place de la Concorde, emptying out furiously from a sort of monstrous hearth, was emerging obliquely from a vast crater in which an entire terrace of houses had been engulfed, at the entrance to the Rue Royale.

I leapt immediately to the conclusion that that this was the main body of the Martian machine, the residue of the Torpedo that had, by some means, projected a scattering of secondary fires over the whole of Paris as it fell.

A white Air Police helicopter—none of those we had passed thus far had paid any attention to us—attempted to prevent us from flying over the burning Seine, but we had already crossed the rim of the tumultuous furnace, whose heat and smoke reached us at an altitude of 400 meters.

The Left Bank offered the same spectacle as the Right: the rutilant fire-generating gas was covering the whole of Paris! But Sylvain had eyes for only one thing amid the disaster: the building that sheltered his wife, No. 7, Rue Dupleix. A frightful anxiety caused his hands to clench on his control-levers, to the point at which our helicopter made an abrupt pitching movement, when he saw that the palace of the Terrestrial Directorate—which had occupied the greater part of the Champ de Mars, immediately behind the Eiffel Tower, for twenty years—was on fire. Three-quarters of the palace was ablaze, and people who had taken refuge on the cornices of the part that was still intact raised their arms towards us, appealing for help—for the fatal tide of red gas had filled all the adjacent streets. Official rescuers were arriving in their white helicopters though, and my friend's anxious eyes had already recognized his conjugal home beyond the Place Dupleix.

"Can you see Gabrielle?" he asked me, in a strangled voice—for he could not release the controls in order to look through the binoculars.

I recognized her, dressed in a white nightgown, among the 15 or 20 people waving on the roof-terrace.

"God be praised!" cried Leduc. "But we have to snatch her out of there!"

"Snatch" was no exaggeration; while our helicopter, having arrived above the building, descended prudently to set down, the refugees jostled one another, gesticulating madly, in the hope of being taken aboard and saved from imminent danger—a danger still mysterious to us, for the flood of poisonous gas could not reach them at that height, and there was no trace of fire in their immediate surroundings.

Our propulsive engines stopped; the supportive rotors maintained us three meters above the terrace, hovering. With one hand, Leduc drew a long white rod from an inside pocket and, after a moment's hesitation, handed it to me.

"It's a matter of necessity, worse luck!" he murmured. "Take the blaster, Léon. You point it like this and you simply press this black button marked F… Not the red one, whatever you do! Don't hesitate to clear the ground. We have two available places, but only Gaby must go up with us; it's impossible to choose another passenger—there are too many! Open the cockpit, lower the ladder, and fire on anyone who isn't Gaby."

As soon as I had carried out his preliminary orders, he shouted at the top of his voice: "Gaby!"

Ten strong hands reached out from a frenetic crowd of men, however, pushing the women aside, to grab the bottom rungs of the rope-ladder. Despite my injunctions, a Herculean specimen clad in blue pajamas with pink roses had already begun to climb up. His apoplectic clean-shaven face was almost touching my blaster, of which I dared not make use, when Sylvain shouted: "Only Gaby! Everyone else back! Shoot them down!" My trigger-finger clenched; a brief jet sprang forth from the weapon, and the Hercules, his head blown away, let go and fell back, as stiff as a tailor's dummy. All the hands let go of the ladder, and our assailants recoiled in fright before the threat of my blaster.

"Gaby!" Sylvain called out. "Quickly, Gaby!"

Hurling herself into the free space, the young woman bounded towards me. She clutched the rope-ladder, but was unable to get her feet on it. With a supreme effort, I lifted her up by her wrists, drew her into the cockpit, then released the ladder on to the howling mob of doomed malcontents. I had not yet closed the door when I was thrown on the transparent floor, on all fours, by our abrupt vertical ascent.

After ten seconds, however, frightful cries of despair became audible. With inexpressible horror, I saw the group of refugees, already tiny, staggering like drunkards; the whole terrace tipped, at an increasing angle, pitching them over the balustrade into empty space. With a thunderous sound of crumbling masonry, the entire house collapsed like a house of cards into the tide of red gas, which closed over its wreckage.

At the sight of the hideous death from which we had just saved her, Madame Leduc fainted in her seat. While trying to bring her round I warned my friend that the controls of the machine demanded his full attention as pilot.

"Anyway," he replied, "we can't stay in the air indefinitely watching Paris burn. We have to land somewhere."

But where? It could not have been more than 20 minutes since our arrival over the capital—an hour in total since the fall of the Martian Torpedo—but in that short time, the catastrophe had assumed immeasurable proportions. The infernal vapors were gaining ground around their seething wellsprings and were infiltrating all the arterial roads, great and small, whose network was traced in red on the enormous plan of the city displayed below us, traversed by the curves of its flaming river, peppered with bloody stains, and smeared with the smoke of rapidly-multiplying fires.

While we moved horizontally, uncertain as to which direction to take and fascinated by the grandiose horror of the spectacle, we saw two or three more terraces of houses crumble and collapse, eaten away at the base by the corrosive inundation, like cubes of sugar melting in hot tea. The noise of these collapses and the cries of their victims, punctuated the formidable tumult rising from the disaster: rumbling and booming sounds; explosions; the howling sirens of police helicopters. The helicopters were whirling like a flock of terrified seagulls, filling the air that was pierced here and there by a roof loaded with refugees, occasionally peeling off to head for one or other of the culminating points spared by the red flood: Montmartre, the Buttes-Chaumont, the Observatoire…

Despite the 500 meters of altitude that Leduc was now maintaining, a ruddy mist was beginning to surround us, and puffs of acrid smoke infiltrated the cockpit through the door that I had been unable to close properly. Gabrielle, revived by that improvised revulsive, coughed, opened her eyes and took cognizance of the situation. She was a cool-headed woman and she was able, this time, to calm her nerves.

The spectacle of Paris, murdered by the Martian gas, drew a long strangled sob from her at first; then, throwing her arms around her husband's neck, she leaned her cheek gently on his helmet and said to him: "What are you doing, Sylvain? We can't stay here—we have to go to Mont-Valérien. We'll get news there…besides which, it's my post." And while Leduc, following this judicious advice, directed our aircraft towards the hill bristling with the gigantic antennas of the official TSF controlling the entire world's communications, the young woman hid her face in her hands, and added: "Oh, are they going to allow all Paris to burn and perish? Why haven't these gas-fires been put out?"

The answer to that question was all too obvious, and Gabrielle provided it herself while we flew at top speed over the outlying districts, not yet as badly afflicted as the city center, whose streets were swarming with panicked crowds fleeing for the suburbs. The Jovian astronomers' error in indicating Nancy as the place where the Martian Torpedo would fall had caused all means of defense to be concentrated around that city. Who knew, given the destruction of the seat of the Terrestrial Directorate, from where the initiatives of the world government would now emanate? Who knew whether a single Director had survived to send orders to Nancy to bring the means of defense back to Paris, with all possible haste?

IV. The Terrestrial Director at Mont-Valérien

We realized, as we touched down at Mont-Valérien, that our fears were only too justified. Apart from a few idle mechanics and a couple of distant night-watchmen chatting on the main steps with the concierge of the TSF buildings, the airstrip was deserted.

One sole helicopter had just set down there, immediately ahead of our own, so awkwardly that it had tipped over half-way and broken its forward propulsive unit. A bare-headed individual stepped down from the cockpit, violently berating his pilot—a civilian, certainly, not a qualified aviator—and came towards our group. He was a little old man in spectacles, gaunt and bald but sprightly, dressed in a frock-coat and black trousers, ripped and stained as if by acid. His feet were bare inside his slippers, and his right hand was wrapped in a blood-stained handkerchief. Despite this sordid appearance, his genially-wrinkled forehead and his features, hardened by an expression of inflexible determination, revealed him to be a leader of men.

Gabrielle recognized him immediately. "Gideon Botram, the deputy Terrestrial Director!" she whispered to us, while adjusting her night-attire as best she could.

Although I was unfamiliar with officialdom, I imitated Gaby and Sylvain, rectifying my stance under the Director's eagle eye. He spoke in a rapid and trenchant voice.

"Why is there no one but you here? Has the entire staff of Mont-Valérien been massacred, along with my colleagues? Yes, I believe I'm the sole surviving Director. They've struck at the head, these Martian bandits! But what are you doing, Mademoiselle? TSF, aren't you? You should be at your post. Has anyone warned the Commander of the anti-Martian forces at Nancy yet? You don't know? Quickly, then, to the controls! You, the pilot-officer"—he pointed his left index-finger at Sylvain's winged insignia—"I'm requisitioning you and your machine for my personal use."

Trotting along in his slippers, the lively old man drew us in his wake towards the central service building, where a few heads were visible at the windows. He looked me up and down questioningly. "And you," he continued, "Who are you, eh?" I told him. "A publicist? We've got work for you. You'll replace my secretary, who's back in the ruins with so many others. Do you know, by any chance, how to treat a burn?" He extended his wounded hand to me. "No? Pity. These Martian gases are much stronger than the red-tinted vapors of nitric acid, for they devour everything. On contact with water, moreover—or flesh, which contains water—they decompose, bursting into flames. Flames, Monsieur! Hell must burn like that!"

At these words, I understood what a horrible death it was to which thousands of my contemporaries had been condemned, but I did not have the leisure to mourn their fate, for we had arrived in the vast control-room, where three employees got up and came to meet their Master. One of them informed him, timidly, that he had taken it upon himself to inform the Commander of the anti-Martian forces, who had demanded official confirmation and precise orders before setting out for Paris.

These orders were dictated, in the most severe terms, by Gideon Botram, whose eyes were glittering with rage behind his gold-rimmed spectacles. It had, therefore, been sufficient for the heads of government be disposed of in the hour of peril—and for the sole survivor among them, the deputy Director, to remain blockaded in his room for more than 50 minutes before help arrived—to paralyze the defenses completely!

There, we put our finger on the hazards of excessive centralization, which is solely adapted to normal circumstances. Today, the salvation of Paris, or that part of it which could still be saved, and tomorrow, the success of the war to resist the brutal Martian aggression—perhaps along with the destiny of humankind—rested on this frail old man, who set us an example of marvelous activity and distributed his orders with a perfectly cool head.

In addition to the forces from Nancy, the airbuses from the suburban depots were sent in haste to the factories of Seine-et-Oise to collect provisions of industrial explosives, for want of engines of war, which had been suppressed for thirty years by universal disarmament—that supreme victory of civilization, which humankind would, alas, regret! They returned under the control of the finest pilots, who dropped the explosives on the fire-vomiting wellsprings in the region of Paris.

I was charged with reorganizing by TSF the communication services that had been suppressed at a stroke by the disappearance of the central telegraphic offices and printing presses of the capital—and drawing up a report on the catastrophe.

Meanwhile, Gabrielle Leduc, having put on her working uniform over her night-dress, resumed her duties and deciphered the most recent news from Jupiter received by the great observatories of Mont Blanc and Gaurisankar. She released a sudden exclamation; then, in a voice tremulous with emotion, pausing at intervals to consult a little dictionary, she began to read to us, translating the string of Jovian signals on the blue strip of the receiver as it came in.

"New projectile launched by Mars towards Earth today.... Supreme Jovian Council met on Ganymede.... After a demand addressed in vain to the people of Mars to cease their unjustified hostilities... in the name of sidereal Fraternity... and immanent Justice... which are the supreme rules of planetary humankinds.... and of which Jupiter has constituted herself the defender on behalf of the Solar System... decides unanimously.... to come to the aid of our sister planet Earth by any means possible... and decrees... in view of the unspeakably obstinacy of Mars... that the aforesaid felon planet is set outside the law of love and sidereal fraternity... and that all the scientific resources of Jupiter will be set to work with the least possible delay to inflict the most exemplary chastisement upon the Martians.... To the people of Earth, courage and fraternity!"

At this unexpected news, a cheer sprang forth from our throats and those of the telegraph-operators—whose numbers had swelled to about a dozen—which the redoubtable presence of their Master could not inhibit. An alliance between Earth and the Planet of Wisdom! A general mobilization of Jupiter against the vile Martians! Gideon Botram himself forsook his Olympian serenity, and had to take off his spectacles to wipe away a tear of sublime joy and gratitude.

I hastened to finish my report on this vague but grandiose hope. It lessened to some degree the demoralizing effect of the destruction of Paris, when a skillful operator placed at my disposal transmitted it from the giant antennae of Mont-Valérien to the reception-desks of all the newspapers in France, Europe and the entire world—which is to say, to the three billion inhabitants of the Earth!

By means of the large bay windows of the hall, our eyes were continually redirected to the distressing spectacle of Paris on fire, but the details of the catastrophe gradually ceased to be visible beneath the ruddy fog flowing in heavy red and black waves, amid which the flying rescue-aircraft—police helicopters and stout airbuses in blue, green or yellow suburban livery—could barely be made out. Some of the latter, each loaded with 50 or 60 refugees, were even setting down on the Mont's airstrip to discharge their cargoes, but contingents of the Senegalese gendarmerie, summoned by the Director at the very beginning, had already arrived from their suburban headquarters and had formed a defensive cordon around his person, ours and the buildings of the TSF, the provisional seat of government. Within the shelter of that cordon, the brain of the Director of the Earth—so to speak—gradually recovered from its confusion.

This precaution, which we were inclined to see at first as a mere formality, soon proved to be necessary. An hour afterwards, it was no longer merely the occasional airbus that was attempting to reach our inaccessible summit from the mounting waves of red gas. Wheeled vehicles of every sort—cars, motorcycles and bicycles, and even the horse-drawn carriage of a self-indulgent millionaire—had followed in a tumultuous and clamorous crowd, amid clouds of dust, along the roads passing the foot of the hill, fleeing towards the distant suburbs.

Once this initial exodus was reduced to a trickle, it was the turn of fugitive pedestrians, already exhausted by walking 10 or 15 kilometers from the center of Paris, who broke off to mount waves of assault upon the Mont, which they attempted to climb in search of shelter for the night. The torrential multitude of these refugees, disgorged by every road, flowed towards our redemptive summit, breaking down fences, uprooting hedges, scattering through the gardens and enclosures, climbing up in their myriads, like an ant-hill thrown into panic by the heel of a strolling pedestrian.

Despite our black guard, we experienced an irrational terror at seeing this mad crowd of invaders moving towards us, with its lugubrious clamor. Men, women, children and old people, they paid no heed to anything—neither the warnings broadcast by megaphone, nor the demands of the gendarmerie—while they attempted to force a way through the military cordon. Inflexible followers of orders, the Senegalese made use of blasters, and the near-silent nature of these terrible weapons augmented the massacre. A few sonorous rifle-shots fired into the air would have made the horde draw back; instead of that, it was not until they saw several ranks of their fallen comrades—the occasional limb or head, three-quarters of their bodies having been blasted away by deflagratory annihilation—that the survivors decided to beat the retreat, with despairing howls of malediction, and to throw themselves back into the horrid confusion of the road, transformed into a human torrent.

What would become of these refugees? How could their disordered multitude be fed and lodged? Would they find the help they needed in the peripheral agglomerations, as they passed through?

We saw, in the Director's frown, that he too was taking account of the difficulties of the situation. The charitable assistance of individual initiatives might do some good, but what else was there? What about all the public services whose exceedingly complex and delicate organization extended throughout Paris, France, Europe and the entire world, whose networks all depended, in the final analysis, on the central administration of Paris? How could the world get by, thus decapitated, until these services had had time to be reconstituted and returned almost to normal?

Gideon Botram cast a pensive glance over the little company of officials—telegraph-operators, civil servants, scientists and so on—that the rescue planes were continuing to disembark in the Mont's internal courtyard. He communicated his resolution to them by loudspeaker.

"Messieurs, the fate of the United States of the World is in our hands. As soon as the fire in the ex-capital is under control, we shall reconstitute the Government in the provinces."

The war against the gas had just begun. Two large canary yellow airbuses, loaded with explosives, were visible in the fuliginous fog—but the task, which would have been relatively easy at the beginning of the catastrophe, had become very difficult. The gas-generators embedded in their dozens in the ground of the unfortunate capital were each hidden beneath an enormous red stain, impenetrable to the gaze but at least ten meters thick, which prevented accurate aiming. It was unthinkable that the flying machines should be instructed to descend into the waves of infernal vapor. It was necessary to stick to dropping the explosive charges as judgment dictated, and continuing until each generator was destroyed.

The first success was fatal to those who achieved it. Their machine descended far enough into the fog and the smoke as almost to touch the effervescent carpet of red gas filling the Place de la Concorde. The sixth attempt must have struck home, for the Martian generator sent up a column of crimson fire, accompanied by an irresistible explosion, to a height that seemed to us to be equal to that of the Eiffel Tower. The airbus, caught in the explosion and doubtless blasted into little pieces, had vanished by the time the spray settled.

The others, rendered prudent by this example, only released their explosives upon the fire-vomiting shells thereafter from a considerable altitude, while moving at speed; this delayed the operations markedly.

At 10:30 p.m., the special defensive apparatus erroneously organized around Nancy came to join the conflict, but their efficacy was mediocre. It required no less than six hours for the aerial fleet to obliterate all 45 of the gas-generators; the long-range deflagrators, which were, in any case, too heavy for transportation by helicopter, would not have helped. This destruction only served, at first, to augment the disaster, for the water from the sewers, which had been breached in many places, caught fire on contact with the infernal substance, and the flames engulfed the islets of houses that had been spared thus far. Save for a few culminating points, the entirety of Paris, from La Chapelle to Vanves and from the Bois de Boulogne to Vincennes, presented nothing to our eyes but an immense furnace, whose light emerged here and there from the layer of smoke that the breeze carried vaguely westwards.

We wept silently, sent back to our tasks by the orders of the Director, who had recovered his impassivity. Sentiments that we had set aside until that moment, of the kind formerly known as patriotic, rent our hearts and drowned us in the regret of civilized men confronted with the most poignant and immediate sorrow of seeing the treasures of art and history—museums, libraries, monuments—thus obliterated: ten centuries of genius and assiduous effort, the glorious patrimony of a France that had ceased to be a geographical expression and an administrative subdivision, and had become again our country, native or adoptive; the corner of the planet dearer than any other to our hearts, where generations had lived and died in times past, in happy ignorance of future scientific progress, interplanetary communications and Martian gas torpedoes!

V. Humankind Condemned

A little after 11 p.m. on the evening of the day when the Earth first learned about the frightful efficacy of the Martian torpedoes, exhausted by emotion and insomnia, I disembarked at Marseilles from helicopter No. 4 of the Directorate squadron. As soon as the last source of rutilant gas had been destroyed before our eyes and orders had been given for the fight against the Parisian fire, Gideon Botram had embarked the 50 or so more-or-less official staff—among which the Leducs and I were henceforth numbered—with whose aid he proposed to reconstitute the body of government on the Mediterranean coast.

Separated from my friends—for it was Ladislas Wronsky, the head of the scientific civil service, who occupied the fourth seat in the Director's helicopter, in which Leduc had obtained a place for Gabrielle—and lodged with seven or eight people unknown to me in a cockpit designed for six, I was too weary to take part in the conversation. I had become drowsy even before the terrifying furnace of the capital disappeared over the horizon, and upon arrival, I allowed myself to be led passively to the room assigned to me at the Prado Airport Hotel.

When I woke up under the warm caress of the morning sunlight, I kept my eyelids closed to begin with, to savor the beatitude, vague as yet, of that return to life. The memories that haunted me, of the Martian missile, desperate flights, crumbling roofs, towns on fire—it was a nightmare, was it not?... A bad dream, which would dissipate at the familiar sight of my bedroom in Saint-Valéry and the bay of the Somme....

I opened my eyes: an unfamiliar room, furnished with the banal and gaudy luxury of accommodation for travelers—and, through the window, the blue waves of the Mediterranean, sparkling brightly in the sunlight. I really was in Marseilles; I had not been dreaming, but had actually experienced that tragic day.

Nevertheless, the horror of my memories was attenuated by the spectacle that I beheld, leaning contemplatively on my elbows at the casement. Beneath the ardent light of the Provençal summer, the white villas and the palm-trees by the road-side extended in a harmonious curve to the chain of hills whose limestone stood out in sharp relief against the azure sky. Yachts with immaculate sails and fishing-boats with long slanted lateen-yards speckled the gulf indolently. Sea-mews as white as snowflakes were skimming the waves, while larger gulls glided slowly overhead at a great height. A marvelous setting, in which everyone breathed the joy of life! Optimism was reborn in me while I shaved. My improvised flying-suit made me smile, and I imagined myself under the orders of Gideon Botram, Wing-Commander, combating the Martian torpedoes. Evidently, we would "get them," as I had read in my history book.

A light drumming at my door recalled me to reality. I opened it. Sylvain came in, his brow furrowed, and shook me by the hand.

"The Master's asking for you, old chap. Your information service won't be idle today: Martian torpedo No. 2 fell on Lyon two hours ago... The same thing as Paris yesterday—the Rhone's on fire, it seems, as far as Valence!"

Without giving me time to digest this calamitous news, he drew me along the corridor to the elevator. For some reason that escapes me—for Gideon Botram was as unostentatious as could be—it was in a dozen automobiles that the staff brought from Mont-Valérien were transported to the Grand Palace of Notre-Dame de la Garde, selected as the provisional seat of government.

That journey through Marseilles in the bright July morning! Marseilles, alive and exuberant, astir with the news—carefully adulterated—of the burning of Paris, but still ignorant of the catastrophe in Lyon and, above all, of the series of torpedoes whose threat was suspended over the entire world. Its citizens did know, on the other hand, that the ancient Phocian city was to replace the Sequanian ex-capital as the implicit center of France and the world, and Massilia's secret envy of Lutèce took satisfaction in this belated triumph.[6] Along the Old Harbor—a forest of masts and rigging majestically overlooked by the svelte gossamer silhouette of the transporter-bridge—along the quays animated by a cosmopolitan population, along the Cannebière with its white buildings, under the shady plane-trees of the side-streets of Meilhan, and other boulevards whose names I have forgotten, the dense crowd massed to watch us pass by greeted the Director's arrival with loud ovations; fervent pride was displayed on almost every face. The fate of Paris was forgotten in the jubilation of seeing Marseilles promoted to the rank of capital of the United States of Earth.

It was the last glimpse I was to have of normal and civilized city life.

Our installation was laborious. The vast buildings, on a hill overlooked by the Basilica and its gigantic gilded Virgin, were scarcely able to accommodate the Directorate's central services. The ministries and administrative offices—all of whose staff and documentation would have to be reconstituted—were distributed across the city. For a week, my duties monopolized me completely, and I was no more sparing of my eighteen secretaries and typists. We were a long way from the three hours of official labor! From 7 a.m. to 8 p.m.—the moment at which I handed over the night shift to an intelligent assistant—I handled incoming messages from the TSF receiver at Saintes-Maries-de-Camargue, of which Gabrielle Leduc had been appointed director; I censored, summarized, corrected; I drew up reports and official bulletins; I transmitted the Director's

---

[6] Marseilles was founded as a colony by migrants from the Greek state of Phocis, when it was then known as Massilia, and later as Lacydon. Lutèce was an ancient alternative name for Paris, which is a "Sequanian city" by virtue of being situated on the Seine, once also known as the Sequanie.

orders. All the news of the world passed before me eyes: calamitous, frightful, of a nature to demoralize the most hardened soul....

The fall of the second Martian torpedo on Lyon had been better observed than in Paris. Observers were able to see the bolide, superficially inflamed by its traversal of the atmosphere, *slow down* at an altitude of several kilometers, before bursting into some 50 fragments—the generators of the red gas, which scattered over the Lyonnaise region to strew death and devastation. The battle was better organized this time, thanks to the initiative of a knowledgeable chemist, Arnold Ginestal, who suggested neutralizing the gases, even before the destruction of their generators by explosives, by means of powerful jets of liquid carbon dioxide. Thanks to this procedure, whose employment was to be generalized, the burning of the Rhone did not even extend as far as Valence, and it was possible to save about a third of the city of Lyon, in addition to the hills of Fourvières and La Croix-Rousse—whereas only a tenth of Paris, at the most, remained standing when the fire was put out.

The shards of the gas-generators, blasted apart by explosives, permitted the conjecture that the shock of impact triggered the automatic production of an indefinite volume of the rutilant vapor, which greatly intrigued our chemists. They baptized the new element that its analysis revealed *Ruberium*, after its color—but it was soon overtaken by the name *Satanite*, coined by a journalist from Bordeaux in view of the infernal properties of the Martian substance— which left the acids and most energetic combustibles of terrestrial nomenclature far behind. Decomposing water with the accompaniment of flame, it devoured animal flesh and vegetable tissue, cement, building-stone and marble, causing all calcareous compounds to effervesce on contact with it, and it worked through a meter's thickness in a few minutes. Steel resisted it quite well, as proved by the metallic bridges, which were twisted by fire but remained in place. The collapse of the Eiffel Tower was solely due to the corrosion of its concrete foundations. Various metals—gold, iridium and platinum—were proof against the action of Satanite, and attempts were made to utilize them in the manufacture of costumes resembling diving-suits, which would permit rescuers to risk going into the heart of the rutilant gas-clouds.

There was certainly no lack of platinum thereafter, nor of radium. The former of these two elements, whose numerous applications had previously increased their market value to unprecedented proportions and threatened to exhaust their terrestrial ores, made up the body-work of the Martian machines, while the latter provided the energy-reserves feeding the production of the rutilant gas! Each of the 30 or 40 generators launched by a Martian torpedo contained, in addition to substances as yet unanalyzed, ten tons of platinum and seven or eight kilograms of radium! Shortly before, that would have represented fabulous riches, a treasure to make the princes of the Arabian Nights, with their sacks of rubies, turquoises, sapphires, emeralds, topazes and diamonds, pale with envy! It was a rain of Danae, amounting to hundreds of millions—more than enough to pay for the material damage inflicted by the gas and the fire!

Despite the relative depreciation in price brought about by the first news of this profusion, a horde of looters swooped on the smoking ruins of Paris as soon as the firemen were finished, and then on Lyon, to carry off the shards of platinum while they were still warm, and to gather up the smallest pieces of radium, at the risk of atrocious burns. Organized gangs equipped with helicopters, in defiance of the armed forces, even attacked the debris of the satanite generators, bearing away considerable blocks of the precious element.

Given that the Martians—as succeeding events were to prove to us—were spying on all the actions of humankind, by means of the television apparatus whose secret had been generously donated to them by the Jovians, how they must have laughed! And how thankful they must have been for the unexpected consequences of their involuntary gift of Artaxerxes! For the possession of all this radium by fomenters of disorder was to hasten the collapse of humankind. International Anarchism still existed, in fact, but had been reduced to the impuissance of vain declarations, strictly contained by the government dictatorship that controlled the secret of the blasters, monopolizing the radium that fuelled them. Now, it appears that this secret had already been in the hands of various occult committees for some time, and that they only lacked the active product needed to manufacture weapons and distribute them to their affiliates, whose ranks swelled in a matter of days into a desperate mob...but I'm getting ahead of myself.

Nice, Rome and London received the third, fourth and fifth satanite torpedoes, and shared the fate of Paris and Lyon. It became impossible to hide from the public the fact that the Martian bombardment was continuing, and the Directorate authorized me to admit it in the communiqué of July 13. We added this advice to the inhabitants of cities: go up to the upper floors of houses at 5 a.m., or even the roofs, to which the rescue helicopters—which the civic authorities had requisitioned in large numbers—would come. Meanwhile, the means of defense were organized: fleets of aircraft, furnished with explosives and cylinders of liquid carbon dioxide, were training in the use of their equipment. The great cities would be preserved, to the extent that was possible, and would not, at any rate, be subject to disasters comparable of those of the earliest days.

These exhortations and official assurances, however, were a feeble counterbalance to the news of successive catastrophes. In particular, refugees from the destroyed cities, some of whom were beginning to arrive everywhere in Western and Central Europe, and in North Africa, seemed to carry a contagion of unbridled terror that diffused around them, adding its influence to the atmosphere of horrified anxiety in which humankind was presently living.

It was on the evening of the destruction of Rome that I saw these unfortunates with my own eyes for the first time. After a day of oppressive heat and excessive mental strain, I was wandering along the Cannebière, alone and melancholy, breathing in the breeze drifting up from the harbor, amid a crowd with drawn features and furrowed brows, whose muteness seemed sinister.

On the terrace of the Café Riche, lit up in its usual sumptuous fashion, people were slumped in front of their glasses, immobile and prostrate, their backs bowed in anticipation of the blow that would strike them down, perhaps in a few hours time, in the frightful agony of rutilant vapor or fire. Others, their jaws clenched, were holding women's hands, staring at them in a near-demented fashion. On the edge of the pavement, 100 curious idlers were gathered around a lamentable group, exchanging opinions.

The group comprised a husband, wife and daughter: Italians with dark brown hair and eyes and dull complexions, with their burned and corroded clothes in tatters, sprawled on packages wrapped in garishly-colored handkerchiefs. An electrically-powered trawler had just disembarked them, after taking them aboard the previous day from the end of the pier at Nice. The daughter, her voice punctuated by sobs, was telling the story of the thunderclap of the explosion: the precipitate flight from their homes at Ponchettes, along the waterfront, amid the fearful tumult of the murdered city—the tocsin, the howls of distress, the helicopters' sirens, the first detonations of the explosive attacking the satanite generators—the flames springing forth from the palace to their right, and the stream of red gas that was emerging on to the street, which they would have to get past to reach the jetty and salvation. She unwrapped the rag enveloping her legs to display the purple scars inflicted by the diabolical substance.

Coins rained down; pity and indignation stirred the crowd; hostile cries were raised, less against the Martians than against the Directorate, powerless to combat them and assuage the miseries of "poor sinners." It was then that I heard, for the first time, our Master called "the Antichrist"—which would soon become the rallying cry of mystical Anarchism…but a squad of Senegalese arrived, who dispersed the idlers and led the lamentable refugees away.

Nice had been struck by a torpedo at 2 a.m., Rome at 3 a.m.; London perished at 11 p.m. One could not even expect the daily catastrophe at a fixed hour, as had been thought at first. That disillusionment was not the least serious; so many people, petrified by habit, clung to the least appearance of regularity, like drowning men to planks, for the salvation of their reason—and the Martians, more knowledgeable about our psychology than we thought, deregulated their fire in consequence.

It was supposed at first in official circles that each gas-generator contained, in some sealed compartment, a Martian who controlled the manufacturing process, but that absurd idea was quickly abandoned. The Martians had no intention of coming to Earth before having, if not exterminated the human race to its last representative, at least destroyed the great cities, pulverized the social organism and annihilated all attempts at resistance. These positivist beings were consummate cowards, and refused to run the risk of a battle—so, in order to colonize without danger, they proceeded in the manner of hunters who gas a foxes' lair in advance; it was a war of extermination that they had declared upon our species.

The Director refrained from publishing these atrocious conclusions, but the masses were not deceived, and the demoralization of knowing that it was condemned to death overwhelmed humankind. Rather than combining all its forces to oppose the peril with a unanimous will, it seemed instead that the universal obsession with carnage and destruction had awakened atavistic instincts, which had been repressed by normal life and which had been thought conclusively defeated by the triumph of civilization and peace. Monstrous though it was, instead of turning these wild instincts of hatred and destruction against the common enemy, humankind turned them against itself and began to tear itself apart, beneath the satisfied eyes of the Martians!

I shall, in due course, describe the abominable scenes of disorder of which, alas, I was to be the witness. The break-up began, here and there, in the early days, even in the numb bewilderment of an as-yet-imperfect comprehension of the eventual fate that was reserved for us, but its manifestations were suppressed by the local police and we only heard muted rumor of them at the Directorate. We were too absorbed in the task—literally superhuman and without precedent—of reorganizing all the services with whatever staff we chanced to have, and putting the great cities on a defensive footing.

The requisitioning of aircraft, especially, gave the authorities a great deal of trouble. The panic that was later to empty the great centers of population had scarcely begun. People restricted themselves to sleeping under their roofs; attachment to one's domicile, resigned passivity and the optimistic belief that the threat was to others limited the exodus to the countryside to a few isolated instances. But the owners of aircraft, believing that they were certain to be able to escape in the case misfortune, selfishly refused to surrender their machines.

The rich, under the pretext of taking vacations and avoiding the heat, flew off to mountain villages, or even to sanatoriums in Greenland, Spitzbergen and other regions neighboring the North Pole, which the Earth's axial tilt would shelter from the Martian bombardment for a few weeks more—and it seemed improbable that the bombardment could be sustained for more than a month after the warrior planet's opposition. Gideon Botram had considered using this means of efficacious salvation on a large scale, but how could the whole human race be transported to these superior latitudes? How could it be housed, fed and provided with the means of subsistence there? The problem was insoluble, and censorship forced the newspapers to maintain silence regarding the immunity reserved for the north pole and its surrounding regions.

The first symptoms of the disintegration of civilization were manifest in the form of a revival of nationalism. The United States of the World had united all the people of the Earth in the same apparent fraternity 30 years before—the highest achievement of scientific civilization, and also the most artificial. The Martian attack, and the explosion of atavistic instincts that was its immediate result, struck it a mortal blow. The Terrestrial Directorate—established, in the event, by force—had continued its reign by virtue of acquired habit and the worldwide prestige of Paris, the political and intellectual center of the globe. That prestige was, however, not unmingled with a certain rancor in the formerly-autonomous nations towards imperialist France, which had reduced them to the status of administrative districts.

Paris, the capital and brain of the world, the universal object of envy and covetousness, still attracted criticism from preachers, even of the official religions, who vituperated against its dissolute splendor and debauchery, and covertly wished the wrath of the Lord upon the "modern Babylon." The tireless propagandists of Anarchism joined in the chorus, seeing the liberation from the "Directorial yoke" as the first step towards communist enlightenment of humankind. The catastrophic destruction of Paris seemed to both parties to be the realization of their most cherished desires: the hand of God, or Immanent Justice—using the Martians as intermediaries—had struck the guilty city, and a new era had opened beneath the feet of a regenerated human race!

In addition to these monstrous sectarian abuses, which considered the death of millions of innocent people to be a negligible detail or a holocaust necessary to the realization of their ideas—coincident, they believed, with the designs of Providence—many regions of United States of the World profited from the occasion by reasserting their autonomy. The radio messages broadcast from Mont-Valérien declaring that the Terrestrial Directorate, in the person of Gideon Botram, was secure, and that the common government of France and the world would be reformulated in the province—in brief, that French dictatorship would continue—were generally delayed or intercepted, and the delegate powers in the capital of each state in the Union simultaneously announced the catastrophic destruction of the central Directorate and the re-establishment of the former nations they represented and governed.

England, Japan, China, Germany and the Argentine Republic were the first to apprise us of their firm determination to resume political independence. Then, the Washington newspapers that reached us after July 11 via the Transatlantic Tube contained insulting and aggressive tirades against the Europe that had obliged the true United States—those of America—to set aside its glorious flag, the stars and stripes, for more than a quarter of a century, in favor of the monogram PAX and the azure globe making up the symbol of the tyrannical Directorate. The Chicago *Tribune,* in particular, commented ironically, with deplorable humor, on the fact that Europe had been selected as a target—quite justly, it affirmed—for the Martian "messengers." America itself was allegedly sheltered from a similar misadventure and, if the worst came to the worst, would be able to defend itself against the "stinking bullets," as it wittily rechristened the infernal torpedoes.

Any attempt at repression would have been illusory, or would have led to conflicts of an incalculable seriousness between the forces of the Directorial police and the black gendarmerie stationed in every state, blindly submissive to the local authorities, whose loyalty to their adoptive fatherland had not been put in doubt for 10 years. It only remained to recognize the *fait accompli*: the Directorate of Gideon Botram no longer held sway outside France, Spain, Italy, Belgium and Switzerland. Our TSF messages no longer broadcast unchallengeable orders to the world, merely daily news of the cumulative disasters inflicted by the Martian torpedoes and defensive Platonic exhortations—for the fratricidal wars that would soon bloody the continents and add their blind horrors to those of the Martian bombardment did not take place between nations.

The gravity of the situation did not escape the local governments; they gave way to national vanity in proclaiming their separation from the French Directorate, but did not go so far as to make war against it, and resisted the pressure of atavistic instincts. Those instincts initially wrought their havoc between classes, and then at random between various human groups. There were only a few instances of sporadic precursors of Revolution seeing fit to destroy the TSF antennae, thus isolating a city or capital from the daily flow of information that was still centralized by the former Terrestrial Directorate. Such places, cut off from the calamitous news, quickly took on a precarious and spasmodic existence, like decapitated ducks still running around and reflexively beating their wings.

In any case, the political disintegration of humankind, revelatory of the profound foolishness of human intelligence, occurred with stupefying universal spontaneity. It was a palpable example of the kind of psychic wave which, then more than ever, seemed to impinge upon everyone's mind at the same time, causing all the representatives of humankind to think and act as one. The various phases of the terrestrial panic, the epidemics of sentiment or resolution that affected every nation in that accursed era, became manifest everywhere simultaneously, like TSF receivers under the influence of Hertzian waves. I had every opportunity to convince myself of that in the course of my official duties—and later, when I was swept away with the government by the vertiginous cyclone of revolutionary panic, I had no doubt that the scenes to which I was a witness were unfolding in the same way, analogously if not identically, over the entire face of the condemned planet.

VI. An Idyll Under the Martian Terror

The sixth torpedo put an end to the relative quietness of America by destroying Chicago and setting the waters of Lake Michigan alight from a distance. The seventh was aimed at Boston, the eighth at Yokohama. The ninth fell far away from any big city, covering the fertile plain of Limagne in Central France with a red tide of satanite and obliterating all human life from its surface. Had the Martians aimed at Clermont-Ferrand and, for the first time, missed their target by a wide margin? No—the example of Paris, attained by the projectile whose trajectory threatened Nancy, was there to demonstrate that the torpedoes were not subject, once and for all, to a single ballistic impulse at the point of their launch towards the Earth, but that the Martians retained command of their "messengers" up to the last, perhaps by means of telemechanical waves. The devastation of Limagne was certainly intentional, and it had the result of greatly increasing terrestrial panic.

People in the cities, who had imagined that they would find a secure haven in the countryside whenever they wished, sensed the vanity of that refuge; people in rural areas, who had selfishly thought themselves safe, came to share the apprehensions of city-dwellers. In addition to the polar region, accessible only to the privileged few, the high altitudes of mountain peaks offered the fearful minds of men the only seeming immunity from gaseous red death and incineration. The inhabitants of every plain and valley, and everyone living in proximity to a watercourse, trembled in the same manner as city folk—but the hour of the great exodus had not come. We still had a further cycle of preliminaries to undergo in our gradual descend into the utmost depths of the inferno of fear in which civilization eventually foundered.

The news of social movements that reached us at the Palais de la Garde from every part of the world became more worrying every day. Cosmopolitan Anarchism loudly proclaimed its schemes of annexation; its secret committees, with new stocks of Martian radium at their disposal, were manufacturing blasters, and their disciplined groups were repeatedly meeting official forces of Senegalese head on. Scenes of vile looting were ravaging entire cities, in which sacrilegious malefactors had spread false rumors beforehand, saying that a message from Jupiter had announcing the fall of the next torpedo thereon—and the horrible confusion of panic inevitably followed.

The disruption of aerial and railway transport increased. The replenishment of provisions went badly; country people no longer went into the cities, and hoarded their produce. The devaluation of platinum dragged down the value of international coinage struck in that metal; bills drawn on the Banque de France were refused; gold and silver disappeared. Storehouses of foodstuffs were ransacked, even those earmarked for refugee camps. Mortality rates among the refugees rose dramatically.

At the same time, the first outbreaks of an epidemic became manifest on the outskirts of torpedoed cities, where millions of corpses were rotting. The physicians designated this virulent contagion by various names, and the popular euphemism of "Martian bronchitis" was calculated to reassure the most timorous, but its ravages were no less incalculable for that. If I recall the descriptions I had occasion to read at that time correctly, its symptoms corresponded point for point with those of the infamous Black Death, which had become the scourge of Europe in the darkest hours of the Middle Ages—to which our own era was becoming increasingly analogous.

It is necessary that I open an intimate and personal parenthesis at this point—not to indulge myself, like some, by laying bare the secret impulses of my heart, but because this confession appears to me to be indispensable to the comprehension of my attitude and my role in the events to follow. Furthermore, I have every reason to think that my case was far from being isolated, and that it will serve as an example to demonstrate the force with which the will to live is manifest, even in the most desperate circumstances, and the force that the illusory power that the essential and ineradicable sentiment which one 19th century philosopher named "the genius of the species" [7] is capable of exerting on a man plunged in the situation in which I then found myself, making him forget the most immediate and frightful dangers and launching him into the future as if he were assured of the greatest and most fortunate opportunities.

An orphan since the age of 20, the bitter competitions of a literary career—which I had eventually adopted after a rather prolonged digression into scientific studies—had taught me soon enough to consider the world as an arena, in which it is only possible to remain standing at the cost of an incessant struggle. Even with the firmest of friends, one must take account of the fundamental egotism inherent in every human being and the too-frequent opposition of their interests to ours. Intimacy, between men, can rarely be more than intellectual—and my experiences with the representatives of the other sex had not had the success I expected, based on the faith of poets and my own illusions. I had run up against futile anxieties, total indifference or incomprehension of any slight elevated subject-matter, which established an obstacle in our commerce and quickly dissipated any initial intimacy. These brief adventures had left me the melancholy memory of an irremediable dissatisfaction.

---

[7] This phrase, or its French equivalent, *"le génie de l'espèce,"* was actually employed by several 19th century philosophers to means slightly different things. Varlet is probably referring to Henri Bergson, but Bergson had adopted the phrase from its German equivalent, popularized by Arthur Schopenhauer and also used extensively by Friedrich Nietzsche.

At first, I thought myself a sentimental monster, with aspirations incompatible with those of my peers, destined to bear the burden of my isolation forever. Then, I reckoned myself the victim of my exceptional moral elevation. Finally, I gradually came to understand that people were all in the same situation, with the rare exceptions of a few fortunately-matched couples. I ceased to hunger for their fate and eventually resigned myself, not without a certain bitter aftertaste, to being alone in the world, in the midst of a desert of human hostility, imprisoned within the strict limits of my individual organism with my incommunicable soul, which no other soul would ever illuminate with fraternal effluvia, in that supreme psychic communion once celebrated by the divine Plato.

Life having been thus denuded, so far as I was concerned, of all sentimental interest, my ambitions turned increasingly to intellectual and philosophical curiosity; I lived, so to speak, by habit, and any incidental successes that accrued from my quotidian existence seemed equally vain with respect to my most intimate consciousness—that internal tribunal, one step removed, which watches over all our actions and thoughts as if from the serene altitude of an essential world, weighing us and judging us, *volens nolens*, from the viewpoint of the Eternal.

In consequence, I only attached a superficial importance to the singular freak of chance that struck me like a ricochet from the Parisian catastrophe, which made me—an obscure publicist 36 years of age—the head of the Directorate's information services, an official personage of worldwide notoriety. Only my external vanity was flattered. When the exhausting demands of my duties left me the leisure to look out of my window at Marseilles's beautiful warm and starry summer nights, my solitude within the universe seemed more bitterly intense than ever. I felt that I was alone among the human race, prey to the panic of its condemnation and the wild surge of animal passions; I felt that I was lost, an infinitesimal globule of consciousness on the surface of the Earth, spinning beneath the Martian threat, beneath the tragic fist of a superhuman Destiny that crushed humankinds, planets, suns at the whim of blind chance...or a supreme Will: the unfathomable ways of Providence, as the ministers of he official religions put it...

I felt useless, empty, broken, with no longer even a semblance of amity; Sylvain Leduc had been promoted to Commander of the aerodrome at La Crau; his wife was directing the new worldwide TSF station at Saintes-Maries-de-Camargue. I had nothing about me but the slyly obsequious faces of my subordinates or the expressionless and preoccupied visages of Gideon Botram and his senior collaborators.

I sometimes congratulated myself on being alone in the world in this fashion, without any charge on my soul, having never given life to an innocent creature to be hurled into the gulf in which humankind was sinking—but I did not succeed in deceiving myself, and quickly came to wish, according to the whim of stoical egotism, that I had a companion heart and mind possessed of a fraternal intelligence. I too wanted to experience sentimental joy, even at the expense of a distressing responsibility—for it would surely multiply tenfold my consciousness of the struggle, of life, whose every form appears precious from our new-found viewpoint of men condemned to death.

But I'm rambling...

News items of the direst sort reached us, that morning, at the governmental Palais de la Garde, and preoccupation with them added to the normal burdens of my work in setting my nerves jangling: the tenth torpedo fallen on Timbuktu; the principal station of Equatorial Alternators annihilated; the general massacre of Europeans in the Saharan oases and the destruction of the apparatus of inter-planetary optical projection; insurrectionist movements throughout Muslim Africa; India afflicted by fire and bloodshed; Martian bronchitis, diffused by air transport, multiplying its hecatombs at unexpected distances from the sources of infection—1000 victims in New York, as many in Cuba, twice that number in Montevideo... And the list was growing longer every minute.

A female clerk came into my office to give me a typewritten note, which I took in my hand without looking up. It was a Jovian message—the second we had received by sidereal TSF—giving the formula for the synthetic food manufactured on Jupiter, whose intensive production, if it was successful, would allow us to avoid the usual difficulties of replenishing stocks of meat and agricultural produce. The note was so badly typed, however, that its errors made it almost unreadable.

"Who typed this?" I asked the clerk, while deciphering the script. "You?"

"I'm new to the service, Monsieur, and it wasn't my trade..."

Her voice touched me strangely, but my nerves were all over the place, and I shouted at her, with a brutality that even astonished me: "That's obvious—in that case, why are you here?"

"I beg your pardon, Monsieur. I'm a refugee from Paris; my fortune was on deposit in the Banque de France and I lost everything in the catastrophe. I'd almost forgotten that I'd learned to type at school... I'm extremely sorry to be good for nothing."

It was only then that I raised my eyes to look at her. What point is there in describing that face, soft and melancholy but radiant with frankness and honesty, for the indifferent? In any case, I don't think I saw anything in that first instant but her eyes. They were a peculiarly rich and profound blue, like the flower of the Alpine larkspur—but that, too, I did not know until later. I only knew, with the conclusive certainty of a revelation, that those eyes—alone among the millions of open eyes beneath the foreheads of humankind past, present and future... alone in the infinite universe, in fact—were the only ones that could penetrate the invisible, impalpable but impenetrable partition of extraneous indifference and hostile egotism that separated me, like a choking carapace of glass, from my so-called human brothers.

Henceforth, I was no longer alone; the implacable law of suspicion and antagonism was suspended for the two of us; our fraternal souls, as was predestined, recognized one another. Exhausted by long solitude, avid for expansion and communion, and to realize the marvelous alliance of the human couple, to concentrate on another the treasures of affection that our youthful enthusiasm had formerly dreamed of spreading throughout the world—the treasures of a love repressed by the harshness of life, by the bitter law of competition, hostility and hatred—we recognized one another.

Our idyll blossomed at a single stroke, without any other prelude than the banal incident that I have just described. We were certainly both victims of that singular and disturbing acceleration which, after the debilitation and metal disarray of the early days, had afflicted the thoughts and actions of human beings, as hectic and fast-moving as a clock whose escapement has broken. The waves of the collective psyche, emanating from the millions of people swarming around us, and billions of others more distant, brought their precipitant palpitations to us, even in the directorial palace, with a vehement, undeniable, quasi-material force. "Make the most of the time you have left:" that contagious idea filled space, vibrating in the manner of the Hertzian waves, incarnate in everyone breathing, realizing itself on the plane of brutal desire or that of ideal satisfaction, according to the character of the individual...

It seemed to us that we had known one another forever, that we were only continuing, in this new life, a long intimacy sealed elsewhere—on the Earth or some other planet—during the double avatar of a radiant anterior life. "You shall die!" was trumpeted in our ears every morning by the news of a new torpedo attack. Tomorrow, it might be our turn. We scorched through the days regardless, in order to savor those joys to the full which had been the most beautiful adventure of humankind since the symbolic Adam and Eve. Vertiginous paradox! The world began, for us, in the midst of the disaster that would finally devastate our species. But the monstrous danger, while scourging our souls, retreated into a sort of phantasmal unreality. Stronger the death—the Martian red death suspended above us like the sword of Damocles—our couple scorned it with a smile, for out marvelous exultation rendered us immortal. It came from much further away than our ephemeral existence; it sprang from the profound source of the Spirit that animated the universe; it was *already* immortality.

During the days that separated us from the weekend holiday, hard-won from the indefatigable Director, I recollect that the typewriter of third-grade clerk Raymonde-Alice Becquart was in my office more frequently that the strict requirements of service demanded!

In addition to the evenings of plenary liberty, our inexhaustible conversations also required the nights, until 3 or 4 a.m., when daybreak made it impossible to ignore our fatigue and the threats of the present. With religious attention and boundless curiosity, we told one another the stories of our lives, effecting, so to speak, and exchange of our individual egotisms, which ended up being fused together—and above this charming and childish babble, our souls experienced transcendental unity, communing in the permanent and silent grip of ecstasy.

VII. The Revolutionary Panic

The delightful Saturday finally arrived. Feverishly, I opened the envelope containing the news sent from the Saintes-Maries station, to the text of which Gaby Leduc had added an amicable personal greeting from Sylvain and herself. Then I read the official communiqué—the 13th torpedo falling on New York; the first attempts to manufacture the Jovian synthetic nutriment on an industrial scale; the repression of the Islamic revolt in the region of Timbuktu; the work urgently begun to repair the Equatorial Alternators destroyed a few days earlier; the discovery by Ladislas Wronsky of a serum effective against "Martian bronchitis"—whose worst aspects I carefully abridged, according to the Director's orders.

At 11 a.m., I left the gubernatorial palace with Raymonde, who was dressed entirely in white. In spite of the summer Sun, we had decided not to make use of the helicopter that had been put at my disposition, along with its pilot, for two days. We needed complete intimacy and absolute liberty, so we undertook our escapade intending to use any means of transport that we chanced upon, or which caught our fancy. The air outside, although hot, was exquisite to breathe after the close confinement of our offices. Arm in arm, as joyful as children, we went down to the center of town at a lively pace, through streets that ere increasingly animated.

"What festival is taking place today?" asked my companion, huddling close to me. "Is it possible for these people to enjoy themselves while humankind is undergoing this frightful crisis?"

"It's more that they're forcing themselves to forget." I dared not call attention to the profound analogy that I saw between their situation and ours.

The world had moved on while days of overwork and nights of exhaustion—during which I was careless of everything except the presence of my beloved—had kept me within the walls of the Palais de la Garde and the artificial atmosphere of the mandarins. In the external world, in people's ongoing lives, consternation had given way to a fever of merriment, and to desperate transports of brutal pleasure. Life had become exaggerated, better to deny death.

Beneath the ardent Sun, in the intense heat of the July noon, faces were already sweating wine, eyes were burning with cynical desires, and voices cracked as they issued falsely jovial appeals to others to join the self-indulgent carousal. While I drew Raymonde along, confused and slightly fearful, I almost regretted not having taken the helicopter.

Old crones with shrill voices, sitting beside heaps of comestibles, launched envious gibes at our excessive elegance. An acrid odor of food fried in the open, with which a crowd of nervous youths, both male and female, were stuffing themselves, nauseated us as we passed by. The furious chords of pianos and electric organs blew over us, emerging from gaping music halls lit up as if by night; weary frenzy carried couples from one dance to another in the sunlit street, gyrating as if death alone could put an end to their vertiginous sabbatical. The bars were overflowing with men and women embracing one another, clamoring drunkenly and dazedly in the tobacco fumes and the odors of aperitifs and spilled wine, some of whom addressed obscene invitations to us.

The brutality and susceptibility of crowds, their irresistible force and blind wrath, as immune to pity or logical argument as a runaway horse or a mad bull, had always inspired the same insuppressible horror in me as a visit to a madhouse. This time, we were in the very midst of the dementia, which some impulse or fortuitous pretext might turn against us at any moment, and we lived through a quarter-hour of painful nightmare—I had no weapon and we dared not run—until we reached streets that were less menacing.

The atmosphere, meanwhile, remained oppressive. There was a sense of the inauguration of a new era, the dawn of a social delirium, of which the term "Martian terror" is as good a description as any.

On a near-deserted boulevard that we went along with some relief, bordered by smart houses and emporia, a racket was suddenly raised as a tumultuous procession emerged from a side-street. A banner of black velvet with silver trim, displayed above a sheaf of funereal plumes, bore a skull-and-crossbones device against a backcloth of emblematic tears, and an inscription in large letters: THE BROTHERHOOD OF MISERY. Behind the flag-bearer came the fanfare: some 20 people armed with various brass instruments and improvised noise-makers. As they crossed the boulevard they suddenly erupted, simultaneously, into a quasi-musical charivari.

It was the hymn of the new society that the members of the column were singing in chorus, at the top of their voices, but it was impossible for us to distinguish the words because of the deafening noise made by the thunderclaps of an over-zealous noise-maker. It was easy to grasp their meaning, however, by reading the inscriptions traced in white letters on the black taffeta bands elevated on poles above the ranks of the enthusiastically-howling crowd:

NO MORE SLAVERY!

LIBERTY UNTIL DEATH!

DOWN WITH THE RICH!

WE WANT TO GO TO SPITZBERGEN TOO!

DOWN WITH THE ANTICHRIST AND ALL HIS HENCHMEN!

BY FREE WILL OR BY FORCE, BUT WITH US ALL THE SAME!

THE END OF THE WORLD IS NIGH, BUT THERE IS TIME TO REPENT!

ALL FOR ONE AND ONE FOR ALL!

And others, even more direct.

The procession filed across the boulevard 20 meters in front of us. I recognized all the sorts and conditions of society: seamen, aviators, mechanics, civil servants, dock laborers, factory workers, businessmen in suits—no less ardent than the rest—and even two or three Senegalese gendarmes, without their helmets, showing their teeth as they laughed and rolling the whites of eyes in their black faces... all intermingled with women, bare-headed or bonneted, linking arms in ranks of 10 or 12, all wearing similarly covetous expressions on their hateful faces, all with the same sinister fire in their eyes, avid for a leveling engulfment in convulsions of hideous joy.

"How are such things allowed?" murmured Raymonde, disgustedly. "Aren't there any police any more?"

"No more police, I fear, my darling, than airbuses in flight or trams on the rails. All the public services are on strike, and our excursion..."

"Oh, my love, we might have to go on foot, but we can't say in Marseilles; all this madness sickens my heart and frightens me."

"Let's go to the harbor, then; we'll get aboard a ship, one way or another, and spend our Sunday further along the coast."

As we came nearer to the city center, the partying crowds gave way to these more conscious and organized manifestations of the same state of mind. It was a society prey to the release of animal instincts. They walked at liberty in every human shape and form, prominently parading their communist, materialistic or mystical imperatives. The ordinary routines of life had fallen apart, disintegrating under the influence of the panic, and its elements were re-grouping in the form of processions, each symbolizing an aspiration, a desire or a threat.

We saw a long procession of refugees filing around the Prefecture, perhaps 10,000 strong, a collection of the most tattered rags and the most disparate costumes that I had ever seen, from women with bare legs and bare feet, clad in mere slips, to men in underpants, crossing their muscular arms over their hairy chests. They were all sweating in the midday Sun, as lean and hungry as a migrating wolf-pack, all howling wildly, while brandishing their fists at the sky, or raising insanely vengeful placards:

GIVE US BACK OUR HOUSES AND OUR WEALTH!
WE ARE THE VICTIMS OF THE DIRECTORATE!
DEATH TO THE ANTICHRIST!
WE DEMAND PEACE WITH THE MARTIANS!
SURRENDER GIDEON THE ANTICHRIST TO US!
GIVE US BREAD OR WE'LL TAKE IT!

Other processions, much less dense and tumultuous, but more disquieting, each consisted of about 100 men—only men, no women—with fiercely resolute expressions beneath the masks of sweat that covered their faces like a uniform. They bore no placards, wore no insignia. These first organized bands of revolutionary Anarchism marched in tight formation, keeping in step like military patrols, each under the orders of a leader. They were apparently armed with blasters, whose black shafts and strangely-formed reflectors testified to their clandestine fabrication.

Blasters had multiplied in unexpected profusion in the last fortnight, almost under the very eyes of the Directorate, which was occupied with other matters. It was easily believable that stocks of these weapons had been laid down for a long time in the factories of Anarchism, only awaiting the ammunition—the radium—that the pillage of he Martian torpedoes now furnished in abundance. Every revolutionary soldier had evidently been issued with his blaster; some allowed their butts or reflectors to protrude coquettishly from their special holsters. One of the contingents we saw, at the top of the Rue de Rome, even exposed all of its black shafts to the sunlight, advancing with arms shouldered, like the troopers of yesteryear.

The few Senegalese who remained faithfully at their posts at the street-corners, their dutiful habits and official hypnotization having not yet been abolished by the contagion of the ambient madness, let them pass. Some looked at them enviously. Two or three, who attempted to re-establish order, were blasted apart in front of our eyes.

Then came the pillage of the Café Riche. The café had opened in the morning, with a staff reduced by the strike, but as noon chimed, all the waiters and waitresses took off their aprons. The managerial staff were attempting to evacuate the dining-room and close the establishment just as we arrived in the Cours Saint-Louis. But a contingent of the Black Guard, turning the corner of the Cannebière, prevented them from doing so. Half of the troop, despite the objurgations of their leader, installed themselves on the terrace, and the other half, carrying bottles, glasses and plates, transformed themselves into a confused torrent of benevolent and derisory waiters, serving their colleagues and the customers. The latter, bewildered at first, began to cheer them amid the popping of champagne corks, whose contents were drunk directly from the bottles, sending foam all over their faces and making the drinkers choke with laughter.

I wanted to buy a bunch of roses for Raymonde, and the crowd was pushing us up against the florist's stall. Suddenly, the crush was intensified as the crowd shifted. Terrified cries went up:

"The Dervishes!"

"A police helicopter!"

"Watch out—it's landing in the Cours!"

But it did not land; it came to a halt hovering two meters above the ground, and a Senegalese gendarme leaned out of the port-hole

The roadway of the Rue Noailles emptied, the crowd squeezing on to the pavement, and an improbable procession of dancing men advanced into the vast empty space between the tramway lines, as naked as worms, each one brandishing an enormous blaster reddened with ox-blood in one hand, like a club, and a long skewer in the other, like a dagger. They were using the latter to score their breasts, their thighs and their cheeks. Every sunburned body was smeared with blood; their bellies undulated to the rhythm of darboukas and fifes punctuated by a shrill chant of "Allah! Allah! Allah!" howling forth from frenzied heads shaking their shocks of hair, with their eyes turned back.

"The Annunciator Dervishes!" whispered my neighbor, whose fat gelatinous belly I felt trembling against my elbow. "They disembarked yesterday evening, from India or Tripoli or God know where. There are already plenty of white men with them..."

I did not hear the rest of the sentence. The Senegalese in the helicopter issued the customary formal demands. His hoarse and guttural voice was instructing the mute and petrified crowd to "Disperse, in the name of the law!" for the third time when the leader of the Dervishes leapt forward, his blaster pointed.

The gendarme's head crackled in the jet of flame; then the craft's white cockpit was cut through as if by a punch, and the machine collapsed in flames on to the flagstones, its rotor-blades expiring.

On the terrace of the Café Riche, the Black Guardsmen got up tumultuously, blasters in hand, to repel the stampede of Annunciators, who had recognized their enemies and were falling upon them, clubs upraised. Cries of "Allah! Allah! Allah!" mingled with those of "Anarchism for ever! Death to the Senegalese!"

The customers, mad with fear, plunged under the tables or threw champagne-bottles with all their might at the assailants. A black skull was split like a coconut. Blaster-beams sprang forth in every direction like jets of soda-water, volatilizing everything that interrupted their trajectories. The roof of our stall had a corner removed by a stray shot. Groups of men burned by the beams were falling on every side, writhing like crabs plunged into boiling water—and explosions came from the brawl, now being fought at close quarters, as blasters fired at one another, mutually detonating their radium ammunition.

With moans of fright, the crowd pressed forward, attempting to flee. Raymonde and I could not move, crushed against the flower-stall. My fat neighbor, who had fainted in my arms, served us as a rampart.

Suddenly, flame sprang forth and spirals of smoke extended over the crowd. The awning of the Café Riche had caught fire and the building too, fires having been ignited in several places by the blasters. The shrill cries of "Allah! Allah! Allah!" resounded triumphantly, drowning out the last few cries of "Anarchism for ever!" and "Liberty!" from the burning café.

The crowded eventually got out of the way, and we were carried by its last remnants along a road parallel to the Cannebière, towards the old port.

"Will we have time to eat, my love?" asked Raymonde, while we drank a very necessary tonic on the terrace of a quayside bar facing the ancient Phocian Lacydon.

"What's the hurry, darling? Isn't it sufficient that we arrive before nightfall? Let's go to Cassis. It'll take us two hours at the most in one of those pretty motor-boats that are waiting for us at the water's edge, bobbing in the sunlight."

She shook her head, with a soft smile, and pointed upwards at the smoke from the fire. Borne by a gentle breeze, it was coming down the Cannebière in thick clouds and drifting out to sea above the port and the ferry. "As you can see, my dear, we're scarcely 200 or 300 meters way, and the fire might reach the restaurant before we've had dessert. The entire quarter could go up like a box of matches. There are no more firemen, no more rescue-helicopters, or anything else. It's the end of the world, isn't it?"

I looked deep into her larkspur-blue eyes. They were serious; she wasn't joking. I shivered as I saw that my beloved, too, was yielding to the contagion of carefree madness that was carrying Marseilles away—doubtless along with the rest of the world—in a vertiginous whirlwind. Then, as if some kind of switch had suddenly been tripped inside my head, the observation she had just made seemed to me to be exquisitely funny. Yes, indeed—it was the end of the world! It was a matter of not stupidly wasting the few hours of respite that separated us from the Martian red death. What did it matter, anyway—we would perish together! For the moment, we should enjoy ourselves!

The restaurant was next door to the bar, where I paid with my last loose change. Before seating us at our table, however, the manager led me politely to the money-changer on the key, an old owl-faced Armenian who accepted my watermarked banknotes issued by the Directorate and gave me in return a few "Labour Bonds of the Revolutionary Committee of Marseilles," crudely printed in white on black paper. Since the day before, the manager told me, these had virtually become the only acceptable currency; in the popular quarters, in fact, payments were more often made in foodstuffs: kilos of sugar, liters of wine, bars of chocolate, oranges or watermelon quarters.

The menu was execrable and very sketchy. The spectacles that had unfolded before our eyes during the last two hours were hardly calculated to encourage an appetite, but the mellow intoxication of our tête-à-tête and the prospect of thirty-six hours of liberty restored our serenity once we were installed in a relatively pleasant corner. The nameless stew of glutinous leftovers that was represented as "*blanquette de veau*" and three wretched potatoes that arrived, watery wine, and a thin slice of crumbling camembert, made an adorable snack.

"Anyway," I said, "if we're still hungry—look at this!" I produced from my waistcoat pocket a box containing the first samples of the Jovian synthetic nutriment, which had arrived at the Directorate that very morning—and I proceeded to swallow one of the large pills, by way of dessert. One might have taken it for chewing gum.

"You'll give yourself indigestion!" my companion joked. Then, more seriously: "Let's hang on to them. Who knows whether we'll be able to eat tonight?"

She had not expressed any such doubt that morning, but our journey through Marseilles had been singularly instructive. The hour we spent at the restaurant, facing the busy quayside, showed us several further novelties.

The illusion generated by the idleness of the holiday, and by our secret optimism, had become fugitive. The funnels and masts of deserted boats were mirrored in the waters of the harbor, as if swollen by the heat; the crowd, impelled into the streets by avid curiosity despite the siesta, was milling around distractedly. Processions were passing in the distance, playing their music and displaying their banners.

There was even an authentic procession of the faithful, which filed along the quay, several thousand strong, singing hymns: an entire clergy decked out with sparkling gold Catholic ornaments, venerable tonsured heads bare despite the deadly Sun; an archbishop under a canopy giving out blessings; a holy sacrament amid the clouds of incense; and an enormous reliquary, a monument wrought in gold and silver, crushing 20 robust carriers beneath its weight, who were substituted every 100 paces. A mystical fervor transfigured every face; women were weeping and sobbing; and young curates with powerful voices were circulating along the procession's length, directing the hymns and intoning the responses of litanies that mounted towards Heaven in explosions of delirious fervor: "Pray for us, Sainte Martine! Have pity on us, Sainte Martine! Sainte Martine, deliver us from the Martians!"

This lamentable invocation sprang from the throats of all the faithful, and the people watching them pass by joined in, including the diners around us, reminded of the desperation of the situation.

Little girls dressed in white and crowned with roses, marching behind the main procession, distributed scapulars and medals bearing the effigy of the saint, which had been blessed, as an infallible antidote to the Martian threat.

Profane amulets were abundant too. A hawker came round the restaurant tables, offering them. Their efficacy seemed did not seem to be in doubt, for I recognized a varied assortment of good luck charms in the peddler's tray—little pigs, No. 13s, miniature helicopters, and so on—that I had seen in numerous buttonholes, and which I had taken for simple badges...badges of the general madness, yes, and of the clouding of heads unanimously returned to the grossest superstitions!

As for the other side of the panic, the rage to forget and the delirium of pleasure-seeking, ten leaflets for dance-halls and cinemas were handed out to us: the Ciné-Mars...eille was offering a program in which the comic and the cynically obscene alternated with newsreels: "The Torpedoing of Chicago;" "The Rescue Airfleet of Nice;" "Dancing in the Final Hours;" "The Academy of New Dances: the Torpillette and the Satanita;" "Dervishes Dancing"—and so on...

Meanwhile, the smoke continued to flow, thickening all the while, above the old harbor, coming from the burning Café Riche and numerous other buildings, which had caught fire in succession in the absence of any remedy. Distant clamors and dull explosions reached us in burst from the Cannebière. A cohort of the Black Guard, with shouldered blasters, emerged from the Rue de la République at a quick pace, heading towards the disaster...and the loot. Louts with criminal faces were coming the other way, loaded down with booty of various sorts, which they displayed to one another, jeering: silver snuff-boxes, clocks, *objets d'art*. Some, with bottles filling their pockets and under their arms, were balancing others on their heads.

As our meal drew to a close, all the people coming from the Cannebière, including the honest families of working men on strike or bourgeois folk, were carrying "souvenirs" of looted shops, laughing heartily, fathers, mothers and children alike loaded down with costly trinkets or functional items: pairs of shoes, umbrellas, packs of cigarettes, bicycle-wheels, baby-carriages, sick-beds...

Banknotes issued by the Banque de France, now mere pieces of paper, were strewn on the pavement.

The sensation generated around us by the fit of coughing that suddenly seized one of the waitresses reminded me that I had forgotten about the "Marti-anitis." And yet that word—the official name of the "Martian bronchitis"—was displayed on every street corner, on the hoardings of emergency clinics, in pharmacist's windows, on the Red Cross ambulances that carried the victims of contagion away amid the reek of phenol. But the vertigo of carelessness—in which we were almost caught up—had become so universal in those demented days that no one worried any more about their comings and goings. Only the use of blasters caused an unambiguous movement of recoil. There was more physi-cal revulsion than mortal dread in the circle that formed around the waitress, who had slumped into a chair, shaken by spasms of coughing, her face blue.

"Are you afraid, Raymonde?"

"No, I don't think so," she said, without taking her eyes off the agonized girl, who was being gently propped up by a bearded priest in a white robe and colonial helmet—but her fingers clenched about my hand, and she added: "What a hideous way to go, beloved! Let's get out of here!"

Our ridiculous meal cost me a terrifying quantity of "hours of work" as imprinted by the CRM, and I wondered anxiously what price the boatmen would demand to transport us to Cassis.

The ancient clock on the Eglise des Accoules, overlooking the Italian quarter, was chiming 2 p.m. The flagstones on the quay were roasting the soles of our shoes, and eddies of acrid smoke, scented with burning leather and rub-ber, made the stifling heat of the fiery Sun even more painful. Our gazes wan-dered indecisively over the crews of motorized yawls, petrol-driven dinghies and rowing boats that seeming to be awaiting, as in former times, the pleasure of amateur sailors.

"Sea trips from here, ladies and gentlemen, inexpensive, two people at a time!" the master of a little coaster called out to us, removing his lips from the neck of a bottle enclosed in wickerwork, while his two sailors put down their soup-spoons to mimic the acting of plying the oars.

Despite their piratical sunburned faces, I was about to accept the offer of an unexpectedly good bargain when my companion whispered: "Oh, no—not them, I implore you!"

She dragged me towards a wretched sloop, from which an old sea-dog wearing a scarlet Genoese cap with a black lining favored us with a paternal wink.

"Day trips from here! Take you as far as you want to go. Payment negotiable. Just climb aboard."

And we climbed aboard, without discussing the thorny question of price. The anchor was lifted, the oars groaned in their rowlocks, and we were glad to see the quay grow more distant. The reflections of the reddening Sun danced on the wavelets in the harbor.

"Do you know what you're doing? Mark me, you've had a lucky escape." The old salt confided to us that the crew of the "inexpensive" coaster was armed, ready for anything, and that it had begun by taking a dozen cargoes of refugees out to sea during the catastrophe at Nice, one after another.

"To sea, lady and gentleman—and they *left them there*, you understand, to come back in search of others at the end of the pier...and it's just the same here with their 'sea trips'—no one ever comes back."

Raymonde, her lovely blue eyes wide with horror, was about to reply when a great clamor went up to starboard, with the characteristic hiss of blasters. A dense mob was astir on the quay. Almost immediately, a thunderous column of fire issued from a huge petrol-tanker painted with red lead, whose mizzen-mast collapsed on the fleeing men, and a flood of burning liquid poured down on to a disemboweled ship at the mouth of the harbor, threatening to cut off our retreat.

"What a bunch of hooligans those Black Guards are!" grumbled the old mariner, redoubling his vigor. What's the point of that—what they just did? Tell me, boss, do you know how to swim? What about rowing? Yes? Then get a move on, with that other pair of oars. Help me, or we're shafted." [8]

Thanks to our desperate efforts, we escaped. But we were still under the ferry-bridge, and the entire width and breath of the harbor was nothing but a sheet of fire. The wind, fortunately, was veering to the mistral, blowing densest smoke obliquely towards the lighthouse. New explosions were going up from boats reached by the fire; cries to port and starboard advertised the commencement of the pillage.

Beyond the transporter-bridge—finally out of danger!—we caught the wind and released the oars. With my painfully blistered hands I helped our boatman raise the sail, which drew us rapidly out into the open sea.

---

[8] The expression the mariner actually uses here is *coïonnés*, one of several argot terms peppering this passage, which could be literally translated as "fucked;" as the use of such terms seems to be intended to contrive a compromise between vulgarity and euphemism, I have exercised a certain restraint in translation.

A piece of paper danced in the air in front of me. I succeeded in grabbing hold of it, and we saw that the air was full of other fluttering white sheets—the last packet dropped by a helicopter in flight that had been distributing them over the southern district: a black helicopter whose flanks bore the emblem of the Revolution: the skull-and-crossbones.

I resumed my place beside Raymonde, who was letting her hand dangle in the foam bubbling up along the side of the boat. We read it together.

The Terrestrial Directorate informs the population that a cosmogram received from the planet Jupiter identifies the city of Marseilles as the impact-point of the next torpedo launched by Mars. The catastrophe will occur on the night of July 20. The message recommends that everyone flee, immediately, and that recommendation is endorsed!

Underneath were the signatures of Gideon Botram and Ladislas Wronsky, quite skillfully forged.

"What a vile thing to do!" cried Raymonde, who also saw through the Anarchists' ruse. "To make the entire population flee, so that they can pillage at their leisure! Oh, my God! These men are worse monsters than the Martians!"

The sacrilegious sheet trembled in the wind between our fingers. I let go of it, numb with shock, wondering what would become of the Palais de la Garde and Gideon Botram, the "Antichrist," the last mainstay of the dying civilization.

"Humankind is committing suicide," I said, in a low voice.

Our old mariner launched a long jet of saliva into the blue sea, switched his wad of tobacco from one side of his mouth to the other, and said: "Bah! When dolphins are caught in the net with the tuna, the dolphins devour the tuna instead of joining forces with them so that they can all get out. We're all in the net together, now!"

VIII. The Cassis Soviet

The fresh saline breeze rustled in the saffron-colored sail deployed against the satin sky. The rocking of our vessel on the crystalline blue waves gradually soothed our nerves. The golden Virgin sparkling on top of the Palais de la Garde and the amphitheatre of the city, half-veiled by smoke, finally disappeared behind the dazzling calcareous pyramid of the Île Riou; the vertiginous tumult of Marseilles ceased buzzing in our ears like the thousand confused voices of a folly-filled conch-shell.

Our eyes, resting from the sight of human agitation, studied the pleasant retreats of the coasts desirously. As wild and deserted as they were 25 centuries ago, when the Phocian migrants arrived, the coves with strange Ligurian names, which the old salt counted off—Sormiou, Morgiou, Sugiton—opened their narrow and profound creeks within the tall, white and bare cliffs, like fjords strayed into the sunny Mediterranean.

Outside the demented civilization, snuggling in the depths of a bay more harmoniously "composed" than the scenery of an opera, between a long promontory of red ochre and white hills half-clad in large stands of pine trees—how peaceful the little port of Cassis seemed to us, from a distance! What pleasant idleness radiated from those pink villas, among the vine-covered slopes and the olive groves, and the quay with its little houses, painted in all the colors of the rainbow and the dawn! Even today, life still offered the prospect of a few indulgent and lazy hours in the cool shade of the plane-trees in that miniature town square.

So, leaving our philosophical mariner satisfied with a few Directorial banknotes—which would, a few months earlier, have paid for a passage to India for both of us—we set of in search of a hotel in which to spend our all-too-brief vacation, begun under such sober auspices.

The first attempt, on the edge of the harbor, was scarcely encouraging. There was nothing available; every room, to the smallest dark cupboard, was packed with refugees from Nice or fugitives who had fled the revolutionary panic in Marseilles. It was impossible to obtain anything to eat; there had been no bread since the previous day, and all comestibles had been requisitioned by the municipal authority. We would not find a room anywhere, the hotelier assured us, not even in private residences or the night-shelter.

The dense crowd swarming in the square, in the shade of the plane-trees, confirmed this opinion, reviving our memories of Marseilles. What madness, under the influence of the contagious radiation ravaging all humanity, had transfigured all these troubled faces simultaneously, like a fit of tragic decision?

We would soon find out.

A drum-roll resounded. The crowed moved back under the forceful pressure of 30 or so young men emerging from a side-street to the left: the Black Guardsmen, with their blasters and sweat-covered faces, were here too! The Hydra of Anarchism, which was thought to have been killed off one and for all when the scientific and rational dictatorship had put an end to the gigantic experiment instituted *in anima vili* by the Russian bolshevists, was triumphant everywhere; it extended its tentacles into the smallest village; with the aid of the Martians, it had conquered the world with dizzying rapidity.

In the fearful semi-circle opened up by the black cohort, bristling with sparkling reflectors, an old man with a vulpine face and steely eyes appeared, mounted on a flight of steps. He was clad in dirty khaki from head to toe and girdled by a funereal sash bearing a fateful silver skull flanked with the letters S.C. Despite the absolute silence—the sea could be heard softly lapping on the shingle, and the purr of a motor high in the sky—the drum-roll sounded again, and the old man read out, in a mordant and venomous tone:

"In the name of human Fraternity and collective utility, the Soviet of Cassis is hereby instituted, with absolute power over the entire territory of the ex-commune, including property of every sort and the individuals of both sexes who happen to be within its bounds at the time of the promulgation of this decree.

"Article One: habitants domiciled in the ex-commune, and they alone, are declared members of the Soviet of Cassis.

"Article Two, Clause One: Access to and abode within the Soviet's territory are forbidden to all foreign non-members of the Soviet, whether refugees, escapees or others.

"Clause Two: Any aforesaid foreigners who persist in residing within the Territory for more than 12 hours, which are accorded to them as a final concession, will be taken to the Soviet's frontier and, in the case of resistance or recidivism, forcibly expelled.

"Clause Three: Under no circumstances may nourishment be given to the aforementioned foreigners.

"Clause Four: However, those who express an irrevocable desire to join the community will be sovietized, in their persons and property, and will enjoy the privileges accorded to effective members, the former citizens of the ex-commune.

"Article Three, Clause One: All previously private property, fixed or movable, situated within the Territory, is established as the common property of all the members of the Soviet.

"Clause Two: The equitable division of victuals, clothing and other essentials will be effected at the discretion of the Committee of the Soviet.

"Clause Three: Every individual of the male sex, without age limit, will be employed according to his aptitudes in agricultural or other labor, in guarding the territory or in the manufacture of weapons.

"Clause Four: Every individual of the female sex, aged between 18 and 35 years, will be requisitioned for the special service of the Soviet Fraternity.

"Article Four: Any infraction of the above-announced dispositions, or any further regulations which facilitate their application, will be punished by death.

"Made and promulgated at Cassis, on July 20 of the old era, day one of year one of the Soviet of Cassis, by the Committee:

"Marius Bizoard, President

"Paul-Emile Cougourdan, Secretary

"Joséphin Malmousque, Chief of Soviet Defense." [9]

Applause burst out, with an enthusiasm nourished by cries:

"The Soviet forever!"

"Cassis forever!"

"Yes, yes—out with the foreigners!"

"We've seen enough of them!"

"Fraternity forever!"

"All for all; everything for everyone!"

Cackling laughter, like that of little girls when tickled, broke out here and there, mimicked by wags. There were a few indignant exclamations too, but the efficacy of the blasters was only too well-known, and any open rebellion against this cynical tyranny imposed upon several thousand men and women by a handful of sectarians would have been in vain.

Bourgeois refugees from Marseilles, seemingly well-to-do, gathered around us, planning a general retreat to the harbor. The armed force had disappeared; the members of the crowd raised their heads and gradually made their sentiments manifest. A group of young mariners, who were keeping familiar company with two or three willing girls, talked about retaining Raymonde and the prettiest of the refugees, but the latter were a dozen strong and resolute in their attitude; we passed without hindrance.

It was impossible to flee that inhospitable burg by sea! Militiamen, blasters in hand, were standing guard along the quay. To leave the commune's territory required an authorization from the Soviet—an authorization to carry out its formal instructions! The imprudent refugees trooped off to obtain one from the town hall. For myself, I did not want to offend the gentlemen of the Committee in company with Raymonde.

The crowd in the distance soon recovered from its initial surprise. It decided to put the new state of things to the test and exercise its "rights." A brawl had already broken out at the entrance to the square; there were feminine

---

[9] Varlet inserts a footnote on behalf of the narrator: "I reproduce this document from a duplicated sheet that was posted and distributed to the public; its text differs slightly from the one pronounced on the promenade on that memorable afternoon."

squeals, blows, cries of rage and pain. Within five minutes, disorder and violence had spread throughout the entire town.

Vibrant with impuissant revulsion against this odious tyranny, shocked by the horror of the face of humanity, like Lot and his wife fleeing Sodom and Gomorrah, we went past the last houses on the waterfront, heading westwards. O joy—the road was not yet under guard. The way to Salvation was open!

Our hearts beating with hope and blind resolution, we decided to follow it until its end, and then turn right, despite all obstacles, to cross the rocky wilderness that separated us from Marseilles by 15 kilometers or so.

We met other pedestrians, including a band of half-drunken quarrymen, against whom I set myself to mount a desperate resistance—but these people were still ignorant of the establishment of the new regime of "All for all" and limited themselves to hurling filthy remarks and ironic greetings in our direction.

After crossing a little plateau wooded with ancient pines, the road descended into the depths of a steep gully and skirted a sort of arm of the sea forming a narrow and sinuous cul-de-sac: the first cove. Within this sunlit fjord the solitude was complete. We passed alongside an abandoned quarry—the one that was still being exploited was on the other shore—then slackened our pace. A mere path, now, climbed the calcareous slope like a ledge, wooded to the right, bare to the left, save for the occasional bush projecting from a cleft plunging steeply down to the somber indigo of the waters that extended, a few 100 meters away, into the sea.

"You must be exhausted, my poor darling," I said, pointing to a large block of limestone shaded by a stout juniper. "Let's sit down. The Sun's already going down; nightfall will overtake us..."

"Bah! We'll make camp at the bottom of one of these pretty coves, of which we have seen so many. We have your nutriment pills to eat—they must be very nice!"

"And tomorrow, we'll have all day to walk, in sight of the sea. There's no danger of our getting lost, but I'm afraid you'll get very tired."

"It's an excursion in the mountains, that's all! And with you, my beloved... Now we're far away from our charming human brethren, I can breathe! What does a little tiredness matter to us, hey? I don't think I'd be able to sleep, so I could go on all night. Do you remember the story in Herodotus? A king of ancient Egypt, perhaps a Psammetichus, to whom the oracle revealed that he would die within a year, ordered that his palace be illuminated round the clock, and he lived by day and night alike in perpetual feasting, in order to double the time remaining to him. I would willingly imitate him...with you, and in this beautiful solitude—for we have no need of round-the-clock illumination."

"We'll have the stars," I said, heartened by the courage of my adorable companion.

We went on along the path on the ledge overlooking the cove, facing the open sea. The Sun set, invisible to us behind the rocky crest. There were tufts of pink cirrus cloud in the fading azure. Cool gusts of wind caressed our right cheeks.

The excited intoxication of rebellion that had surrounded us like a cloud since we left Cassis gradually diminished. The serene majesty of the landscape infected us without our being aware of it. Our deflation had not lasted long, however, when we suddenly found ourselves at the extremity of a point with no exit, behind which was another cove, less steep but much larger than the first.

"Yes, it's annoying," said Raymonde, when I expressed my disappointment. "We've reached the end of a useless path…but then, since night is falling and we won't be able to go much further today, wasn't it a stroke of luck that brought us here, to make camp in sight of such beautiful landscape, sheltered from human turpitude!"

We were on a natural terrace surrounded by a chaos of calcareous rocks, which sloped gently downwards. Their base was bathed by the languorous lapping of the waves in the sumptuously blue bay, which extended its peaceful solitude to the marine horizon and the long cliff of the far shore, which was reddening like a wall of brass in the last rays of the setting Sun.

"See, my love!" she continued. "There are still shelters for our love, even in this era of catastrophe and madness: the countryside, as we used to call it. Despite the Martian torpedoes, revolutions in the cities, and Soviets in the towns, we shall have had our holiday!"

Fugitives though we were, dogged by threats from Heaven and Earth, and destined to plunge back into the maelstrom of calamities—even sooner than we imagined—those few hours of grace in the midst of eternal Nature were the supreme consecration of our spousal ideals. The marvelous conversations of the preceding days—how many had there been? Four, five…or years?—had revealed our terrestrial pasts. The whirlwind of the panic and the dangers we had run together proved to me the nobility of her fraternal soul. That evening, for the first time, she and I revisited, and not in any imaginary sense, a scene from our previous life…

We had prepared a bed of pine-needles—they were more abundant on the other slope of the point—and juniper branches, in order to be as comfortable as possible. By way of a repast, one tablet each of the Jovian nutriment procured us the sensation of immaterial euphoria and lightness of spirit that must have led other people astray, but which delighted us from that first experience. They we lay down on the edge of the terrace.

The stars came out one by one. The landscape around us lost its color in the increasing darkness. The sea scarcely made a sound.

Terrestrial nature no longer solicited our senses; the egotistical aspect of our being was asleep, its duty accomplished, in the absence of immediate anger, and our spirits, absorbed all day by the tyranny of colors and forms and drowned in the imperious terrestrial light, became gradually detached, in the manner of constellations veiled by day by a screen of cloud or the blue of the sunlit atmosphere.

The universal Spirit incarnate in our ephemeral forms forgot its excessively human quotidian interests, and revealed itself in sole concern with the Eternal.

The Spirit reduced our insignificant parcels of life, intricately engaged in the extremely complicated game of the struggle for existence—for the possession of terrestrial matter—to our true importance; it overcame those infinitesimal bodies of flesh, confounding them with the vital flourishing of the Earth...the immense Earth, whose globe is surrounded by our conscious atoms...the globe of the planet Earth floating—in the mysterious snare of gravity!—more and more distantly, minuscule in the infinite space whose absolute and undeniable reality we were contemplating...

The infinite space of the Universal Heavens, whose real Presence enveloped us with its sovereign vertigo...

And my soul, spreading its wings, familiarized by long nights of solitary contemplation of sidereal profundities, drew its twin soul in its wake, in an ever-more-expansive flight, balanced by the two wings of Science and intuition....

Resting her cheek on my shoulder, however, in an anxious voice, she pointed.

"Mars! And that star there, very close to Mars and almost as red, in a fan of four stars spreading westwards-tell me, my love, what is it?"

"Antares...Antares in Scorpio."

"Scorpio! That's strange. You'll think I'm silly, but I've never been able to look at that constellation, for as long as I can remember, without shivering. It's a mystical, superstitious horror, an irresistible and insensate dread, which stirs me to the very depths of my soul like the memory of a frightful past of pain...even now, the enemy planet Mars, which has sworn to exterminate terrestrial humankind, only inspires a human dread, limited to my present existence. My soul must once have lived an unhappy existence on Antares in Scorpio, whose distant memory still haunts its new avatar—even with you by my side, my beloved, and in the certainty that the force of our love will reunite our souls beyond our present life..."

There was also the unforgettable bath we took, that night, in the lukewarm and phosphorescent water—that bath where her young and slender body, as luminous as some divine siren of yesteryear, drew in its wake a trail of blue sidereal lace...

There was...but what would be the point?

IX. In the Skies of Marseilles

Midnight had passed. In anticipation of the next day's long march, I was resigning myself to talk about the necessity sleep, when all of a sudden...

"Oh! Quickly, look at that beautiful falling star!"

The Martian torpedo, whistling as it fell, slow and red, from the zenith burst over Marseilles, into 100 artificial tears. The rippling explosion was followed by another, almost as powerful, then a third, dull and prolonged.

Marseilles delivered to the red gas! Would the Palais de la Garde escape? At a stroke, we became once again the civilized collaborators of Gideon Botram.

I had put my arms around Raymonde's shoulders. Her teeth chattered; her hands came together; by the light of the stars I made out her wide-open eyes. Eventually, she spoke first: "The cosmogram from Jupiter! It was true, then? Why wasn't Marseilles evacuated, then? Why have so few airplanes and helicopters flown past?"

"Because the Directorate gave the lie to the rumor and no one budged, except perhaps the common people. The coincidence can only have saved a few lives: our Master, with the best brains that remain to humankind."

"We can't stay here any longer. What's happening over there? Oh, my love, curiosity's devouring me—it's not just feminine weakness!"

"Yes, we have to get going. But the night's too dark...and go where? The Soviet of Cassis behind, Marseilles too far ahead..."

"Far? But look—that fire is close by!"

"That's a pine-wood burning. Marseilles is out of sight. The sky's already red over there—and look at those moving stars coming towards us: the lights of those who are fleeing by air."

She got up and surveyed the narrow terrace, a dark form set against the vague whiteness of the rocks and the luminescent sky. The throbbing sound of a helicopter passed directly over our heads, 200 meters up; we were able to discern two fugitives and two vacant seats through the hyaline walls of the illuminated cockpit. Then there was a stout and noisy airbus, further to the left, over the sea. A vague sound like an invasion of gigantic crickets filled the darkness, which was speckled with the red and green positional lights of aircraft and striped in every direction by long searchlight beams. They passed to the right and the left, and directly overhead.

"Quickly, quickly! They have to see us, to take us away...the signal...let's light the aviators' distress signal!"

It was our only chance, very slight, but which we had to try. Our mass of resinous branches and pine-needles was divided into three lots, distributed about the terrace in the form of an isosceles triangle, and set on fire with the aid of my cigarette-lighter. Their flames now illuminate the two of us at their center. There was no possibility of keeping the fires going; they would only last for a few minutes. But the bulk of the aerial fleet had passed over; the lights and buzzing sounds were thinning out.

One of our torches was already dying when the dazzling beam of a searchlight picked us out, causing us to close our eyes. When we were able to open them again, a millionaire's super-silent helicopter was hovering a few meters above our heads. At the porthole was the reflector of a blaster and a hook-nosed face, plump and clean-shaven, which examined us suspiciously.

"Who are you?" a curt and imperious voice enquired. "What are you doing there? What assistance do you need?"

I replied just as laconically: "Two employees of the Directorate, on a trip. We were obliged to flee Cassis, which is in the power of communists…"

"Have they confiscated my château?" asked the millionaire, phlegmatically.

"Without a doubt," I said, "and sovietized women between the ages of 18 and 35."

A little cry of alarm was audible in the cockpit, but the man with the hooked nose did not wince. "You haven't told me what you want."

"To be taken to the Director, if he's escaped."

"He escaped, thanks to the steadfastness of Ladislas Wronsky. The false news—or, rather, the premature news—released by the revolutionaries, was contradicted at 4 p.m., and very few people left the city…unfortunately. The anticipated pillage thus became impossible. But at 10 p.m. the entire population of the proletarian quarters marched forth under the leadership of the Black Guardsmen, to cries of 'Death to Gideon the Antichrist!' They were about to surround the Palais when Wronsky forced the Master, who wanted to resist, to flee with the Government in helicopters. They should have arrived at the La Crau airfield an hour before the destruction of Marseilles."

"Take us to the camp at La Crau, then." I was about to add: "The Directorate will compensate you"—but I simply said: "You'll be safer there."

"Than in my château in Cassis? And our wives too. That's settled—climb aboard, both of you."

As delicately as a dragonfly, the helicopter touched down on the rocky terrace, which had never been subject to any similar contact since its emergence from the waters. The cockpit door opened and we climbed into a luxurious cabin, where an excessively plump woman with peroxide blonde hair and a discouraged expression, dressed in a pink silk kimono, welcomed us with a wan smile. The man with the hooked nose placed us in the vacant seats, closed the cockpit again, and the machine rose up, without any unsteadiness and hardly any noise.

"Not too fast, Isaac, I beg you," murmured the blonde woman, nervously sniffing a bottle of smelling-salts, "and don't go too close to the fire!"

"Don't be afraid, Rachel," growled Monsieur Isaac, manipulating the little control levers on a control panel not much larger than a typewriter.

The noise of the engines was so discreet, the resonant voices so sharp, and the cabin so well-appointed, that one might have thought one was in a drawing-room. At first, the contrast between that plush interior and the solitude of the marine rocks where we had been preparing to spend the night claimed our attention—but the interior lighting was distracting our pilot, who extinguished them abruptly. The spectacle of the night became visible through the transparent walls of our aerial vehicle. The silhouette of the heights that still hid Marseilles from us now stood out against the vast reflection of the fire, while out to sea, on the surface of the waves, a single isolated flame was writhing like a red firework.

"A satanite generator that fell into the gulf," said the guttural voice of our driver. "Well, it's not the only one."

Gradually, the entire sea-lane revealed itself to our eyes, strewn with fires that illuminated everything like a nocturnal festival. Between these improvised lighthouses, an entire fleet of ships was visible—coasters, tugs, even a great transatlantic liner—fleeing in disarray, lit up in red on the bloody waters.

And the image of the Apocalypse appeared: Marseilles on fire, kilometer after kilometer along the coast; L'Estaque, the detonation of whose explosives factory we had heard, was a volcano of green, yellow and blue flames; the piers and basins of Joliette, as visible as in broad daylight; warehouses burning here and there; the old harbor still alight, spreading its flood of burning petrol every-where; and throughout all its breadth, mounted in stages above its amphitheater, the city erupted with the yellow flames of its oil refineries and soap factories, mingled with the red whirlwinds of satanite.

Over the length and breadth of the city, as far as the outlying districts, loomed the giant torch of the Palais de la Garde. In the distant agricultural lands, burning pine woods hemmed the profile of the hills, testifying, like the igneous plumes in the gulf—among which there was one solitary Stromboli in the open sea, near the Planier lighthouse—to the expansive force of the Torpedo. None of the disasters that had struck the terrestrial capitals equaled this one in its extent.

Despite the distance—we were just passing over the Château d'If—we were terrified by a voice that drowned out the vague tumult of the conflagration: the magnified voice of a loudspeaker with which some unfortunate surrounded by the gas was advertising his presence. His distinct and repeated cries of "Help! Help me!" desperately howling into the air, seemed to be the unanimous voice of he murdered city. The rescue helicopters were widely scattered, though; per-haps thirty in all, gliding hither and yon amid the red reflected light and the smoke. The strike of airbus personnel and all other means of transportation had paralyzed the rescue effort. A single disciplined airborne squadron was arriving belatedly from Toulon; its searchlights and sirens were behind us briefly, slant-ing down upon the burning city, while we moved out over the sea without stop-ping.

The voice of our host jerked us out of the state of grief-stricken hypnosis that had overtaken us.

"There's money to be made down there," he murmured, as if talking to himself—and repeated, as if by habit: "Money!" He raised his voice, at first for his wife and then for us: "And we need it, my girl, because this strike has cleaned me out. The Directorate won't be in a hurry to indemnify me for my property in Marseilles, my factory in Timbuktu, my bank in Paris or my château in Cassis. Apart from this meager machine that's transporting you, Monsieur and Madame, I'm as poor as Job right now—but I started with even less, and I defy all the Martians in the world to prevent me remaking my fortune. As true as my name's Isaac Schlemihl, there's money to be made from a little scheme I've just cooked up. Well, Monsieur..."

"Léon Rudeaux," I said, astounded to see this businessman setting his desire for money and wealth against the destruction of a capital city and the collapse of civilization.

"Ah—you're the one who draws up the governmental communiqués? My congratulations...well, Monsieur Rudeaux, I've got you out of a tight spot, and Madame too, without any fuss, you must admit, and I'm counting on you not to refuse me a small favor. You have the confidence of our international Gideon; introduce me to him as your temporary pilot and put in a word for me, so that he'll grant me a license for the exploitation of the ruins..."

"What? What about the looters? The Black Guardsmen?"

"Don't worry—they'll help me. In any case, they won't take everything, and I'll be operating legally and methodically. I can count on you, can't I?"

A strangled "yes" was my only response. Disgust and admiration were choking me. Avidity and presumption pushed to such a degree made this Shylock a kind of hero!

Meanwhile, we were leaving the hot zone of the city of Marseilles and the gulf's gigantic fireflies behind. In the darkness, which seemed more intense by contrast, we no longer had anything to guide us but the lights of the airfield at La Crau—a distant agitation of beacons, searchlights and colored signals beyond the surface of the Berre reservoir to our right, darker than the sea to our left, pricked by a few minuscule navigation lights—and, becoming more distinct as we approached, the Faramam lighthouse and the airstrips of Saintes-Maries, our objective.

We touched down at 2 a.m.; the field was as animated as an air show, but I was struck by the disarray and insufficiency of the police service: five or six Senegalese, who dared not even prevent an airbus from disembarking some twenty menacing refugees, mostly armed with blasters, before their very eyes. Blasters had become as common as the rifles and pistols of the bellicose era. Bitterly, I recalled the first governmental exodus to Mont-Valérien, and its inviolable cordon of troops. This time, it would only require one or two helicopters loaded with Black Guardsmen to abduct the Director!

The latter was asleep, it seemed, no one knew exactly where. It only remained for us to imitate him. As the moment was hardly propitious for seeking out lodgings, we accepted the hospitality offered by Monsieur Isaac and spent the rest of the night sleeping on the comfortable pneumatic armchairs of the cockpit-drawing-room that had just transported us.

X. The Abdication of the Directorate

Gideon Botram had waited until the last possible moment before yielding to the exhortations of Ladislas Wronsky and fleeing the Palais de la Garde in face of the immediate threat of insurrection. He refused to believe in the danger, and that no preparatory measures had been set in place to evacuate the governmental staff. Only he and the ministers got away aboard the few available helicopters, while ordering the Air Force at La Crau to send an aerial flotilla at the earliest possible moment to transport official documents and the other inhabitants of the Palais to Saintes-Maries. The latter, it was hoped, had nothing to fear from the popular hostility aimed specifically at "the Antichrist and his associates," not the subaltern employees who were victims of the "tyranny." What fate the Black Guardsmen had in store for them, however, remains a matter for conjecture, for the first units of the Guard had not yet reached them when the Martian Torpedo projected a satanite generator on to the Palais, and the torrents of red gas flooding the hill devoured all those who escaped the fire.

Our Master seemed to me to be singularly depressed when I was introduced into his modest room at the Hôtel de la Plage, with Raymonde and Isaac the ex-millionaire. He thanked the last-named for having brought back his most devoted colleagues safe and sound; then, having dismissed him with a promise to satisfy his request, he returned his attention to us momentarily to ask us for a few details of our adventure. When we had declared ourselves ready to resume our duties straight away, he shook our hands benevolently, and with unaccustomed emotion.

"Thank you, my friends." Then, resuming his "official" tone, he added: "Mademoiselle Becquart, would you please present yourself at His Excellency Monsieur Wronsky's office; you'll replace his missing secretary. Monsieur Rudeaux, follow me, we have to draw up a communiqué and reinstitute the Terrestrial Information Service."

He lowered his voiced, though, as he pronounced the last phrase, as if the ex-Master of the World were ashamed of his eventual powerlessness.

There was no underestimating the significance of the series of measures that he had been obliged to take: the transference of the capital to Marseilles; the replacement of Mont-Valérien by the giant station of the Camargue as the central terrestrial and interplanetary TSF station—a chain of fatalities that had inevitably resulted in the flight to Saintes-Maries. Even at the height of its glory, the Directorate of the United States of the World considered the communication service that permitted it to serve as "the world's brain" essential to its existence. That service measured out the life of its ideal organism and dispatched its sovereign orders to the most remote regions of the globe. At each stage of its political diminution, the relative importance of pure Information had increased. Now, it had become unique and predominant.

The stranded remnant of the Directorate that had finally run aground in the wilderness of the Camargue—a mere dozen individuals lodged in the white-washed walls of a cheap little hotel in a petty seaside resort, devoid of ministers, archives and staff, save for a few clerks at the TSF station, one typist and one supervisor, without any other military support than a single brigadier and four Senegalese—was a mere phantom of government that was no longer anything more than a global Press agency, a theoretical and superfluous organ, like a lucid intelligence surviving within a body struck down by paralysis.

In effect, the Terrestrial Directorate had ceased to exist, since the reawakening of nationality and the political schism of the extra-European countries. The United States of Latinate Western Europe had only survived dismemberment for a few days.

Even if Gideon Botram were only taking temporary refuge in Saintes-Maries, as was his intention, he had not transported anything to his new capital but an authority reduced, at the very most, to France—which is to say, the few large cities that not yet fallen prey to revolutionary panic.

The end of Marseilles had struck the final blow to his political authority. The last countries faithful to the former Union founded by France's scientific dictatorship—Spain, Belgium, Switzerland and Italy—gave notification of their withdrawal on July 21 and 22. By virtue of a curious phenomenon of habit, however, a vestige of his former prestige continued to surround the person of the Master in the eyes of neighboring governments. Almost without exception, the latter punctually remitted the news previously destined for the central power and asked for "assistance" in resisting Plague and Anarchy.

Both these scourges gained ground. As if primed by the fall of the torpedoes, both extended their contagion around sources that grew more numerous by the day. While the former mowed down individuals and dissolved their corpses, the second struck down supportive institutions, and, incapable of replacing them with a viable and coherent social order, broke up into local soviets independent of and hostile to one another.

Gangrene disintegrated the formerly united and vigorous body of humankind, converting it, by a retrograde evolution, into an aggregation of countless municipal "cells," debilitated and corroded by dissent.

Oh, the work of the torpedoes had been swiftly accomplished, and all resistance broken! The Martians could have disembarked from the next "celestial messenger;" we were ready to submit to their enslavement! Presumably, though, we still seemed to be too strong; their cowardice recoiled before the least possibility of danger, or virtue...

The torpedoes were still falling; the flow of disasters continued. Meanwhile, we stayed at Saintes-Maries. The dispossessed Master seemed to have been struck by a paralysis of the will. There was no more question of reorganizing a Directorate, in France or elsewhere, Bordeaux, Lille, Brussels, Geneva and Le Havre having been mentioned at first. The ex-Leader of the World, Gideon Botram, with his keen sense of reality, understood that the time of political power had passed. He was resigned to the spiritual authority of a sort of Pope-in-exile.

Our global communications center became humankind's last line of communication, its intellectual consciousness—and the "rulers" of each country, inflicted to various degrees by the same political decay, in the midst of the contagious madness of he masses, held on with all the might of their subsistent reason to this unique wellspring of civilization. The powers of darkness were gaining ground, though, and the cells of its cerebral subdivisions atrophied one by one in the progressive paralysis; some stations ceased to respond, each deliberately and arbitrarily disconnected by the sedition of a populace refusing to have anything further to do with "The Antichrist."

We were astonished, at first, that these protestations were as platonic as they were, and that no general crusade was preached and dispatched against us, but the extravagant popularity of Gideon Botram, born no one knew where or how, persisted in thwarting such ambitions. I have referred to him, explicitly, as a Pope—an anti-Pope, perhaps, but the analogy holds. Every day, he was solemnly excommunicated and accursed as he Antichrist in every temple of Christianity, and abused as a "foreigner" in 498 dialects by a good two billion souls of every other religion, but his apocalyptic prestige was his safeguard. An aureole of superstitious terror surrounded him, even in the eyes of non-Christians. To attack him would have been a sacrilege, an impiety against the designs of divine Wisdom. The fire of Heaven had spared him twice, and that must be because he was reserved by Providence for some more frightful and spectacular punishment, destined to serve as an example to every nation...

Our existence organized its routines on the model that the hazards of the first day had assigned to us. I left the hotel with Raymonde at 8 a.m. to go to our duties at the TSF station a few 100 meters away. Gideon Botram, formerly so active and early-rising, sometimes accompanied us. All arrogance, as well as all initiative, seemed to have deserted him; he chatted with us casually about the mosquito-bites he had suffered during the night, about the radiant morning light, about the cicadas that maintained their deafening concert. Walking in the shade of the plane-trees, we had the appearance of a trio of petty clerks going to their office as late as possible. The members of the government, overtaken by the same torpor of abdication, ambled around, waiting for their Master beneath the old nettle-trees on the terrace.

Ladislas Wronsky, the chief scientist, who rose at dawn, was the only one already at work. When Raymonde went into his office, rosy-cheeked, freshly-washed and scented by the sprig of Spanish broom that she had tucked into her waistband, the old scientist looked up from his papers with a severe expression, stroked his long white beard and said: "Half an hour late, Mademoiselle! Let's get a move on—and throw away those flowers, which are poisoning me." I would have cursed the indefatigable ardor for work that he alone conserved in the midst of everything, and which he attempted to share with his new secretary, had it not been for the numerous visits the latter paid to my office every day, to bring me some new communication to broadcast, or to ask for the text of a response that was late in coming.

Wronsky sometimes came in person to the operations center and, taking the place of a clerk, sent long dispatches with delicate finger-work; following his departure, I tried hard to decipher his messages from the reel of the telegraph machine, but their meaning remained enigmatic. Among many other vain questions, he was determined to discover at any price what mechanism a Martian torpedo might contain—or, rather, the basal unit that projected the satanite generators. And he implored every country, collectively, to open one up intact for him, rather than destroying it with explosives! It was a fine time to satisfy the puerile curiosity of an out-of-work scientist!

My working days caused a long sequence of news-items to unfold before my eyes. Torpedoes fell on Berlin on July 22, Moscow on July 23, then on Calcutta, Peking, Antwerp and half of Flanders—whose dikes were not high enough to hold back the tide of infernal red gas. There were the ravages of the plague, the emigrations of city-dwellers, submerging the country-dwellers, who resisted them with weapons in hand, forcing a retreat to higher altitudes, where they thought they might find safety, and where they perished in thousands of hunger, cold and exposure. There was the general refusal to consume the Jovian nutriment, although we were hoping, by that means, to spare the world the scourge of famine; it was falsely accused of causing "Martian bronchitis," and people joyfully set fire to the stocks that helicopters from La Crau distributed to the cities. The workers at the factory making it at Saint-Louis-du-Rhône fell prey to this dread, so we gave up....and every morning, regularly, this laconic and sibylline cosmogram arrived from Jupiter: "Have courage! Examine the torpedoes!" Were they, too, like our Ladislas? It was definitely a mania.

The passive languor holding sway in the atmosphere of the offices overwhelmed me. I fulfilled my duties to salve my conscience. All this information, and the reports in which I summarized it, seemed to me to be utterly tedious and vain. What good did it do to keep humankind up to date with the new misfortunes that struck the race? What was the point in thus poisoning its final days?

At 6 p.m. I handed over to one of my two auxiliaries and lit a cigarette in the doorway. Then Raymonde joined me and we went for a stroll together on the narrow strand of fine sand isolated between the low dunes and the blue, tideless sea. The coast extended indefinitely beneath the implacable azure, flat and monotonous; the only two "features" of the countryside were the wrought iron obelisks supporting the network of TSF antennae and, lower down, the ruddy roofs of the village grouped around the ancient church, built in yellow stone gilded by the perennial sunlight and crenellated at the top like a Medieval fortress.

The luminous melancholy of this world's-end penetrated our souls, causing us to forget external anxieties. We said very little, content to enjoy one another's presence—or, rather, allowing nature to be a third party to our intimacy. Raymonde had a passion for botany, her mastery of which had long surpassed mine, so we studied the flora of the sands and the salty plain: plants covered with silky hairs or prickling thorns, or with swollen and glaucous tissues, blue thistles, yellow poppies, bouquets of thrift of an exquisite lilac color, sweet-scented sea-lilies…

We went back there in the evenings, sometimes alone, sometimes with Gaby Leduc, whom I had already seen during the day, in the course of business. Her husband occasionally accompanied us—my old friend Sylvain, whose dutiful steadfastness sustained the Air Force at La Crau and whose vigilance ensure the provisioning of the Directorial staff, the TSF station and the greater part of the village of Saintes-Maries. Not once did we go back to the hotel after dinner, with the distinguished refugees and minister's wives, because those haughty hypocrites with their lorgnettes sickened us with their vainglorious and slanderous gossip. Not once was Raymonde able to play the piano, thanks to those Tartuffes in skirts.

For ten days, we lived the pedestrian and stagnant existence of bureaucrats by day, and modest village folk by night—and every day, the funeral bell tolled for new victims in the region, prey, like the rest of the world, to the Plague, to the red death of the torpedoes, to Anarchism, to the dementia of the panic and to desperate pleasures. It seemed to us that all of that had been going on for years and might continue indefinitely, like the Martian bombardment.

XI. What the Air Force Commander Saw

I never found out the real reason for the long five-day excursion which the head of Air Force operations at La Crau undertook during that dark interval. Officially, he was commissioned to sound out the dispositions of the governments of countries detached from the Union, but we guessed that there was something else behind this pretext.

Isaac Schlemihl, rewarded with his license for the exploitation of Martian radium, had chosen Avignon as his center of operations, and the proximity of the ancient papal city was too tempting for the commander at La Crau, with his insatiable curiosity and his spirit of adventure, not to pay the audacious businessman an immediate visit. I have every reason to suppose that our friend Sylvain undertook his official tour with a few kilos of radium hidden in his cockpit, destined to resupply the constitutional powers in Spain and Algeria, who had run out of the precious metal. What commission did Schlemihl give him on the price of the sale? In what currency were the transactions completed? Was Gideon Botram mixed up in the business? There were so many points that it is impossible for me to elucidate, because our friend Sylvain restricted his account of his voyage to an episodic narration.

The story that he told Gabrielle, Raymonde and myself one evening in our room at he Hôtel de la Plage contained facts so curiously characteristic—not to say tragic—that I made haste, the following morning to write them down. These notes, preserved through the most perilous adventures, have aided me in composing my memoirs.

Sylvain Leduc and his mechanic Champoreau had taken off in their favorite helicopter—the "old crate" that had already over flown a capital city in flames with me as its passenger, and was destined to have a near escape from yet another torpedo.

The shoreline of Languedoc, and that of Catalonia, whose curving line they followed rather than cutting straight across the Gulf of Lyon, offered them a spectacle—normal in that era—of seething disorder: cities, towns and villages establishing their local Soviets, the swelling numbers of the Black Guardsmen, flags displaying the skull-and-crossbones, blasters and mass executions. Mystical processions wound through the countryside, and the pilots of those pirate helicopters of Anarchy that were not flying towards the obliterated cities to pillage the ruins were amusing themselves by sowing death and panic in the ranks of those miserable sheep.

Barcelona, faithful to its traditions, had already rebelled against Soviet power; from one end to the other, the superb Rambla was nothing but a confused battlefield, and several public monuments were on fire. Analogous scenes were occurring in the other towns, and Leduc, habitually blasé, summarized what he saw in Valencia and Seville with this lapidary statement: "People were demolishing them without knowing why, and there were fires everywhere." In the Sierra Morena and the Sierra Nevada, the forest clearings were swarming with people, as if the entire population of the region had come to camp out on their peaks.

"All that was banal to me, you understand," Leduc said. "And my brave Champoreau yawned as if to dislocate his jaw. He had just asked me whether we would still find *moukères* [10] in Algeria as we were arriving at Gibraltar, when I saw a flag fluttering in the wind on top of the famous Rock. I thought I was seeing things, and told Champoreau to take us down to 200 meters—there was no mistake! It was the English flag, the so-called Union Jack—and, even better than that, columns of what looked like red ants winding along the spiraling roads and on the ramparts: the old Redcoats! There was still an English garrison at Gibraltar! Although there were no more national flags, no more governments, hardly any more society, while everyone else was pitching camp where he pleased, these damned Englishmen had found a way to reinstall themselves on their Rock as if nothing had happened! That took me by surprise.

"We had opened the portholes, because of the heat, and we scented the characteristic odor of Albion—that cumulative perfume of Navy Cut tobacco, brandy, whisky, rum, plum pudding, roast beef and tea. On the parade-ground of the fort a company of redcoats was standing motionless. They had rifles, surreptitiously conserved in bunkers along with the uniforms, and they fired a volley as the flag was lowered and hoisted three times, saluted with regimented cries of 'hip, hip hurray!' Where had they dug them up, these Englishmen of Gibraltar? They were 30 years behind the times!"

The Englishmen in question had maintained all their fine traditions, however, and out two aviators had to pay the price for their curiosity, for a shell, bursting 10 meters from the helicopter, reminded them that "no one flies over Gibraltar."

In Algeria, Leduc found a situation less advanced than in Europe but just as serious. The Islamic uprising in Timbuktu had already spread, even to the peaceful tribes of our old colony; the Atlas mountain region was beset by fire and bloodshed and the large coastal cities, especially Algiers, were resisting with difficulty. I don't doubt that Schlemihl's radium was gladly received there. Poor Champoreau did not have the leisure to make the acquaintance with the anticipated *moukères*, though, for, after a brief halt at Bône—Constantine had fallen into the hands of the Khroumirs and there was no longer a single living European in Tunisia—Leduc set a new course for northern Italy. The southern half of the country had been provided with radium by the Rome torpedo; Sicily and Calabria, overrun in every direction by troops of anarchist marauders, of-

---

[10] There is no English equivalent of this French adaptation from Arabic, which refers to women of easy virtue.

fered scant temptation to our explorers, who were so inadequately armed that they carefully avoided getting close even to a lone helicopter.

It was in the open sea south-west of Sardinia that they encountered the American millionaire's yacht.

"Some kind of eccentric, who did not even have a radio aboard—deliberately, too, for he wanted to take a complete vacation, ignoring all business matters, just fishing and drinking cocktails on his boat...leading the life of a natural man, no less! Left America two months before. Last landfall at Monaco three days before the first torpedo. Always on the move thereafter, around Corsica and Sardinia, in absolute ignorance of events. The Jovian cosmogram announcing the projectile? A rumor! He had seen Cagliari burning from the sea, but that was insufficient to inform him, wasn't it? So his yacht, which I perceived as it was hauling up its fishing-nets like some vulgar lugger, was carrying the colors of the United States of the World, with an America ensign in the corner, according to maritime custom before the cataclysm. That was the detail that gave me the idea of going down for a bit to talk to him...not without being hailed to come aboard, because I didn't want to be shot at, as in Gibraltar. On the contrary, though; he welcomed us as old friends.

"His English threw me—*Yes, damn it* is all I know—and he didn't speak French, or even Italian. Fortunately, Champoreau, who's done a stint in Australia and has a gift for languages, played interpreter. Our old crate was moored to the bridge by the lascars and we had a chat with the boss, W. J. K. Dervanbilt—yes, the Cannery King in person—in the fancy stateroom, around a collection of glasses and bottles: whisky, Benedictine, kummel, chartreuse, and cigars with gold bands, like in the old days. But that wasn't all, brother, and as soon as I had twigged the situation, I amused myself by letting him go on...

"He had his bully beef factories in Chicago, and—a quirk of which he seemed proud—all his title-deeds, bonds and banknotes in the *Esmeralda*'s strong-box. The crew? Oh, that strapping fellow would have broken one of them over his knee and clobbered the rest with the pieces; anyway, he had a real bulldog as second-in-command and loaded blasters in his pockets. Would they form a sea-borne Soviet when they had taken in what Champoreau translated on my behalf? At any rate, W. J. K. Dervanbilt's eyes widened like soup-plates when he understood that his home town had copped a Martian torpedo. Chicago razed! Factories gone, banks gone, government gone—everything gone! A smash worse than all the *Grand-Soirs* [11]... and I showed him cuttings from the Ameri-

---

[11] A *Grand-Soir* [Great Eve] is a day of revolutionary upheaval, when an old order comes crashing down and anything seems possible; the phrase was beloved by the French Marxists and Anarchists of Varlet's day, who had the revolutions of 1789, 1830 and 1848 to look back on—even though none of them had really lived up to that billing—but it has no English equivalent because the English never went in for that sort of thing.

can papers, proclamations, communiqués, my official papers and Isaac Schle…well, in brief, enough to convince Saint Thomas.

" 'Well,' he said, finally, putting his fat cigar down on the edge of the ashtray. 'Well, it's finished!' Then, taking a key from his waistcoat pocket, he went to open a big strong-box that took up a whole corner of the stateroom. 'Please help me,' he added, taking an armful of title-deeds and banknotes.

" 'He's asking us to help him,' Champoreau translated, flabbergasted by these heaps of papers that represented thousands and millions of dollars.

" 'Overboard,' the millionaire directed us, heading for an open porthole.

" 'He wants us to throw it all in the sea!' protested my Champoreau.

" 'What do you expect?' I said. 'It's no good for anything else!'

"In five minutes, the clearance was finished. As if nothing abnormal had happened, our man offered us one last cigar, gave us one last handshake, and, while two crewmen were untying our helicopter, phlegmatically instructed the others to cast the nests again. Bah—that Cannery King wasn't about to die of hunger; there are plenty of fish in the sea."

That devil Leduc had a rather simplistic manner of putting things!

He also had the cruelty to hold us breathless with a prolonged description of Florence, which he flew over during the burning of the Pitti Palace and the neighborhood of the cathedral, while the historic Dome swam in the smoke 'like a golden pumpkin;' it extended as far as the lagoons of Venice—but the jocular manner was unsustainable, and he cut it short.

"Well, yes," he resumed, after a pause, "I saw that torpedo close up. Gaby must have told you. When I think about it…brrr! What you don't know, though, is that, in falling, it saved our Gideon. We were coming back from Venice, heading straight for La Crau. We were between Brescia and Verona, within sight of Lake Garda, when we came across a dense column of people on the march, which must have taken up a good six kilometers of road…talk about dust! Fifty thousand strong, at least. Men, women, children, a mixture of all the national costumes of the region—Venetian, Tyrolese, all the way to the depths of Dalmatia and Herzegovina. All as ragged as could be, dragging their feet, loaded down with bundles, sweating under the hot Italian Sun, bawling hymns with one voice, led by priests of every sort, sweating more and howling louder than all the rest.

"I've seen my fair share of processions, pilgrimages, migrations and the like, but that one, which I saw close up by going down and running along its course from east to west, astonished me. With a mystical fury in their eyes and voices, they shook their ridiculous weapons at us—knives, sticks, broken scythes—aggressively. For them, our helicopter was obviously a diabolical messenger. They threw stones at us…which fell back on their heads, causing them to abandon the sport in short order.

" 'Can't you hear what they're shouting, Boss?' Champoreau said. '*Antecristo, Antecristo! Abassa, Antecristo!* Death to the Antichrist!' I certainly could hear it! And I saw, too, that all of them had large crosses made of white cloth sewn on their left shoulders. Non doubt about it, it was a crusade—the last crusade—marching against the Antichrist. That, undoubtedly, was our Gideon!

"What they might have been able to achieve, I have no idea—and they're incapable of doing it now, for a very good reason—but you can imagine how interested we were. The head of the column had just come to a halt, on the orders of a singular upstart mounted on a donkey, escorted by a dozen burly fellows who hailed from Brescia. What the Devil did he want of them? And why were these Crusaders obedient to his least gesture? What mysterious authority did the individual on the donkey exercise? His bare feet were brushing the ground, protruding from his white tunic. His long red hair, parted in the middle, together with his beard, created a solar radiance around his face. I couldn't see his eyes—from above you understand—but they held the crowd in absolute thrall. Christ's double! He had an electrifying impact on that crowd of fanatics, who were only attentive to him.

"The rearguard of the column was still advancing, overflowing the road on both sides, gradually spreading further and further into the fields, on to the terraces of vines, climbing the fig-trees and olive-trees, surrounding our Christ and his 12 apostles, over whom our helicopter was hovering, like the Holy Spirit! You know me—this mystical nonsense leaves me cold, doesn't it? Well, if I hadn't had shuddering and vibrating controls beneath my hands and feet, I think I might have yielded to the contagion of that crowd. That incorrigible street-arab Champoreau had stopped talking; he was very pale as he listened to that Christ, who had dismounted from his donkey to harangue the crowd from the crest of a mound.

"He spoke to them about the iniquities of men, who had drawn the wrath of the Eternal Father down upon them and had merited that deluge of torpedoes. 'The fire of Heaven will consume the entire Earth, and the End of Time is at hand,' he went on, in a clear and vibrant voice that filled the countryside. 'One means alone remains by which to suspend the judgment of my Father, and that is to renew the sacrifice of Golgotha here; to offer me on the cross as an expiatory victim for the salvation of humankind!'

"He was undoubtedly ready to do it, and the delirious multitude assembled around him, believing his words to be as hard as iron…but they were all horror-struck at the thought of raising a sacrilegious hand against their Saviour. 'Sure!' Champoreau was finally able to say. 'He knows full well that no one would dare…'

"But someone did dare. A little man, bent and broken, in a dirty overcoat, with a long white beard and a hooked nose, detached himself from the crowd and came forward to prostrate himself before the Christ. 'Here I am!' he said. He lifted up his head. I thought I was looking at Isaac Schlemihl…who was also the Wandering Jew…who was also Judas! An enormous clamor went up, of horror, relief, triumph. Freed from its anxious delay, the crowd followed the example and precipitated itself forward to accomplish the immutable ritual.

"Coins rained down at the feet of the Wandering Jew, who gathered them up one by one, avidly. 'Enough!' said the Christ, taking hold of his arm. 'You have your settlement—30 pieces of silver, AS BEFORE!'

"Two young poplars by the roadside fell beneath the axe, were stripped of their branches by 100 mad woodcutters, who got in one another's way, and were tied together with a few loops of rope to make a crude cross, which was dragged up to the impassive Christ. The Judas-cum-Wandering Jew set it on his shoulder. 'Walk!' he stammered, tremulous with rage and holy terror…and amid the horrified rumor of those 50,000 spectators, the scene followed its inevitable course.

"Beneath the whips of Catholic and Orthodox priests, playing the parts of Roman soldiers with demonic frenzy, the Christ, bowed down by the burden of infamous wood, fell and got up again three times while climbing the Golgotha of a small hill overlooking the calm water of Lake Garda.

"The Christ was stripped of his white tunic, for which the priests played dice; he lay down on the cross…but there were no nails. 'Here they are!' laughed Judas mockingly, taking from his pocket three long iron skewers, ringed with rust, one by one. 'They're the ones FROM BEFORE, Master; I gathered them up and saved them carefully. ONE NEVER KNOWS.'

"And the rite was completed! He was a contraband Christ, to be sure, but that's not important; he was a son of man, flesh and blood like you and me; they were real nails of rusted iron that were driven into his hands and feet, clenched in atrocious agony; it was real blood that spurted forth and trickled down, once the cross was stood up and wedged into its hole with three heavy stones. It was a real human cry that the agonized Christ released amid of the frightful silence of the apocalyptic multitude accumulated on the gradient of that improvised theater.

"We were still hovering at 20 meters, gorgonized, when…oh, my friends! There was a VRRR directly overhead, a crescendo, and…KABOOM BOOM BOOM BOOM! The bolide! A Martian torpedo was falling into the crowd, the principal section 100 meters away from us, sprinkling the human swarm with its generators, which began to belch red smoke amid the deafening howls of people devoured alive by satanite…and nailed above it all was our Crucified Christ, expiring on his Golgotha, an intact islet within the rutilant flood!

"Don't think for a minute that while I saw all that I was as tranquil in my helicopter seat as I am in this armchair now. Oh, my friends, what a thunderbolt from the God of wrath! 'Damnation!' I said to myself as I saw the blow coming. The bolide explodes; we catch a serious gust of wind and are sent spinning towards a generator, which rips off one of our rotor blades and comes down 100 meters away. The helicopter pirouettes, I'm thrown into the air and almost through a porthole—but the engine keeps going. Champoreau hasn't let go of the controls; he's gripping them like a monkey, with his head down. He brings the craft up again, minus at least one rotor blade, and we climb again, using our propulsive engines instead of the rotor blades, above the tide of satanite in which our thousands of Crusaders are howling like the damned souls they are…and the Christ, on his cross…he had asked for it, but if Champoreau had let me, I would have taken him down, the poor devil…not that it matters, in the end…

"And then, we ended up arriving, not much the worse, at Brescia, where I was able to get my hands on a new rotor blade in exchange for a few grams of radium, which I just happened to have…"

XII. The Invisible Aegis

The sudden, unexpected and imminent hope of deliverance for humankind visited the TSF station first. For seven hours we alone, along with a few engineers in the tropical regions, bore the burden of anxious expectation. In fact, Wronsky, the instigator of that hope, saw fit to reveal it to us—which is to say, the official staff, including the ex-ministers, Gideon alone having already been informed—on the evening of July 31, and swore us to secrecy. If the experiment failed, we, the last civilized men whom he deemed worthy of subjection to such a rude proof, would be alone in suffering the disappointment. The rest of the world would only be informed in the case of the success of the means of salvation on which, for several days, all over the terrestrial sphere, thousands of workmen had been laboring feverishly, without being aware of the end they were pursuing, maintained at their posts by a few 100 discreet and devoted engineers.

The concise and lucid explanations that Wronsky wanted to give to us before communicating them to the world caused me to admire the sagacity of his genius and blush with shame at my doubts regarding the mysterious radio messages sent forth by the old man.

The deviation of the first torpedo—headed for Nancy, according to the Jovian astronomers, but which had actually fallen on Paris—had been attributed by the majority of journalists to an error on the part of the said astronomers. Some, however, had voiced the suspicion that the torpedoes were being carefully tracked by the Martian engineers and redirected shortly before their explosion by means of Hertzian waves acting on some telemechanical mechanism.[12] The partisans of this hypothesis also remarked that the extraordinary slowness of the engines' fall did not correspond with the ballistic rapidity of a projectile launched towards Earth from Mars and following its trajectory freely. The torpedoes must, therefore, be equipped with a "brake" activated by the same mechanism. The much more numerous partisans of the other hypothesis replied: "not at all!—it's a simple parachute that opens by itself as it reaches the upper layers of the atmosphere, so that the retarded machine inevitably deviates from the anticipated point of impact in a direction opposite to the Earth's rotation, as

---

[12] This kind of steering-mechanism would be impractical, because the distance between Mars and Earth, even at opposition, requires several minutes for information to be transmitted back and forth at the speed of light, making reactive adjustments difficult. As the reader will see, Varlet consistently has difficulty in accommodating the limiting velocity of light within his extrapolations, although he is aware of some of its implications.

evidenced by the fact that Nancy and Paris are situated on the same line of latitude in a westerly direction."

The inquiries of Wronsky's that had seemed silliest to me concerned the meteorological conditions in the various regions successively torpedoed at the moment when the machines struck. The unanimity of the responses had even struck me as I transmitted them to my superior—but he knew that they were a striking confirmation of his hypothesis. *Every torpedo had fallen in a zone of fine weather*. Thus, perfect visibility and the ease of locating lighted cities standing out against the dark face of or planet had enabled the Martian engineers to follow and rectify the course of their projectiles. Had they had been launched once and for all, their points of arrival would have been mathematically determined, with no account taken of the clear or cloudy state of the terrestrial atmosphere.

The good weather that invariably reigned in areas as varied as those of the numerous points of impact—in frank contradiction of the calculus of probabilities—sufficed to demonstrate that the torpedoes had been accelerated or decelerated (the times of their fall varied), and deviated to a greater or lesser degree (since they maintained approximately the same parallel) in their course, in order to arrive in a zone of good weather, there to be steered to their final target.

Wronsky told us that he strongly suspected that the "brake" and the "Deviator" comprised a system of turbines, in which the dissociating atoms of radium acted by reaction, in the manner of an artificial firework, and whose trigger was activated by the influence of waves of a specific frequency sent from Mars. The description, so carelessly given to our "brothers in space," of the telemechanical apparatus used on Earth had doubtless furnished the model for theirs. Waves emitted by the Earth at a given moment ought, therefore, to be able to counterbalance—indeed, to overwhelm—the Martian waves and render the torpedoes harmless. Only an exact frequency, however, could operate such an apparatus, which would otherwise be indiscriminately obedient to all the waves traversing space. It was, therefore, necessary, in order to attempt this means of protection, to know the details of the trigger mechanism placed by the Martians in the main body of their torpedoes. That was the research recommended to us by the words contained in the daily cosmograms from our friends on Jupiter: "Have courage! Examine the torpedoes!"

The old scientist had almost despaired of ever obtaining this indispensable information. All the basal bodies of torpedoes recovered thus far had been so badly damaged by the rescuers' explosives that their mechanisms were reduced to inchoate debris. The task of the scientific commissions in every country charged with that examination—without suspecting its capital importance—was also hindered by the bands of looters in quest of radium destined for the Anarchists' blasters.

It was not until July 29 that the torpedo which had fallen on Peking yielded its secret to a few valiant heroes. With intrepid folly, even before the red gas had been neutralized and dissipated by the jets of carbon dioxide, three Japanese engineers, sacrificing themselves for the salvation of humanity, had dressed themselves in platinum diving-suits—with which no one had yet dared to experiment, save for radium looters who had not come back—and made their way down to the basal unit, which proved this time to be almost intact. They had re-emerged covered with atrocious burns, despite their protective vestments, their lungs eaten away, dying—but they bought back the frequency-activated mechanisms, whose exact description was immediately transmitted to Saintes-Maries.

"Then," the old scientist continued, "we were able to get started...

"Those among you who are attached to the interplanetary TSF know that the observatory on Ganymede has not ceased to advise us, every morning, of the heading that the daily torpedo is following, followed from space by the penetrating eyes of the televisors. However, as the deviation imparted to that machine at the last moment could displace it by 1000 or 1500 kilometers from the anticipated point of impact, the zone under threat became so large that its evacuation was quite impracticable. Thus, the torpedo that caused the death of our unfortunate colleagues in the Palais de la Garde seemed to be destined for Cairo! The publication of Jovian cosmograms only succeeded in generating disorder worse than the catastrophes themselves—hence the solemn oath of silence that we had to exact from the employees to whom I have just alluded.

"We are informed, however, of the trajectories that the Martian 'messengers' follow through the skies. On several occasions, our large telescopes at Mont Blanc and Gaurisankar have been able to pin-point them before their fall. I have been informed that the Mont Blanc instrument has already got a fix on the torpedo that is intended to strike the Earth in a few hours time. It is at the zenith of San Francisco. Where the final deviation will take it, I don't know—but I do know that we possess the desired means to determine that deviation ourselves!"

While delivering this improvised conference-speech to his audience, grouped in the control room, Ladislas Wronsky had never ceased striding back and forth. He stopped, his legs apart, his arms folded across the breast of his frock-coat, and, while surveying us with an expression redolent with joy and pride, he hammered home his conclusion: "At this very moment, my friends, the last connections are in place and the last adjustments are being made. When the projectile is within range of terrestrial radiation, we shall attempt...the salvation of humankind.

"The distribution of electricity will be briefly interrupted all over the world; the 25 central Equatorial Alternators will run at their maximum, and the total current—200 million kilowatts—will be launched into the oscillators and transmuted into electromagnetic waves, in order to deflect the torpedo and send it to ravage the polar deserts or to be engulfed in the Pacific Ocean!"

There was no applause; not a single cry was raised, nor a single word spoken. The entire auditorium seemed to be overwhelmed by the enormity of the news: the dread of an atrocious disappointment prevented us from welcoming this hope—so imminent, so rational, so luminously deduced—as real. Our minds, hypnotized by three weeks of disaster, resigned passively to await the Red Death, dared not believe it. It took several minutes for the meaning of the peroration to sink in to out inmost consciousness. Then, in the silence, a strangled cry of ecstatic joy went up from a group of female operators—and, as if we had been waiting for that signal, old Wronsky's enthusiastic confidence went through us all like an electric shock.

I didn't know what was happening around me; I was blind to the external world. My arms had spontaneously embraced Raymonde, who was beside me; with my face buried in her hair, I breathed in its perfume spasmodically. In a dazed trance, among the ringing bells and distant clamors filling my ears, I heard two alternating voices—hers and mine—repeating endlessly: "Saved!…it's over!...we're saved!...the world's saved!...saved!"

No one dreamed of leaving the room. We all remained seated in the places where the news had taken us by surprise. Fragments of incoherent and feverishly familiar sentences went back and forth among the ranks of chairs; in the brightness of the arc-lamps, all the faces wore the same fixed and prolonged smile, painful to behold at length, as irritating as any tic. At intervals, strange silent intervals came from nowhere to set aside the chatter with which we veiled our anguish.

After an hour and a half, the lights suddenly went out. There were two or three cries of alarm, then a mute darkness in which one could hear one's own heart beating. The equatorial oscillators had begun to function; the invisible aegis of terrestrial science was finally opposed to the Martian red death!

We waited, motionless, shivering in spite of the warmth. The starry night was visible through the open windows. A distant owl sounded its monotonous two-note cry.

When half an hour had elapsed—a seeming century!—the lights suddenly came back on. A bell rang; a telegraphic receiver began clicking. Wronsky, his long white beard resting on Gaby Leduc's shoulder, deciphered the message in a low voice. We held our breath.

He drew himself up to his full height again. He had recovered the impassive voice of a geometer at a blackboard.

"My friends," he said, "I have the honor of telling you that the experiment has succeeded. The direction of the Martian torpedoes is henceforth in our hands. The one that our waves captured has just fallen in the Pacific, between Hawaii and the Californian coast. The Earth is saved. Humankind can get back to work!"

Part Two: The Sign of the Beast

I. The Earth Delivered

The little that we saw of it, in our minuscule village of Saintes-Maries, suf-ficed to give us an idea of the wave of enthusiasm and veritably frenzied joy that overran the Earth that day. Europe and Africa were still plunged in night but most of the towns were woken up by the sound of bells and loudspeakers pro-claiming the Deliverance; the illuminated streets filled up; people embraced, acclaiming the triumph of human ingenuity over Martian perfidy. The name of Ladislas Wronsky was on all lips; that of Gideon Botram became popular again, his nickname a badge of glory; in the heat of the first enthusiasm even the para-doxical cry of "Gideon the Antichrist forever!" was heard. And dances were organized, to the accompaniment of every imaginable musical instrument: an epidemic of dancing that carried couples away, aggregating them by twos and threes and agglomerating them in masses of rhythmic joy, monstrous sarabands uniting entire towns beneath dazzling illuminations…and beneath the vigilant eyes of the Martian televisors.

It was daylight in Asia and Oceania, evening in America, but the demon-strations were similar. As soon as the peril was past, Humankind imagined that the evils it had generated had would vanish, as if by a wave of a magic wand, disappearing and giving place without transition, to the former state of things.

That illusion was perhaps stronger at Saintes-Maries than anywhere else, if that were possible. The people of the locality, including the numerous refugees, had only tolerated the presence among them of "the Antichrist and his associ-ates" reluctantly. Their obsequious falsity had only smiled as we passed by be-cause of the provisions generously distributed by the governmental helicopters. That morning, at least for several hours, their sentiments were purified of any admixture. Ladislas Wronsky and Gideon Botram were carried in triumph to the old fortress-church, while we, his collaborators of every rank, shared the honor of being harangued by the old parish priest beneath the ancient vaults and hailed as the ministers of divine Providence. The solemn *Te Deum* was followed by a ritual farandole, and we were paraded through the village once more, amid ova-tions to which the eight or ten local Black Guardsmen prudently joined their voices.

There was no serious disorder, but the license of a population, so to speak, *in delirium* quickly forced us to retreat to our room. The TSF service being as-sured by a handful of employees, our Master had granted a day's holiday to the rest of the staff—but Raymonde, as Wronsky's secretary, and I, as the head of the Information Service, were obliged to attend an extraordinary Council of State, which discussed what measures might be taken, in view of the new situation. The dissident states, Gideon Botram thought, would undoubtedly offer to reconstitute the United States of the World.

The session was fixed for 10 a.m. It was 7 a.m. when the vague distress I had been experiencing for hours, and which had imposed itself upon me since my return to the Hôtel de la Plage, finally laid me low. There was a sharp pain in my side, like a red-hot iron, my throat was sore, my lungs felt as if they were clamped in a vice, and my head as if it were filled with lead: the first symptoms of "Martian bronchitis," as described to me by Gaby Leduc, who had suffered a slight bout a few days earlier. Staying on my feet became intolerable.

I felt obliged to make that confession to Raymonde, but I did not have to; the moment I opened my mouth, she told me to go to bed with anxious solicitude. I was very pale, she suggested softly. She could have said "livid;" the dirty mauve tint of my hands, resting on the covers, filled me with profound disgust.

How hideous I must seem to her, I thought. *Poor darling! What a memory she'll retain of me, if I die!*

The inevitable crisis of coughing and suffocation ensued, and made me forget these vain anxieties. Knowing the futility of trying to find a doctor in that time of popular rejoicing, Raymonde watched, powerless and despairing, as the agonizing pain made my writhe on the pillows. There was, in any case, no serum in Saintes-Maries, and all other treatments were ineffective. Life or death depended on the patient's strength of resistance. In the absence of serum, one could only let nature take its course.

I soon entered into a kind of stupor, characteristic of the malady, the sight of which inspired great pity in observers. From my point of view, on the other hand, it was a period of extraordinary detachment, I might almost say of radiant serenity. At the outset, my consciousness still recoiled from external sensations, before taking refuge in the illimitability of the brain to await the outcome of the battle enjoined by my entire being against the illness. My fever-veiled gaze fixed itself with secret despair on the anguished face of my beloved. I resisted; I did not wish to die! To die in the very hour when the Earth as delivered! To die when our relationship had only just begun to live! When the garden of the liberated planet was on the point of opening around us, in which we could expect to experience all the inexpressible joys of love and of civilization restored to its apogee…!

Little by little, the seething of that revolt eased. My soul ceased to indulge itself in the feverish evocation of that beautiful future. The beloved hand placed on my burning forehead penetrated me with benevolent effluvia of infinite gentleness and resignation.

I understood then that death is nothing, that there is no death! What importance was there in living a little longer, or not quite so long, on *this* planet, given the relativity of he time that reigned here? Were not our souls, emanations of the universal Soul incarnated in our perishable bodies, linked by mysterious bonds of affinity which had always predestined us for one another? Would we not find one another again on other planets, ever more radiant and noble, until the cycle of our successive existences finally consummated our supreme union in the bosom of the unique and perfect Being that was, is, and always will be, Eternity?

I understood clearly, then, and was astonished by Raymonde's mute desperation. Had I been able to speak, I would have shared my conviction with her, and told her that even the pain of such crises of asphyxiating coughing was minimal, almost foreign to my paralyzed consciousness. It was like a morsel of petty suffering distributed among a multiplicity of petty "subconsciousnesses," each of which was vibrating independently under the gaze of my true soul, which had become serene.

I was suspended between life and death for two days, alternately tended by Raymonde and Gaby Leduc, who found it very simple to render us that service of close friendship. Then my convalescence began, which proved almost as rapid as the onset of the illness—as is the general rule with cases of "Martian bronchitis" whose outcome is fortunate—and I was able to take an interest in worldly affairs again. For a few days, however, I retained a vague nostalgia for my "nirvanic" state.

The inopportune illness prevented me from taking part in the Directorial tour that was decided by the Council of State on the second. Gideon and Ladislas, accompanied by the ministers, took off from Saintes-Maries the same day—escorted by Sylvain Leduc, at the head of a squadron of gendarmes—to visit Europe and North Africa and investigate the chances of a restoration of Directorial power. I did not regret having to miss the spectacle offered by great cities in those circumstances, though, since I would have had to see it without Raymonde. Women had been rigorously excluded from the touring party, because the Soviets still ruled the majority of communes and the presence of females might have occasioned disastrous conflicts.

There was trouble enough without them. The delirious joy that stirred their towns along with all the rest did not prevent certain Anarchist committees from remaining on the defensive, fearful that the news might only be a ruse from which the bourgeois parties might profit by recovering power. In many instances, the Directorial mission was welcomed by megaphone announcements—"It is forbidden to disembark on Soviet territory! Sheer off!"—supported by battalions of Black Guards, hostile and resolute. Russia, in particular, obstinately refused to allow "Gideon the Antichrist" to fly over her territory. It was the same with southern Italy, Sicily, the North of England and Spain. At Lille, four aircraft of the Soviet defense gave chase to the mission's squadron and forced one of its planes to land.

Towns where the joy and dancing were unconstrained—which were numerous—received "Ladislas, Savior of the World" and his companions with acclamation, but none of them offered to restore power to Gideon Botram. In two or three instances, when the latter made a speech emphasizing the urgency of governmental restoration, howls of reprobation drowned him out, and—a detail that a member of the mission recounted to me in horror—among all the assembled crowds that had interrupted their dancing to listen to the orator, thousands of arms were raised, offering the threat of the black blasters of Anarchism.

Humankind was dancing in the ruins, but it was dancing armed with weapons. The ancestral bestiality that everyone carries in his heart had shaken off the chains of the law and the habits of morality; the tiger had tasted blood, and woe betide anyone who attempted to put it back in its cage!

The mission returned to Saintes-Maries on August 7, without having accomplished the tour's purpose, disappointed by the reception it had received in Europe from the organized authorities. The news from the rest of the world was no more comforting.

The torpedoes continued to arrive, deflected every time with the same success, projected to the bottom of a sea or an ocean, where their satanite generators fulminated for days, like an archipelago of Strombolis. Humankind could no longer doubt its deliverance. Its mad rout of pleasures lost its dismal and desperate character—but, far from easing, it developed into a chronic condition.

Here and there, a few strikes had ended, and a few public services—most of them having passed into the hands of Anarchists—were re-established, after a fashion. Nothing was done, however, to reconstitute the stocks of food in which the looting, the partying and the destruction of large cities had made irreparable breaches. The gravest of all the symptoms of the popular state of mind was that the former local governments were powerless witnesses to the reign of brutal force that had been reinstated upon the debris of civilized justice.

A single month of disorganized panic had sufficed to return humankind to the primitive barbarity from which it had taken centuries and millennia to raise itself—and the acquired momentum persisted beyond the moment when the cause of the madness had disappeared, still drawing the race down that fatal slope.

How could it be stopped? Ladislas Wronsky extolled the re-civilizing influence of scientific committees disseminated in every country, receiving the orders from a central Institute. Gideon did not cling obstinately to political power in a personal sense, but deemed its re-establishment to be the first priority. That supposed a general disarmament of the population, though, and to recover the blasters that had become as common as the revolvers of yesteryear, it would be necessary to deploy superior armaments that remained to be found.

The conclusion was, therefore, inevitable. The Directorate of Saintes-Maries had to resign itself, for the time being, to its new role as the thinking organ of the world, to centralize news items and retransmit them *urbi et orbi* with the initial fundamental intention of reviving confidence in the future. That confidence was insufficient. Despite the undeniable deliverance, the Anarchist

Committees, interested in the prolongation of the disorder that facilitated their reign, did their utmost to sow and foster mistrust.

The Transatlantic Tube came back into service—it was discovered that a broken-down train full of passengers had been "forgotten" during its abrupt abandonment by the strikers, stranded beneath a 1000 meters of water off the Azores—bringing us the American newspapers, of which a certain number had begun to reappear. The troubling question of what the Martians might do next was raised there, viewed in the most pessimistic light.

These extracts from the August 15 edition of the *Minneapolis Daily Soviet News*, printed in demi-folio in view of the paper shortage, are among the most characteristic:

No, comrades, you must not let yourselves be deceived by the affirmations of the former Boss of the World [13] *and his damned French clique, which are stuffing your heads with humbug.*

The danger is past, they say? Why? Because the Martian artillery ceased firing on the day when they saw that our Wronsky had discovered a trick that would sent their missiles to the Devil? So be it—they would lose no more of those costly machines. But can you believe that they have renounced their enterprise of blowing up the whole Earthly shebang?

No, comrades! These people of Mars have acted with a scientific method and practical know-how that would be worthy of Americans if they had a little more personal bravery. They certainly have vast technological means at their disposal and unlimited stocks of radium—but the preparations for their main business are bound to take them several years. This is serious. They have resolved to emigrate to the Earth and will not desist, no matter what—be sure of that. This setback cannot make them change their minds; that is impossible. They have too many good reasons for quitting their home world: lack of water, increasing cold, thinning atmosphere, and others that we cannot see through a telescope...

You know, comrades, that the two planets have not ceased to approach one another since the moment when the Martians judged the range appropriate at the end of June, but the distance will begin to increase again in two or three days. In a month, six weeks at the most, not only will we be out of range of their cannon—if there really is a cannon—but the line of fire between Mars and the Earth will come closer and closer to the Sun, whose extreme mass would perturb the course of the projectiles excessively.

Only six weeks, therefore, at the maximum, remain for the Martians to finish us off. If they let the opportunity pass, they will have to wait nearly two

---

[13] This is one of several phrases in the quoted passage for which Varlet offers his own tentative English translations, most of which I have modified slightly into more likely forms.

years—until the end of June 1980—for the astronomical positions of the two planets to become favorable again.

They cannot wait, and they will not wait!

They can see us, remember! They know how to construct televisors, for which those other soft-heads, the Jovians, gave them the plans. They are following all our actions. Be assured that they are taking a good long look, laughing heir heads off as they see us dancing because we imagine that we are sheltered from their next step.

What will that be, exactly? That I don't know; I have no televisor in my pocket. But I can give you a guarantee that they have something good up their sleeve. Perhaps they'll arrive here in person, a whole colony of them, armed from head to toe, ready to make us jump like a jack-in-the box. And if we do not close ranks, comrades; if we bite the bullet and dispose of our bonny blasters, as that mooncalf the Antichrist proposes, we shall be like lambs bound for slaughter—by the claws of the bourgeois tyrants if the Martian do nor come...

As for the famous promise of the Jovian astronomers to come to our aid—in a pig's eye! It's understandable that they dare not explain it via the TSF—there's a third party on the line—but they were able to tell us that their guillotine, or whatever other vengeful blade these high justices propose to apply to the Marian felons, will not be ready until the next opposition. "Have courage! Hold on until then!" they added. They don't get out much! No, between now and then—in a few weeks time, comrades!—we'll all be put through the grinder...

Let's live in the meantime, comrades! Let's help ourselves to what we can! If we must die, let's not die without first having our fill of the enjoyments that the filthy Capitalists have shamefully monopolized until now!

We've had enough of wage-slavery and the unjust privileges of our employers! Everything for everyone! All for one and one for all!

In the time of order and Directorial censorship, of course, not a single line of these scandalous statements would have been published, and the cynicism of these appeals to the basest passions gave us the measure of the social decay in which humankind was complacently wallowing.

Nevertheless, it must be confessed that, beneath the brutal buffoonery of that gross style, it was our own fears that were being echoed—fears that were the subject of constant discussion in the "governmental" milieu of Saintes-Maries, as we called it by force of habit.

Although I abstained from talking to Raymonde about them as we wandered along the deserted beach in the exquisite gentleness of the Mediterranean night after a hard day's work, such apprehensions still obsessed us. Suddenly falling silent, we would embrace one another urgently, shivering as we saw the bloody topaz of Mars rising above the southern horizon, in close proximity with Antares in Scorpio.

II. Isaac Schlemihl, Monopolist of Soviets

Although the re-establishment of the Directorate to political supremacy remained a distant dream, the material conditions in which it members lived were ameliorated. Two hotels were entirely reserved for them, and the village of Saintes-Maries, proud to accommodate Ladislas Wronsky and the spiritual authorities of intellectual society, cast out refugees from the communes and people suspected of subversive opinions. The indefatigable Leduc maintained food supplies to our Lilliputian Versailles despite the increasing difficulties. Monsieur Van Culden, in his capacity as ex-Treasury minister, dealt with financial problems quite cleverly.

The most obvious progress, however, concerned our security, so ill-assured at first by the five local gendarmes. Eight hundred Senegalese—escapees from the destruction of Marseilles, the fury of Anarchism or revolutionary contagion, who came to offer us their services or were collected throughout the region, some from as far way as North Africa, by Leduc's emissaries—mounted a vigilant and devoted guard around our refuge, the supreme sanctuary of Order and Civilization. It was comforting to see all these superb black men in white uniforms and colonial helmets marching in military formation on the parade-ground of the airfield next to the TSF station, practicing anti-aircraft maneuvers or embarking rapidly on the ten white-painted military helicopters bearing the Directorate's arms. We were no longer at the mercy of an arbitrary strike; it would have required a veritable army to get through our defenses.

One morning, at 10 a.m., the clarion sounded unexpectedly; while the engines of the air-fleet roared as the helicopters took to the air, commands blared forth from the loudspeakers: "Approaching aircraft! Stop here! It is forbidden to fly over! Steer away or be fired on!"

I ran to my office window. Like bizarre black bats against the beautiful summer sky, three helicopters bearing death's-heads were hovering, facing a semicircular formation of our white birds. How did they dare? But a guttural and forceful voice cried from above through a loud-hailer: "Friends, it's comrade Isaac Schlemihl, who begs comrades Gideon Botram and Ladislas Wronsky to grant him an audience!"

"Land behind the antennae!"

The ringing of my telephone prevented me from seeing any more. Our Master wanted me in his office.

There, I found myself in the company of the "Savior of the World."

"Sit down, Rudeaux," said the latter. "You can make a record of the conversation. What can this Schlemihl possible want from us?"

The sound of military footsteps was audible in the corridor. Schlemihl appeared, flanked by a Senegalese escort and followed by two singular individuals.

One, whose thick black moustache connected to his side-whiskers, wore a crimson uniform trimmed with collar-badges representing the fateful death's head. He clicked his heels and raised his hand to his helmet.

Schlemihl bowed deeply, and introduced us to him. "Excellencies," he said, "I have the honor of presenting to you Comrade Peter Kropatchek, my good friend and Generalissimo of the United Soviet Forces of Provence and various other places." He moved aside to display the other person, who bowed his head in embarrassment. "This is my devoted pilot, Chelra."

Beneath a flying-suit shaped in a provocative feminine form, I recognized the blonde woman from the helicopter, Isaac's wife.

Isaac smiled at my astonishment. "Yes, it's a little obvious. She's not yet 35, you know, and it's necessary, when dealing with our friends, to observe certain principles; this concession satisfies them." On seeing Wronsky impatiently drumming his fingers on the arm of his chair, however, he continued: "But your time is precious, Excellencies, and so is mine, so I'll put my cards on the table."

He explained to us, succinctly, the results he had obtained. He did not attempt to conceal the manner in which he had used his official privilege. With the cooperation of honest citizens as well as the approbation of Anarchism—obtained God knows how!—this indefatigable businessman had organized the systematic pillaging of ruins, with particular respect to Martian radium. His traveling salesmen had offered radium to Soviets ill-supplied with this indispensable product, in exchange for airbus-loads of goods and foodstuffs, which had been heaped up, in anticipation of dark days, in his warehouses in Avignon.

"And despite everything, Excellencies, I still have tons of radium. If the bombardment had continued, I would have been able to offer you—in return for certain guarantees, of course—enough to fuel the propulsive engines of a number of vehicles adequate to transport yourselves and anyone else desirous of making the voyage to the safety of the polar regions...but here we are, tranquil. Business goes on—my business, I mean—and this isn't the time to leave the country. What I propose to you, Excellencies, is a Restoration..."

Ladislas frowned, but Gideon's eyes sparkled behind his spectacles. The idea brought a smile to his face. "A Restoration of the Terrestrial Directorate?" he asked, eagerly.

"Terrestrial...hmm. Not immediately—but that would come. European, for the moment, is what I'm offering you. You're formulating the ideology, gentlemen—I've read your communiqués: the consciousness of the planet, the refuge of true civilization, and so on. It's very nice, but this isn't the time. While going about my humble business, I've observed that society would like nothing better than to be reorganized—but on a new plan, gentlemen! The revolution has taken place, and there's no longer any question of going back. The hour of communism has sounded! It's necessary to resign ourselves to that. The new world is in place, gentlemen, and it will only accept power under that label. I say 'label,' for, once the inevitable era of transition is past, friction will be reduced and everything will be reconstituted, under different labels, exactly as it was. That is already happening among our comrades. They accept the notes issued by my Avignon bank because they are printed in white on black paper with the death's head and the inscription "Reward of Labor"—and my divisional coinage is made of chocolate. Don't laugh, gentlemen; that's one of the reasons for my success. Everyone eats, in my house; there's plenty of everything, because I'm not afraid of words—while your banknotes are refused everywhere and you sit here, nibbling away at the remains of the old regime, waiting for the world to submit benevolently to your orders!

"It's true that I don't govern… I'm just a humble merchant, poor Isaac Schlemihl, gentlemen, although His Holiness Pope Benedict XXII has deigned to accept hospitality in the ancient Palais d'Avignon, renewing the tradition of his distant predecessors. He has even conferred on me the titles of Chevalier de Saint-Grégoire and Comte-Venaissin,[14] by reason of that small service and a few others…the enlightened Pontiff, you see, is not afraid of words himself. I've confided my plans to him, and he approves of them…

"But I've told you that I don't go in for government. I lack the prestige; I know that. My excellent friend here, Peter Kropatchek, has it—he's the great-grand-nephew of the glorious Bolshevik Lenin—but only among our comrades. He's used that prestige to organize an army. One by one, all the Soviets in the region have linked up with him. Do you think yourselves strong, gentlemen, with your four battalions of Senegalese? We—or, rather, General Kropatchek—can count on 28,000 Black Guardsmen, who are only waiting for the order to march. Six hours would be sufficient for my commercial airbuses to actualize a general mobilization of those forces and concentrate them in Avignon. All the Soviets in France will follow. Russia is won to our cause, and will help us if necessary…but that's not all we need to conquer Europe; we need a name, a name that is known. It's yours, Monsieur Gideon Botram! To reassure the bourgeoisie, the timorous men, who are legion…all those who are afraid of words! Antichrist or not, only a Terrestrial Director can give a new regime established by the power of blasters the stability necessary to moral order and commerce."

Isaac Schlemihl collected himself momentarily. Then, striking the classic pose of Napoleon I, with his right hand tucked into his frock-coat, he continued solemnly: "In the name of all our comrades, in the name of their Generalissimo, here present, and in my own name, I have the honor of offering Your Excellency the title of President of the Communist Republic of the United Soviets of Avignon and the Provençal Region!"

---

[14] This title refers to an ancient term for Avignon; the Comtat in question was a feature of the days when the papacy was divided, one of the two rivals being established in that city.

The former Master of the World had gone pale. The desire for power, the horror of the means that would assure him of its possession, and the price that humankind would pay for its culpable weakness, were visibly tormenting his mind. Twice he opened his mouth and closed it again, without being able to utter a word.

Ladislas came to his aid. "Monsieur," he said to Schlemihl, in a dry and peremptory tone, "my esteemed colleague"—he emphasized the word—"is overwhelmed by the vast confidence you have in him; he is incapable of answering you, but I know his mind well enough to serve as his interpreter. I admit that you have at your disposal the required military forces..."

"All our Soviets march as one man!" cried the great-grand-nephew of Lenin, impetuously.

"Shut up, Kropatchek," said the commander of the Restoration. "You're not a diplomat, that I know!"

"You'll spoil everything, General," whispered the disguised woman, pleadingly, placing her chubby hand on the warrior's arm.

"The required military forces," Ladislas repeated, without seeming to notice the incident, "to impose our power on Europe and to drown any trace of resistance in blood. I admit that to be so. I also admit that we would resign ourselves to that extremity in order to re-establish and re-affirm social order. But it is not social order—it is, on the contrary, the usurpation of Anarchy—that you're proposing that we sanction. It's chaos: the negation of all the fundamental principles of family and society that are implicit in the very title that you're offering us. No, Monsieur Schlemihl, you are free to make alliance with the Revolution, and you are free to dupe the last few men of property, even including the venerable leader of Christendom, but you shall not draw a single member of the Directorate into your net! Even if our refusal provokes your wrath, and that of your satellites; even if your execrable army makes us pay with all our lives for our fidelity to truly liberal principles, completing the work of the Martians by trampling down the last defenders of Civilization, I give you and your Janissary chief, here and now, our response in a single word: never!"

Standing up with his hands upraised to the sky in heroic testimony, quite transfigured, the old savant, ordinarily so cool and composed, vibrated with the faith of a martyr. Galvanized by that contagious enthusiasm, our Master got up in his turn, and pronounced, in a clear and resolute voice: "No, never!"

I almost added my own voice to that sublime oath.

As for the envoys of Darkness, Kropatchek was a deeper shade of crimson than his uniform, and was rolling his furious eyes. The pilot with the nice hips was trying to calm him down. Schlemihl, with an expression of scornful pity, shrugged his shoulders and muttered between his teeth:

"*Alter Meschuge...Chalaumes mit Backfish!*" [15] Then, in a louder voice, he said: "Words, gentlemen, nothing but words. I admit your hesitation, and I respect the motives for it without sharing them...but you'll think about it, I'm sure, and you'll end up realizing that I'm right. Within a month, Monsieur Gideon Botram, I shall have the pleasure and the honor of seeing you crowned leader of the New Society by His Holiness Benedict XXII, to the unanimous acclamations of the bourgeoisie and our valiant Soviet army. Have your response sent to me in Avignon by helicopter; our TSF apparatus has been put out of action, as you know. And with that, gentlemen, I have the honor...come, Rara; let's go, Kropatchek."

And, followed by his two companions, flanked by the Senegalese, the Tempter made his retreat. Five minutes later, the sinister helicopters were bearing the odious trio towards the northern horizon.

I was not party to our Master's subsequent regrets, or the exhortations that Ladislas must have lavished upon him in private to prevent him from going back on his word and sacrificing the sacred cause of Civilization to his thirst for political power. I only know that Monsieur Schlemihl was not seen again in Saintes-Maries. But who knows whether, despite everything, that evil suggestion might not have ended up victorious, and that cynical prediction being realized, if further events had not completed the demoralization of humankind and the absolute obliteration of all constitutional power?

---

[15] I have reproduced these phrases exactly as Varlet renders them; he includes a footnote explaining that the Yiddish words translate as "Old fool! What a load of rubbish!"

III. Ladislas Wronsky's Idea

In speaking instead of, and on behalf of, Gideon Botram to answer Isaac Schlemihl, Ladislas Wronsky had done nothing but affirm his true position. In fact, he was the one who held the first place in the new Directorate, which became the recrudescence of the spiritual authority of the old savant's genius over the scientific minds of every country.

I have no doubt that, if he had wanted to, Ladislas could have seized political power at the moment of the Deliverance, when the crowds hailed him as the "Savior of the World." The leaders of the Anarchist committees prided themselves on their science, and would probably have recognized him as their nominal president. If such possibilities ever occurred to him, though, the old man's integrity would have refused to entertain them for a single second. He judged himself entirely unqualified to exercise political power; if anyone had offered him the sovereignty of the world, he would have immediately handed it over to Gideon Botram. His only ambition was to bring all the force of his intelligence to bear on the progress of humankind.

Among the enigmas of the human heart that remain indecipherable to me, I place the singular and quasi-paternal affection that this churlish and misogynistic old man of 69 saw fit to bestow on Raymonde and myself. I cannot see what interest he—a fanatical devotee of science, scornful of what he called "literary gossip"—could possibly find in me. The only one of my novels he had riffled through, at Raymonde's instigation, drew the severe verdict: "What does it prove? There's no conclusion!" And yet, he loved me like a son.

As for his secretary, he did not spare her his reprimands; when he invited us to his residence "for a chat" he shut her mouth with a comment like, "You're very sweet, of course, my child, but, as a woman, you can only have general ideas," if she happened to express a serious opinion. Nevertheless he cherished her like a daughter.

Did he sense, beneath the feminine airiness that he affected to attribute to her, the rare qualities of that beautiful soul: the proud independence, the rectitude, the loyalty, the horror of lying that had to bring forth fervor for the truth? Or was it just the whim of an old savant, lovelessly celibate, skeptical with regard to habitual flatteries, touched by the sight of our spontaneous sympathy towards him? I never figured it out.

Whatever the reason was, I thought that I ought to mention that affection, because it had a powerful influence on our destiny and launched us into subsequent adventures whose narration might be useful for the edification of Humankind—if the reign of Humankind on Earth ever resumes!

I shall not overemphasize the sudden change of opinion that overtook the governmental "court" when our favored situation was no longer in doubt. The venomous smiles of the Ministers' wives, and their backhanded sneers regarding that irregular couple, the "petty Chief of Information" and "Monsieur Wronsky's little typist" were a thing of the past, as was their malicious pleasure in lingering in the drawing-room for the sole purpose of keeping us from the piano. Now it was all graceful bows and the vilest groveling to obtain the presence of one or the other of us at "afternoon tea"—and when our clear resolution to decline any invitation of that sort had been politely but firmly signified, their toadying became even more flagrant, to the extent of leaving the drawing-room and piano to us "out of respect for the inspiration of the exquisite musicienne..."

Ladislas' infatuation for our company resulted in daily conversations with him, either in his office, under the pretext of service, by day, or on the terrace of the station in the shadow of the nettle-trees in the late afternoon, or even in Gideon's lodgings in the evening—but never in his hotel room, which he had arranged with stoical simplicity, and where, he said, we would have had nowhere to sit.

The news of events and the threats of the future, terrestrial and Martian, formed the habitual subjects of these conversations, but not one terminated without the old savant holding forth on the project dearest to his heart: the foundation of a Conservatory in which the world's savants might be kept safe until better times: the very spirit of Civilization.

The theory on which the notion was based—although much too absolute, in my humble opinion—was original and seductive. It had, in any case, the advantage of sustaining our morale even after the second catastrophe. Here, succinctly summarized, is his reasoning.

The present lapse was only a superficial accident, whose consequences could be easily arrested by the good will of the intellectual elite. Indeed, he said, *civilization*, as it is ordinarily understood, is an illusion. It is necessary to distinguish, within its bosom, the Gifted Minds—men endowed with active intelligence, who are the truly civilized—from the remainder, whose passive intelligence merely reflects the thought of the former: the "human material," as the old savant expressed it.

Active intelligence is a rare phenomenon. The Gifted Minds form, so to speak, a variety of the human species—a spiritual variety whose representatives are born in various places, according to as-yet-unfathomable laws, independent of the general carnality. In them, intelligence, with its disinterested love of Truth and scientific curiosity—the civilized man's notion of the sacred and the sole justification for the existence of humankind within the plan of creation—predominates over animal existence. It is only given to a small number of individuals, however, to attain this goal, or, at least, to pursue it consciously. They alone are *efficacious*; they alone *exist*, in the absolute sense. The remainder, whose number appears to constitute Civilization, are only "human material:" souls as deprived of real thought as the will of a hypnotized "subject," reflecting the ideas of the Gifted and passively following their progress. The habitual fabric of their lives and the quotidian object of their preoccupations are the instincts and appetites of the "ancestral Beast," and civilization can only manifest itself in them if those instincts and appetites are sufficiently bridled and dulled.

It is in the domain of morality that the passive man, the "human material" finds his opportunity to raise himself up and render individual and social life harmonious and beautiful—offering to the truly civilized, the Gifted, a milieu favorable to the maximum development of intelligence, which then projects on everyone, indiscriminately, the aureole of Civilization.[16]

Now, before our eyes, the work accomplished over centuries by the efforts of the Gifted had perished in a few days. The mass of those "civilized by contagion" had escaped the "polarization" of the Elite, and, by a sort of inverse Visitation of the Spirit of Darkness, had returned to the atavistic instincts and repudiated Civilization.

The only means of conserving the gifts of progress was, therefore, to abstract them, in the person of their true depositaries, from a milieu that had become worse than unfavorable—actively hostile, in fact—and to bring the Savants and the last men of good will together in a single central Institute, where their reciprocal company would shelter them from animal instincts and evil suggestions.

Gideon Botram had stopped openly opposing this project, but I suspected him of taking pleasure in increasing the difficulties of realization with which he obstructed Wronsky's impatience. The latter was, in effect, the President Designate of the "Conservatory of Civilization," and its advent would reduce the phantom authority still attributed to the former Director to naught.

---

[16] Varlet inserts a footnote on behalf of his narrator: "Ladislas Wronsky thus subordinated moral perfection to the search for Truth—the Saint to the Savant. With regard to the Artist, he had nothing to say. I had some trouble getting him to admit that the Artist also plays a preponderant role and that he is as Gifted with Intuition as the Savant is with Intelligence."

IV. Three Penetrative Shells

The days went by. The evenings extended and became cooler. The song of the cicadas became more discreet. The grapes were ripe; the harvests began. Storm-clouds sometimes appeared in the everlasting azure of the Provençal sky, breaking in benevolent downpours over the Sun-baked ground.

We were finally getting close to the fateful date of October 1, which the most pessimistic had fixed as a limit to the possibility of a new bombardment of the Earth by Mars during this opposition. The disquiet of the provisional state in which we were living would then disappear, we thought, along with the desolate feeling that a "mainspring" had been broken—the mainspring of Humankind's hope and confidence in the future.

After mid-September, it seemed to us, the Martian menace would be thwarted, for the date of October 1 concerned the arrival on Earth of a projectile, and it was necessary to allow a fortnight for its trajectory from the red planet. We would therefore be safe if no shot was detected by September 15 or 16—and the astronomers of Ganymede were on watch; day by day, the Jovan cosmo-grams told us "Nothing new on Mars" and added a laconic: "Courage! The punishment will take place"—at the next opposition, in two years' time.

The disappointment was all the more irritating for being so long delayed. The fatal blow renewed the anguish that we alone, of all humankind, had to support until the projectiles' arrival! On the morning of September 12, Jupiter sent us the message: "Shell departed from Mars towards Earth." There was identical news on September 14, and again 15—then nothing more; the "season" was closed, conclusively.

We repeated to one another endlessly that the waves from the oscillators would deflect these three shells, like their predecessors, but we were no longer able to believe in the efficacy of that protection, for the Martians would not have wasted their efforts gladly. If they had decided, after a month-long interruption, to send us these projectiles at the last minute, they must have employed a novel means to ensure that they would strike their target!

While the three new "messengers" were making their way through the in-terplanetary void—tiny twinkling flecks, followed by the televisors of the Jovian astronomers intent on calculating their trajectories and the points on the terres-trial surface from which the unknown flails hidden within their metal flanks would reach out—hope and apprehension succeeded one another in those of us *in the know*, like light and darkness on a stormy day.

Would three shells, if they escaped the deflective network of the tele-mechanical waves, be enough to make Humankind renounce its will to raise itself up again? Gideon Botram enumerated the favorable symptoms that had multiplied considerably in recent days, modest as yet, but clear enough to demonstrate that a recovery was taking place all over the world. The folly of pleasure was dying down. Certain groups—electricians, mechanics, transport workers and public servants—were returning to work. Factories were reopening their doors. TSF stations that had been deliberately put out of action were being repaired. Newspapers were multiplying; their tone was becoming less pessimistic, beyond the Atlantic as well as in Europe.

The *Nouveau-Paris*, the great daily whose premises had escaped the fire—along with enough others for Paris in ruins to retain nearly 60,000 inhabitants—was looking forward to the reconstruction of the capital, considerably bigger and better than before. Towns were no longer subsisting entirely on the reserves of food in their warehouses; country folk were beginning to provide fresh foodstuffs again. Local currencies were being issued everywhere; the Banque de France had re-opened its counters—under Communist control, admittedly—and was printing bills in Bordeaux that were accepted even by the Soviets. The latter were letting their most outrageous regulations fall into disuse. They were losing territory, expelled by newly-organized White Guards, Blue Guards and Pink Guards. Provence was getting ready to shake off the yoke of Kropatchek and to rescue the Holy Father, who was, in fact, Isaac Schlemihl's prisoner in the Palais d'Avignon. Southern California, Texas, Florida, Guatemala, the island of Chiloe, Bengal, Egypt, Ireland, Scotland, Belgium and Switzerland declared themselves autonomous bourgeois states. Moreover, the ravages of "Martian bronchitis" diminished in the northern hemisphere with the end of summer, and the disease only manifested itself in the southern hemisphere, at the beginning of spring, in an attenuated form.

In brief, without the threat of the shells, still unknown to everyone on Earth save for 15 or 20 individuals at Saintes-Maries, the situation would have seemed quite encouraging...

But no, alas! In a few days time, the whole world would know—and the only-too-probable ravages of the deadly machines would cause the temporary success of the Deliverance to be forgotten. The 20 months that would then elapse before the next opposition would seem to be a negligible surcease, useful, at the most, for those condemned to death to "enjoy the time they had left." The sketchy reorganization would be carried away by the explosion of a new panic, this time irremediable.

For Raymonde and me, that fortnight's delay was far from being the period of sterile anguish that I initially feared. After September 15, Gideon Botram finally committed himself to Lasdislas Wronsky's projects. I accepted, as a signal honor, the responsibility of conveying the good news to all the savants of Western Europe who would form the nucleus of the "Conservatory of Civilization," whose seat would be in Montpellier, in the buildings of the Faculty of Medicine; the preparations for the journey took up all my time.

It was not just a matter of gathering a cargo of savants but of sounding out the most notable—in France, Belgium and England on this occasion—and convincing them to go to Saintes-Maries, where Wronsky awaited them. In principle, I should have traveled alone; I only needed a pilot. It was despite my resistance and the amicable representations of Ladislas that Raymonde obtained permission to accompany me.

"It's a sacred mission that has been entrusted to you," she said to me, "and I'd be the last person to get in your way, but it's a dangerous mission too, and I don't want to be separated from you at any cost. I want to be by your side, until death...and I'll make myself useful, be sure of that. You can't travel alone. However perfect your helicopter might be, you'll need a devoted pilot...and I'll be that pilot. As we're going into Soviet lands, I'll follow Madame Schlemihl's example, and I certainly hope that I'll make a better aviator than she did!"

She took some trouble to disguise herself. Her short-cut hair, her upper lip darkened by artificial down, her contralto voice and her slim, lithe figure gave her the appearance of a handsome adolescent. She had a mischievous impulse to try out her new personality on our old friend. Wronsky addressed her gallantly as "young man"—it was the last time I saw him laugh. After that day, she never forsook masculine dress, in order to assimilate the congruent attitudes and gestures.

It still remained for her—and for me—to familiarize ourselves with the operation of our helicopter, a machine lovingly prepared by Leduc in person: a marvel of precision and flexibility, which a child could maneuver.

In normal conditions, our preparations would have taken a few hours. At present, an adventure into the prevailing social disarray was an expedition requiring every possible precaution: on-board sleeping accommodation; changes of clothing; some food supplies—especially of the Jovian nutriment, which we were beginning to employ as a staple; two blasters apiece, with ammunition; an abundance of bills drawn on the principal European banks; not to mention aeronautical charts and my precious letters of introduction for the different countries we were to visit.

The taste for adventure that we both had in common was reawakened by the prospect of our imminent departure, and we lived in a state of feverish enthusiasm during these preparations. Despite the dangers we were about to run, the mission seemed to us to be something of a honeymoon trip. We almost forgot the fatal deadline. It was solely a question of fixing our departure for the day after the arrival of the third Martian missile—we could have been ready sooner, but an obscure and ill-formed sentiment pressed us to spend those days together at Saintes-Maries—and then we avoided the subject. Botram and Wronsky, aware of the futility of conjectures and hypotheses, only spoke about the future Institute, the individuals that it was most necessary to co-opt into it, and the other details of my mission.

As a matter of conscience, the current from the Equatorial Alternators was employed in an attempt to deflect the projectiles. One after another, though, on September 28, 29 and 30, the three shells broke through the protective network of waves as if it were a spider's web, without deviating from their course. It was no longer dirigible torpedoes that we had to deal with; these were purely ballistic missiles, penetrative shells that fell, one after another, into those regions where volcanic activity denoted the minimal resistance of the Earth's crust.

Arriving at a terminal velocity of 30 kilometers a second, these bolides, loaded with enormous penetrative force, breached the solid tegument that separates us from the igneous mass filling the interior of our globe, and three new volcanoes opened up—the first a little to the south of Fujiyama in Japan, the second on the flank of Popocatepetl in the Mexican Cordilleras and the third in the ancient Solfatara of Pozzuoli, west of Naples—giving free passage to the central fire.

The famous explosion of Krakatoa on August 16, 1883, which ravaged more than 1000 square kilometers of the Indonesian archipelago, crushing burning and drowning 300,000 or 400,000 victims under showers of rocks, torrents of lava and tidal waves, had already given a glimpse of the particularly devastating nature of eruptive phenomena due to the sudden violent emergence of a crater rather than the normal play of plutonian forces. This time, the Earth had three Krakatoas. The detonations of their successive "bores" were audible to us, the first two in the form of muffled thunderous rumblings, distant but as clear and powerful as the explosion of large ammunition-dumps, the third resounding and prolonged, accompanied by palpable tremors, giving the tragic impression that a cataclysmic earthquake was about to occur. Then, a few hours later, the tidal wave—a foamy barrier four or five meters high—seemed to hurl the entire sea in an assault on our dunes. Several houses in the village collapsed, and the Camargue was lost to sight, swept by an inundation that stranded us in the TSF buildings until the following day. The helicopter set aside for our expedition was submerged in its hangar, and the necessary repairs delayed our departure for two days.

The great meteorological perturbation overtook us in the interval, born in the vicinity of the giant valves releasing continuous jets of vapor and subterranean gases hitherto compressed at a 1000 times atmospheric pressure. For six days, a furious tempest, blowing northerly at ground level, from the south east in the heights, prevented us from leaving Saintes-Maries, where the first news of the disaster arrived. Although confused and summary from Japan and Mexico, where the violence of the catastrophe was at its maximum, the news demonstrated adequately that the material damage and loss of life caused by the earthquakes, cyclones and eruptions far surpassed the results of all analogous catastrophes and those of the deadliest wars—including the World War of 1914-18, with its 15 million victims!

In Italy, the reaction to the sudden formation of a new crater had caused a resumption of the activity of already-existent volcanoes: Vesuvius, Stromboli and Etna. The first combined its fury with those of the Solfatara. As in Saint-Pierre and Martinique in 1902, a fire-cloud had engulfed Naples, the happy city, where 99% of the population had perished. The seismic shock had drowned the islands of Nisida, Procida and Ischia, a portion of Pausilippe and the point of Misene. The "Phlegean Fields" had disappeared under enormous flows of lava. Others reburied Herculanuem and Pompeii forever, and advanced into the gulf in promontories destined to equal the one at Sorrento. Volcanic "bombs" had fallen on Capua, pumice-stones into the Adriatic, and "lapilli" reached as far as the ruins of Rome, where plumes of smoke were seen by day and columns of fire by night.

As for the moral effect, what little we learned via the TSF exceeded our worst fears, and what we would soon see would complete our conviction that the unexpected blow had caused all the hints of reorganization to be forgotten, and brought back the darkest days of the "Season of the Torpedoes."

V. In Search of Men [17]

The northerly tempest slackened during the night of October 7 and 8, and at 8 a.m., Leduc, who had come from La Crau for that express purpose, installed my beloved pilot and me in our aircraft. Gaby had also left her office to bid us farewell. Gideon Botram shook our hands energetically. Ladislas Wronsky, more emotional than he wanted to appear, stammered his final instructions, cutting them short to embrace us both paternally. Then, putting all of them aside, I got under way. Two minutes later, we were flying northwards, with our rotor blades whirling at top speed.

We were off! Intoxicated by speed, I was sufficiently familiar with the operation of the machine to savor the exhilarating sensation of manipulating the control levers. Our helicopter had two sets of controls, and I could see Raymonde out of the corner of my eye, sitting beside me and looking eagerly out over the countryside fleeing beneath us: the green meadows of the Camargue, where free-roaming bulls raised their moist muzzles anxiously, and solitary lakes where flocks of pink flamingoes rose up from the reeds to follow us. In the distance, the branches of the Rhône, bordered with poplars, converged on the town of Arles, over which we would bear to starboard.

"Wings, my beloved!" my companion said, eventually, above the gentle purr of our aerial progress. "Here are the wings so long invoked by the desire of poets. It's Pegasus that's carrying us through the open sky, far from the pedestrian routines and rampant baseness of quotidian life. It's the marvelous escape towards the unattainable horizon, towards that Elsewhere which, even today, makes life—ours especially, my love—worth living. Oh, I implore you, let me take sole control! Let me feel the beautiful bird of human genius obey my orders as if my will were infusing it, and as if I were one with it, my heart beating within its heart of fire, my wings cleaving the air, forgetful of weight!"

Leduc had declared her to be the most brilliant pupil he had so far trained, and he had not exaggerated. I knew her to be an authentic pilot, capable of relieving me for part of the journey. Barring accidents, our first day's flight would easily accomplish the planned 1000 kilometers; we would be able to lay over in Lille, at the home of Doctor Malgras, the doyen of the Faculty of Medicine, whom Ladislas Wronsky had notified of our arrival.

We had passed over Arles, with its russet roofs and the ovals of its ancient arenas. At present, we were flying over the valley of the Rhône, between the

---

[17] The title of this chapter, "*A la recherche des hommes*," is a deliberate echo of Proust's carefully multilayered "*A la recherche du temps perdu*," which is notoriously difficult to render into English; I have adopted the simplest and most literal translation.

greener expanses of Languedoc and the cypresses and olive-groves of Provence, striped with white rectilinear roads. The intoxication of our departure had not made us neglectful of the manifestations of human life, and the first anomalies did not strike us before we reached Tarascon. The little town that I had previously found so lively, joyful and carefree seemed deserted. One the flat roof of king René's château, whose stone turret overlooked the entrance to the Pont de Beaucaire, a dozen human ants—the only living beings in the entire city—were busy about a slender and elongated object strongly reminiscent of the cannon of yesteryear.

The countryside, on the other hand, became more animated as we came closer to Avignon. Confused crowds of singing men and women and troops formed up in parallel ranks were advancing along every road towards the Papal city, from which spirals of smoke rose up. People were fighting furiously in the outlying districts, around the gates, in the streets and the squares.

"General Kropatchek's army does not seem to have the upper hand," I said, seeing the scarlet uniforms of the United Soviets everywhere in retreat.

Carried away by curiosity, we descended to 100 meters above the Rue de la République. The blasters' range scarcely exceeded 20 meters, so we were safe at that altitude—at least, I thought so. Over the racket of the riot, however, a characteristic sound of detonations was audible, with increasing clarity.

"Rifles! They've got rifles!" Raymonde exclaimed, hurriedly pressing down the ascension controls as far as they would go. A crackling salvo of shots was directed at us, without inflicting any more damage than a single bullet embedded in the padding of my seat.

Out of range, at 1000 meters, we flew over the incomprehensible battle that was raging throughout the city for another ten minutes or so. Around the Papal Palace the massacre was horrible; the square was crowded with scarlet uniforms, but the insurgents' firearms were driving back the Soviet blasters everywhere. New fires were breaking out at every moment. On the left bank of the Rhône a fuel-depot was on fire, and the smoke driven by the mistral was spreading its sinister black spirals all over the city.

"Poor Isaac!" I murmured. "Look what his fine projects have come to!"

"If it were only his!" replied Raymonde, taking us northwards at full speed.

That vision of horror repressed the initial joy of our aerial excursion. We were no longer schoolchildren on an escapade or a young married couple on honeymoon, as my cheerful travesty had suggested; we were the last envoys of civilization in search of Men worthy of that name, spared by death and the Spirit of Darkness that was ravaging the country and the entire Earth.

The symptoms of decay revealed themselves to our attentive eyes. To the right and left of the Rhône, the railways formerly overrun by the wheels of gleaming electric convoys were empty, tarnished here and there by rust. The stations were abandoned. The one at Valence was no more than a heap of scrap iron twisted by fire, and looters were busy throughout the surrounding district, which was still burning. Two trains were lying on the tracks, telescoped and overturned. The highways were either deserted or blocked by rows of motor-trucks and armed troopers. There were no cars and no solitary pedestrians, save for a few on minor roads. At the entrance of a town near Livron, an embankment of earth blocked the road, surmounted by cannon and a red flag. Several times, sentinel helicopters whose sides were panted black or scarlet obliged us to make prudent detours, and we accelerated our speed to avoid encounters with suspect aerial flotillas.

The madness of war and devastation had taken possession of Humankind again.

We were almost happy when clouds hid the ground from our view shortly after Vienne. For four hours we flew over the sea of fog, beneath a sky blurred by a sort of vaporous dust, which had filtered the glare of the Sun since the great eruptions. Our helicopter made progress with admirable regularity under out alternate direction. At about 5 p.m., if the indications of the compass and the anemometer could be trusted, we would be in Lille.

We would have done better, though, to follow Leduc's advice and stop at Dijon. When we passed over the zone of cloud we found ourselves 100 kilometers north-east of Rheims; then we met an east wind that delayed us to such an extent that the Sun was brushing the horizon as we passed directly over Cambrai.

I took over the controls again, because I knew the country, through which I had often cycled in my youth, and I steered without hesitation as the Sun set. Douai! Scarcely thirty kilometers separated us from Lille; we ought to have been able to see the beacon lights of the aerodrome—but there was nothing.

The same dread overtook us both.

"There are no lights anywhere," Raymonde eventually remarked, anxiously.

"Perhaps an accidental break in the cable. Then again, it's not dark yet..." But I understood the significance of the total absence of electric light as dusk fell only too well. The failure of the Equatorial Alternators, anxiously expected for several days, had finally occurred. I imagined the gigantic workshops at Timbuktu, Lake Chad and Khartoum, which fed the entirety of Africa and Europe with electric current, virtually by themselves, besieged by the furious hordes of Islam; I saw their engineers waiting in vain for the help that we could not send them, defending themselves and their staff to the death before succumbing to the weight of numbers, martyrs to duty. The destruction of the Alternators would suppress the function of the TSF and plunge Africa and Europe into darkness—a further retreat of Civilization before the invasion of Darkness!

The tall chimneys of Lille, its roofs and bell-towers, were silhouetted by the last rays of the setting Sun. At the Ronchin aerodrome, petrol fires were lit as improvised landing-lights, but I hesitated before putting down. A frightful anxiety, a nameless despair, gripped my heart at the sight of dark Soviet city spread out like a menacing trap. I cursed my temerity in having attempting this journey in such conditions, my folly in having ceded to Raymonde's insistence...

"What are you waiting for, darling?" she asked. And I committed myself, with a deathly chill in my heart.

Once on the ground, my fears eased slightly. No doubts were expressed as to the sex of my pilot; our passports—in which I had prudently folded a bill for 20 "labor units"—seemed satisfactory to the absent-minded clerk. The salty local accent that sounded around us had something familiar and reassuring about it. A young man of good bearing came towards us when I pronounced my name and that of Ladislas Wronsky and introduced himself as Professor Malgras' envoy.

With the helicopter berthed, our mentor drove us in a fine limousine through unlit streets that grew darker and darker. The city seemed to be dead, the journey across it to the Boulevard Vauban interminable, and its roads in an atrocious state. Recently burned-out houses made mountains of debris, obliging us to make detours. These were the traces not of a Martian torpedo, but of recent riots.

We were welcomed cordially by the professor and his wife, in a candle-lit drawing-room. There again, Raymonde passed without further ado as my younger brother Raymond, and was introduced as such to the guests that were soon looking us over: the scientists forewarned of our arrival.

We were sitting down at the dining-table when the entrance of two women who had not been expected created a sensation that seemed bizarre to me. They had rosy complexions, shining eyes and radiated a sort of challenge. The other women clustered around them, questioning them volubly. The word *Zézèphe* was repeated insistently.

"That's right," my neighbor murmured, smiling at my intrigued expression. "You've come a long way and you're not up to date. *Zézèphe* is a euphemism for SSF, or the Service Soviétique Féminin. The women are always interested in fulfilling their new duties—although they're still optional, in fact, for the most part. In this case, for example, they've had dealings with an old man who, in exchange for a bill of 25 labor units, has added the necessary stamp to their statutory card." He turned to my pilot. "You see, young man, the Soviet regime is powerless to strip handsome lads of their natural privileges...the regime has been established for more than two months, and it's had time to humanize itself."

"What harm will it do, anyway," put in a thin individual of Mephistophelean appearance—Doctor Rambeaux, I think—"if the law is applied integrally. It would set a few precedents for us..."

But no one noticed the incongruity or the sudden redness of my pilot's cheeks, for the master of the house introduced the subject of my mission to them—a subject that took up the entirety of the second course, which consisted of a meager can of corned beef. That treat succeeded half a smoked herring each, and the bread was replaced by corn-flour pancakes.

I perceived, to my surprise, that Ladislas' generous idea was running into unforeseen difficulties, Our Lillois "scientists" were more concerned with their personal comfort than the future of Humankind. Doctor Goulliard and the chemist Cogniet, both bachelors, were the only ones who gave me their immediate support and promised to set off for Saintes-Maries within a few days. The others, who had families, refused to abandon their university posts, their local connections and so on. The status given to men of science by the municipal Soviet was acceptable, they claimed; the good of Society demanded their presence here, where they were working to improve public-spiritedness…

"Will you take long to improve it?" objected Doctor Goulliard, sarcastically. "Don't you see, gentlemen, that your efforts can do nothing, here, against the mounting tide of atavistic instincts freed since the 'Season of the Torpedoes' and excited to madness by the sentence of death pronounced by the penetrative shells and these Krakatoas, pricking the Earth's crust—like iron banderillas in a bull's spine before the final sword-thrust? Perhaps communism isn't the kind of order that everyone dreamed of, but it's order of a kind, and what the newly-unchained instincts are tending towards is disorder and anarchy. The regression will continue; after the 'municipal cell' we'll arrive at the horde. In the meantime, individual madness gets nearer and nearer. Think of the epidemics of the Middle Ages, the moral contagions of the year 1000. Do you think that anyone will respect science, when the destructive mania breaks out in its fullest extent?"

But these dismal and only-to-probable perspectives were more than the women were able to support. Our host's spouse dissolved in tears. "My God! My God!" she moaned, "We'll never see our old lives again, so easy, so placid, so happy! What will become of us?"

As soon as the roasted acorn beverage had been drunk and a cigar smoked, we went out with the gentlemen to finish the evening at the Café Bellevue in the Grand Place. It was a comfort to us after the dark streets, to find the illumination of that luxurious establishment, which—uniquely, in the whole city—produced its own electricity.

The hall was packed, and I immediately recognized in the customers that feverish haste to enjoy life which had struck me so forcibly in Marseilles two and a half months earlier—but the atmosphere had something even more distraught and funereal about it.

"They all have the eyes of the Annunciator Dervishes!" Raymonde whispered in my ear.

The extinction of the lights for the cinema session was greeted with cynical growls of joy from men and women alike, and I had to exchange places rapidly with my young and charming pilot to interpose myself between "him" and his neighbor. The luminous images on the screen catches a sufficient fraction of everyone's attention, and the scenes of horror, in particular, redouble the avidity not to waste a single second of the supposedly-brief time remaining: the Solfa-tara seen from Capri, launching its jets and bombs into the sky and pouring smoke from its cone; the towns on the gulf burning amid inundations of lava; the burning of Catania by the fires of Etna; the burning of Milan by the Anarchists; the Revolution in Brussels, the city retaken by the bourgeois party and set alight by the Soviet forces; the Anarchist fires in Glasgow, Rotterdam, Strasbourg, Lille...

Zzing! A clash of cymbals; the picture is extinguished. A searchlight-beam pierces the smoke-laden atmosphere of the hall to illuminate a *real* nude dancer on the screen, amid a brutal explosion of improvised drums and the frightful, heart-rending howl—"The torpedo! The Martians!"—of someone leaping on to a table...and the blaster-jets striking heads all around us...the lights come back up—and, further away in the room, another cry springs forth from the panic-stricken throng: "The sky's on fire! Fire everywhere! Fire!"—and another blaster jet springs forth, frantically mowing people down.

"Enough, enough!"

"Get out while you can!"

"But kill them!"

"Kill! Kill! Kill!"—from a population instantly bristling with blasters and revolvers, spraying death in every direction.

It was the scene in the Café Riche all over again, but more brutal and more hideous, with nothing conscious or organized about it, but with an imperious and irresistible magnetism—which, I confess, to my own shame and my beloved's, brought our blasters dizzily into our hands, and *obliged* us to fire, and fire again...*ffrrr...ffrrr*...into the crowd, our nerves twisted by the atrocious delirium of satisfying that animal contagion.

Our little scientific troop retreated through dark streets, leaving the major-ity of the guests behind on the way. Some distance from the city, there were confused clamors and detonations; the light of one fire turned the sky purple towards the Boulevard des Ecoles, another towards the Porte d'Isly.

Walking with the two of us and our host, Doctor Goulliard analyzed the crisis of collective hysteria that we had witnessed in clinical terms: "Reflexive imitation," he said, "released from the inhibition of rational control. The psychic disintegration seemed to be in suspension during the liberating Respite, but it was *incubating*, and its latent progress *developed* today, like a photographic print. In fact, the madness of humankind, which was still embryonic while the torpedoes fell, has found its outlet under the influence of the new catastrophe. The animal instincts, perverted and hallucinated by the destruction and the deaths, dream of completing the work of the volcanoes, repudiating individual and specific conservation to realize its two goals to the fullest possible extent. Arson and massacre, henceforth without pretext—for the sheer love of it—are in the process of exciting a new fanaticism in demented Humankind."

We lowered our heads before these frightful truths; self-disgust agitated our hearts, at having participated in these monstrous rites. I felt the last civilized hope flickering within me as I recalled that this cold analyst of the mounting folly had also been in the midst of the mob a little while before, his features contorted and his mouth agape, with a smoking revolver in his fist!

VI. The Savants' Failure

We stayed in Lille throughout the next day. I saw the city in which I had spent my youth turned upside-down by the fury of its own inhabitants, full of crumbling ruins, some of them smoking, watched by mute and somber groups avidly drinking in the spectacle, ready to renew it in their turn a little further away. I witnessed communist distributions, interminable queues outside the doors of Soviet buildings, from which people emerged clutching a smoked herring, a can of preserves or a handful of dry legumes, which had to be defended against the brutal covetousness of passers-by.

Two instances of murderous rage further revealed the abominable crisis before our eyes: the preliminary howl of "A torpedo! The Martians! Fire!" followed by indiscriminate blaster fire, and the convulsions of the wretch writhing in the road, finished off by the stamping heels of the audience. The "Martian bronchitis" was also laying low the healthiest of constitutions debilitated by insufficient nourishment. The majority of women had the same gleam in their eyes as the two in the dean's home. Dresses were rare, and those on display—gaudy, extravagant, low-cut to the basses of the sternum in spite of the cold—were completed by an SSF armband. Children were playing at "Martians" and I saw a group of them on the Boulevard de la Liberté sprinkle petrol on a luxurious house abandoned by its owners and set fire to it, without anyone trying to stop them.

After we had spent a second night under the roof of the amiable Dean, the latter took us back to the aerodrome, where our aircraft was returned to us, not without difficulty. A few liters of fuel were sold to us at a high price. Two hours later, after a journey favored by good weather, hardly troubled by cloud, we disembarked in Brussels at the University's private airfield in the very heart of the city.

There, too, ruins were numerous. The entire quarter situated between the Parc and the Hotel de Ville, where civil guards and Black Guards had been fighting doggedly eight hours before, was nothing but a heap of debris. There too, the noise of rioting and distant explosions had replaced the placid rumor of the capital. There were no trams and no taxis, only a few cars with blacked-out windows and a few furtive pedestrians.

"A great many Italian refugees have arrived here," said our host, biology professor Jan Vlaminck. "They contributed to the spread of the panic. They affirmed that the Martian shells were continuing to fall every day, and exasperated criticism of the government—Soviet now—which was accused of hiding the fact. It was an unpopularity in which we scientists shared. Since yesterday, I dare not show myself in the city. We've been accused of complicity with the Martians, by virtue of not having advertised the arrival of the projectiles this time. We're accused of not having been able to prevent their fall or ameliorate their ravages. We're accused of having cut off the electricity."

"These idiots," continued Monsieur van Himmeln, director of the Observatory at Uccle, "have forgotten—if they ever knew—that there are such things as falling stars. Yesterday evening, there was a riot in Schaerbeek because people mistook the luminous track of a meteorite for the arrival of a torpedo. Two or three of them even committed suicide on the spot, for fear of Martians! That is the consequence of a crass ignorance of astronomy, about whose dangers I advised the public authorities—when there were public authorities!"

I had hoped to communicate with Saintes from Brussels, but the TSF was still not working and it would be days, in the present disorder, before local dynamos were rigged up and ready to substitute for the current of the Equatorial Alternators.

It was on my own authority that I decided not to visit Holland, for Monsieur Vlaminck assured me that I had no hope of finding any recruits there for the Conservatory of Montpellier. The choice of a French city as the site of the institute would be no more acceptable in Leyden than in Brussels, and would excite the same repugnance. "I'm astonished," he added, "that our savant colleague Monsieur Wronsky did not think of Brussels! Brussels is the only capital in Europe worthy of the name that is still standing; it is entirely appropriate to shelter the hearth of human thought and hope for a future recovery!"

Only one university member, Doctor de Witte, gave me his support and promised to make his way to Saintes-Maries, by a means which presently remained hazardous, all regular transport services by rail and air having ceased. Doctor de Witte was, however resolved to make the journey on foot if necessary. Despite the mild joy his enthusiasm caused me, I was unable thereafter to dissimulate the hopelessness of my mission, and the full extent of the moral collapse. The *Sign of the Beast* had not even spared the elite. The savants had participated in the narrow nationalism that was compartmentalizing the Earth; they had, in sum, refused to leave their countries, their "familiar surroundings," in order to constitute the sacred Phalanx of civilized Redemption. They refused to understand that their ideal union, formerly ensured by the facility of communication, would become impossible, and that, in isolation, they risked succumbing to the contagion.

It was in Brussels that I first heard mention of the "Eternal-Nightists" whose baneful doctrine—if one might call it that—was destined to achieve worldwide extension, and gradually to draw into its hallucinated intoxication the sectarians of every religion. My guide could not give me any precise information about them, though. He included them, under the general label of "anarchists," within a sort of vague "fifth estate" formed by all the appetites and animal rages, whose irresistible tide was engulfing the communist "fourth estate" in its turn.

On leaving Brussels after a sojourn of 20 hours, we would have been easily able to visit the ruins of Antwerp and reach Oxford in the same day, but the spectacle of London attracted us more, and we headed straight across the North Sea. On the outskirts of Ghent, the traces of the tide of satanite that had destroyed "the glory of the Scheldt" were visible in the sterilized landscape, the dead trees and burned-out farms of the coastal region, contrasting with the green Flemish countryside. We were flying high and fast, and the only indications of social disorganization that struck us were the abandoned railways and canals, where the barges were randomly grouped in confused masses. Bruges had been burned out, and the Casino at Ostend was still on fire; its smoke served us as a reference-point when we flew out over the waves, struggling against a rather violent north wind, which drew thick clouds across our course, enveloping us before we reached the English coast.

I headed for the Thames Estuary, so that I could follow the river's course without any risk of getting lost. Moving slowly at a low altitude—for the sirens of helicopters, invisible in the fog, came close on several occasions—we flew along the broad river, once animated by intense traffic but now deserted save for a few electric launches and a white ferry-boat broken down in the middle of the estuary. Boats of every shape and size were laid up along the interminable quays, and in the basins fringed with warehouses, which bordered both banks all the way to the Pool of London. Beyond Gravesend, they had all been within the reach of the fires and the red gas.

Upstream of Woolwich, the effects of the torpedoes became more and more complete. Blurred by the fog, fragments of charred wall loomed over the debris of riverboats; empty shells like pontoon bridges filled the burned-out docks, whose quays had collapsed. I tried in vain to make out the location of Greenwich. As far as the eye could see, there was nothing still standing. The once-majestic Tower Bridge had blocked the river with an inextricable mass of rubble and twisted metal. London's other bridges had all suffered the same fate, their heaped-up debris making barrages from which the current tumbled in cascades between banks whose ruins extended beyond the horizon.

Everything, from the docks and residential districts of the East End to the fine buildings along the Embankment, had been devoured by the egalitarian satanite. Beyond Westminster Bridge, the tower of the Houses of Parliament remained intact, by virtue of one of those freaks of chance that the vulgar qualify as miracles, as if it were turning a monstrous eye upon the nightmarish devastation…and upon a gathering of human beings more sinister still.

In a vast square, around what seemed at first to be a fire, a procession of thousand ragged individuals, men and women, was moving in a circle. The memory of the fusillade in Avignon prevented me from descending low enough to read the inscriptions on their banners or make out the words of the hymn they were singing, but I could see that the pseudo-fire was only a sort of brazier. Each in his or her turn, as they passed by, threw upon it a handful of some substance that produced a thick red smoke, whose eddies gradually spread an opaque pall above the square. The sharp tones of three harmoniums, like those previously used by the Salvation Army, accompanied the joyous hymn voiced by all the demented wretches.

The incantation of that funereal music and the pillar of purple smoke rising into the sky like a monstrous prayer—rites of some ignominious mystery celebrated in the midst of that necropolis, displaying the abominable obsession of its ruins for mile after mile—brought our horror to its peak. It became so poignant that I did not wait for Raymonde's plea, and, blessing the clouds that my unhealthy curiosity had initially cursed, we gained altitude. Their pitiful shroud closed again over the corpse of the murdered city.

We descended again in the vicinity of Windsor. The intact castle dominated the pleasant town and the woods decked out in their autumnal shades. A quarter of an hour later, we were in Oxford, at the airport of the ancient University, where I was surprised to see the British Union Jack flying, as in days gone by. The mere sight of that flag could have told me the response that Wronsky's propositions would receive.

Lord Higgins welcomed us with perfect politeness, but refused categorically to allow me to complete my mission with respect to his colleagues. While he lived, he declared, not a single member of the University would leave Oxford to establish himself in a continental city. A global Institute? That was all very well—but what point would there be in looking for a new seat? That seat was entirely ready; it already existed, populated by an elite which, if they so desired, the savants of merit living abroad were welcome to join. Oxford would willingly open its doors to them. Outside of that rational solution, however, no project could be viable or worthy of consideration. No Englishman would lend his hand to it. The University of Cambridge,[18] although it was Oxford's rival, would undoubtedly give me an identical refusal. In short, I could dispense with further travels and return as quickly as possible to France.

To tell the truth, Lord Higgins did not express himself in such brutal terms, but his discourse tended to that conclusion, without the slightest ambiguity. I would have persisted nevertheless and continued to Edinburgh, where at least two recruits awaited us, their support having been guaranteed in advance, had it not been for the news that reached us in the evening.

Lord Higgins did us the extreme kindness of putting us up "until tomorrow morning, when I believe you'll have good weather for traveling."

After dinner—I admit that we took considerable sensual pleasure in consuming two slices of an admirable and most unexpected joint of roast beef, bloody and juicy—we all went into the drawing-room, here our host regaled us with a reading from the Bible: a chapter from the Apocalypse, as I recall, quite

---

[18] Varlet actually refers to "the University of Eton" but I have corrected the egregious error.

appropriate to the situation. Then the two Lady Higginses, mother and daughter, retired while we men stayed to drink "a glass of wine" while chatting.

The advertised glass of wine was succeeded by whiskies and cognacs. While our host was in the middle of a dogged apology for the Anglo-Saxon race, and therefore oblivious, I was able continually to exchange my empty glass for Raymonde's full one, my poor love being unable to cope with these libations. A liveried servant then came in, bearing a silver tray. "The TSF correspondence, my lord," he said. "The central station in France resumed transmission half an hour ago."

One of the radio messages was addressed to: "Léon and Raymond Rudeaux, in the course of a Directorial mission to Brussels, Leyden or Oxford."

"Oh, what luck, my darling!" cried my pilot, forgetting "his" role in the heat of emotion "They've got a dynamo going again!"

Lord Higgins started and looked at us oddly. "Yes, *gentlemen*, the station at Saintes-Maries has been able to re-establish one dynamo—but ours isn't turning as yet, so our antennae can receive but can't transmit…"

I was no longer listening. My anxious gaze was following Raymonde's finger as it ran beneath the text signed by Wronsky: *Anarchist riots throughout Provence. Helicopter squadron dispatched to relieve Kropatchek has not returned. Are blockaded, with insufficient forces, by nihilist bands. Send help if possible. Hope mission successful. Good wishes from everyone.*

"My God! How terrible!" cried Raymonde—and her tears ate into the virile make-up on her upper lips. We must send them help. My lord, I implore you, in the name of science and humanity, don't refuse…"

"Impossible, *Madame*," replied our host, bowing. "I regret it, but we only have a few policemen in Oxford. They're indispensable to the safety of our colony. All our good wishes go with you—but that's the most I can do."

"Thank you, my lord," I said bitterly, supporting my poor companion, who was about to faint. "Your kindness is overwhelming. We'll leave alone, then, at dawn tomorrow, to rejoin our friends and fight alongside them, to the death, for the sacred cause of Civilization!"

VII. The Breakdown at Dury

We were flying at top speed above grey rain-clouds, which hid the ground. I had not even had time to fill up with fuel, and Lord Higgins did not offer me any as he bid us farewell with a glacial attitude. It would, therefore, be necessary for us to land in the course of the day, for our half-empty tanks would scarcely take us any further than Clermont-Ferrand. In order to be ready for any Soviet eventuality, Raymonde had become my pilot Raymond again. Her eyes gleaming with urgency and anxiety, she looked back and forth between the compass, the anemometer and the infinite sea of cloud.

"We must be over the Pas-de-Calais by now," I declared. "In 20 minutes we can go down in search of fuel—at Arras, if my calculations are accurate…"

Either they were not, or the wind had thrown us off course, for it was the grey and dismal surface of the Channel that soon appeared below us. The rain had stopped; a coastline of deserted dunes was visible to port, forming a sort of profound gulf towards which I steered.

"The mouth of the Seine?" Raymonde guessed.

"There would be cliffs, my love, not dunes…"

Suddenly, enlightenment dawned: those sands uncovered by the ebb-tide; that estuary extending deep into the flat countryside; those lines of poplars…

"It's the bay of the Somme!" I exclaimed. And I recognized the port of Hourdel, then Le Crotoy, and, further away to the south, the green pastures and the dike of Saint-Valéry, where—three months earlier, in the immeasurably distant past of *Another Time*—I had contemplated the effects of clouds, sunsets, and the periodic transformations of the bay as it was dried out to a vast extent and re-invaded by the tide, when the fishing-smacks returned under full sail, in a line of ten, twenty or thirty, following the sinuous course of the channel with the grace of dancers: the "ballet of the boats," as I called it!

But the thought of our friends, in danger at the other end of France, forbade any distraction. After rapid glance over the ancient elms of Cap Hornu and the little town, which, like every other, bore the stigmata of the era of calamity—the outlying district of La Ferté was reduced to ruins, and a cloud of purple smoke extended from the floodgates to Pinchefalise—we went up the valley of the Somme at top speed.

The sky became clearer. It seemed best to make the most of the clear conditions rather than refueling, so we flew over Abbeville at speed, and 20 minutes later I left Amiens—still dominated by its majestic cathedral—to port in order to veer southwards.

"Why are you slowing down, my love?" Raymonde asked, noticing the change of direction.

"I'm not slowing down—look, the control-levers are flat to the boards. It's the motor that's weakening. It'll soon stop, I think..."

The rotor-blades were only turning jerkily; further ignition got them going again, but then they stopped completely. We had broken down—at 800 meters!

Used to helicopter descents, the unexpected deployment of the parachute-planes threw us into confusion; a moment's hesitation caused us to miss a field suitable for landing, and we touched down within the walls of a large estate, in which there appeared to be a vegetable-garden, where some 15 individuals were at work. Bizarrely, not one of them raised his head or attempted to get out of the way. We got down without injury, though still dazed by a slightly rough landing, but all the people continued placidly plying their spades and hoes. Even those who must have been brushed by our slipstream as we went by seemed to be ignoring the presence, ten paces away, of the helicopter that had plunged out of the sky directly on top of the glass covering a melon-patch!

We climbed down from the cockpit without thinking, in our surprise, of arming ourselves with out blasters. I made a circuit of the machine and discovered a slight fissure in the tank from which the fuel must have leaked—the sole cause, undoubtedly, of our breakdown. Then Raymonde drew my attention to four further individuals: three men in formal but decorative frock-coats and an exceedingly fat woman, who were advancing toward us.

"It's not always Soviets," I murmured. "They have a rather doctoral air about them..."

"Well, gentlemen," commenced the tallest, having arrived within two paces of us, "that's a singular means of introducing yourselves! You're the first patients to have come to us by air—but that doesn't matter; we'll care for you like the others... Our philanthropy knows no bounds. Isn't that so, Miss Tarry?"

The fat woman, whose black silk bodice was decorated with academic palms, replied in a shrill voice and a strong English accent: "Perhaps they aren't patients, though, Monsieur le Directeur. The young man, especially..." And she addressed a gracious smile to "Raymond," on whom she feasted her eyes.

The so-called director's eyes disturbed me; bright blue, they had a fixed stare so intense that I turned to look at his more normal acolytes.

"Monsieur," I said, "We have been commissioned by Doctor Wronsky to recruit affiliates for a new Institute that he is founding at Montpellier, in the Faculty of Medicine..."

The man with the magnetic eyes interrupted me. "Ah, Montpellier! That's another thing altogether! You've come on behalf of Doctor Maigret, then? A bit dotty, old Maigret... Jealous of my success, no doubt? But it's necessary, between colleagues... I won't hide anything from you, since you're doctors... You are doctors, aren't you?"

I mumbled a few vague words. The man positively intimidated me, but I was attempting to correct the misunderstanding when the fat woman, who had placed herself a little behind the rest of the group, began signaling to "Raymond" to be careful.

His eyes as disquieting as ever, the "director" rubbed his hands and continued: "You seem like reasonable men, in fact. No need to go to extremes with you. My philanthropy will seduce you, I'm sure...but we must take care of your machine first, since you're here at the house—for a long time, I hope!" He tapped his foot with sudden violence and shouted: "Let it be, damn it! I forbid you to touch it!" He had interposed himself, threateningly, between me and the helicopter. A shouted "Hey! Come here, everyone!" had caused the gardeners to come running, and he gave them an order to roll it into a nearby shed.

What madness it had been to leave our blasters in the cockpit, entrusting ourselves to the apparent safety of this non-Soviet domain!

Raymonde darted an anxious glance at me—but what could we do against 15 resolute men armed with spades and pickaxes, obedient, with canine docility, to the fascinating state of the "director," to whose magnetic ascendancy we were submissive ourselves? Would not a protest be sufficient to compromise the situation irredeemably?

Pushed by vigorous arms, our helicopter disappeared into the shed—an old automobile garage, in which I saw, with a beating heart, several drums of fuel which seemed to me to be heavy, and therefore full!

But the "director" cornered me again, the obese Miss Tarry took "Raymond" by the arm, and, followed by the other two "doctors," we were obliged to go into the main building, where the dinner bell was ringing at full volume. Having become jovial again, the "director"—who told me that his name was Doctor Landru—completed my confusion with a continuous stream of questions relating to Montpellier, Doctor Maigret and his pupils; fortunately, he did not listen to my replies, and leapt from one subject to another, even putting in jokes: "Oh yes, an excellent doctoress, Miss Tarry; her first name is Odile, so I call her 'O. Tarry'—*Otary*, you understand? Ha ha ha ha!"[19]

And he stopped in order to laugh more easily, racked by a fit of contagious merriment in which the two doctors and Miss O. Tarry herself joined.

Raymonde took the opportunity to move closer to me and whisper; "Be careful, darling. Above all, don't mention..." But her fat companion drew her away. Doctor Landru invited me to climb the front steps, and I did not under-

---

[19] An otary (*otarie* in French) is an eared seal, or sea-lion. The names in this passage have a familiar ring to them nowadays, but Georges Simenon had yet to invent his Maigret in 1920 and the alleged serial-killer Henri Landru, who used "lonely hearts" ads to attract his female victims, had not yet been brought to trial for murder when Varlet wrote this passage. Landru had, however, been arrested in 1919, and the name might well have rung a bell with some of Varlet's readers even before the *cause célèbre* generated by the murder trial—which began on November 7, 1921—made the name notorious.

stand the signs that Raymonde was making by way of completing her thought. What was it that I must not mention? What danger was looming over us?

We arrived in a sort of grand refectory, which reminded me of my schooldays. On a platform elevated by two steps, a table was set for six, at which we took our places. On the inferior level, further tables were furnished with benches. The gardeners, who had followed us in, occupied two of them. Then the door opened to admit a file of peasants carrying hand-baskets. Walking automatically, as if entranced, these newcomers came up to Landru one by one. He clasped their hands, while the doctors emptied the hand-baskets: turkeys, ducks, chickens, rabbits, slabs of butter, cheeses—heaps of victuals that gradually filled up two vast baskets. I counted 28 peasants, who sat down in their turn with the gardeners.

"All our patients are here?" intoned the director. "Yes—begin serving!"

Four domestics in green aprons appeared, pushing compartmentalized carts full of steaming plates that were deposited in front of each diner: a dozen boiled potatoes.

"Eat!" ordered Landru. "Eat these fine Arcachon oysters! They're good—tell me that they're good!"

Meekly, the troop of gardeners and peasants released little cries of gastronomic delight, while avidly sinking their teeth into the potatoes.

"Eat! It's chicken with *petit pois*! Drink! It's chilled champagne!"

"It's chicken with *petit pois*! It's chilled champagne! Oh, it's good! Long live Doctor Landru!" exclaimed the unfortunate "subjects" competitively.

The sinister truth had finally become apparent to me: Doctor Landru, a master hypnotist, had mesmerized all these men; the gardeners and peasants had become his slaves! The swine had profited from the present disorder, which put him beyond the reach of justice, to indulge himself to the full, at no other expense than the magnetic passes designed to obtain the obedience of those he called "his patients."

Indignation choked me; it was impossible to swallow a mouthful of what was served at our table—chicken with *petits pois*, authentic in this case—or sip the champagne that was bubbling in my glass. Raymonde had also understood, and darted horrified glances at me clandestinely across the table, while the fat "doctoress," leaning towards her, looked longingly at her with eyes illuminated by wine and concupiscence.

"The latest news!" Landru announced, stemming the flow of his incoherent pleasantries to take a newspaper from his pocket. "Here are the day's *true* news items, the only ones in which you can believe. Listen! Those who tell you anything else are liars! All goes well. The great boxer Jim Frangicrane has become world champion. Monsieur Gideon Botram, second Terrestrial Doctor, laid the first stone of a new hospital for stray dogs in Pantin yesterday. An interview with Monsieur Ladislas Wronsky on the prospect of connecting America and

Asia by means of a Transpacific Tube similar to the Transatlantic Tube. The first tests of a turbine-driven helicopter…"

I was no longer listening. The sight of all those poor deluded men, stuffing themselves with potatoes that they believed to be oysters and chicken, welcoming last year's news, presented as today's facts by the impostor Landru, with beatific smiles…the absurd monstrosity made me literally lose control of myself.

"This is madness!" I shouted. "Pure madness! So you don't know anything, here? The torpedoes, the Martian shells, the devastated cities, a third of Humankind killed by the gas, the fires, the earthquakes, the plague! You don't know…."

What an uproar! "Liar! Liar!" howled the "patients."

"Villain! False brother! Spy!" the two "doctors" shouted in my ear, while holding me down and punching me vigorously. O. Tarry grabbed "Raymond" round the waist.

"Ah! A trickster! So you're a patient too! Well, don't worry, we'll soon see to that!" jeered the "director" as he leaned over me.

I was helpless. I felt the terrible blue eyes fascinate mine, irresistibly; they poured vertigo and confusion into my brain with very passing second. Ah! An inspiration! Pretend! Pretend to fall into a trance *before* the hypnosis actually has that effect! And I pretended: rolling back my eyes, letting my eyelids fall half-closed, I slumped into inertia.

"Are you asleep?"

"Yes, I'm asleep."

"You belong to me now. You will believe everything I tell you! You will do everything I order you to do!"

"Yes. I will believe it. I will do it."

"To begin with, you will go to work with your fellow patients. You understand. Potard and Bahut,[20] I confide him to you. Put him through his paces—he's a 'new boy.' Get going! Move!"

And I was obliged to get up, mechanically, to take my place among the gardeners, hiding my anguish with respect to Raymonde under an inert and somnambulistic mask. I remembered with relief that she was unresponsive to hypnotic suggestion—but would it occur to her to pretend?"

"Now for the other!" said Landru. "What's the matter, O. Tarry? Why are you turning your head away?"

"He's so young! So nice!" pleaded the doctoress.

"He's a patient—I have to cure him!"

---

[20] Some of the names Varlet uses harbor insulting double meanings, usually lightly veiled; these two are brutal in their simplicity. A potard is a dispensing chemist; a bahut is an item of kitchen furniture, the Breton equivalent of a Welsh dresser.

"A colleague…" one of the doctors put in, in his turn.

"I'm getting angry! Enough, in God's name! Don't pester me any more, or I'll hypnotize the lot of you!"

With extraordinary promptitude, the new "subject" appeared to be plunged into a hypnotic trance. O joy—she was pretending!

"You see," said Landru. "That didn't take long."

"He went off very quickly," objected the shorter "doctor."

"Pah! Who can resist me? And you…besides, look!" While I stifled an exclamation, he pricked Raymonde's arm vigorously with the tine of a fork. "He's fast asleep!"

And he completed his orders to the "new boy" with this suggestion: "You will *also* obey O. Tarry!"

My dear companion played the comedy necessary to our salvation even better than I did. Without addressing the slightest sign of intelligence to me, she came to stand by my side among the gardeners. All afternoon, as if they had received an order, the latter watched us closely. Until the bell sounded for "supper," we had to work with all our might digging up potatoes in the vegetable-garden where we had set down, only a few steps away from the shed in which our helicopter was locked, without being able to exchange a word—for hypnotized subjects do not speak unless ordered; it gets in the way of work!

Raging internally, our hands blistered and grazed by the pick-handles, we had to return, in line with the other "patients," to the accursed refectory, to eat the meal—boiled carrots, this time, relabeled stuffed calves' brains *en tortue* and vanilla ice cream—to the accompaniment of the sniggers of the accomplices on the platform, who were guzzling those dishes for real, and to submit to the news from a *Grand Parisien* of the previous year.

Then came the injunction: "Go to bed!" One of the domestics led us to a room on the first floor where he left us alone in the dark, without even turning the key in the door, such was his absolute confidence in the suggestive power of the "director."

After we had washed ourselves silently, Raymonde told me in a whisper about the new danger that confronted us: O. Tarry had commanded "Raymond" to join her in her room at 10:30 p.m—in two hours! All was lost if we could not find a means of escape before then. But what were we to do? Our windows, looking out over the grounds, were furnished with stout bars; besides, ferocious barking proved to us that there was no chance by that route. Inside, there was silence. Everyone was asleep. The helicopter! If we could get to the shed, and if the two drums were indeed full…there would be enough fuel to reach Amiens! No, there was no other way to save ourselves.

On our way, then! Taking every precaution, groping our way along dark and silent corridors…the staircase…the hallway…the garden…still no one. And there, in the starlight, the dark mass of the shed….

Alas, a sonorous snore alerted us that someone was asleep in the garage. But no—we could not retreat in the face of that obstacle. Seizing a spade abandoned on the threshold, I opened the door. The snoring ceased.

"Your electric torch!" I said to Raymonde, "switch it on!"

In the luminous beam, a man appeared, propped up on his elbow and rubbing his eyes.

"Quiet, or you're a dead man!" I told him, my weapon upraised.

Instead of obeying, he threw himself towards me, with a prolonged howl. With one blow, struck with all my might, I split his skull, and finished him off with two more blows.

"Quickly, quickly!" I hissed at Raymonde, who was petrified with horror. "Light a lamp so that we can see what we're doing! Open the fuel-tank—I'll see to the drums."

Three of them were intact! The task of filling up was executed as if in a dream, but so very slowly, in the context of our frantic haste, made more acute by the distant sound of shouting coming from the main building!

The barking was coming closer…opening the garage doors wide to let the helicopter out, I threw myself into the cockpit behind Raymonde and closed the door. What a joy it would be to be under way!

The motor started purring just as two furious dogs hurled themselves against the rotor blades. They turned, striking the dogs down and drawing us out of the shed, into the midst of the crowd of our enemies, who were running and howling.

Its members were mown down; our downdraft became violent, crushing their bodies. In the open air that was finally above our heads, the supportive blades whirled at top speed, and we rose up from the ground—saved!

We headed straight for the lights of Amiens, a few kilometers away.[21]

---

[21] Varlet inserts a footnote on behalf of his narrator: "We were told a few hours later that we had escaped from the famous hypnotist Landru, who had been imprisoned six months earlier in the departmental Asylum at Dury. After the directors had fled, during the revolutionary panic, he had hypnotized the warders, then the patients and since then had maintained control of the Asylum, along with his accomplices, two former interns and an English nurse, thanks to the protection afforded him by the peasants of the neighbourhood, who were gratefully amazed the Pantagruelian feasts that he committed to their memories every time they brought him their modest tributes of rabbits, chickens, butter, and so on. A fine example of the general moral laxity in that era!" Splitting the skulls of innocent dupes with spades and mowing them down with helicopter blades—not to mention making no attempt whatsoever to liberate them from their slavery—evidently does not count, in the narrator's opinion, as further evidence of "moral laxity," although the reader might take a different view.

VIII. Amiens, Supreme Refuge of the Arts

Ten minutes later, at 9:30 a.m. exactly, we set down without difficulty at La Hotoie airport. I hoped to refill our fuel tanks in a matter of minutes and depart that same night, but the mechanic showed me other cracks that were ready to open up to create even more leaks. It was absolutely necessary to replace the entire rear wall—work that would take about twelve hours!

Our consternation was ameliorated by the news that the Amiens TSF had been working again since the previous day. The Post Office was closed at that late hour, but the manager only lived a short distance away, at number four, Rue Morgan...

We ran there. The manager opened the door himself at the first ring of the doorbell and, on seeing our official papers, generously introduced us into his office. In response to our anxious questions, he admitted with ill-omened embarrassment that the Amiens radio station had indeed been transmitting since the day before, and that he had received two radio messages addressed to us, one from Saintes-Maries and the other from La Crau...

"Give them to us, quickly," Raymonde cried, feverishly. "Are they saved?"

Without saying a word, the functionary took two forms from his desk drawer and held them out to us. We pored over them tremulously.

Directoire Saintes-Maries, October 11, 9:17 a.m.

Besieged in TSF station by Anarchist forces on ground and in air. Helicopter hangar destroyed in explosion. Leduc's aid arrived too late; could not get through to us. Fire has reached dynamo hall and control room where we have taken refuge. Bomb. Adi...

"We did not receive the end of the message," murmured the manager, looking away. "The transmission was abruptly cut short. Look at the other one."

Raymonde was devastated, sobbing on my shoulder. I read through my tears:

La Crau, October 11, 8:02 p.m.

Our blasters useless against Anarchist machine-gunners. Saintes-Maries station destroyed this morning. Gideon Botram, Ladislas Wronsky, Gabrielle Leduc and all personnel died for civilization. Crau airborne squadron returned decimated. Awaiting news of Léon and Raymond Rudeaux.

Sylvain Leduc.

The excellent Amiénois abstained from offering us the banal consolations of awkward pity. He helped us to contain our grief by asking for a few details of our late friends and our mission, then about ourselves. These confidences softened our sentimental regrets slightly; simultaneously and conversely, however, our comprehension of the consequences that this misfortune would have for us only became sharper. Without a home, having no role to play any longer, with-

131

out any goal in the precarious existence that had been gifted to us, undeservedly, by our absence, it seemed to us that all external support had been suddenly removed, and that we were sliding into a sort of moral abyss, inextricably and desperately bound together by our love, but powerless to resist the blow.

When I had finished telling my story—and I gained confidence to the extent of revealing my companion's disguise—our interlocutor began to speak.

"Monsieur et Madame...or, rather, *gentlemen*, for security is so problematic in our sad epoch that I advise you to persevere in that prudent measure...your situation is such that nothing any longer compels you to leave Amiens. I am sure that you will agree with me, once you have seen the exceptionally favorable state of affairs that pertains here. Even if the functions that I continue to exercise—oh, by habit and by inclination, for nothing remains of the PTT[22] but the name, save for a few radio stations—even, as I say, if my job did not keep me here, I would spend the few remaining days of my life in Amiens. The vicissitudes of the day have deprived me of my wife and my four children, and I live in a house that is much too large for me alone, which I would be happy to share with guests as distinguished as you. Since you make use of the Jovian nutriment, you will fit in with my regime, and if you have tastes that are in any measure artistic, you will not find society and distraction lacking."

I thanked the kind functionary warmly, and, after having consulted Raymonde for form's sake, I accepted his generous hospitality. Then I asked him for an explanation of his last remark.

"Chance, gentlemen, fortunately for us, is a most singular thing. My story will help you to understand that our city is an anomaly of the first order. To cut a long story short, the Jovian nutriment preserved us from the communist revolution. I have no doubt that if that experiment, which demonstrated the perfect innocuousness and nutritive virtue of the product, had taken place sooner, while communications were easy and widespread, the popular prejudice that 'the nutriment causes the plague' would have been easily vanquished and that its general employment would at least have attenuated the crisis that has wrecked civilization. It's too late now, alas! Amiens must be a special case...

"You are familiar with the tyranny of 'fashion' and you remember its power before, and even during, the 'Season of the Torpedoes.' Well, by virtue of one of those sudden vogues which once made it practically obligatory for the entire artistic population of Paris to visit some place in Brittany, Provence or the Basque country, Amiens became the rendezvous of all the capital's painters, sculptors, musicians, writers and so on—or, rather, those who escaped the disaster, who were numerous in the quarters least affected, Montmartre and Montparnasse.

---

[22] Like TSF, this is a formula commonly used in France, but not in England, even though the English equivalent (Post, Telephone and Telegraph) would be identical.

"A simple freak of chance was the origin of this movement; during the rescue process, a dozen airbuses loaded with escapees of this sort found it opportune to set them down in Amiens. They became infatuated with the cathedral and declared our city 'the only one possible,' telling all their dispersed colleagues—communications still existed at that time, remember—who hastened to join them.

"You were at Saint-Valery, you say, on the morning when the first torpedo fell? Two days later, you would have found numerous 'artistic refugees' there, for Saint-Valery shared the fashionability of Amiens during the summer. Everyone gathered hereabouts at the beginning of September, and, because the normal population had diminished by three-quarters during the Great Exodus and in consequence of the 'Martian bronchitis,' the artists easily found lodgings.

"As for nourishment, Monsieur Leduc could tell you that ever since the industrial manufacture of the Jovian nutriment first began, he has dispatched considerable stocks of it to Amiens in response to its inhabitants' demands. It is a unique case, I believe, but all those who have artistic inclinations and tastes are enormously appreciative of the particular spiritual stimulation provided by that form of nourishment, with involves no digestive effort or waste. Others followed suit, and everyone here has lived exclusively on that admirable product for some considerable time.

"Thanks to that circumstance, there was no soviet in Amiens. I should add, though, that the most dangerous elements of the population set off for Paris, with the aim of pillaging the ruins, and that few returned. Besides, from the very beginning, a few hearty fellows among the artists and sculptors constituted a 'Phalanx des 4-z'arts' [23] and the idea occurred to them of adopting the old firearms from the museum as their munitions. They did not have any trouble putting down attempts at popular insurrection, in view of the limited range of radium blasters."

"I saw that in Avignon," I put in.

"The idea has run its course," Monsieur Zambeaux continued. "It's a fatal regression, progress in reverse. I have no doubt that we shall see the return of bows and arrows, and then stone axes. In sum, we are living here under the dictatorship of Art, as the Earth was formerly under the dictatorship of Science. Our domain is more restricted, though, for—except for a little colony at Saint-Valery—it reaches its limit in the suburbs. The peasants are mistrustful and remain distant, quite peaceful but refusing all commerce with us. The Soviet

---

[23] The "Bal des Quat'z'arts," usually further abbreviated as "4-z'arts," was a carnivalesque festival held annually by the students of the Ecole Nationale des Beaux-Arts in Paris, so-called because it brought together students of Architecture, Painting, Sculpture and Engraving. It was first held in 1893 (at the Moulin-Rouge) and continued until 1966.

towns are hostile to us, and since the dawn of anarchy bands of Eternal-Nightists have been roaming around the surrounding country."

"I think I saw some of them in London—but I don't know what they are."

"The Eternal-Nightists were born of an enormous flood of propaganda that reached us from America when the Transatlantic Tube was temporarily restored to use. You might well have read their tracts, without attaching any more importance to them than to the manifestoes of 20 other new sects—but this one succeeded. Its hour had come, and it undertook a formidable development, which was uninterrupted by the failure of communications, because its members were wanderers. There has been a snowball effect since the penetrative shells and the revelation of the volcanoes. In brief, since you don't know, Eternal-Nightism is a cause—or, rather, a kind of mysticism—which proposes to save humankind by establishing a veil of opaque smoke all around the Earth, intended to impede the Martian shots.

"The 'zones of fine weather' in which the first telemechanically-directed torpedoes had to fall provided the principle from which the promoters of this ostrich-like scheme departed. And the general obscuring of thought, the decline of the intellectual level, reached such a point that the penetrative shells, designed by the Martians to strike without deviation, did not cause them to abandon their idea. On the contrary, the example of volcanic plumes—which they could see in actuality or in the cinema—was an encouragement to them.

"The American tracts included a very simple formula for a compound that produces prodigious volumes of purple smoke, opaque and persistent, of which the adepts of the new cult make considerable use. You must have noticed fires of this sort in the course of your expedition. In addition to that, though, they set light to anything prone to produce smoke as it burns: wood-piles, haystacks, tanks of petrol or kerosene, even houses—for Eternal-Nightism is nothing but a destructive version of nihilism; it's rumored that its secret rites include human sacrifice and cannibalism.

"Thus far, we've been sheltered from their attacks, but their bands are growing larger every day. Winter is approaching, and they'll need to find new food supplies—for the Nutriment inspires them with extreme horror. After the pillage of the countryside, it will be the turn of the cities. Will our 'Phalanx des 4-z'arts' be able to hold them off? I doubt it; the air force at Le Crotoy seems to be leaning towards their doctrine, and only ten helicopters remain in Amiens since the exodus from the cities. Your friend Leduc might be the defender our 'artistic station' requires."

That seemed obvious to us, and we composed a long radiogram to Sylvain in which an explanation of the situation of Amiens was appended to news concerning us and our condolences on the sad loss of Gaby. An aerodrome is not easy to move, however; the white birds of La Crau were acclimatized to the skies of Provence, and it required repeated messages to persuade Sylvain that, following the obliteration of Saintes-Maries, the asylum of Science, our duty was to defend Amiens, the asylum of Art.

Introduced by Monsieur Zambeaux into a literary salon in the Rue Delambre, our scientific affiliations initially obtained us a reserved, almost suspicious, welcome, but the story of our adventures and Raymonde-Ramond's "original" costume soon made us a successful curiosity in the Amiens-wide artistic community, which ceased to consider us as outsiders and eventually admitted us.

How friendly and sympathetic that little society seemed to us, despite its petty faults and imperfections, and the inevitable friction between its members, during the long months that we were fortunate enough to live within it! We were, to be sure, surrounded by egotism, but—in sharp contrast to what had happened in other human aggregations— it had not submitted to the crazed contagion of atavistic instincts. Reduced by their "artistic temperament" to the role of slaves to the instinct of Beauty, these people had channeled the manifestations of atavism into works of art, resulting in nothing other than a crop of masterpieces. Beneath the thumbs of sculptors and the brushes of painters, clay was modeled and colors were juxtaposed in radiant forms. Printing-presses manned by the authors themselves ground out immortal poems; sublimely-imagined plays awoke echoes of classical drama in theatres habituated to the dismal drone of "repertory;" and the crowds filling the vast naves of the cathedral were ecstatically infused, to the accompaniment of mighty organs, with the souls of composers of genius.

We lived in an atmosphere of sublimely unreal art, in the divine world of Beauty, which seemed to me then to be the most noble goal of human activity, the supreme justification of the existence of humankind upon the Earth, even higher than the pursuit of Virtue or that of Truth. We forgot the calamities that had dissolved upon the globe and had delivered the remaining millions of our contemporaries to the madness of despair.

Leaning against the balustrade of the flat roof on one of the towers of the cathedral, with 100 other fervent admirers of sunsets, we learned to see nothing but a supplementary magnificence in the fantastic coloration that the Sun's fires took on, thanks to the increasingly dense dust and vapor spread into the atmosphere by the distant eruption of the fire-vomiting mouths expelling the flaming entrails of the globe. The columns of purple and black smoke rising here and there from the countryside, like the pillars awaiting the future dome of the Eternal Night, brought joy to painters and provoked admiration among mere amateurs of beauty.

Beauty! She, uniquely, in all her forms, preoccupied the population of Amiens. It would require a whole book to enumerate the manifestations that she revealed in that hothouse of Art! Even costume, liberated from vulgar prejudices, participated in everyone's fantasy. In the streets, silken doublets, brocade mantles, pointed shoes, Henri IV ruffs, Greek chlamyses, Egyptian *calasiris*, delighted our aesthetic sensibilities at every step. In the well-heated drawing-rooms, Olympian forms had no fear of exposing themselves without veils to gazes purified by the exclusive and permanent worship of beautiful forms.

The former Musée de Picardie, with its frescoes by Pierre Puvis de Chavannes and its renowned treasures, was no more than a minor appendage to the new galleries that monopolized, one by one, the Prefecture, the Palais de Justice and the Gare du Nord, similarly adapted to lodge masterpieces of the past acquired in sovietized towns in exchange for foodstuffs drawn from Amiénois storehouses, rendered redundant by our stocks of the Nutriment.

On two occasions, my beloved pilot and I set off in our helicopter, in convoy with an airbus on an expedition of this sort. The first, to Lille—which brought us, among others, the delightful "wax head" attributed to Raphael— gave me the opportunity to see the unfortunate city again. The Soviets were succumbing to the daily incursions of Eternal-Nightists, who had already reduced Roubaix, Croix-Wasquehal and Tourcoing to ashes, sparing only the factory chimneys, which they employed to pour torrents of purple smoke—whose pall covered the entire region—into the atmosphere. In Lille itself, the mid-day Sun had the appearance of a sinister carmine Moon. Doctor Goulliard, whom I saw again on that occasion, attributed the recrudescence of frenzies of murder and arson to the "dynamogenic" influence of that light.

It was soon necessary to give up that sort of expedition, for the cities were falling, one after the other, into the grip of anarchy, and we were almost captured in the course of our journey to Rouen, which we believed to be still sovietized.

It goes without saying that, at the outset of our sojourn in Amiens, I had voluntarily enrolled, along with "Raymond" in the "Phalanx des 4-z'arts." Once a fortnight we undertook tours of sentry-duty—or, rather, our helicopter did— designed to protect the city against a surprise attack by the increasingly bold and threatening Eternal-Nightists. By day, their columns of smoke wove their fateful veil indefatigably, while it was the bright red fires of their vile "altars" that we observed on the fine nights of that unexpectedly mild winter…mild to the point that the Venetian festivals they organized in the water-meadows often offered us the spectacle of their moving fires reflected in the placid waters, while snatches of song and languorous music drifted up to us—making a poignant contrast with the sullen hymns of the hordes and their monstrous rites dedicated to darkness.

It was the beginning of spring when Sylvain Leduc finally yielded to our solicitations and brought the entire airfleet of La Crau to the North. Half of it was accommodated at Hotoie, the other half at Le Crotoy, where it assumed an authority over a staff whose fidelity was more than dubious—which reassured our colony at Saint-Valery and encouraged a large number of Amiénois to search out the coolness of the bay of the Somme at the end of June.

I doubt, though, that Leduc would have chosen our artistic "outpost" if we had known sooner of the existence of another civilized outpost—this one scientific—which was revealed to us by TSF soon after his arrival.

Our apparatus had limited range, as no doubt did the other stations disseminated over the surface of the globe, equipped with whatever dynamos they happened to have following the loss of the Equatorial Alternators. Our unskilled electricians had been unable to reconstruct the detectors specifically developed for interplanetary communications, and messages from Jupiter no longer reached us. Signals too weak to be deciphered informed us of the existence of enigmatic stations outside Europe.

From time to time, a Soviet town, having been silent for a long interval, would abruptly announce an attack by errant hordes, a desperate battle, and issue an appeal for help: SOS, SOS, emitted spasmodically...and we would hear no more news of that town.

One the other hand, Mont Blanc—whose astronomers we had believed to be dead and buried—emerged, as it were, out of the blue one morning, to begin transmitting its daily message once again. An entire scientific colony was living up there at present, occupying part of the vast system of bunkers hollowed out in the flanks of the Giant of the Alps following the first announcement of the Asian invasion, and subsequently used as storehouses by the observatory. Thirty scientists had taken refuge there, from Switzerland, Alsace and northern Italy, with a few men of good will, and they were all working actively for the amelioration of their sojourn. They said that they were still capable of tripling the number of their inhabitants.

We were so comfortable in the delightful snare of our artistic Capua that the news only generated a feeble and quasi-theoretical emotional response in Amiens—but Leduc hastened to mount an expedition to Mont Blanc and returned full of enthusiasm. I believe that only the difficulty of accommodating his air fleet at the observatory, or at Chamonix, prevented him from leaving us.

The pure atmosphere that surrounded our brothers in civilization was, in his opinion, a particularly decisive argument. At that height, the most tenuous dust projected by the volcanoes occasionally formed a sort of haze veiling the Sun, but, even so, it was still the Sun, rather than the kind of brick-colored Moon that extended an increasingly dismal and sinister light over us. There was blue sky, instead of the ceiling of reddish smoke that had long been spread out over our heads, and which obliged us to live in the stifling atmosphere of a greenhouse whose windows were smeared with ox-blood.

The winter, as I have said, was unusually mild. The advent of summer made very little difference. The semi-translucent covering imposed on the region—and presumably on the whole of Europe, if not the entire world—smoothed out the seasons by retaining beneath it the calorific radiations of the Sun that penetrated it, thanks to its red tint.[24] The parts of the spectrum endowed with the chemical properties indispensable to the growth of vegetation,

---

[24] The effect nowadays known as the Greenhouse Effect, to which reference is made here, had first been identified by Fourier in the early 18th century and had been further popularized in the 1890s by Svante Arrhenius; it is not surprising

chemical properties indispensable to the growth of vegetation, however—especially the ultra-violet—were blocked. What was for human eyes a simple obscuration was, at least for plants, already an Eternal Night; the earth no longer produced any but stunted shoots with discolored leaves, like those lettuces that are cultivated in caves.

The grass in the meadows was a creamy yellow color, which seemed red in the light of the eclipse, and the livestock refused to eat it. The fruit trees did not come into flower; the ears of cereals were empty. The peasants, thus far the most obtuse of people in comprehending the full extent of the terrestrial catastrophe, despaired on seeing the bosom of the Earth, which had faithfully nourished humankind for countless generations, dry up.

No famine in history had ever been advertised by such complete and inexorable signs. It was, in an absolutely literal sense, a year without harvests.

---

that Varlet concludes (wrongly) that the effect of expelling vast quantities dust and smoke into the atmosphere would be to produce a mild winter, by virtue of retaining more solar heat.

IX. The Triumph of Eternal Night

It was on July 12 that I escaped the destruction of Amiens by the Eternal-Nightists. For only the second time in our marriage, I was separated from Raymonde; a slightly sprained ankle had kept her in Saint-Valery while I undertook my tour of aerial guard-duty above Amiens.

The tedious routine got on my nerves, and must have caused the painter Nibot to regret, more than once, the offer he had made to accompany me. The Eternal-Nightists seemed to me to be prowling in greater than usual numbers around their fumigenic fires; suspicious airships were moving on the horizon. When I landed, at dusk, I was oppressed by dark presentiments and I almost refused the invitation extended to me on behalf of Madame Blagatzky in favor of an immediate return to Saint-Valery—but "rationality" got the upper hand; I suppressed my feelings and went to the celebrated Theosophist's house, the former Hôtel Belfort, facing the new Musée de la Gare, to witness "experiments in levitation by the medium Zébia Baradino." [25]

There were about 20 of us assembled in the large drawing-room, and the lights had just been put out, when the warning sirens sounded lugubriously outside, immediately followed by a fusillade and the detonations of bombs and shells. In the drawing-room itself there was an outburst of laughter and the characteristic *ffrrr...ffrrr...* sound of a blaster wielded by the false medium, followed by a blinding shock, the thought of my beloved—and then darkness.

Amid confused voices, my body was manhandled and palpated brutally; there was a sharp pain over my left ear, and I distinctly heard these words: "Don't bother—leave him, he's a goner. They're all done for here—set the hovel on fire and we'll look further afield!"

Consciousness returned, and strength, despite the heaviness of my concussed skull. The footsteps faded in the distance; I opened my eyes and saw that I was surrounded by corpses—the guests at the Blagatzky soirée! Flames were growing at the bottom of the curtains...escape?

Inside the house, the crackling of the fire; outside, the clamor of the horde that was master of the city, pillaging, killing...and Raymonde, my poor beloved!—must not Saint-Valery be suffering a similar fate?

I got to my feet and staggered across the drawing-room. Smoke was swirling in the stairwell. I went down to the ground floor. Howling mobs were filing through the square on the other side of the door. The smoke was getting thicker; flames gushed out of an antechamber. I went forward, feeling my way,

---

[25] Like several of Varlet's casually-dropped names, these are minimally adapted from those of real individuals: Madame Blavatsky, the founder of Theosophy, and the famous medium Eusapia Palladino.

opened one door, then another…a descending stairway…then a vaulted cellar, spacious, vaguely illuminated through a ventilation shaft at the far side. I reached it, climbing up on a block of wood supporting a cask…

And the spectacle that I beheld made me forget the mortal danger of my situation, imprisoned in that cellar between the fire above my head and the cannibals filling the square.

Cannibals? Yes! A few meters away, a crowd was swarming around a lighted brazier in the roadway. The shadows of the cellar hid me from them, but I could see them—all too clearly! A man in a red apron leaned over to plunge a knife into the throat of an unfortunate captive laid at his feet, bound and blindfolded. There was a gurgling death-rattle; the jet of blood was received in a beer-tankard by a bare-breasted red-haired woman, who drank first, as the volume of the shouting redoubled:

"Me, me!"

"The Martian's blood!"

"Again! Another! Let's all drink!"

"We'll live!"

"Glory to the Eternal Night!"

And the tumultuous crush hid the disgusting scene from me, while horror caused me to release the bars of the grille and slump back on the cask.

The successive consumption of burning floorboards unsettled the vault of my cellar and smoke began to seep in. Even so, the masonry held firm and the fire did not last long. All night long I remained there, half-asphyxiated, with my face plastered to the grille, without daring to draw back the simple bolt that retained it, making no attempt to escape. The dismal light of the buildings set on fire by the victors left me in no doubt that such an attempt had no chance of success.

Every time that a gap appeared in the tempestuous mass of the nearest mobs, I was a furtive witness to some new scene of the abominable bacchanalia celebrated by the triumphant Horde. Four ritual braziers were ablaze in the Place de la Gare. I saw the corpses of prisoners, my unfortunate fellow citizens, sputtering upon them, having first had their throats cut and their blood drained, a hideous beverage. I saw the precious paintings, engravings and manuscripts from the nearby museum go up in flames, while convulsive debaucheries were perpetrated everywhere and the shrill sounds of harmoniums and accordions cut through the incomprehensible hymns bawled with all their might by the dancing and quivering crowd.

And incessantly, at every new horror glimpsed or overheard, there was the heart-rending obsession of thinking that my beloved might perhaps be meeting the same fate…

Dawn broke, the reddened light of the new Sun made the flames seem less bright, and the foul features of the Eternal-Nightists, in their verminous rags, with amulets suspended around their necks, seem even more repulsive. The lassitude of the orgy wearied them little by little, and before mid-day they were all asleep in heaps, like animals. Several had their backs to my ventilation shaft, blocking my view, giving off such a stink of sweat and old leather that I had to retire to the depths of the cellar, from which the smoke was, fortunately, beginning to clear.

My frightful captivity lasted all through that night and the following day. I would not have been able to bear a mental agony so prolonged had not its very excess, perhaps combined with the confined atmosphere, put me into a comatose torpor that deprived me of consciousness. When I came to again, the opening of the ventilation shaft was clear; in the square, an indescribable scene of ruin and carnage, there was no longer a soul to be seen; the Horde had gone on its way.

Hoisting myself up on the cask, I emerged into the open air and breathed in the odor of burned and roasted flesh avidly, as if it were a salutary breeze. In the distance, towards the center of what had been the city—smoking ruins and charred walls—suspicious sounds revealed the presence of looters. Although I had not so much as a club with which to defend myself, I did not waste time searching for a weapon. As the day died, oppressed by the anxieties that were torturing me, I went along the boulevards, which instinct selected for me as the safest course, and the one least obstructed by the debris of burned-out buildings.

Like a man in a trance, I headed towards the violet light of the setting Sun. What did Amiens, the last refuge of the Arts, matter to me? As I stepped over corpses, avoided the fall of burning beams, and went around the heaps of rubble strewn across my route, I had only one thought in my mind: to find my beloved! For I did not want...for my entire being refused to believe...that she too....

Several times I saw marauders hide as I approach; at the corner of the Rue Beauvais another took a step towards me, but refrained from attacking me—and I arrived without hindrance at the Gare Saint-Roch, where I set out along the railway line. There would be less risk of losing my way in the darkness, and I hoped that I would run less risk of dangerous encounters on the way.

I learned very quickly to step on the sleepers without touching the ballast. My pace became steady, and I went forward quasi-automatically, my eyes fixed on the rails, like a cockerel which sets its beak on a chalk line.

I had not eaten anything for 24 hours except a single Nutriment pill that I found in my waistcoat pocket; I had no more left because the wretches who had thought me dead had rifled my pockets and stolen my pill-box, along with my watch and everything else, with the exception of a notebook. Hunger tormented me, and I had a frightful taste on ink in my mouth, but I did not want to stop at some well and search for food. Besides, my empty stomach was not without its advantages; it caused a slight fever to run through my veins, and my anguish was sometimes eclipsed by the scenes unfolding in my imagination.

What if the colony at Saint-Valery, menaced by the Horde, had embarked on the aircraft at Le Crotoy? What if Leduc, seeing Amiens destroyed, had given up the idea of landing there and profited from the opportunity to emigrate with the survivors—saving my beloved first!—and transport them to the inviolable summit of Mont Blanc? I would find Saint-Valery in ruins, Le Crotoy evacuated; I would have to go after them on foot, and alone!

And I imagined the vicissitudes of my journey to come; I heard its story, as if someone were telling it to me: a narrative voice speaking in the intimacy of my cranium as if commenting on a cinematographic film. In truth, *I* was no longer there! I was witness to *my* imaginary adventures; I listened, and was amused by my cruel uncertainties, for there was no mention of Raymonde.

A hopeless enterprise! 700 or 800 kilometers to cover, alone, across a country more dangerous than the jungles of Borneo: France surrendered to the Hordes; France returned to Paleolithic barbarism. The necessity of avoiding the approach of my "peers" as if they were wild beasts. I saw, as if taking dictation, silhouetted against my memories of being an aviator, cities ravaged and deserted, cities destroyed, where solitary looters fought against dogs, cats and pigs nourished on corpses, which had become redoubtable in consequence. I made a long detour to the south of the Parisian conurbation, the lair of bandits who fell upon the cities sacked by the Eternal-Nightists. I traveled by night, fearful of the jet of some helicopter-pirate's blaster, hiding in the bushes by day to sleep...

And the chapters of the novel extended endlessly while I followed the rails in the ruddy darkness, striding somnambulistically over each successive sleeper, putting one foot in front of another, from one sleeper to the next.

....I tack between the Hordes, revealed by their stink, fearful of being discovered, alone, always alone, surrounded by their execrable fires and the pillars of purple smoke sustaining the dome of Eternal Night. By chance, I discover a blaster abandoned on a battlefield—without ammunition, alas! The weapon is no more use to me than a hazel twig. No matter: I put it under my arm; one never knows...

Hold on! The Wandering Jew! The first human encounter in the hallucinatory world of my tireless nocturnal marches. The Wandering Jew accosts me, but I recognize him despite his long beard and dirty overcoat with grotesquely-bulging pockets: oh yes, it's Isaac Schlemihl, now a tramp, damn it! And who, instead the legendary five *sous*, takes a large piece of radium from his pocket. He makes me a gift of it—to me, "his pretty rara"—because I'm an old acquaintance, and he winks at me, and explains with a sly expression that he "does business" with the Hordes, who have run out. For a gram of it, "Their Excellencies the Chiefs will give...ah! ah! ah! They sometimes have very pretty daughters, those Gentlemen of the Hordes!"

...The Wandering Jew has left me. Thanks to my weapon, I introduce myself into a Horde, more savage and degenerate than all the rest. They have lances and javelins with flint tips, and my blaster soon wins me a prestige equal to that of their leader. At close range, I see their customs, their superstitions, their amulets, which reduce the to the level of Papuans; they do not even know any longer how to divide time, save into "day" and "night," and they are beginning to tattoo themselves in red and blue with the *ripolin* [26] they have discovered. But they are docile to my advice, and I dream of regenerating and re-civilizing them, and building a new society with them. The leader's wife, veiled like a muslim, is especially taken with me. She pursues me with dangerous assiduity...

The wandering Horde eventually arrives on the shore of the Mediterranean. One night—one radiant night, starry as of old—the leader's wife unveils herself to me alone, on a terrace of rock. I have foreseen this moment; I have been waiting for it: She has Raymonde's features...oh no! She *is* Raymonde, abducted by the Horde and forced to become...O horror!

And I cut the reel of film, to find myself moving once again along the rails, distinct in the red-tinted darkness. The Moon, in its last quarter, had risen. A dog was barking in the distance...

An immeasurable hatred swelled up within me, against the Hordes: a hatred as ferocious as their cannibal rages. I bitterly regretted that, in Amiens, we had rejected the proposals of Leduc, who wanted to exterminate them. I plunged with all my heart into the desire for massacre; I invoked the images of the Eternal-Nightists that I had observed, in order to kill them in a thousand various ways, with atrocious refinements of torture, one by one or in hundreds, or thousands, and to line up their bloody corpses side by side, kilometer after kilometer, their heads and feet crushed with iron bars.

I saw them, those iron rails and those bloody cadavers; I trampled them underfoot, one after another...

No! The railway sleepers, visible at this hour in the gathering daylight...

My murderous delirium frightened me, and I was also fearful of my solitude, a panicky and puerile fear; and I was afraid of the light—that sinister purple light, to which we had grown increasingly accustomed, in the city, but which appeared to me now, for the first time, in its monstrous character...alone on that abandoned railway, alone in a world surrendered to bestialized Hordes, alone in that ravaged landscape, invaded by the vegetation of the Eternal Night, that vegetation which I knew to be white but saw red, that stunted and deformed flora disturbing my botanical consciousness, hideously appropriate to the new planet on which I was wandering alone, in quest of my lost beloved, beneath the red Eternal Night!

I sensed that it was necessary for me to eat and rest, if I did not want to lose my reason entirely. After searching for a while I discovered an old field of sugar-beets. I dug one up, scarcely larger than my thumb, and chewed it slowly; it revived me somewhat, in spite of the rebellion of my stomach, accustomed to the Nutriment.

---

[26] Ripolin was a 19th century brand of paint, which became sufficiently famous for its name to be preserved as a trivial noun.

Then I lay down beneath the disturbing red-and-black foliage of a little wood of fir-trees, and drifted off into an incomplete slumber, as if in the grip of a long nightmare, with the illusion of marching and marching forever, without ever arriving...

When I awoke, bathed my feet at the edge of a marshy pool and got under way again, the nightmare continued. I congratulated myself, in the midst of my distress, on having chosen that railway, so little frequented, instead of the road. Only twice was I obliged to hide to avoid encountering solitary pedestrians. On the road, I would inevitably have been taken by surprise by one or other of the suspect gangs whose footsteps and loud voices I had heard, for it would have been impossible for me to run for three strides.

I dragged myself onwards. To avoid a detour of a few 100 meters, and even though the twilight was still clear, I took the risk of going through the station at Abbeville. It was deserted, fortunately, as were the buildings into which I glanced as I passed by, and where I saw two naked corpses. I was so exhausted that it took me all night—seven hours, at that season—to cover the last ten kilometers: an interminable Calvary! Without the helicopter, I firmly believe that I would not have reached Le Crotoy.

Yes, Le Crotoy: for the truth that I suspected, which seemed to me indubitable, was confirmed a little further on than Port-le-Grand station, in the first faint light of dawn. In the distance, beyond the bare, flat fields, were the light of fires and columns of purple smoke. The Eternal-Nightists were celebrating their execrable triumph in the ruins of Saint-Valery! On the other side of the bay, however, high in the air, two helicopters were mounting guard over the Air Force camp. My beloved *had* to be there. With all my failing strength, I clung to that hope: the "Herons of the Somme"—Leduc's squadron—had had the time to save the villagers—or, at least, my Raymonde!

What an anguish devoured me, though, despite that *certainty*!

The daylight broadened. I approached Noyelles—how wretchedly slowly! Twice already a white helicopter had passed overhead without seeing me. I was in despair. I wanted to lie down on the side of the railway and wait for death.

Finally—finally!—my shirt, which I had taken off to wave, by way of a signal, attracted the attention of a third pilot. Ecstatically, I saw the helicopter pause, hover and descend towards me...and it was the painter Nibot who opened the cockpit door and helped me up into the rear seat, saying: "Well, Rudeaux, you have all the luck! Everyone thought you'd died with the others at Blagatzky's! Only your wife insisted on waiting for you. Even so, the exodus to Mont Blanc is decided. A few hours more, my poor friend..."

Faint with emotion, I went into the hangar where the escapees from Saint-Valery were still asleep on improvised couchettes. The red daylight came in from the vast bay, along with the morning breeze. *She* was lying there, her head on an outstretched arm...

She sensed my presence. She opened her lovely eyes, swollen with tears, and sat up to welcome me as I feel to my knees beside her, breathless.

"Oh, my love!" she murmured, hugging me. "I knew that you'd come back!"

X. The Bunkers of Mont Blanc

The Mont Blanc colony, where we were resident until the end, comprised two quite distinct parts linked by the funicular railway that had been established, in civilized times, for the benefit of tourists unused to tiring climbs. At Chamonix, the principal aerodrome, the plant manufacting of the Nutriment, the workshops for construction and repair, and the turbines furnishing electrical energy for heating, lighting and so on, accommodated a population of 300 mechanics and artisans, whose unusual intelligence had preserved them from the "animalizing" contagion and who had offered their services spontaneously to the scientific "colonists" from the very beginning. Higher up, at 4800 meters, the buildings of the observatory were occupied by about 30 astronomers and an equal number of university men, whom Leduc had assembled as a complement of the last representatives of civilization. As for us, we were lodged in the vast bunkers hollowed out in the rock, beneath the thick carapace of the eternal snows, whose depths contained stories of every sort—enough for us to sustain a two-year siege.

The cannon, machine-guns and other weapons in that arsenal of yesteryear—which had escaped the destruction ordered by the Directorate—set up in batteries at strategic points, would permit us to resist the combined barbarian hordes of Europe, in the highly improbable event of their venturing to such an altitude, above the domain of Eternal Night that they held sacrosanct.

An impregnable fortress of civilization, our summit stood up amid the blue sky. Even Chamonix, at 1034 meters, was free of the reddish veil that we perceived, far below, as a sinister sea of purple clouds, beneath with his hideous humankind of the hordes pursued its regression towards the ancestral Beast. Around us, the grandiose landscape of mountains draped in inviolable snows extended infinitely, and we spent hours, warmly wrapped in furs, walking along the terrace of the observatory. Never tiring of blue sky and sunlight, after our confinement beneath the bloody shroud, whose retrospective horror made us exclaim indignantly against the stupidity of having endured it for so long, we caressed the vault of the firmament, restored to the original purity of the beautiful profound indigo that dresses the sky at high altitudes, with ecstatic gazes. Gratefully, we followed the course of the regal star that bathed us with its dazzling radiation. We savored the play of the light on the grandiose panorama of the Alps, which offered its snow-capped peaks, angular glaciers, ravines and torrents to our binoculars—and sometimes the minuscule silhouette of a chamois, immobile beneath the immense enchantment of the setting Sun.

In the meantime, the night offered us the inexhaustible marvels of its constellations and its planets, which the persistent covering of red clouds had hidden from us for six months. We had never seen them in an atmosphere so clear, by means of instruments so perfect, with s competent a guide—for the Director of the Observatory himself, the amiable Abbé Romeux, observing our astronomical zeal, was kind enough to authorize us to use the large equatorial, and we gradually became used to spending entire evenings beneath the cupola.

These sublime contemplations gave Raymonde and me the impression of floating above life, and the year of our sojourn at Mont Blanc was a period of elevation—I might even say spiritual serenity—in which our love, renewed by the anguish of that separation which had proved not to be final, burned more ardently and more purely than ever.

We did not go so far, however, as to abstract ourselves from the communal life that made our station into a family of sorts. The greater number of Mont Blanc's guests gathered every evening in the largest of the bunkers, transformed into a library-cum-drawing-room. The scientists and the artists had both learned to forget the slight mutual distrust that had once separated them, and they no longer considered one another as anything but equal representatives of Civilization. In the peaceful atmosphere of that electrically lighted and heated hall, the noise of general or particular conversations was reminiscent of that of a club of olden times.

In addition to the subject of the material situation of the world—Leduc, an indefatigable explorer, brought us daily accounts of what he saw beneath the dome of the purple Night—there was no lack of news for our commentators. Materially isolated, the TSF station, well equipped this time, put us in communication with other final representatives of civilization, who were scattered around the circumference of the globe in seven other colonies.

Two of these were associated with the sister observatories of Mont Blanc, lodged on the summits of Gaurisankar and Mount Wilson. The former, which remained purely astronomical, was in the town of Simla, the former summer residence of English officials in India. It brought together on the slopes of the Himalayas the largest number of men resolved to defend the conquests of intelligence again the empire of Darkness. Mount Wilson was more closely analogous to Mont Blanc in the composition of its personnel, though perhaps more exclusively scientific. It was the only center of civilization that remained in the entire extent of the two Americas, at least so far as we knew—for it was possible that a colony worthy of the name, although deprived of TSF, had gathered together the survivors of a superior humankind in South America.

This hypothetical colony had, however, escaped the researches of the Japanese aviators of the Nagasaki station, whose long-range explorations made our friend Sylvain pale with envy. On the other hand, they had discovered an unexpected terrestrial paradise flourishing in Tahiti, Samoa and several Pacific atolls, whose natives, liberated from the vile domination of the Whites (who had been killing one another since the beginning of the crisis) had recovered their natural folkways and their happy and innocent barbarity.

At the southern tip of Africa, Cape Town had passed into the hands of Boers, who were taking revenge for the Transvaal and valiantly defending an agricultural colony a few dozen kilometers square against the incursions of the Zulus—but towards mid-January, they ceased sending us their news.

Cairo held out until the end: an island of Western civilization grafted on to Arab fatalism, which astonished us by its vitality.

Finally, much closer to us, Edinburgh, where the arrogant dons of Oxford had been very happy to find a refuge—under the British flag, it is true—was the least interesting; their messages only concerned theological disputes with no connection to actual circumstances.

Thus, so to speak, the selection had been made. The human species had divided into two distinct sub-species: on the one hand, the regressive elements, the Hordes delivered to atavistic instincts and dying in millions every day; on the other, the 12,000 or 15,000 civilized individuals of the "stations." But what did our small numbers matter? It was the sacred fire of intelligence of which we were the guardians, and the slightest preservable spark might suffice to reanimate the flame that we had seen burning so brightly when Civilization was incarnate in three billion representatives. Had not all the innumerable oaks of the future forest first been contained in a single acorn? It is sufficient that a seed finds fertile ground; it was sufficient for us that the future would open up again.

And it seemed that it did open up again.

First of all, the Eternal Night dissipated, in the course of the winter in which I devoted my leisure time to drafting the greater part of these memoirs.

It seemed certain that the combined efforts of the Eternal-Nightists would have been powerless to create the funereal shroud if the volcanoes opened or reanimated by the penetrative shells had not lent them their effective support. Indeed, the great plutonian manifestations, which were attenuated towards the end of spring, died down almost completely in the course of the summer—and the veil of purple clouds dissipated in the winter. It is true that the ranks of the Hordes were thinned out, mown down by the redoubled force of the epidemics that found these degenerate and verminous creatures an admirably fertile terrain. As they ran short of combustible material, the harvest of smoke failed, and their rites were reduced, among the survivors, to mere symbolic gestures.

All that winter, from November to March, snowstorms kept us confined to the warm bunkers—it is possible that, without that prolonged confinement, I would not have written these pages—and deluges of rain, at lower altitudes, succeeded in sweeping he atmosphere clean. The distant landscapes reappeared, illuminated by the Sun to the depths of the valleys, and the earth, liberated from its sterilizing shroud, covered itself once again with green vegetation. There was no shortage of habitually-cultivated regions to recover their fecundity. Leduc was already talking about reconquering agricultural land, and we discussed the opportunity thus presented for the war of extermination that he recommended: a general massacre of the remaining hordes, which some of us simply wanted to herd into "reservations" analogous to those in which the Americans had accommodated their Redskins. We imagined the city of the future hopefully.

Interplanetary communications had been re-established, after many attempts, at the beginning of March, and the cosmograms from Jupiter inspired us with a new confidence in the future. "Earth shall live," our wise protectors affirmed; we need no longer fear attack from Mars. No torpedo, no penetrative shell would come to ravage our globe. The punishment of the criminal planet would be an accomplished fact within a few months, at the outset of the new opposition. Since making its solemn promise to their brothers in space, the Jovians had devoted all the resources of their immense planet, all the genius of their intellectuals and al the efforts of their population—which was numbered in hundreds of billions—aided by a gigantic technology, to preparing the means of carrying out the sentence handed down by the high court of the Solar System. The general mobilization of Jovian society against Mars was an accomplished fact, and when the time came…

The masters of Jupiter did not, in fact, reveal the exact means to be employed—in order, they said, to avoid the abuses that might be made of them by the humankind of our world, which was certainly worthy of their pity, but was still so far from their perfection and too little advanced to share in the redoubtable secret of "Solar Accumulators." Our large equatorial at Mont Blanc, however, permitted us to distinguish modifications of the surface of the planet of wisdom that revealed prodigious building-works, which the guilty Martians, thanks to their televisors, had to be following tremulously. The bands of cloud that we had always seen, dense and continuous, reigning over almost all of the Jovian disk, now appeared to have retreated to the higher latitudes, and to be divided along the equator by a black zone, in which our most advanced optical instruments clearly discerned a large number of "cells" designed to capture solar radiation in the same way that a soot-blacked box absorbs them—with the difference that the Jovian "accumulators" had been storing billions and trillions of calories of radiant energy for months, which the would when the time came, re-emit them all at once, for the tragic execution…

Nevertheless, no one quite understood the role played by a slender line of light, formed from the combination multiple points extended over the entire circumference of Jupiter, in the exact center of the black zone of Solar Accumulators traced around the equator. Even Abbé Romeux was perplexed and shook his head with a pitying smile when Raymonde hazarded the hypothesis that it might be a railway line extending all the way around the planet's girth.

As the date fixed by the high court for the accomplishment of their irrevocable sentence and the conclusive liberation of Earth drew nearer, we became increasingly impatient to see the denouement of he drama of which we were passive audience, and which was taking place millions of kilometers away, as inaccessible to our intervention as ancient Fate.

"The planet Mars, which has sinned by fire against sidereal Fraternity will be punished by the fire of immanent Justice, of which Jupiter has instituted itself as the champion. This fire, borrowed from the radiance of Our Father the Sun, will be unleashed upon the aforesaid planet Mars on June 22, by the terrestrial calendar, and the Execution will commence at midnight, Mont Blanc time."

Such was the wording of the avenging cosmogram that we discussed every evening, as the opposition approached, while tracking the two planets as they drew inexorably closer to one another, following the inevitable laws of universal gravitation. By a disturbing coincidence, however, the Earth was also moving forward in its orbit, in such a manner that the criminal planet would not only come into opposition with its judge and executioner but with its victim, the Earth—so that, on June 22, the three planets would be very nearly in a straight line extended from the Sun, and that, at the moment when the Jovian Accumulators could finally take effective action against the vile Martians, thee latter would similarly arrived at their minimum distance from the Earth.

To what desperate gesture might the certainty of punishment impel them?

Part Three: The Martian Paradise

I. Jupiter's Thunderbolt

Wrapped in furs, all the inhabitants of the upper station and those from Chamonix, brought by a special train, were walking around the terrace of the observatory, waiting for the fateful moment when we would witness the formidable and unprecedented spectacle of an interplanetary punishment, as the mysterious dispositions of whose true nature and effect we were still ignorant were activated. The ice-cold and clear night shone overhead and all around us, deploying the familiar splendors of the constellations. To the south, close to Antares in Scorpio, dazzling Jupiter and ruddy Mars were separated by a distance equal to twice the diameter of the full Moon, which was shining with a steady and placid light.

The warm and sonorous voice of Abbé Romeux drew us from our anxious reveries: "Five minutes gentlemen!"

Everyone took up his observation post.

All the portable instruments at Mont Blanc had been distributed among the notable members to the colony. In addition, the observatory's optician had constructed several hundred rudimentary telescopes by inserting photographic lenses into lead tubes, and everyone had been provided with one. Abbé Romeux's benevolence towards Raymonde and me had, however, extended to making us part of the privileged circle using the eight rotatory ocular prisms connected to the large 220 telescope.

My eye was glued to the cold copper circle. The Jovian globe suddenly appeared, against a round velvet-black background speckled with tiny stars, giving me that indefinable, and yet quite clear, impression which invariably "grabs" the experienced observer as well as the simple amateur: the impression of astronomical Space.

That globe, isolated from all the rest, with the apparent size of a little pumpkin, was visibly floating in the void, escorted at an oblique angle by its four large satellites, like blanched cherries. Visibly—one might almost say palpably—the system was an enormous distance away, in a remote abyss, which further increased the imperceptible trepidation of the image caused by the electric motor responsible for keeping he telescope pointed at the celestial sphere in an invariable direction, from which the rotation of the Earth would otherwise displace it in a matter of seconds.

Before that sojourn at Mont Blanc, photographs, maps, descriptions and figures concerning Jupiter, drawn from books, had spoken only to my intelligence, but here I had incorporated those abstract notions into my sensibility. When I put my eye to the eyepiece, my imagination was immediately engaged, perceiving the reality of distances and volumes directly.

That globe I was seeing, less luminous than our Moon, was certainly a world. Fawn-colored in general, it was cut in two by the black zone, which was itself divined by the mysterious shining line traced along the equator. It was the giant of the Solar System, 11 times greater in diameter than the Earth, whose surface, 120 times larger, sheltered that population of noble and disinterested beings who had just spent two terrestrial years in the realization of the grandiose project inspired in their wise leaders by the vile conduct of the Martians.

We felt the presence of those 300 billion Jovians, scattered beneath the clouds they had carefully withdrawn to the superior latitudes, or grouped in the equatorial zone, around the apparatus receiving the avenging energy, every workman at his post, the fingers of every engineer upon his controls, his eyes on the gauges, all religiously awaiting the signal they would be sent in a few minutes time by the great leader of Jovian society. The latter was based on Ganymede, the third largest satellite, so modest in its dimensions by comparison with its planet but more voluminous nevertheless than Mercury and not much inferior to Mars.

On Ganymede, the great leader was sitting in the midst of his Constituency of astronomers and sages, an impassive tribunal of judges, poised to erase a planet from the map of the Heavens, because its inhabitants had misused the gift of intelligence and contravened the law of sidereal Love and Fraternity!

At that level of magnification, the telescope's field of view could not contain Jupiter and Mars at the same time, and the condemned planet was still hidden from us, but we would soon steer our instrument towards it. Beneath the cupola where the privileged spectators waited, eyes glued to the ocular lenses, the twelve strokes of midnight fell one by one into a profound silence.

Then, on the brilliant thread of the Jovian equator, a luminous point was born, intensified, became as dazzling as a solar fleck, and extruded a sort of white-hot needle sideways from the vast globe, which moved slowly along.[27] It

---

[27] Had Varlet showed this passage to the real Abbé Moreux rather than delegating its explanation to the fictitious Abbé Romeux, the astronomer would have been able to explain to him why this image is doubly ridiculous. It reproduces what was to become a classic erroneous cliché of science fiction in assuming that a radiation beam would be visible in a vacuum from an angle. Searchlight beams show up in the atmosphere when seen side-on because of light deflected by air molecules; in space such beams could not be seen at an angle. Moreux would also have pointed out that observers on Earth could not see the weapon fire until photons conveying that information reached Earth, which would have to travel at the same pace as the beam itself; the arrival of that information on Earth would be followed almost immediately by evidence of the impact, so ob-

attained the side turned towards Mars, extended therefrom, and pursued its development into the night-black darkness...

Through the open door, as well as the oblong bay in the cupola itself, we heard cries of surprise exclamations of admiration, and even jokes from every part of the terrace—but it was for the benefit of the privileged few at the large telescope that Abbé Romeux gave his commentary on the spectacle.

"That luminous thread you see developing with such apparent timidity is, in fact, propagating towards Mars at the speed of light: 300,000 kilometers per second! But think of the distance separating the two planets, diminished for us by their immense remoteness and perspective, just as electric express-trains traveling at 200 kph appear to us, when seen on the horizon, to be toiling like snails—but don't forget that the distance between Jupiter and Mars is actually more than three times that between Earth and the Sun. Three and a half times 150,000,000 kilometers is 525,000,000! I will, therefore, take 30 minutes for the tip of that luminous-calorific jet to reach the surface of Mars. A marvelous and unprecedented projection, to be sure, since it is due to the genius of the creatures inhabiting Jupiter, but comets, those enigmatic entities dispatched from the hands of God, have achieved almost as much. The tail of the comet of 1811 measured 175,000,000 kilometers; that of 1843 extended 300,000,000 kilometers; that of..."

The worthy Abbé interrupted himself, though, and we heard him strike himself resoundingly on the head. "Madame Rudeaux!" he cried. "I offer you an honorable apology! You were right: that slender shining thread really is the track of a giant railway girdling the Jovian equator, Yes, it all becomes clear to me now...we do not know the exact nature of this dart of light and heat which is extending into space before our eyes, this fantastic pencil of fulminant energy which will strike the Martians, but I can see therein an application of the principle employed by Archimedes when he set fire to the triremes of Marcellus, which were besieging Syracuse, with the aid of ardent mirrors. Jupiter is using an analogous method to launch the solar energy stored in its Accumulators. But if this Apparatus X, the projector that we have just seen unmasked, were stationary on the planet's soil, it would be drawn away by the planet's rotation and would not be able to remain permanently aimed at Mars. But look, its aim remains fixed, while Jupiter had already been turning sensibly upon its axis for twenty minutes. There's no doubt about it: Apparatus X, the fulminant projector, is mounted on a mobile carriage which is moving along the Jovian equator on those shining rails in the opposite direction to the planet's rotation, and with an exactly equal velocity."

---

servers on Earth would not be able to watch the beam's "wave-front" making the kind of slow progress here described.

A murmur of admiration went up, addressed to the clarity of Abbé Romeux's explanation as well as to the genius of the Jovian astronomers for that masterpiece of grandiose simplicity: the egg of Columbus!

But everyone soon feel silent, for the celestial spectacle required all our attention.

The formidable dart of vibratory energy had continued its elongation. It had gone past all four of the Jovian satellites, and we imagined with awe the sight that the monstrous beam of their Justice must have presented to the astronomers of Ganymede as it extended over their heads, a few 1000 kilometers distant, towards the criminal planet. The latter had finally been accommodated in the field of our telescope, Jupiter having been eliminated therefrom, and it appeared, as large as a plum, facing the rigidly-extended thread of fire, whose dart was coming closer and closer, as if to perforate it.

We recognized the geography of that familiar globe, drawn with the clarity of a miniature Persian rug: the white caps of polar snow, one—the southern—much larger than he other; the narrow and elongated seas, whose green color varied in darkness according t their depth; the rounded black stain of the Solis Lacus; and the fawn-colored continents, tinted to a greater or lesser extent with orange, striated with a network of canals that was scarcely visible, due to the dryness of the season. We thought about the Martians, who could see the inexorable Sword extending towards them.

I imagined those millions of beings, powerfully intelligent but devoid of any moral scruple, cowardly and perfidious, akin to fallen angels, awaiting, with despair in their hearts, the unknown and terrible Visitation that would be their End-of-the-World. How they must be repenting, at this moment, their inexpiable crime! Or not, in fact! Those creatures were incapable of repentance; it must be the rage of their powerlessness that was torturing them, the crazed exasperation of perishing without vengeance, the regret of having to submit to that pitiless talion for nothing…solely for the pleasure of having broken the resistance of Earth; the regret of having delayed too long, of having used the last days of the previous opposition to send those vain penetrative shells to terrify a demoralized humankind, which was at their mercy, instead of profiting from the panic created by the torpedoes by gathering the fruits of their first bombardment and expediting their departure from their own world, crammed into interplanetary vehicles, the Martian colony that would have ensured the future of their race on the new planet!

Now, they did not even have the consolation of telling themselves that other sons of Mars had landed on the Earth and would sooner or later establish their supremacy there. All the sons of Mars, without exception, were about to the slain by the Sword of judicial extermination!

Jupiter's Thunderbolt had finally completed its prodigious development; it reached the globe of Mars—but without producing the sudden and catastrophic effect that our imaginations had calculated, more or less complacently. We could not retain a murmur of anxiety, while the crowd on the terrace, less discreet, complained loudly of its disappointment, as if at a firework that had just fizzled out.

This time, the Abbé used his loudhailer to reassure us. For the guests in the cupola, his voice resonated bizarrely, doubled up, as one might say: natural first, then amplified by the apparatus and echoing from a distance in the icy nocturnal air:

"The point of impact of the fulminant Dart is hidden from us, my friends. Remember that Jupiter is situated well beyond Mars, almost behind it relative to us, and the rigid jet of its projector cannot bend so as to strike the face turned to us simply to be agreeable to us and give us a better view! Have a little patience. If I am not mistaken, the conflagration that must presently be devouring the continent known as Elysium, which may be its capital, will soon be revealed to us by the distant effects that must result from it in the Martian atmosphere, while we wait for the rotation of the planet to place its devastated face before our eyes—which we shall see tomorrow night, for in an hour, as you know it will have disappeared beyond our horizon."

Soon, in fact, a thin fringe of white cloud edged the disk of Mars, coming from the opposite face. It was no more, in appearance, than slowly-extending light cloud, but, in reality, it was the sign of the frightful conflagration caused by the Thunderbolt!

In a flash of intuition, I imagined the Martian crowds assembled in the streets and the squares of the capital of Elysium, seeing the dazzling tip of the Jovian Projector growing at their zenith, into which their gazes were plunging, so to speak, like that of a condemned man into the muzzle of the musket that will shoot him. Here, though, the fatal shot had taken 30 minutes to reach them, and their dazzled pupils must be opening wider and wider upon the final nullity—an immeasurable, monstrous Sun invading their sky with phantasmagoric acceleration; a cataclysmic deluge of 1000 infernos falling at the same time on ten square kilometers; the volatilization of a city and its population in the fiery hurricane of the captive solar radiation, stored and projected in an annihilating beam.

No refuge could withstand the Jovian Thunderbolt: the ceilings of caves and subterranean tunnels would melt into liquid lava under an elevation of temperature which the Abbé Romeux's spectroscope measured at 3000 degrees Centigrade. The seas themselves could not have provided an adequate shelter, for they were reduced to whirlwinds of dense vapor, which mingled with the other products of the combustion.

And Mars, turning slowly on its hypothetical axis like a chicken on a spit, successively offered all the points of its surface to the avenging Thunderbolt—which, for eight long days, swept all the meridians one after another, charring the soil, volatilizing the seas, all the way to the two poles, where the ice-caps melted, spreading out their whiteness in liquid cataracts, as in times of flood, filling the canals, which were attained and dried up in their turn. Eight days, during which a formidable warfare between water and fire, until the definitive victory of the latter, must have been pursued beneath an increasingly dense swathe of vapor, whose eddies and momentary gaps permitted us to glimpse the progress of the devastation—the accomplishment of the great work of Jupiter's Justice.

But I'm getting ahead of myself. That first night, when the telescope only showed us the traces of the fire lit on the invisible face of Mars, reserved an event designed to disturb the joy of the conclusive deliverance that the cremation of the enemy planet signified for us.

It was 3 a.m. Mars and Jupiter, linked by the incandescent thread of the Thunderbolt, had vanished over the horizon. Dawn was about to break. On the terrace, the majority of the occasional observers, equipped with instruments that were too weak and disappointed by the insignificance of a spectacle that they had anticipated very differently—Mars bursting into flames, I suppose, like a wad of cotton wool soaked in kerosene—had left the party. Those who remained were discussing without any enthusiasm the future that the final defeat of their enemies in the sky had secured for humankind.

Beneath the cupola, around the big 220-centimeter telescope, we were just directing one final glance at the pitiless Dart digging into the heart of the red planet, our satisfied hatred and still-timid joy of deliverance mingled with a sort of pity. Raymonde had just expressed everyone's private sentiment by murmuring "Poor Martians! Were they really *all* guilty?" when a disturbance began in the crowd outside, composed of confused exclamations of indignation, anger and discouragement.

A single rough voice rose above the tumult momentarily, saying: "Filthy swine! It'll be a good thing if they fry to the very last one!"

There was a noise of hurried footsteps; the clamor drew nearer, and an electrician from the TSF appeared on the threshold, brandishing a paper breathlessly.

"Monsieur l'Abbé!" he stammered. "Monsieur l'Abbé. They've... they've fired again!"

II. The Survivors' Shell

"If the beast is dead, its venom is dead"—the proverb was contradicted by the facts. That lair of sidereal bandits, Mars, was crackling in the flames of a monstrous inferno; its last survivors were subjected to the torments of asphyxia while they awaited final extermination—and yet, the Jovian cosmogram informed us that a new projectile was on its way toward us. On the day, perhaps at the very hour, of the punishment, perhaps at the exact moment when the fulminant Battery had been unmasked on Jupiter and the destructive Fire had been launched towards them, the ungovernable Martians had "fired" one last time. And because, at the moment of opposition, the face of Mars turned towards the Earth had escaped the investigations of the Ganymedean televisors, the projectile had not been perceived by them and signaled to us until a few hours after its departure.

The broadside of cries of hatred unleashed by our fellow citizens on the terrace betrayed such a veritable demonic fury that Abbé Romeux—the uncontested but untitled head of the "political establishment" of Mont Blanc—hesitated to transmit the news to the other civilized stations of the world, which were not equipped with interplanetary TSF. All of them had already manifested their impatience to be delivered from the Martian threat once and for all; at that time, three of them—Edinburgh, Cairo and Cape Town—had just witnessed the execution of the Jovian sentence. Mount Wilson was at the telescope. Nagasaki, Simla, Gaurisankar had been informed. Should we spoil their joy, or dash their hopes, by plunging them once again into anguish and discouragement, risking demoralizing the weakest, who were at the end of their resistance?

However, the contrary thesis, supported by Leduc, quickly rallied the majority of the scientific votes and decided the Abbé: better to make the announcement before the idea of deliverance had sunk in; the disappointment would be less precipitate, and serious measures could be taken in all the centers of civilization to oppose the Martians' final shot, which would conclude with their disembarkation.

We did not have a single instant of doubt about that, and our brothers' responses all expressed the same opinion: the projectile destined to reach terrestrial soil on July 6—in seven days time, at the moment of writing!—encloses at least some of those Martian colonists for whom the torpedoes and the penetrative shells had prepared the way. The hypothesis that they might have launched another dirigible torpedo was flagrantly absurd, since there were no longer any Martian engineers to transmit the directive waves. A penetrative shell or some other merely destructive device? Equally inadmissible. The ravages caused on the Earth by the bombardments of the opposition of 1978 had let nothing for the most ferocious and cowardly of skyborne enemies to desire. The way was

157

open—they knew that—and their intention was certainly to profit from it this time. The Jovian Thunderbolt had surprised them in all-out preparation for a methodical invasion of the Earth; its operation had simply coincided with the first departure of Martian colonists. Without that opportune intervention, more projectiles would have followed, stuffed with invaders finally resolve to set foot on the coveted planet.

Yes, this time we will have to deal with the Martians in person—but that idea ought to reassure us, if our anxiety is accessible to reason. This interplanetary vehicle is unique. According to the model of its predecessors loaded with satanite or penetrative explosives, it cannot contain more than a few dozen combatants at the most, with weapons and baggage. Even supposing that they are equipped with new and powerful means of destruction, any one of our civilized groups ought at least to be able to hold them in check, which will give time for help to arrive. And such help will be near at hand, given that the helpers will already be on their way to the threatened point, which the Jovian astronomers will determine for us a day or two in advance.

Provided, therefore, that the Martians do not have the privilege of increasing their number with a rapidity that is, on Earth, reserved to inferior animals, we shall soon get to the end of their small number. The worst that can happen, in the highly improbable case that their vehicle's point of descent escapes Jovian observation and the attention of men, is that they might be able to install themselves in a deserted region—or one inhabited by the savage hordes, which comes down to the same thing—and found their colony there. We would then have two heterogeneous races resuming their development...until the moment of the fatal collision, "when the better would triumph," as Leduc put it.

Let us put that last hypothesis aside, though. In reality, we shall do everything possible to engage in battle at the earliest possible opportunity, to settle the fate of humankind once and for all. Leduc has just told us that he has put his aerial squadron on a war footing.

The present date of June 29 has seen the extinction of the Thunderbolt, the punishment of Mars being complete and all life abolished on the surface of that planet. It is also notable, from my point of view, for another reason: it is the day when I have finished writing the previous pages, begun last winter and interrupted several times, recapitulating I the form of memoirs all that I was able to see and learn in these last two years that is worthy of interest. They are finally up to date, and I propose to continue them henceforth on a daily basis, as events transpire.

July 1. The muted demoralization that I have omitted to mention until now, because of its vague and ungraspable character, and because it has not been expressed in words, is making troubling progress. Something serious is going on at Chamonix, if I read Leduc's concerned attitude correctly. He mutters to himself about the insubordination that is rife down there, especially among the aviators.

Since the spring, he avows, one might think that they have been subject to the contagion of the de-civilized atmosphere in which they undertake their exploratory expeditions. Stocks of wine, canned food and biscuits, recovered from the ruins of Lyon, and which their leader ordered to be stored in Chamonix, have been retained by them and consumed in secret orgies in which the inhabitants of the lower station participated. Since then, their appetite for meat has revived and the Jovian Nutriment is no longer sufficient for them. The announcement of an expedition in which they have been instructed to take part has been greeted by general protests, and it required all Leduc's authority to force them to consent to make the necessary preparations.

At Mont Blanc itself, a singular nervousness is increasing. The population of artists, in particular, is manifesting disturbing symptoms. Nibot and the majority of the painters have abandoned their brushes; the writers openly repeat an opinion that drew a contemptuous exclamation from me shortly after my arrival in Amiens, at a salon in the Rue des Trois-Cailloux: "Why bother, since there's no longer an audience?" The women, especially have changed; they organize dances on a daily basis, not only in the Bunkers but at Chamonix—and they are careful not to invite Raymonde and me, for they sense our disapproval of these new mores. It has even reached the scientists; the insufficiency of their laboratories and libraries, and the installation's discomforts, provoke fits of bad temper that degenerate into bitter disputes—and the Abbé Romeux has great difficulty calming these outbreaks and re-establishing an ephemeral harmony.

As for Raymonde and myself, love preserves us from the contagion; we are closer than ever, and we derive our scorn for death and the new calamities with which the future seems replete from the notion that we shall suffer them together. Nevertheless, we too feel a kind of bizarre enervation, and sudden fits of apprehension without any definite cause—a secret anguish that translates into a sharp desire to be *somewhere else*. It seems to us that we have been stuck in the cold of high altitudes for a year, and that we are reawakening from that lethargy, weary of the monotony of spending our lives shuttling between Mont Blanc and Chamonix, weary of the ever-present faces of our fellow detainees, avid to see other people, avid to rediscover new horizons, even on the devastated Earth.

It seems to us both that occult and evil influences are lurking all around us, in the atmosphere of the Bunkers. We have decided today to join Leduc's expedition, if he will allow it.

July 3. The mutiny of the aviators has reached its denouement, which almost turned to tragedy. It has, at any rate, deprived our station of effective means of cooperating in the defense of Civilization against the supreme assault that the sons of Mars will mount against it.

This morning, at 10 a.m., the 80 pilots and mechanics at Chamonix, with only a single exception, refused to obey Leduc, who was astonished to see them assembled in front of the hangars instead of separately attending to their assigned tasks. With them were about fifteen female "artists," ex-models or "blue-stockings" in traveling costumes. The leader of the band spoke for them. They had had enough, he said, of "toiling like slaves under the orders of a tyrant," of "dying of cold in the mountains," and being fed on "some rubbishy pharmaceutical product" which left their stomachs empty from dawn till dusk. The helicopters belonged to them—they had risked their hides often enough up above—and they were going to use them to find a place where they could "recover from their fatigue and take things easy," far away from the likes of Romeux and Leduc...and the Martians. Tahiti or Tuamotu would suit them, and would also suit these ladies, who were accompanying them...and the leader gave the order there and then to get under way.

Leduc attempted to stop them, but nothing could be done, either with pleas or the threat of his revolver—which only resulted in his being disarmed by the mutineers. Tied up and helpless, he had to watch his ex-subordinates and their companions embark and take off in the eighteen helicopters of out airfleet, which disappeared over the southern horizon. He wept with rage as he told us the story of this vile desertion.

"The swine have deserted me!" he repeated "Well, it can't be helped. I'll do it alone, by God! Yes, I'll fight the Martians on my own!"

He was exaggerating. He will not be alone, firstly, because he still has one loyal young mechanic—the one who prevented the mutineers from killing him and freed him from his bonds after they had gone—and, secondly, because he has Raymonde and me, who are persistent in our resolve to take part in the adventure. One of the two remaining machine is the one with which we arrived at Amiens, the one that Nibot succeeded in saving and taking to Le Crotoy on the night when I escaped the massacre and the fire. That is the one that Leduc has chosen, in view of the large capacity of its fuel tank. If the shell's point of descent is situated within a radius of 3000 kilometers, we shall be able to reach it without being obliged to stop and search some town for a fuel-depot spared by fire and looters.

Everything is ready and we have two machine-guns aboard, along with revolvers and blasters, with which we will be able to lend some small assistance to whichever civilized station we are sent to by the Jovian cosmogram we are expecting at any moment.

III. From Mont Blanc to Cairo

July 6. What a grandiose and poignant poetry emanates from the desolation and solitude extending over the country over which we are flying, at top speed, aboard the helicopter that has transported us—Raymond and me—so often before. Nothing that we saw in France, Belgium or England equaled today's spectacle.

For 18 months the ruins have been, so to speak, brand new. One felt that normal life had only just stopped in those towns where the fires were still burning or bands of looters interrupted their work to threaten us with their weapons. In the rural regions there were the Eternal-Nightists lighting the first altars of their monstrous rites, hordes or battalions on the march; there were cultivators, deaf and blind to unprecedented dangers, lifting their heads as we passed over their ancestral fields, where they were tracing the last furrow of the year-without-harvests; there were carmine vines, still-green meadows where the last domestic herds were grazing; there were fragments of intact nature, autumnal forests with yellowing leaves....

Today, there is the reign of death, and even the vegetal world, exhausted by its struggle against the red darkness, hesitated to extent the green shroud of compassionate nature over the heaped-up ruins. Although it is mid-summer, the trees along the roadsides are leafless, skeletal, as are those of the forests, the majority of which have been burned. Fields invaded by sickly brush, then a farm still standing, then a domestic animal—sometimes, at the sound of our rotor blades, a famished ox staggers to its feet and flees at a stiff gallop across the wild and fence-less countryside, scattered with vague skeletons picked over by flocks of crows and packs of dogs...or perhaps wolves.

But the most poignant thing is the absence of humans. One might think that our race had already disappeared from the Earth! Not once, since our departure from Mont Blanc, not once in ten hours of flight, have we glimpsed a single member of our species who was not reduced to a skeleton, or at least to a cadaver. The plains of Lombardy, once so fertile and so populous, are as deserted as the glaciers of the Alps! A desert!

Turin in ruins, Milan a desert, burned during the great Anarchist uprising, nothing but unrecognizable corpses in the rubble-strewn streets. Florence, where the Dome, spared by a caprice of the fire, still stands amid the ruins of palaces and museums, a desert....

Tuscany, a desert, where the emigration of an entire town seems to have been struck dead at a single blow—10,000 corpses, perhaps, filling the roadway along the banks of the dark waters of Lake Trasimeno, as in Hannibal's time! All of Italy a desert, beneath the bright rays of the Sun, from the Alps to Rome—where we set down for a few minutes, at Raymonde's request, in the ancient Forum, whose 2000-year old ruins were still standing, as were those of the Palatine and the Coliseum, in the midst of other ruins that the Torpedo had created two years before. The Martian satanite, which had broken down the stone blocks and stucco of the neighboring buildings, the banks and palazzos of the Corso and the Via Nazionale, the 360 churches of the Eternal City, including St Peter's, and the Vatican and the Quirinal, had scarcely achieved any further corrosion of the heart and bedrock of Imperial and Republican Rome. The only difference between these sets of ruins was that the more ancient preserved more traces of beauty—but the same backcloth absorbed them all: the backcloth of a past without perspective, that of conclusive death.

"All this will never be revived!" said Raymonde, remembering the desert over which we had traveled. "Humankind will never regain possession of the Earth!"

"It will require several centuries years for man to reclaim possession of his domain," I said, considering the three columns of a temple—that of Castor and Pollux, I think—surmounted by a fragment of architrave, which stood out, fawn in color, against the dazzling azure of the sky like a melancholy hope.

"Centuries?" jeered Sylvain Leduc, withdrawing the water-filled canvas bucket he had just plunged into a fountain whose edges were ornamented with the remains of sculptures. "Possibly. What does it matter? Evolution has no lack of time. Hold on, through—look over there instead of going into ecstasies over these old stones. There's someone who has already reinstalled himself in his domain!"

Indeed, at the far end of the Forum, we saw the first survivor of the indescribable disaster. It was the young mechanic whose piercing eyes had discovered him and alerted his master in a low voice. In the shade of an old portico, the unexpected individual was studying us from afar while smoking his Neapolitan pipe—and beside him, on a column, was the baroque inscription *Custode del Rovine*: custodian of the ruins! Raymonde was the first of us to burst into nervous laughter.

But Leduc had only consented to top in order to find a little fresh water. He cut the interlude short, and we embarked again....

While I am scribbling these notes, we are flying over a mountainous landscape—deserted, of course—in which my memory of classical studies situates the lands of the first peoples conquered by Rome: the Aequians, Sabines, Volsci, Hernici—but I scarcely dare mention their names to Raymonde, installed beside me in one of the rear seats. Leduc, who is at the controls with his faithful lad, greets any poetical, or even slightly elevated, reflection with mocking laughter or vulgar jokes. He has also acquired the habit of swearing roundly at every opportunity, and his company is becoming less and less agreeable. He refuses to make a slight detour, so that we can get a better view of the vicinity of Vesuvius and the Solfatara, which we are leaving behind to starboard, along with Naples, enshrouded in lava, and the gulf into which new promontories extend. He only permitted me to take five or six photographs with a telephoto lens, which will show us scarcely anything....

We have crossed the Apennines; the twilit waters of the Adriatic are on the horizon. Our pilot will not stop. He wants to keep going all through the night, he says...the night during which the Martian shell will fall, "in the vicinity of Cairo," at 11:42 p.m. I shall try to sleep for a while, to the monotonous rhythm of our rotor blades, with Raymonde's head on my arm. Shall I dream of bats again, as on previous nights?

July 7. Yes, I was subject once again to that obsessive nightmare. I saw the crepuscular bats again, flying around me and coming in turn to present their humanoid faces to me, with staring, hypnotic eyes whose gaze penetrated me with a quasi-premonitory fear.

The strangest thing is that Raymonde has had the same dream! But Leduc—who never dreams, he says—mocks our "idiotic" terror and attributes our visions to the fact of being in the helicopter. I'm wary of discussing it with him, because he's in an atrocious mood this morning. When I expressed my regrets at not having seen Ithaca, Olympia and Cythera, which we had overflown—especially when I raised the subject with my beloved of the previous life we must have lived in the light of antiquity—he began swearing volubly: a string of oaths that left no time to draw breath...and he struck the little mechanic, who was gazing at him with the eyes of a faithful dog, with his fist. I excuse him, for he has had difficulties with the engine and has been awake all night. But, even so, I think he's a little excessive! There's no reason for it, although he hasn't seen the luminous streak of the shell's fall, as he had hoped....

We're flying over the sea—the glittering Mediterranean, displayed all around us in an uninterrupted circle. Only Crete broke that uniformity momentarily; we saw its mountains, the highest of which still bore traces of snow, but we only caught a distant glimpse of it, to port. Despite my reminiscences of antiquity, I kept quiet—because I only had to murmur the name of the Minotaur for Leduc to turn round, with a sardonic smile. Fortunately, he kept his joke to himself

The heat is becoming suffocating as the hot Sun turns our cockpit into a greenhouse; we had to open the forward porthole, and that has slowed us down a little, because of the resistance of the airflow, but even our indomitable pilot admitted that the artificial breeze was necessary. Besides, he knew that he had to conserve his engine, which was overheating dangerously. What would we do if a breakdown deposited us on the surface of the sea, in which ships no longer circulate? Far from seeking to reassure us though, friend Sylvain cursed "that damned swine of a mechanic, who was made expressly to annoy him." He talked to his engine as if to a real person, insulting it, accusing it of "taking sides with the Martians against us" and challenging it: "You wouldn't have the cheek to fail for good and all here, would you? You'd be going head-first into the drink with the rest of us, with no one to pull you out!"

We're alarmed by his intensity, and it sometimes seems to us that the engine might take him at his word, when it produces a series of misfires, as if in response to his crazy objurgations.

Finally! The Egyptian coat is in front of us: the Nile Delta... and now the growing silhouettes of palm-trees, terraced houses like white dice among the islets of verdure surrounding the mirror-like flood...to starboard, the indistinct ruins of Alexandria...but it's not entirely deserted here; the native villages have a few inhabitants, who raise their arms in their large white sleeves towards us...and on the roads, before we reach Cairo, the occasional camel with its driver, or a donkey loaded with baskets of vegetables...and in the distance, behind the city, whose minarets are still standing, on the far side of the Nile, the suburb of Giza and the pylons of the TSF station, where we'll head first to obtain information as to the shell's point of descent, of which we've seen no sign anywhere...

IV. The Attraction of the Perfume

July, 9 p.m. Here we are at the TSF station in Cairo. I'm writing by the light of a mosque's night-light, while a strong southerly breeze shakes the mosquito-nets covering the windows and continually brings us strange gusts of intoxicating perfume....

On the other side of the room, even though the apparatus has stopped working, Nazir Bey persists in tapping out a distress signal: SOS...SOS...SOS...three sharp clicks, three slow clicks, three sharp clicks. Raymonde, lying on a divan, is watching him do it. Outside, on the terrace where the irrigation canal laps gently at the feet of the tall palm trees, Leduc has chosen the helicopter's seats to take a brief nap, in the company of his young mechanic. Furtive footsteps continue to sound along the road, en route to the Pyramids...and the Martian shell.

And I'm writing this, because *I'm afraid to go to sleep.*

We arrived at 5 p.m., after flying over the city, whose entire northern sector is in ruins but whose southern part retains enough intact houses to lodge between 1000 and 2000 inhabitants. Their oriental fatalism has preserved them from the panic, but not the epidemics and the attacks of Eternal-Nightist hordes from Port Said and beyond the Suez Canal. On the road to the Pyramids, 1500 meters from the suburb of Giza, we found the TSF station, whose white buildings shelter the civilized colony: some 20 intellectuals, the elite of Egypt, took refuge there more than a year ago, and was able to sustain itself there under the direction of Nazir Bey, the head of the TSF station, an ex-student of the Polytechnique.

A solitary servant in a pink turban and a long blue robe appeared on the threshold, parting the mosquito-net made of pearls of multicolored glass, when our helicopter landed on the terrace in the shade of the palm-trees. It astonished us that he was alone, but the heat was still overwhelming; we assumed that the staff-members were still taking their siesta. Leaving the young mechanic to guard the machine, we followed the servant, who jabbered a voluble explanation—in Coptic, I imagine.

In the corridors, several sub-bronzed servants were sleeping on the yellow-and-blue-tiled floor, as if suffocated by the torrid air—and also by the violent and indefinable perfume that we had initially attributed to he flowers of the terrace, but which pursued us into the apartments.

As we entered, Nazir Bey raised a face ravaged by insomnia from the TSF apparatus, whose elements were making their cicada-like stridulations, and looked at us with haggard eyes. Sylvain introduced him to "Léon and Raymond Rudeax, Sylvain Leduc, sent by the station at Mont Blanc to cooperate in the defense of Cairo against the Martian invasion."

With mechanical politeness, the Egyptian bowed and put his right hand to his heart; then he took his sweat-inundated forehead in both hands and said, in a voice full of anguish: "I beg your pardon, gentlemen; I thought that it was…them. Our aerial squadron took off at 1 a.m. to fight the Martians…yes, the shell arrived last night, as announced…very close to the Pyramids…it was visible at dawn, like an enormous keep…inert, moreover—nothing came out of it…

"All my colleagues were aboard the airfleet…but no one—no one, you understand, gentleman…has come back! They had machine-guns aboard, rapid-firing cannon, explosives…but nothing has been heard; there has been no battle…

"They simply stayed there…all of them! My 18 colleagues, 63 aviators and 25 aircraft!"

"Come on!" cried Leduc, while Raymonde and I sat down on a divan, our legs cut from under us by emotion. "Come on, Monsieur—you can't expect us to believe that all of them been captured by the Martians, spirited away without a shot being fired, just like that!"

"Monsieur, I dare not tell you all that I suspect, but strange things have been happening in Cairo since the arrival of that shell…"

At that moment, the monotonous crackling of the TSF apparatus ceased abruptly. Nazir Bey spoke a few words of the native language into a telephone receiver, listened to the reply, and resumed: "This time, it's our dynamo that has jammed. There has already been strange interference, apparently deliberate, which is making the replies from the other stations indecipherable. Have they even received my signals? I'm a positivist, gentlemen, and I have looked at the previous catastrophes in the cold light of reason, but in the face of what has happened today, I give in: there's a mystery here."

"What's mysterious about a little interference and the breakdown of a dynamo?" Leduc relied, shrugging his shoulders. "It's the recalcitrance of the material. Every mechanic knows that machines have their preferences, their whims, their eccentricities, just like people…and as for your Pyramid story—it's too pyramidal![28] Let me get a couple of hours sleep—it's hellishly oppressive in your country—and I'll go put one over on your Martian magicians all on my own, and get back all the people you mention, even if they're holding them prisoner in the shell, like Jonah in the whale!"

But this comic-heroic bragging made no impact; Nazir Bey's words increased our dull malaise and inexpressible apprehension. "Don't tempt the unknown, Monsieur—and above all, if you can take my word for it, don't go to sleep." He repeated the last sentence: *Don't go to sleep!* That's dangerous, here."

---

[28] In French, "pyramidal" has a double meaning, being used metaphorically to signify "amazing" or "excessive."

These elliptical statements exasperated Leduc. "Ta ta ta! I've just spent 33 hours piloting a helicopter. I'm sleepy and I'm too hot—I'll grant myself a brief siesta in my machine, on the cool terrace—and then, Martians beware! Why should it be dangerous to sleep? I don't believe in the supernatural, I warn you."

"Do you believe your own senses?"

"I don't believe in anything else, damn it...that and my reason!"

"Consult your sense of smell."

"That perfume, you mean? Well, it's very strong, and you've put it everywhere, but we're in the land of ground-nuts and patchouli, and I don't see...."

"It's not a perfume—or, at least, not a *natural* perfume," Nazir Bey pronounced, with a gravity that sent a frisson through our entire bodies, and imposed itself momentarily on Leduc. "It's...something else...and it's coming from the direction of he Pyramids. But that's not all. Look out of the window."

We obeyed, mechanically. Alongside the terrace, in the darkness, with a slight sound of sandals on the sand, furtive shadows were moving, one by one—and I saw, with an inexpressible fear, that these mysterious passers-by were waving the large sleeves of their dark robes in the air...and I recognized, by the light of the stars, the "bats" of my dreams. Raymonde released a stifled cry—she had recognized them too!

Nazir Bey took advantage of our fearful silence: "And do you know where they're going? They began to set out last night, when the south wind brought the first gusts of the...perfume...from the Pyramids. They're going to meet that effluvium; they're attracted by it, like a mesmerist's subject—literally, gentleman—because...they're asleep! *They're asleep*, Monsieur Leduc. Do you finally understand that you *mustn't go to sleep!*"

But the intrepid aviator had recovered his self-possession.

"It's one thing for natives to let themselves get wrapped up in these mystifications. Personally, I won't be going anywhere. Enough fairy tales. I'm sleepy. I'm going to sleep—and at midnight, I'll pay a visit to these conjurers from Mars. Goodnight, everyone."

And we are now alone. Nazir Bey, his attitude profoundly serious, is tapping his SOS...SOS...which no longer go any further than his manipulator. Raymonde, lying next to me on a divan, is following his gestures without seeing them. The servant is sitting on the tiles with his back against the door. And the mosque's night-light is quivering in the gusts of the ardent southerly wind that brings us the Perfume, ever stronger, whose suspect origin does not make it any less delightful, as we grow increasingly accustomed to it.

Any other perfume would already have sickened us by its persistence. This one varies from minute to minute, incessantly renewing itself, as if all the sweet odors of the Earth were included within it. It reminds me of the perfume-markets of Tunis and Qayrawan; all kinds of flowers extend their essences there: carnations, lilies, jasmine, roses, and so many others whose names I have forgotten but which my sense of smell recognizes of its own accord, and which I savor with delight, one by one, like voices that fuse and harmonize with one another—and sometimes there is a prodigious chorus, a triumphant symphony that will surely guide us to the embalmed gardens, to the marvelous oases from which this perfume emanates...or rather to...

Has Nazir Bey not said to us, in fact, that what they are attributable to is "not natural?" What does that mean? I remember reading somewhere that not all perfumes are necessarily material, and that the subtlest of all simply correspond to vibrations of the Ether at a particular rhythm. Suppose that the Martians know how to amplify these vibrations? But to what end? It's absurd!

10 p.m. I admit it, now; I'm afraid too. As Nazir Bey says, there's mystery in the air. That incessant procession along the road, of furtive footsteps and shadows agitating bats' wings....

And Leduc, Sylvain Leduc himself, has just abandoned us!

Five minutes ago, the soft and refreshing sound of the irrigation canal bathing the feet of the palm trees on the terrace sudden seemed to increase, to grow immeasurably...to become the purr of the helicopter where Leduc was asleep, and which took to the air without any warning! And I arrived at the door to see it rising up into the air, vertically at first, and then depart, in its turn, towards the south, towards the Pyramids—towards the Perfume!

What will happen now? Nazir Bey has interrupted his vain endeavor; he has a strange smile on his lips...he goes to the doorway, calls out to the servant, who has disappeared: "Ahmed!" His voice echoes bizarrely in the warm night. He hesitates, then goes out on to the terrace, where I catch glimpses of his white form going back and forth in the blue shadows, beneath the stars, which he seems to be invoking with his upraised arms....

He's going! I can hear his light footsteps descending the stairs...passing beneath the window...and drawing away, in the direction of the Pyramids!

We're alone now, Raymonde and I, beneath the night-light of the mosque, which quivers in the gusts of the southerly breeze, charged with the perfumes of the warm and ineffable Night....

V. Between the Sphinx's Paws

What have we done? By what fatal attraction have Raymonde and I been led here? Even though, after Sylvain Leduc's escape and the departure of Nazir Bey, I swore that I would prevent us, at any price, from falling asleep tonight!

We have not slept, though!

Why, then are we here, refugees in this abandoned bar which bears the name: *Sphinx View*, while the all-devouring sunlight blazes all around us, on the desert sands, the Sphinx, the Pyramids and the formidable Keep of the Martian Cylinder.

I can still see us, as if in a dream, beneath the quivering lamp of the mosque, ready to go out and leave us defenseless against the mysteries of the Night, which the all-powerful Perfume was charging with a languorous intoxication of desires and irretrievable nostalgias....

Raymonde had made me a necklace of her arms, and, hanging around my neck, was reciting poems full of vast regrets, drifting in the heavenly radiance of a vanished past, like the enchanted golden clouds of a long summer sunset, on the shore of a phosphorescent sea, solitary and hopeless...

Illumination and seraphic music alternated with the supreme majesty of the infinite sadness of a farewell without return...the kiss of an eternal separation united our lips...

And the Perfume overwhelmed us—the Perfume of the glorious oases, where our new love was alive, rocked by the palm-trees, to the song of cool rose-water trickling into shallow bowls, served by handsome slaves pouring us nectar from crystal flagons beneath a tent from the Arabian Nights...

The perfume guided us along the route, and the irresistible appeals of the denser gusts are resonating in our souls. The palms-fringed pathway opened into the blue and starry Night: the ineffable Night, warm and perfumed...in the distance, on the horizon, were the Pyramids.

Shadows went past us without seeing us. We were no longer of this world. We went on under a charm, towards a greater charm. I thought of Dante and Beatrice. Raymonde was suffocating with benevolent ecstasy. She waved her arms slowly, tilting her head back, with her face raised towards the sky.

"It's paradise," she murmured.

Her words did not surprise me, but her voice! Her voice was entirely new, as tremulous as that of a little girl....

The starlight was very bright; I would have been able to read...I could see her face...and yet I no longer recognized her...and she appeared to be unable to see or hear me.

But we were not asleep! I swear that we were not asleep!

And it is because we were not asleep, and because we were walking so slowly, that we have been saved!

For the Sun rose as we arrived at the Sphinx—and the sight of its mutilated face stopped me abruptly, like a warning of some approaching danger, the threat of imminent death.

In front of us, the somnambulistic pilgrims went on towards the Pyramids, rose-tinted by the dawn...and towards the shining Keep, from whose heights the Martian Magi were drawing them with their incantations.

Cloaked in red—or were those actually true wings?—their luminous horns evoking the idea of Satans, they were performing the ritual gestures from which the perfumed waves were born. They were flying down to the ecstasized pilgrims and bearing them away, clutching them tightly—still bats!—to the platform of the Keep. Nearby, the grounded helicopters sat idle....

But in the purple and gold dawn, the silent flock of Magi went to stand on the tallest of the Pyramids, and their salute to the rising Sun rose into the air like a fanfare of perfumes...

By means of a heroic effort, however, I had vanquished the paralyzing torpor, and I dragged Raymonde into the interior of this little abandoned bar, whose door was wide open...and it was through the window that I watched the Magi regain return to their Keep and shut themselves inside it—for they seem to dread the bright light of day...

The Desert is empty, at this hour; the lonely Pyramids are standing up against the blue sky, vibrant with heat...the Perfume has weakened...the sleep-walking pilgrims no longer pass by...

But we must not go to sleep!

To keep us awake, Raymonde is playing strange improvisations on the bar's piano, and I am writing this...and the Sphinx, with its mutilated face, is watching us through the window...

Glory to us! Glory to Thee, Our Father the Sun, which I come to approach once again!

Glory to our victory!

Despite of the enemies of our holy race—the degenerate occupants of that vast abode which is known here as Jupiter—despite the impious fire that they have drawn from Thine rays, O Sun, to bring the End-of-the-World to our beloved Fatherland,

We have transmigrated by way of the Etheric fields, and reached our promised Eden, which those other presumptuous demons, Humans, call their Earth!

Humans! We shall be among them henceforth, O my brother Martians, more numerous and powerful than ever! Better than our messengers of death, the genius of our Magi will make them bow down before us in thousands, and deliver their bodies to our souls!

O perfume of Eden! O joy! I breathe you in, sacred Sign of Rebirth, which my soul had tasted three times over since its first awakening from nothingness— to Thy pure light, Sun!—up there, beneath the marvelous Arch of Saturn!

Then an avatar on white Venus—another on wild Mercury—and delivered, Sun, from the travails of life, I shall drink the Flame forever in Thy eternal bosom!

Our Father Sun!

So shall it be!

Was it me who wrote that? What is this unknown and monstrous prayer? What is this awkward and hesitant handwriting, as if I had learned to write all over again, with a strange hand?

Have we been asleep? No. She is still playing the piano. And me? Could I have dozed momentarily? I would not have allowed myself to be...invaded...by this Presence that lays siege to me...by this soul that is trying to supplant me in my own body...which will profit from my sleep by displacing me conclusively from my body, of which it has already made use to write that prayer...

Ah! That *Martian* prayer!

I understand! I understand! It's as if I have experienced a Revelation...as if a Spirit has informed me of these things...

Yes, indeed! It is the *Other* that knows, the other soul that has just profited from my inattention, my temporary drowsiness, to visit my brain, which it covets...and within my brain, that visitation of the Martian soul has left traces...

I understand! I understand!

The Bat-Magi, the Satan-Magi, have come to Earth to aid in the reincarnation of Martian souls, to introduce them by means of their perfumes into human bodies and secure them in place by their incantations, after having expelled the human souls!

For the Earth is the Martian paradise, the *place* necessary to Martian souls after death; it is on our planet that these souls are ordinarily reincarnated in the bodies of new-born babes, which become in consequence violent and bellicose individuals, criminals and warriors...and because the population of Mars is four or five times less than that of the Earth, these errant souls find themselves rapidly reincarnated, and the ex-Martians are a minority among human beings....

But the cremation of their planet by the Thunderbolt from Jupiter has liberated millions of Martian souls at a single stroke! They have arrived on Earth, their paradise, hoping to begin the new existence that will eventually permit them to pass on to Venus, then Mercury—necessary stages of the transmigration that is destined to end in he supreme beatitudes of the central star: the Sun!

Now, there being few or no births among the few tens of thousands of surviving humans, adult bodies, already provided with souls, can be *forcibly* taken by other souls, in exceptional circumstances.

The Martians knew that. They knew that the Thunderbolt would destroy their planet. They sent their Magi to Earth as quartermasters of souls—the Magi whose perfumes create exactly that exceptional state in which a human body is susceptible to receive a new soul...

Where and how is the exchange of souls effected? What becomes of the souls dispossessed of their bodies? Is the perfume designed to serve the Martian souls as an atmosphere or a vehicle? Does it require the presence of a large number of those souls? What is its exact role? Would the *possession* by the new soul be temporary without the intervention of the Magi? How does the new soul learn to make use of an adult body that has never been its own? So many questions, which I might perhaps be able to answer...if I were more familiar with Spiritualist and Theosophical doctrines, to which I was wrong to pay too little attention...or if I allowed myself to be invaded again by the *Other*, by Martian soul that has chosen my body as its terrestrial residence...

I sense it, invisible, prowling around me; I can feel its fluid feelers brushing my coveted brain, whose activity it is studying, in order to learn how to use it...

If I fall sleep, if dreams distract my soul for a single instant, the *Other* will take possession of my vacant body! *It* has already done so once, a little while ago, when *it* used my hand to write its sacrilegious prayer; but *it* did not know, thanks to its inexperience of my bodily functions, how to retain its hold against the return of my soul. Will I be as fortunate another time? Will *it* not grow bolder, fortifying the place where *it* has already left an imprint?

What's this? Raymonde is repeating the same few notes indefinitely, having already played them three, four, ten times over...

She was asleep! She was playing mechanically! Her fingers were continuing to play of their own accord, reflexively, but she was asleep! And the Martian soul that coveted her has taken advantage of the moment...

She is *possessed!* It's over. The nameless misfortune, the monstrous adventure, has arrived...it's my fault, damn it! And there she is, extended on a divan in front of me, asleep, asleep without my being able to awaken her, with a face that I no longer recognize—with the reflection in her features of the Martian soul that possessed her: a fixed and haggard smile—a smile of madness, I would say, if I did not know the abominable truth!

It's my fault! Because we did not flee this accursed place at daybreak. Because I could not overcome the mysterious torpor of the incantatory Perfume, which constrained us to take refuge here, in this abandoned bar, within sight of the Pyramids polluted by the Magi, within sight of their Keep, within sight of the mutilated Face of the Sphinx. Because I did not dare to cross the desert in the blinding sunlight, instead of waiting for the twilight and cool of the evening...

Alas, my lost love, even if you had resisted until then, would we not have succumbed to the redoubling of the Perfume when the Night sent the Magi flying to the Pyramids, from which they would send forth their fluid passes again?

What does it matter now? Why fight on? Why not go to sleep and surrender my body to the *Other*? No, no, no! I don't want to! I don't want to! An enormous jealousy makes me rebel, makes me huddle within my body; I refuse to yield it to the *Other*, who, incarnate in my place, will love her. Love her? *Her*? But it isn't *her*! In our two bodies, there will be two new souls. It is a couple of Martian lovers who will love one another!

In the moments when the *Other* insinuates itself into me surreptitiously, in those instants when I no longer recognize my own gestures and scarcely recognize my thoughts as they cut across currents of *strange memory*...then *She* (the new one!) seems to emerge from her lethargy and recognize the new me...she loves him. *Him*, with a new love that does not know *me*...and when it is *me* who reigns again within my body, she turns her head away, and I no longer hold anything in my arms but the inert and de-souled body that was once my Raymonde.

But I sense that the *Other* does not love her as much as I love her: that my new *me* will make the new Raymonde suffer cruelly, and a frightful distress adds to the rage of my impuissant jealousy. But what is her new soul to me? To me, to my true me? Nevertheless, I do not want to! I do not want to leave my body...I shall resist the invader until the end!

Oh, if I could concentrate all the power of my will! It seems to me that I would regain my strength, that I could chase the intruder from my body, conclusively. And who can tell whether I might also be able to exorcize my beloved, to restore her true soul, which is perhaps still here, beside me—beside us!—without being able to manifest itself, cut off from the world of the living, prey to the malevolence of other Martian souls awaiting their fleshly resurrection?

But no! It's the Other that will expel me from my body forever, as soon as I stop writing, as soon as I give way to sleep...

See how the mutilated Face of the Sphinx is darkening mysteriously in the twilight...

My de-souled beloved is shivering voluptuously under the redoubling of the paradisal Perfume...

The somnambulistic pilgrims are beginning to go by again...

Up there, in their sinister Keep and on the Pyramids, the Magi of Mars with luminous horns are moving their bats' wings in the hot evening, toward the horizons of the Promised Land...

BOOK TWO

THE AGONY OF THE EARTH

Part One: The Terrestrial Port of Call

I. Disincarnate!

We were dead—really dead! Our souls—our astral bodies, as the Spiritualists put it, which is perhaps closer to the mysterious truth—had already stopped watching over our henceforth-unusable bodies. By no means cadavers attained by decomposition, we were drifting towards the reward or proving-ground of a new incarnation! We were, at least, free from the sentiments that had attached us, in a derisory fashion, to the material world of living beings in which we were now incapable of action. That impuissant solicitude did not keep us captive in any way, did not continually draw us back to the neighborhood of our bodies—our living bodies, which we had inhabited for so long that our present beings were like their imponderable effigies; our living bodies, which had fallen into the power of invaders, who *possessed* them, and would animate them from now on!

Hours must have gone by since the moment when, finally expelled in my turn, I had eventually recognized among the hostile crowd of strange fluid forms—my beloved! Dedicated to one another by years of love, our new beings had been attracted to one another, had penetrated into one another and fused into a single unique nebulosity of sapphire fluorescence, in which our united but distinct selves were localized.

Then: a long vertiginous bewilderment, such as a chrysalid must experience on its metamorphosis into a butterfly; the joy of our mutual survival; an insuperable loathing for the fluid forms whose dull red light was roughly etched with hateful and desperate faces; the haunting of our bodies possessed by those foreign souls…

Little by little, resignation to the inevitable soothes us. The fact of our corporeal envelopes ceases to interest us exclusively.

Thoughts of a strange synthetic vigor—intuitions—emerge in the "twin mirrors" of our two spirits and excite our curiosity with regard to our new existence.

We have lost all means of acting upon material reality. By way of compensation, however, that reality reaches us directly, without the mediation of senses. In consequence, our astral bodies now participate in the "fourth dimension" of the universe. Space and the impenetrability of matter have ceased to exist for us in the way that they condition the three-dimensional sensibility of "living" beings. As freely and instantaneously as thought moves from one point to another, a simple "volition" displaces our astral bodies.

Timidly at first, hindered by its very facility, we learn not to pay any further heed to the material objects that habit represents to us as barriers. We leave the little Sphinx View bar by going *through* the re-closed door, to follow our bodies as they head towards the Martian Cylinder amid the crowd of somnambulistic pilgrims arriving from Cairo in response to the summon of the Magi.

Night has fallen, but giant floodlights have been mounted on top of the Keep and the Pyramids, distributing a cold green light, like that of glow-worms. The Perfume's vibration is increasingly intense—I say *vibration* because we have ceased to perceive it by means of a sense of smell, and that is the best available translation of my present intuition—and it causes us to experience a veritable horror, which we have to overcome in order to penetrate into our invaders' lair.

The metallic walls of the Keep offer no more resistance to our intrusion than a window offers to solar radiation.

We explore the 20 floors of the monstrous bolide, which are packed with dismantled machines—pistons, wheels, strange pieces of machinery—measuring instruments, and stocks of unknown chemical products. There are also cabins for the Magi, and we come across one who is busy writing. He has folded his bat-like wings, which seem to be composed of a rubbery fabric the color of mahogany, behind his back. The protuberances on his forehead, which I had mistaken for Satanic horns, are elongating and retracting, following the rhythm of his thoughts. His golden eyes, with vertical pupils like those of cats, are momentarily directed towards us—but we are invisible, even to this familiar of the Occult.

On the upper platform of the Keep, which is almost as tall as the neighboring Pyramids, there is an enormous agitation in the wan light.

The unfortunate Terrans who have yielded to the appeal of the Perfume are brought up by the flying Magi and introduced one after another into a sort of solenoid, whose mysterious currents ensure the conclusive empery of the Martian soul. And these neo-Martians—Terromartians, rather—whose gestures are awkward, go to rejoin the troop of their own kind busy at the foot of the Cylinder.

I think I recognize the man who is directing them—yes, it really is Sylvain Leduc organizing the assembly of the machines. Constructions are rising up before our very eyes. Rails are being laid down that will connect up with the Pyramids' railway. A helicopter takes off, then another, and a third...the process of taking possession of the Earth is beginning!

There are two other individuals beside Sylvain Leduc, however. The first one, whose red cape and horned cap makes him resemble a Magus—that's *me*! It's my stolen body, my body animated by the spirit of some great Martian leader! And his similarly-dressed companion is Raymonde—it's the stolen body of my beloved!

Their gait is no longer as hesitant as it was the last time we saw them; their new personalities are expressed in their curt and authoritarian gestures—and, instead of the anxious solicitude of the first hours, they inspire an atrocious revulsion in us. It adds to the loathing we feel for the fluid faces grimacing all around us from the dull red glimmers, which seem to us to be laughing scornfully at our dispossession, and to the nausea of the Perfume, which penetrates us with horripilatory vibrations. The brutal atmosphere of the Martian colony is becoming increasingly odious and intolerable.

By way of reaction, our desires are ardently raised to the Heavens!

II. Which Will Startle Readers Who Care Little For Astronomy

And our new faculty of displacement at will, which we still have not mastered, transports us into the heights of the atmosphere, hundreds or thousands of meters up.

Surprised by our unexpected deliverance, far from trying to moderate the phenomenon and curb this glorious levitation, we exert all our will to activate it. The Martian floodlights on the Pyramids and the Cylinder have vanished into the distance, and are also carried eastwards by the rotation of the Earth—which continues to sink into space, diminishing, resolving itself into a planetary globe as seen through a telescope!

Knowing no corporeal needs, careless of the barometric pressure that is doubtless already reduced to zero, and of the ardent solar radiation that reaches us again as soon as we move out of Earth's conical shadow, we bathe in the infinite serenity of the velvet-black night, in which the Sun and the stars shine simultaneously, thanks to the absence of any veil of air.

O purification! Marvelous recompense for having dedicated so many hours of our terrestrial lives to the disinterested joys of Astronomy!

What a miserable larval [29] period disintegration must be, for souls that have only ever exercised the material part of their beings! How well the expression "souls in torment" must apply to them, once deprived of organs susceptible to satisfaction by means of the only appetites they have developed!

Would not we, ourselves, be disorientated and maddened by the spectacle of the sidereal space that surrounds us, if it were not for our astronomical cultivation? Would we not hurry to regain the sole familiar ground of the Earth, where we would be reduced to wandering, prey to regretful memories of the base routines and vulgar interests of quotidian existence, amid the rabble of Martian souls aspiring to reincarnation, that being the only mode of existence intelligible to the grossness of their appetites?

Ah, how clearly I understand now that the supreme sacrament is the disinterested search for truth!

A sublime intoxication carries us away: a passionate desire to explore this Space into which our will has transported us of its own accord. The long evenings formerly spent at the telescope have been a fecund initiation; they have prepared our spirits for the joys of the infinite! How much better, though, than all the accumulated figures, with which I took the trouble impregnate my imagination in order to obtain a paltry perception of distances and volumes, is the

---

[29] The word "larva" has a double meaning in French, crucial to Varlet's discourse; as well as referring to an embryonic entity destined for metamorphosis, it also means "ghost."

direct intuition that now allows us to perceive the relationships of the stars to one another and the actual disposition of the Universe.

In the marvelous Night that surrounds the Milky Way, the Sun astonishes us with its new brilliance. Instead of the white disk with marked contours that seems to be visible from the depths of the terrestrial atmosphere, a vast aureole in the form of a luminous housing envelops the regal Star. Around its circumference, an effervescence of rosy flames launched forth, as from a gigantic bowl of punch, to the right and the left, long rectilinear plumes similar to the "rays of glory" that sometimes spring forth from clouds as sunset approaches—two wings of light on which the God of daylight and life—Ra, the sacred Hawk of ancient Egypt—hovers...

Lost in the radiation of that dazzling aureole is the minuscule planet Mercury; more distant and more voluminous, Venus, twin sister of the Earth, displays itself in a phase akin to a "young" Moon—the Moon whose orbit we surpassed in little more than a second, at the speed of light, which we adopted as son as we were out of the atmosphere. In about eight minutes, it would have taken us to the Sun; but it is in the opposite direction, towards Mars, that our flight is taking us...

Four minutes, and the planet previously swept clean by the avenging Thunderbolt passes before us, escorted by its two tiny moons, its face still enveloped by the opaque clouds of the frightful conflagration.

Half an hour at the speed of light—which is extremely fast on the scale of terrestrial measurement, since light could go round the Earth seven and a half times in a second, but which adapts to the millions of kilometers of the planetary scale and ceases to appear enormous to us while the familiar Earth is reduced in the vicinity of the Sun, as Venus was a little while ago, to a large blue diamond juxtaposed with a white satellite—will bring us to the giant Jupiter, whose brightness increases gradually as we pass through the zone of the minor planets.

One of these boulders—I don't know what name it bears in the catalogue—attracts our curiosity as we pass by, and we deflect our course towards the surface of the irregular spheroid, whose diameter is inferior to that of Paris: miniature continents, whose cliffs, a few centimeters high, are lapped by the waves of Lilliputian oceans...forests of unknown vegetation grow as tall as a finger's length...animate beings, species of red and black ants, emerge from their subterranean cities in tight columns, which march to meet one another in the middle of a clearing, exterminating one another furiously, biting, slashing, breaking their adversaries' heads, necks and legs with thrusts of their mandibles!

Horror! Here too there is war, the inexorable struggle of life against life, the destruction of life by itself! Does the animator of worlds not know, then, how to do its work without this perpetual wastage of energy? Is destruction an integral part of its plan? Or is there no plan at all, no goal within Creation? Might the universal Consciousness be an impassive and serene witness to the play of forces that interact within its bosom—the same forces that hold worlds and the universe in equilibrium, in the network of gravity, and result in the internecine battles of ants and humans...and Martians against Terrans? Is the universal Spirit insensible to evil? Or do we qualify, within the narrow limitation of our prejudices, as necessary accidents?

We have fled, revolted by that spectacle of warfare, at a strangely accelerating speed. Jupiter, the planet of wisdom, has passed before our eyes, its gigantic face obscuring half the sky, momentarily eclipsing the luminous spindle of the Sun, which is already reduced to a fifth of its diameter as seen from the Earth...and the Sun is still diminishing; Jupiter is soon no more than a dot drowning in its fire...

Saturn, the enormous Saturn, only slightly less massive than Jupiter, girdled by its triple ring, has just been surpassed, distant in its orbit...Uranus...Neptune...then the other planet, the Transneptunian planet anticipated by terrestrial science...

Unless we have lost all notion of time—which is possible, now, in the absence of reference-points—it is no longer light that is transporting us; it is some other vehicle, more rapid still. The Sun has lost the privileged aspect that is conferred upon it by its proximity to the Earth; it is no longer the day star, no longer the astral ruler of a harmonious cortège of planets on which its rays support life. All the planets have disappeared; the entire system enclosed within Neptune's orbit, which light takes eight hours to cross, has been reabsorbed into a single shining point—a star like the others, barely of the first magnitude, reddened like Aldebaran, whose neighbor it is, close to Algol in the constellation Perseus.

Unprecedented solitude! Extreme isolation in the sidereal Night! We experience here, in reality, that which our imagination once made an effort to conceive, in abstracting itself from the support of the material Earth, which hid the entire celestial hemisphere situated beneath our feet from our eyes. Then, there was an *up* and a *down*; the weight against which the verticality of our bodies battled furnished us with a stable reference-point, imposed upon us, of its own accord, something of the atavistic illusion of being at the center of the universe, and it required a great effort of meditation to forget the presence of our fellow humans, to whom we clung instinctively when seized by vertigo as we looked into the infinite Void...

No more people around us now, close at hand or far away; no more maternal Earth, here; neither *up* nor *down*; space in every direction, swarming with stars, which accumulate in a luminescent zone: the Milky Way. The only reminder of our condition as spirits born on the Earth is the forms of the constellations, which are still similar.

No terror at all. A sacred wonder. The sense of the infinite that sometimes brushed us, too fleetingly, when we forced ourselves to penetrate its actual presence, when an intuition passed through us of our true place in the Universe, of the vertiginous profundities of the space that surrounded us, in which the Earth was plunged, in the neighborhood of the Sun, in the bosom of the lenticular mass of stars that appeared to us, seen from within, in the form of the Milky Way...

What a sublime augmentation of Mystery, now that we are no longer reckoning sidereal space according to the scale of our human senses, now that the egotistical animality of the body has ceased to impose its puerile terrors and prejudices on our spirits!

That star which is growing in size in front of us—in the part of the sky unknown to the inhabitants of the northern terrestrial hemisphere, next to the scintillating Southern Cross—which is doubling into two twin suns rotting around one another, is Alpha Centauri, the "Proxima" of astronomers, whose light is transported to us in a little over four years. But what we are riding at present is the mysterious gravity ray, whose transmission seems *instantaneous* at any distance...*gravity*, perhaps no more than a word. Do we know what reality is hidden beneath that appearance, about which we know no more than its numerical law? Are we not concerned, not with a force, but with the connective fabric of the universe, of a simple modality of the Ether whose hypothesis necessarily entails that of the "fourth dimension" and the continuity of all existent things within a single WHOLE? [30]

Alpha Centauri has passed before us like a station lantern glimpsed by night through the window of an express train; we are traversing light years in seconds, and new stars are strung out, one by one, along our route. Descending the scale of stellar magnitudes, the Sun that lights our Earth gradually retreats into invisibility. It is now at the humblest rank of all, and it requires our sustained attention not to be lost in the rapid dislocation of the constellations. Cassiopeia flattens out. The square of Pegasus is constricted into a lozenge. Orion and the Southern Cross are unrecognizable. And the familiar magnitudes are modified: Capella, Vega, Deneb, Arcturus, all the stars of the northern hemisphere, fade like the Sun, and seem to multiply, while the seed-bed of stars in front of us becomes sparser. Black gaps, like the famous "Coal Sack" in the vicinity of the Magellanic Clouds, are opening in the sidereal fabric, like "eyes" forming in the iridescence of a soap-bubble that is about to burst.

The black lacunae grow, join together; a few last suns are passed...and it's finished! The soap-bubble has burst—we have emerged from the Milky Way,

---

[30] The capitalized word that I have translated as "WHOLE" is "PAN," which is the proper name of a Greek God as well as a trivial noun signifying something all of a piece. The theory of general relativity, which reinterpreted gravity as a kind of fourth-dimensional spatial curvature, had been published in 1916, but Varlet ignores other consequences of that theory, as many other armchair cosmic voyagers before and after him found it convenient to do. Camille Flammarion's *Lumen*, of which in this passage is strongly reminiscent, also credits disincarnate souls with the ability to travel faster than light, but has a naïve view of the relativity of time and space, as is expectable in a work first published in the 1860s.

leaving it behind us with its millions of suns, including our long-lost place of birth. The Galaxy elongates, and finally appears in its entirety, seen from without instead of within, in the form of a vast and dense mass of stars disposed in spiral lines—rather like the luminous jets that emerge from the fireworks that are called "Catherine Wheels."

And the Blackness, the Void of the Outer Universe, into which our flight plunges us—in pursuit of the Great Secret—remains populated with distant luminescent formations: Nebulas in which new universes are elaborated, slowly rotating on their axes as they flee through Space…to encounter other Nebulas, immense and amorphous clouds of ancient matter, disintegrated worlds, chaos awaiting the penetrating, fecund and rejuvenating shock—just as the conjugation of cells gives living matter the necessary impulse to develop new beings once again!

And from Nebula to Galaxy, from one universe to the next, again and again, in the bosom of the illimitable All, our hectic flight continues obstinately, desperately, towards the impossible wall of the External Nothingness…

And the dimensions are abolished. Large? Small? What do these notions signify in relation to the Infinite All? Masses of stars…Nebulas…Universes? Atoms? Every sidereal whirlpool is, on a different scale, the whirlpool of ions and electrons that make up the invisible elements of matter! Analogous, their relative distribution; of the same order, their velocities! Formidable questions: might these Sidereal Atoms be grouped like he atoms of matter into Molecules of a superior degree? Might those, by their aggregation, form living entities of an ineffable order of vitality? Might universe-blood-corpuscles be circulating in the arteries of an incommensurable Being…inhabiting in its turn a world…itself embodied within…[31]

And then! What then! Why that Being? Yes, why? Why is there anything at all? Why this and not something else? Is there actually anything, in REALITY? Might not ALL be an illusion—equal to NOTHING?

And in the intoxication of that ideal vertigo, amid the infinite blackness where the Nebulas were vague glimmers and the Galaxies drifted—isolated in the material Void and yet bathed by the Unity of the essential gravitational Ether, which makes everything One—our sublime spirit, which has just explored and measured the round of Universes, is swallowed up in despair beneath the overwhelming Mystery. Our distress makes us human again, and turns humbly towards the security of the maternal Earth, aspires to the equilibrating ballast of

---

[31] This was not the first time that the notion of an infinite hierarchy of universes in which the nebulas of one cosmos form the atoms of the superior macrocosmos had been deployed in scientific romance, having been featured in R. A. Kennedy's *The Triuneverse* (1912; published as by "the Author of *Space and Time*"), but it is a striking inclusion in Varlet's attempt to update and outdo Flammarion.

the material organisms from which our prideful lust to know the universal Truth rejoiced in being freed...

O previous Life, far from this formidable black tableau of eternal cosmic Night in which the supreme Formula, beyond the reach of our original weaknesses, is set out in stellar hieroglyphs...

O simple animal reality of the maternal Earth: dawn over woods glittering with dew, larks singing in the morning sky, rose-bushes flowering in the spring sunlight, the serenity of a sunset over the sea...

And that desire to cross space draws us back, through the exterior Night streaked with the fulminant flock of universes in flight—masses of stars— nebulas...the lenticular Milky Way opens up, receives us among its stars, which regroup into familiar constellations...Sun! O Aldebaran and Capella, growing Star...

Divine Sun of terrestrial humankind, and your cortège of planets...here's Jupiter...Mars...here's the Earth, a blue diamond juxtaposed with a white satellite...

But what sovereign influence, against which the will of our couplet stiffens in vain—what irresistible attraction—which must resemble what a steel needle experiences in a magnetic field—is drawing us past the Earth—is carrying us, precipitating us towards that white planet: Venus, enormous, filling the entire nadir with its disk padded with dazzling clouds?

III. The Master Initiate of Venus

"Spirit of Earth, are you there?"

I perceive these words by hearing them spoken in an unknown language, whose sounds gradually translate themselves within my brain—for I have a brain, at present: a brain to which an elaborate network of nerves brings me the sensations of a beating heart, legs and arms, material and weighty. My attention loses itself therein; an overwhelming confusion replaces the beautiful intellectual lucidity of before. I am horribly ill-at-ease in this body, which is not mine, and in which an unfamiliar force retains me—like an external compression, without which I would escape violently. Oh, I am sad, weeping in this body. I am in distress here, alone...alone? Ah! Separated from my beloved! Why? What has happened...?

And I remember our fall towards Venus, through cloudy opacity, and then that heart-rending agony, that tearing apart of our couple, leaving my beloved outside this body, where an all-powerful will has reincarnated me.

I sigh profoundly and raise my leaden eyelids.

A peach-pink daylight, entering through oval windows, reveals three people standing in front of me, dressed in white togas of a fine aristocratic type, with faces like marble, who might as easily have been 40 or 80 years old—and I know that the one who has me in his power is the Master Initiate of Venus.

"Spirit of Earth," he repeats, "are you there?"

"I'm here," I say, finally. Timidly, I add: "Master, what has become of my beloved?"

"Don't worry, child," replies the voice, charge with an ideal tenderness, "She is by your side. I have separated your two fluidic bodies in order to incarnate yours in the organism that will serve as your medium. She will be returned to you when our conversation has concluded and I have informed you of your highest duty...

"For a long time, my brother initiates and I have known that strange and calamitous events were happening in the superior stars, but only a Terrestrial or Martian spirit detached from the fluidic tumult of its fellows—where it would be deaf to our appeals—can give us a detailed account. We watched out for the flight through space of a disincarnate soul. You and your companion are the first that a sublime curiosity has caused to flee the terrestrial atmosphere, the first who came within our mental range...

"Tell us what you know."

And I told the story:

"All the people of Earth were living in peace, the animal passions vanquished, the reign of intelligence affirmed every day by a marvelously accelerated scientific progress. We had learned to communicate with our planetary

186

brothers on Jupiter and Mars—but while the former generously exchanged their wisdom with us, the latter appropriated our most powerful secret in order to use them against us. With an end in mind that we did not grasp at first, they wanted to invade our planet.

"As cowardly as they were perfidious, the Martians resolved to obliterate any trace of resistance in advance. Their machines, propelled by an unknown force, rained down upon the Earth, pouring out a red death of fire and corrosive asphyxia. Our capital cities were destroyed one after another; the animal instincts, liberated and exalted by the panic and the social disorganization, added the madness of blind fratricidal warfare to the horrors of famine and plague, then to the calamities of earthquakes and volcanic eruptions provoked by the last Martian shells.

"After the criminal planet's orbit had carried it far enough away from us to oblige it to cease its bombardment, most of these scourges continued to increase of their own accord, eventually demoralizing humankind and reducing its numbers so completely that, during the following opposition, the invaders would have been able to disembark on our world without fear of serious resistance.

"In the meantime, the Sages of Jupiter, noble champions of the law of love and sidereal fraternity, had resolved to punish the felon planet and to render it incapable of harming the unfortunate Terrans as soon as the proximity of the two celestial bodies—Jupiter and Mars—rendered the operation viable. For two terrestrial years, the entire population of the immense planet put all the resources of its science and industry to work in order to charge Solar Accumulators, in which the calorific energy of the Central Star were finally condensed with an unprecedented potential.

"When the propitious moment arrived, this energy, reconstituted by a projector, became a monstrous Thunderbolt, which we saw launched into space at the speed of light, reaching the criminal planet 30 minutes thereafter—where the ravages of the Fire were pitilessly prolonged for a full week, until the surface of the planet was completely incinerated.

"By a fatal coincidence, however, the opposition that had brought Mars into the vicinity of Jupiter similarly brought the Earth within range of Mars, and at the last moment—when the avenging Thunderbolt was already extending its dart through space—a final projectile was launched from Mars!

"One sole projectile, whose occupants had, well before their arrival on Earth become the last survivors of the Martian race; one unique projectile, instead of hundreds, or perhaps millions, that would have contained their mass emigration…

"You know, O Master, that the savage religion of the Martians sees the Sun as the ultimate end of their transmigrations. According to their Magi, it is on Saturn that their souls are born and incarnated for the first time. Following one or several existences, according to the merits of each one—whatever might qualify as merit in respect of these bandits—metempsychosis takes them to Ju-

187

piter, or the little satellites that are its prisons, and from there to Mars. Such is the origin that they attribute to themselves. Their next abode is therefore situated on the Earth, where their souls, guided by his invincible faith, render themselves after death.

"Until now, the population of Mars being much inferior in number to that of the Earth, these Martian souls were able to reincarnate freely among the new-born, and only formed a violent and bellicose minority of criminals and warriors among humankind—but since the End-of-the-World that the Jovian Thunderbolt has inflicted on their planet, millions of Martian souls have come to descend upon the Earth, hopeful of reincarnation in the corporeal avatars through which they must pass in pursuit of their exodus towards the Sun, by way of intermediate stages on Venus and Mercury. Are there even 100,000 humans on Earth at present? Perhaps not. Every human is thus coveted and besieged by a swarm of Martian souls, which aspire to take possession of him..."

The Master Initiate interrupted me: "But, child, a disincarnate soul cannot take possession of an adult organism and expel the spirit that has developed therein, except in very exceptional circumstances. Without the direct intervention of Magi..."

"That, O Master, is exactly what the last projectile has brought to the Earth. By means of a perfume with occult virtues, with which they are charging the atmosphere, they are drawing defenseless humans to the vile Keep in which their incantations perpetrate the odious theft. My beloved and I only needed to go to sleep for a moment under the influence of the Perfume to see ourselves irrevocably expelled from our bodies. It is a Martian leader, I think, and his companion who have taken possession of our terrestrial bodies."

The Master Initiate turned to his two colleagues. "Here, brother, is an exact account of what we have glimpsed confusedly in the magic crystal. The danger that the protective Powers reveled to us a long time ago is very near; it threatens us; it will descend upon our dear and gentle world: the Titans intent on the conquest of the Sun!

"Having escaped the judicial Thunderbolt, will not the Magi overturn the assigned order by means of their sacrilegious maneuvers, despoiling the Earth's survivors for the profit of the Martian rabble?

"O God! Divine Apollo! You inspire me to clairvoyant enthusiasm! The future opens before my eyes—an abyss of horror! I see the monstrous activity in all the factories of Earth, to which the Martians will hasten furiously! They are afraid of the supreme punishment—for Jupiter is ready to annihilate them, this time irremediably. Flee! They want to flee that globe before coming back within range of the Avenger!

"Drunk with the immeasurable power of their accursed science—by the vertiginous acceleration of their progress—their sacrilegious folly will surpass the eternal Laws; they will destroy the Earthly stage and disembark on Venus in their present bodies! See them, O Brothers! The bolides fabricated by them on

Earth: ten—100—1000—a flamboyant hail of bolides raining down upon our peaceful abode and ejecting these exterminators, intoxicated by destruction, into the midst of our people, ignorant of all arts save those of Beauty!"

The Great Initiate tottered, prey to prophetic emotion; the other two Pontiffs respectfully assisted him to sit down on the ivory throne set behind him, and then knelt down beside him.

He kept his eyes closed for a few moments, as pale as candle-wax, rigid and hieratic. Eventually, opening his eyes again, he resumed in a steadier tone; "Tell me, child, what was your intention in returning to the ground fouled by the invaders?"

"I don't know…perhaps to make another attempt to recover my body, and that of my beloved."

"You would have failed again. I alone can give you the indispensable secret. I shall not exact any oath from you. Your probity, and that of your companion, has been obvious to me since the instant when my will-power deflected your couple's flight towards the planet of love. You are the Children of Light, I know that. You will be our allies against the Children of Darkness. There is a dogma with which the religions of your celestial fatherland are familiar, with varying degrees of obscurity: that of protective geniuses. The sage Socrates had his *daimon*. In truth, I inhabit a world younger than yours, but I am your elder in the cycle of existences, and I want to be your guide, your inspiration. Distance is only a word for souls, when sympathy unites them…a mental link is established between us now; henceforth, I shall follow all your footsteps on the Earth, to which you will return. You will recognize my voice in your thoughts, and I shall guide you through the hazardous combat that you will undertake.

"The first necessity is to comfort your human brothers and to preserve the greatest possible number from the influence of the Magi. Go among them in your astral form and visit their spirits, to which you will give courage. After that, when you judge it necessary, recover your natural body…you will do it like this…"

The peach-pink daylight in the windows was fading away and the room was dark. I experienced a sort of nausea, like the prelude to a fainting fit; I felt my self expelled from my borrowed body, and I immediately recovered the clairvoyance appropriate to astral sensibility. A phantasmal blue radiance revealed a new daylight that surrounded me.

I saw Raymonde straight away, a beloved face of nebulous sapphire; I greeted her with all my heart, but was unable to reunite our couple. The influence of a superior will kept us separate, and I perceived that it emanated from the Master Initiate. He approached us, followed by the two Pontiffs, but his astral radiance, which formed an aura extending as far as the hem of his robe, was much more powerful. Even though his lips did not move, his thoughts reached me directly, as if they were born within me.

He pointed to the recumbent body that I had just quit, where the spirit of the medium was completing the re-condensation of its pale pink fluorescence, and he said: "Look into that brain carefully. See that palpitating red granule, as large as a pea, lodged between the two hemispheres. That is the center of application of psychic force, the vital node, the junction-point between spirit and matter." *The pineal gland, the seat of the soul, according to Descartes,* my own mind added. "While it is red and turgid, replete with consciousness, the liaison between body and soul is firm and assured. But watch carefully. When you see it pale and wither under the influence of sleep or prolonged distraction, seize the moment! Exert the force of your will abruptly and directly upon that minuscule point, exalt your consciousness therein...you will regain mastery of your body, and I shall help you to keep it, all the more easily because the Magi will have ceased their operations, and your antagonist will not have the assistance of the Perfume...

"Spirit of Earth, I have spoken.

"Remember that the future of Venus, as well as the fate of the humans worthy of that name still living on Earth, depends on you...perhaps on you alone! Remember that your devotion to the sacred cause of Light might break the fatal thread spun by the Martians. Remember that my brothers and I are watching over you and your companion now, and that we are following our every action. Courage, my child! Be strong, and do not hesitate; the time has come to choose between your terrestrial happiness and your sidereal duty!

"And now, go!"

The power that kept me separate from my beloved let go; instantaneously, our fluid couple reformed, of its own accord, in a vertiginous rush of joy and hope. In the peach-pink daylight, we glimpsed the Elysium of the gentle planet, the happy Venusians crowned with flowers, frolicking in the azure flower-beds beside limpid streams, their naked bodies reminiscent of Classical sculptures, in a perpetual festival of poetry, music and love...then the clouds...then, protruding from their cottony white bed, the summit of a mountain, the cupola of an observatory...and the flight through the starry night of the intersidereal void, towards the bright blue diamond of Earth.

IV. The Business Premises of Mars & Co.

Regretfully, we are leaving the planet of love to fly to the Earth, to which duty calls us—and our hesitation translates itself as the relative slowness of our progress through space. As soon as the enlarged natal globe offers us the familiar contours of the Old World, though—Europe, Africa and Asia, almost entirely plunged in night—our will becomes firmer and our intention more precise. The most important thing, before anything else, is to reconnoiter the Martian colony, to see how it is progressing—so we steer along the long green serpentine formation of the Nile valley, skirting the yellow Libyan desert, spotted with oases like the hide of a leopard.

The shadow of dusk still has the entire Red Sea to traverse, but beacons of cold light are shinning already, pale glow-worms, in an Egypt resuscitated by the feverish and wasteful activity of a forced industrialism. The Equatorial Alternators at Khartoum have been repaired. In the environs of Aswan, enormous batteries of parabolic mirrors—Solar Accumulators!—are gathering the last rays of the setting Sun. Further to the North, the Martian octopus is extending the tentacles of its central colony across the face of our unfortunate planet!

On the edge of the Nile, quite distinct from the old half-ruined Cairo, where the desert of the Pyramids was a few weeks earlier, there is a new city, an immense city. And above that prodigality of lights, above that agglomeration of factories, numerous enough to make one believe that the entire surviving population of the world is already reunited there, looms a formidable monument, which immediately monopolizes our attention and inspires us with an astonishment mingled with fear.

This monstrous symbol of Martian power comprises seven stages of terraces superimposed in successive retreat, like the Roman Pharos of Alexandria or the walls of Ecbatana—but every one of these steps is as steep as a cliff. At the very top of this cyclopean assembly, on the huge plinth, at an altitude of at least 600 meters, stands the Martian Shell itself, the Shell whose 20 floors I explored, the newly-polished metal Shell that reflects the red rays of the setting Sun and the pale projections of the floodlights; and a giant Magus with wings unfurled—an effigy twice the size of the Statue of Liberty in New York—looms above the head of the Shell, whose tip it caresses with its left hand, while its articulated and mobile right arm is imperiously raised, following the course of the Sun, designating the final goal and recompense of the labor that animates the city spread out at its feet.

To add to the fantastic aspect of this apparition, the Magus and the cyclopean assembly of terraces, to the full extent of their height, are made of milky glass, lit from within—so brightly that, in the gathering twilight, the fateful Shell and the leader of the Titans loom up as a prodigious pyramid of light. It recalls both the legendary Tower of Babel and the America advertising hoardings where giant babies soap themselves in public at the very tops of skyscrapers. It is both grandiose and grotesque, absurd and sacrilegious. The Pyramids of the ancient pharaohs, which remain in a corner of the level esplanade in which this monument to pride and folly is set, seem ridiculously small by comparison, like playthings fashioned out of breadcrumbs by idle fingers at the end of a meal, in times gone by.

But what is happening in the palace of red glass that occupies the third side of that esplanade? A swarming host of cars and motorcycles is hastening over the flagstones; helicopters are depositing their human cargoes, which are meekly swallowed up by the entrance porch in the flank of that species of artificial mountain. Others are filing out in gangs and troops, heading for the industrial city...

Despite the horripilatory vibrations of the Perfume, which escape from the lair to propagate the Martian summons over the entire continent to the last remaining humans, overcoming the odiously familiar nausea, we go into and enormous hall full of methodical and terrifying activity. There's no doubt about it, it's the Hall of Reincarnation!

But we have come a long way since the timid trials of the early days; the procedure has been industrialized, for it is a matter of putting the Martian stamp on the entire remaining population of the Earth. And we have considerably underestimated that remaining population, which the approximate calculations made in our final days at Mont Blanc set at a few tens of thousands! A battery of 15 solenoids, operated under the surveillance of the Magi by a numerous staff, is entirely engaged in the conclusive "Martianization" of the heterogeneous crowds accumulating on the lower floor of the hall, contained by barriers like those of the Parisian metro in the days of affluence.

There are pilgrims of every kind there. Some have been swept up by aerial missions, still in possession of their humanity, rolling their fearful eyes. Others, having already been invaded by Martian souls for some time, are quivering with impatience, for they have come spontaneously, some on foot, from the depths of Europe, Asia or Africa, attracted by the magnetism of the Perfume: people from the Hordes, ex-Eternal-Nightists, ragged, dirty and verminous; muzhiks in lambskin coats and fur hats; Hindus in loincloths and large yellow turbans; Chinamen in blue silk robes with slanting eyelids; tattooed Africans, showing all their white teeth when they laugh...and among the last contingents of the Old World, I shudder to see a Boer in a broad-brimmed khaki hat beside a Zulu. The civilized stations have not been spared! What has befallen our friends at Mont Blanc? Those on whom I was counting above all others! Are they still resisting? Or have they already gone over to the enemy?

The features of one of the overseers in the cap of a sub-Magus seem familiar—yes, it's Doctor Landru, the hypnotist from Dury, who is devoting himself gladly to his new "patients." Singular patients, these totally naked dark-

skinned creatures, to whom five solenoids are dedicated. Those bestial, progna-
thous and hairy faces, those long arms, those feet with opposable thumbs! Apes!
They're apes, whose repressed souls have been recruited from the equatorial
forests, brought by helicopter from as far away as Java and Borneo—entire me-
nageries of apes, awaiting their turn to be elevated to the dignity of Martians!
Doubtless it was in error, at first, deceived by the resemblance, that their souls
took possession of simian bodies—but now, the robust orangutans, gorillas and
chimpanzees are hunted methodically, as equals of the last humans.

And, indeed, for beings as deprived of aesthetic and signified sensibilities,
for beings as basely utilitarian as these Martians—cornered, moreover, in a
frightful impasse, for want of human bodies—are not these "anthropoids" an
admirable substitute? Will not that sturdy gibbon make a worker replete with
strength and dexterity? Will not its brain, delivered to an exclusively practical
spirit, careless of the heights of speculative thought, know exactly how to send
to its vigorous muscles and agile fingers the orders of a Martian will? Yes, of
course! It will not take long for us to see, when we visit the city, that this subterfuge, dictated by urgent necessity, has given very satisfactory results to our invaders, whose number has thus been doubled, enabling the Terromartians of
human origin to be reserved for the more delicate tasks.

Before leaving the Hall, we see the strange excess to which a mad desire
for reincarnation can press certain souls. In addition to the apes there are numerous postulants who have adopted the bodies of cattle, dogs and hyenas. But the
Magi refuse to sanction these monstrous borrowings—which cannot be useful to
society, for want of hands—and these wretched animals only pass into Landru's
solenoids in order to be electrocuted and then delivered to the butcher: a fine
example of the ferociously utilitarian organization imposed on the Colony!

Outside, we find that night has fallen. The Monument, illuminated from inside, is a monstrous mountain of light, at the top of which floats the fateful Magus and the gleaming Shell, in the crossed beams of searchlights installed on the
ancient Pyramids. On every side, cold floodlights replace the daylight with a
white clarity and establish a phosphorescent halo above—the City!

Geometrically laid out and paved with glass, the streets of that fantastic
Chicago are swarming with crowds of Terromartians: humans and simian forms,
males and females, naked or dressed any old how—save for the uniform head-
gear, a cap with two distinctive horns, of the Magi and overseers—devoid of all
elegance, hypnotized according to their social function, identified by a registration number, usually attached to the collar. Streets? Tunnels, rather, with the
iron-and-glass walls of phalanstery [32] habitats, shops, busy workshops, and
ceilings made up of a dense network of various and innumerable cables, con-

---

[32] The term "phalanstery" was popularized by the Utopian socialist Charles Fourier, with reference to the communal living-quarters that would accommodate
the inhabitants of his hypothetical society.

ductive wires and conduits, loaded on to pylons distributed without any aesthetic care—all of it temporary, formless, improvised.

There is an incessant movement along elevated monorails—vertical, horizontal and oblique—of luminous bolide-wagons, filing in every direction to the groaning, grinding, humming, quivering factories, shaken by blows from giant pile-drivers, with chimneys pouring out plumes of chemical vapors into the luminous mist of the floodlights. They are the only chimneys, for combustion has been banished from the city; it is the Equatorial Alternators of Khartoum and the Solar Accumulators of Aswan that activate all the machinery. Unfamiliar motors rotate madly beneath sheet-metal hangars or complex superstructures. In steel foundries several kilometers square, serpentine channels of molten metal diverge from an infernal well which vomits liquid iron extracted directly from the plant's igneous core! Thunderous rivers of fire cataract into the circular molds from which the future cylinders of sidereal escape will doubtless emerge.

Other works are manifold and incomprehensible: pulleys, giant cranes, automatic loading-machines pouring out hills of material into railway stations, using the old network of Tantah and Alexandria; airports, vertical floodlights, transport helicopters, airbuses full of conscripts or volunteers, immediately steered towards the Hall of Reincarnation…it is to lodge them that the city expands incessantly, its glassworks transforming the sands of the desert into crystal and molding the paving-stones for the streets, slabs stood on end, shaped into walls, partitions, floors, welded by solar heat—houses built in a quarter of an hour, fitted out and furnished, ready to receive their new inhabitants within an hour!

Despite the awareness of duty that oppresses us, the interest of this tremendous spectacle holds us spellbound for some time. The midnight shift has taken over while we are still wandering through that atmosphere of hectic activity, of which the busiest cities of America can only give the faintest idea.

I had always experienced a sort of vague unease in seeing and hearing industrial machinery in action—grinding mills, shredders, elevators, trolleys, collieries, furnaces, steelworks, metallurgical workshops—firstly because of their noise, which made my nerves jangle, but above all because of the deleterious social ferment that I was by no means alone in attributing to the blind and excessive application of Mechanization. Naivety? How may "human cogs" of the most ferocious industry kept their individuality, followed their personal interests, through the stampede of our machines to goals that were, in the final analysis, various…and innocent?

Here, the character of these prodigious forces, assembled everywhere and converging upon a unique finality, seems to have developed a clearly *satanic* paroxysm. One senses, here, that the city at work is participating, in its entirety, in a dogged and mysteriously hectic haste, whose pace seems to be dictated by the action of the luminous Magus, which is replicated in the forced trepidation of the atmosphere, and in the features of these dehumanized Terromartians, by their new expressions, hard and blinking at the same time, distorted by a grimacing contraction of willful avidity, common to all, from leaders and overseers to simple workers of every race—white, yellow, black—and hairy laborers of various simian species.

Back to the airport, beneath the white, cold light of the floodlights. Twenty airbuses are being filled up with fuel, ready to take off: a methodical tumult in which white overseers and black pilots intermingle with the ape-mechanics that I cannot quite get my head around. And yet, they are all Martians; they evidently consider themselves *natural* to the same degree, in spite of their disparate and heterogeneous envelopes. Those ape-mechanics are no more peculiar and out of place among them than African stokers and Malay lascars used to be among us.

An irritating shock of surprise: in one of the two leaders wearing purple capes and the caps of sub-Magi who are overseeing the preparations—the one smoking his pipe—I recognize Sylvain Leduc. Oh, he was entirely ripe for rendering himself to the Martians, already converted to the furious folly of Mechanization and all its consequences; he threw himself into the wolf-trap, so to speak—and I wonder whether his new soul differs greatly from the old one!

The other leader—superior to Leduc, as indicated by the larger horns on his Valkyrie's helmet—has his back to me, but I recognize him unhesitatingly even before seeing his face and the thick beard that formerly framed it. It's *me*; it's my stolen body, which I will have to win back from its present possessor one day, perhaps soon. The fight will be hard, for the Martian seems to be endowed with a rigid and imperious will, but the spirit of my beloved—where is her body now?—reminds me of the Master Initiate's secret. My victory is sure…and what might I not accomplish on behalf of humankind—the Last Men—once I am introduced into the Supreme Council of the Martians, in the guise of that highly-placed leader, whose authority must be considerable, to judge by the crawling deference of his subordinates, including the prideful, brusque and gruff Leduc.

A sharp curiosity draws us closer to the two leaders. They are speaking French. That surprises me at first, but, on reflection, it is entirely natural, since that is the language in which both their brains are accustomed to think and express themselves: the memory of the language is inscribed in the cerebral circumvolutions, and their Martian souls are obliged to adapt themselves to that quasi-material habitude.[33] I catch the names of cities—Rome, Nice, Lyon, Paris, London—but all that is already agreed between them.

---

[33] This is an obvious narrative convenience—for much the same reason, most of the aliens in Anglo-American SF speak English—but it gives rise to a lingering confusion with which, as the reader will see, Varlet struggles to cope. The Martian body-thieves seem perfectly well able to communicate with one another, apparently in French, even though—according to this logic—most of them must be pre-adapted to speak different languages, and the Martianized apes presumably have difficulty speaking any language at all.

"Moreau!" Leduc calls out—and a Terromartian advances, simultaneously respectful and swollen with a childish pride. It's our friend Sylvain's young mechanic: the one who accompanied us to Cairo, and has now been promoted to admiral of the expedition that is ready to take off—with a purpose that is unknown, but of which I sense the importance.

Leduc gives him his final instructions: "Everything's understood, isn't it, lad? Make straight for Italy, and go up as far as Rome—first stage—tomorrow evening. Leave one helicopter and enough people—a gang of shaggies and a white man, Schlemihl perhaps—to scrape the *solar* from the base-unit. Pay attention, now—no mistakes! Work by night and seal the cases! Then to the rendezvous, double quick. Detach one or two helicopters to clear out the last hordes, if there are any, from the nearest ports of embarkation. There are torpedo-boats at Brindisi and Genoa ready to repatriate the volunteers. You'll continue with the main body of the fleet. At Nice, there's another torpedo base-unit. You repeat the business with the *solar*. One helicopter and one crew. Ditto at Lyon, Paris, Antwerp, London. Ah! Mont Blanc...do as you like with that lot, but don't rush things; go gently to begin with, leave the heavy stuff for later. Tempt them as you pass by, but leave taking them—aboard your own machine, in their case—until you've cleared out France, Belgium and England—the ones in Edinburgh too, although I think they're already on their way..."

Our friends at Mont Blanc are alive! They're still holding out! What luck! We shall attempt to save them!

V. Calling for Volunteers

Fly straight to Mont Blanc—that's our first thought. But what good will it do? We need a plan of action first. And how can we keep them safe if we don't know exactly what danger our friends are facing? Our disincarnate condition, though conferring on us the levitational ability to displace ourselves at will, is not combined with lucid clairvoyance: the thoughts of the Martians remain closed to us unless they express them, and in order to be informed in a useful fashion of the young leader's intentions, we shall have to follow him.

As invisible guests—supernumeraries that will scarcely tire the engines—we take our place with Moreau and his general staff in cabin A of the flagship-helicopter, a powerful airbus with three sets of supportive rotor-blades and two twin hulls. At a word from the Great Leader—my Martianized body—Leduc blows on his whistle; the signal lights turn green, and all the engines of the air-fleet begin to purr. A second blast of the whistle—red light—and the twenty machines take off in a mathematically-precise formation.

At and altitude of 500 meters the immense Martian city seems to us to be fully illuminated by its millions of floodlights. With the flagship-helicopter at its head, the squadron, formed into a triangle like a flock of wild birds, veers around the illuminated Monument bearing the Shell—and we discover on the head of the artificial Magus, looking down from this height, a minuscule Magus of flesh and blood, lit up by a searchlight, who gives us his blessing, while a formidable acclamation rises up from the crowd assembled in the Grand Plaza of the Pyramids.

The lights of the Martian city decrease; we fly at full speed over the Nile Delta, where the evil activity of the invaders is revealed by the numerous lights of electric convoys filing along the railway and transport helicopters bringing their cargoes of recruits. We fly over the resuscitated port of Alexandria and out over the Mediterranean, whose vague phosphorescence seems to reflect the starry night.

In cabin A, having given his orders, young Moreau sits down at his table and pours champagne for his general staff. Isaac Schlemihl is there, having es-caped the massacres by some prodigy, with his wife Rachel, who is similarly wearing the brick red flying suit of the Martian pilots. Nazir Bey is there, still wearing his fez. But they and the three others—there are seven in all, counting Moreau—are no longer human, save in appearance. Their savage Martian souls are hypnotically fixed on their abominable duty; the hope to "convert" the re-mainder of true humankind, to make them willing or unwilling recruits to "Mars & Co." as they say. For they all speak French, the international language after the catastrophe, as before, although they speak it with an atrocious new accent, hoarse and jerky, which elides vowels and seems to multiply the consonants, cutting through them like blades through bucklers.

It is August 15, apparently. Five weeks have gone by: a mere five weeks, since the Cairo Shell and the arrival of the Magi! What sinister progress they have made in that brief interval! And the Martians of the general staff, as they all empty their champagne glasses, rejoice in the work accomplished. The entire population of Africa, Asia and Europe, with only a few exceptions, has gone to Cairo: 123,000 Terrans and 210,000 apes, or "shaggies," have fallen into the power of Martian souls and have passed through the Solenoids of Reincarnation!

But here are a few frustrations. Nazir Bey regrets that the Perfume's zone of influence could not be further extended. It has reached its maximum development and its limits are approximately those of the Old World: a circle, henceforth unextendable, traced around the Magi. And the Magi, for occult reasons, refuse to displace themselves on Earth. Moreau criticizes them bitterly, and the entire general staff joins in the chorus, except for Nazir Bey, who comes to their defense.

Poor Magi! They are sufficiently preoccupied in directing the mysterious and religious aspects of the enterprise! If only they were all still alive, the only Martians to have reached Earth integrated in body and soul—but death has already cruelly thinned out their sacred phalanx; of the 21 occupants of the Shell, nine have been carried off by microbial maladies unknown on Mars. Have the survivors acclimatized, or will they face further perils in their turn? Will the dignity of Magi, the origin of which is lost in the night of time, and which has been perpetuated through innumerable generations in the Martian caste privileged—miraculously, they claim—by the provision of wings and cephalic antennas, pass into profane hands. Will it be so far reduced that the successor to the Sovereign Pontiff Egregore XII,[34] the mystical instigator of the Expedition will be a vulgar Terromartian?

And these "vulgar Terromartians" who surround us agonize over that thorny question with all the passion of their true Martian souls. There are some who scarcely dare discuss it, waiting until Nazir Bey, a fervent and exclusive partisan of the Magi, has gone to make a round of the engine-room and the crew stations. Even then, voices are lowered, as if in dread that spies might hear. The young admiral, Schlemihl, Rachel and their associates are all partisans of Leduc, whose popularity is growing among the aviators and the shaggies.

The majority of their allusions escape us, to tell the truth, but one thing is clear: that Leduc, the chief technician of the Martian endeavor, disapproves of the Magi, who want to limit the Great Work to a pure and simple exodus to Venus. Probably for reasons of personal ambition, and perhaps also by virtue of

---

[34] An egregore is a sort of psychic vampire feeding on the "vital energies" of others; the term was popularized in France by Jean Lorrain's story "L'Egrégore" (1887; tr. as "The Egregore").

forceful mechanist convictions, he supports a project that is bringing together all the dissidents, extremists more Martian than the Magi.

What is this project? A mystery. Moreau contents himself with making a discreet allusion to it, but that is enough to electrify the entire table, which rises in tumult. Glasses are clinked, and everyone drinks enthusiastically: "To the Grand Central Tunnel! To the Atlantic Ocean!"

An absurd, crazy toast! But the hideous and hateful laughter that greets it tells us that it embodies a frightful menace for the Last Men.

And that's not all. Leduc openly extols persecution, while the Magi favor the exclusive use—already too efficacious!—of the seductive Perfume. If the Technical Director gave seemingly benign orders just now, it's because he was giving them in the presence of his superior, the Great Leader, who is on the side of the Magi...

The Last Men! They are tracked down everywhere; vile trickery is employed to bring their resistance to an end—for not everyone surrenders meekly to the call of the Perfume.

Little by little, in the course of that night and the following day, spent on board the admiral's helicopter during the Mediterranean crossing, the fate of our Terran brothers is revealed by the cynical conversation of these beings, who inspire an invincible horror in us. The force of habit makes us see these Terromartians as renegades against humankind, although their souls alone are culpable and their bodies, like ours, are unconscious and unfortunate captives.

It can be assumed that the Hordes of the Old World—all that debris of people barbarized by the great panic sparked by the Torpedoes and the penetrative Shells, and by the subsequent contagion of animal instincts; vague nomadic hosts spreading death and devastation in their wake while maddened themselves and decimated daily by hunger, cold, heat, epidemics, ferocious beasts and fights between rival tribes; errant specimens of inferior humanity whose psychic degradation made them a ready-made prey for the Martian souls—have already been "recovered." Most of them have reached Cairo; others are en route from the extremities of Asia, Africa and Europe, making the pilgrimage in isolation or in caravans joined together by a snowball effect.

The Martian souls of all these *possessed* individuals are rejoicing in their new bodies, and their prayers celebrate the Mecca in which they are waiting, the Hall of definitive Reincarnation, and the prospect of laboring on the Great Work in company with their brothers. The latter are waiting for them impatiently; special missions are sent to meet them in autocars and airbuses, which renew their food supplies, bring them news of the Martian triumph, encourage them and take aboard the weakest, who cannot finish the journey on foot, or those in whom a more persistent Terran soul is pursuing its just claims and threatening to displace its dispossessor before the irrevocable consecration of the solenoid...

It is true that this kind of "repossession," when successful, is of little benefit to the poor human, for his Terromartian companions, hasten to murder him or to deliver him securely bound into the hands of the "missionaries"—and, once transported to Mars Central, the hypnotic maneuvers of the Magi quickly put paid to the recalcitrant.

There is an entire hemisphere, however, into which the Perfume has not yet penetrated. America and Oceania still contain free Hordes, and the question of what action to take against them is one of the causes of division between the Magi's party and Leduc's. Lacking the support of the Perfume's influence, the Martian souls have only won isolated victories on those continents. Jealous of their prerogatives, the Magi insist that total conquest must be accomplished by the extension—increasingly problematic—of the Perfume. Leduc, for his part, advocates emptying the Americas by means of great hunting-expeditions, which would extend when necessary into the South Seas. On his own authority, he has already sent out several expeditions, which have carried out fruitful and facile sweeps. The Pacific islanders, in particular, succumb to Martianization without resistance, and look hopefully to the horizon from their individual islets for the helicopter or torpedo-boat that will "repatriate" them.

As for the civilized stations, uniquely capable of ensuring the salvation of humankind, I am grief-stricken to learn that almost all of them have fallen.

The Boers of Cape Town, already weakened by the Zulus who destroyed their TSF station in January, were the first to share the fate of the scientists and citizens of Cairo—but they were taken by surprise, and the other stations would have been able to hold out longer had it not been for a Machiavellian ruse which everyone credited to Leduc. The Hertzian waves emitted by the Magi since the arrival of the Shell had sabotaged the TSF appeals sent out by Nazir Bey. The other stations were, in consequence, ignorant of the true nature of the Martian threat. It was only too easy to send them an apocryphal version of events and to invite them, under the pretext of the common utility of humankind, to come together in Cairo with weapons and equipment!

Two stations fell into this trap with an incomprehensible naivety. The Japanese of Nagasaki, indefatigable explorers, came in haste, 2000 of them in a fleet of 300 helicopters. Dazed by the influence of the Perfume, and seduced by the grandiose spectacle of the Martian colony—which they mistook for the new capital of civilized humanity!—they undertook a tour of the workshops without any suspicion. They were all disarmed in the course of the tour and sent to the solenoids.

An analogous adventure was reserved for the men from Simla, who arrived in an imposing column of motor lorries escorted by armored cars—but their bellicose character became manifest at the last moment and it was necessary to crush them with the jets of the Martian blasters.

The observatories at Mount Wilson and Gaurisankar, being more prudent, and only having a few helicopters at their disposal, each sent a dozen astronomers on reconnaissance, who returned to them possessed by Martian souls, with an airbus escort, in order to inveigle the remainder with appropriate lies. Mont

Wilson was entirely taken in, but a few suspicious scientists at Gaurisankar, without realizing the abominable truth, refused to leave the observatory and were massacred beside their telescopes by the exasperated neo-Martians.

I could not quite grasp, amid the broad jokes, threats and boasts that were exchanged around he general staff's table, the exact fate of the Edinburgh station. I think that an appeal has been made to the philosophical enlightenment of its members, and that they have regretfully left their beloved university to go to a port of embarkation, from which they are being transferred to Cairo. Is there still time to disabuse them?

The Mont Blanc colony itself is holding firm to its summit, which the magnetic vibrations of the Perfume do not reach. Around the Abbé Romeux are grouped our friends, artists and scientists, whose numbers have not yet been educed by any defections. They might be saved! While listening to the horrible threats proffered by the young admiral, if they will not comply with his injunctions to go to Cairo, we are searching for a means of saving them. No definite plan of action has yet been decided—against them by Moreau, or in their favor by us—when our air-fleet reaches its first stopping-point, in the evening, in the ruins of Rome.

VI. During the Salvage of the "Solar"

This is where we are leaving the first crew, intended to salvage the *solar*.

Although the word has cropped up frequently in the last 24 hours in the conversations of the general staff, the reference still remains mysterious. I have gone over my knowledge of chemistry, reciting the names of the elements, searching among the inorganic and organic compounds, but I do not know what it is. I understand that it is part of the casing of the base-units of Martian torpedoes, from which it must be recovered with care, for it seems to be indispensable to the proper functioning of the shells under construction. Its rarity is even inspiring grave concern, for the few tons that have so far been recovered are insufficient, and the Terromartian factories are not producing any yet.

The Supreme Council has put the word about that this is a mere matter of temporary technical difficulties, but Leduc's partisans hold the Magi responsible for the difficulty. It must, in fact, be due to the lack of a certain substance that is common on Mars but for which they have searched the soil and superficial rock-strata of our planet in vain. Leduc affirms that it must be contained in the world's core, and that his famous Central Tunnel will encounter deposits of it in its course. By way of objection, the Magi point to the negative results in that regard produced by the well furnishing liquid iron—but that drilling operation, to a depth of 31,200 meters, was deliberately directed towards one of he "igneous pockets" situated relatively close to the surface, of which a rapidly-increasing "geothermic cline" previously gave evidence of the proximity of the "central fire." The latter is, in reality, situated at a much lower depth, and, by way of selecting an appropriate point of attack, the famous Central Tunnel will be extended to at least 1000 kilometers!

Leduc's partisans insinuate that it will require the disappearance of all the Magi to bring about the project's triumph...

Is this some obscure sympathy towards the Great Leader incarnate in my body? Is it a presentiment of disastrous results for humankind, which the execution of the Tunnel will bring about? It seems to me that, given a choice, I would prefer the Magi to triumph...

For the moment, though, the actual salvage-operation might perhaps shed some light on this enigmatic *solar*.

Guided by cold floodlights, the body of the fleet is set down on the aerodrome of the Villa Borghese—of whose marvelous shady woods only a few branchless pine-trunks provide a reminder—and its fuel tanks are re-filled. Moreau profits from the pause to get the salvage work under way. The base-unit of the Torpedo, on which the operation must be carried out under cover of darkness—in accordance with Leduc's strict orders—is close at hand, in what used to be the Gardens of the Pincio. The flagship-helicopter leads a bulky airbus there, which disembarks a detachment of shaggies and the appropriate machinery.

In ten minutes, the ape mechanics, along with lights and excavators, have deployed around the base-unit, and the work commences, watched by Moreau and Schlemihl.

I understand why this cladding of *solar* escaped the investigations of Terran scientists! Carried out in haste, amid the madness of the catastrophe, usually under the threat of looters of radium and platinum, the official researches of the government employees were directed to the *interior* of the units. This one—and all the others were similar—is embedded at least 20 meters deep at the bottom of a crater created by the shock of the torpedo falling from intersidereal space. It was thought to be an inverted gas-jar. Even the looters never once thought of exploring the external surface, which is the only thing with which our gang of shaggies concern themselves. By means of the excavators—chromium-steel ploughshares and scoops that dig into the soil precipitately—a sort of large well is hollowed out beside the metallic wall of the cylinder. Into this well workmen go, equipped with scrapers and pneumatic suction-pumps, whose nozzles soon begin to disgorge streams of a granular substance the color of egg-yolk, which glistens with a bizarre brightness. Other shaggies collect it, pack it into aluminum cases whose lids are immediately welded shut; then they are stowed in the helicopter's hold.

The scene has something infernal about it. All this clandestine nocturnal activity to salvage the mysterious product reminds us of the necromancers of old collecting the herbs destined for their magic brews by moonlight. The same suspect and guilty atmosphere reigns in that narrow zone of white light, surrounded by the darkness of the night and the ruins of the Eternal City. The advanced technology that replaces the cabalistic sickle, and the methodical manner in which the operations are carried out, with the purr of the engines and the scraping of tools substituting for formularistic incantations, only serve to augment our sense of the tragedy and horror of these sinister rites—behind which we sense the will of the Magi, and whose objective must be some new scourge for humankind.

But we only witness the beginning of the salvage operation. As excavations around the periphery of the base-unit progress, the circular slot from which the workmen are removing the *solar* is braced at the other side, in order to keep the enormous weight of the cylinder wedged in place. Evidently, its metal could be recycled, but no consideration is given to that possibility because of the difficulties of transport, and that fruit of the Martian labor will be abandoned to the vicissitudes of the climate; only the precious *solar*, cases of which are piling up in the helicopter's hold, is destined for the factories of Cairo.

It is the overseer Schlemihl who will supervise the operation for several hours until morning—for it is extremely important that the Sun's rays to not catch the shaggies at work. Moreau insists on that once again, darts a final

203

glance at the work in hectic progress and goes back to his helicopter. He rejoins the squadron, which has finished refilling its tanks, and gives the signal to get under way.

It is midnight. It will reach Mont Blanc at about 10 a.m. The stopover in Nice will be brief; there is no need to refuel there, merely to deposit a second gang of shaggies. They will not be idle while waiting for nightfall in order to proceed with the salvage operation in the dark, for the base-unit at Nice is sunk in the bed of the Paillon, which must first be diverted.

But we know now what Moreau's intentions are. He imagines that the majesty of his person and the number of his helicopters will intimidate Abbé Romeux and his companions. He will give them an ultimatum, if need be, giving them 24 hours to decide to accompany him, while he goes on, heading for Edinburgh. But he is counting primarily on his own oratorical talents…as are we, for the conceited young ass will not hesitate to make allusions to Martian power, and thus put our friends on their guard with regard to the fate that awaits them if they give in to his threats.

Yes, it is necessary that they see the young admiral, his helicopters and his Terromartians, including the shaggies—for that will horrify them, and help them to understand the information that we shall attempt to communicate to them…

And, this time using the full scope of our levitational capability, we concentrate all our will power…

VII. The Last Men

Mont Blanc: silhouetted in ink against the serene and icy night, the Observatory...

What a contrast with the ostentatious illumination of the cold light and the frenzied activity of Mars Central! The last refuge of Terran civilization seems to be dressed in mourning for humankind.

There is not a single lantern or sentinel on the terrace or at the entrance to the Bunkers. Everyone is asleep—or perhaps not...someone is awake under the cupola, where the motor that makes it turn in an opposite direction to the rotation of the Earth, maintaining the stars within the field of the large equatorial, is throbbing softly. We go in.

Vaguely lit by the minuscule lamp whose beam is concentrated on a table loaded with papers, Abbé Romeux, his eye to the ocular, is moving his fingers delicately over the levers and controls that surround the extremity of the gigantic tube. The threads of the micrometer are in place; everything is adjusted for observation...

A long minutes passes; the astronomer focuses on a shining planet—Jupiter!—which is visible up there, against a star-strewn background, through the oblong trapdoor opened in the dome. He leaves the ocular, consults the indicators on the gauges, and turns to the table to scribble a few notes.

He face is gaunt, his features wracked by insomnia and anxiety—but in his eyes, habituated to the spectacle of the infinite, the flame of intelligence shines more clearly than ever. Here is a man who will not repudiate civilization, and will not yield to threats or promises. Even if he were taken down to a lower altitude and plunged into the magical atmosphere of the Perfume, I doubt that a Martian soul would be powerful enough to subjugate this man.

It is obviously him that we must warn, in preference to any other. Alas, though, he is not asleep; his fully conscious and active mind will reject my suggestions as easily as it is repelling the attempts of the Martian souls that are floating sadly around him...

The advice of the Venusian Master inspires me at this critical moment; let us leave the Abbé, who will be up all night, and search among the sleepers in the Bunkers.

A nostalgic emotion takes hold of us in these familiar vaults. Here is the great library, empty now, where we spent so many peaceful evenings chatting with our friends and discussing the situation—which appeared quite dark and desperate then, but was calm and idyllic by comparison with the present, and, above all, the future that is reserved for us!

Here are the sleeping-quarters, divided into apartments—the fourth on the right as ours! Who is sleeping there now? Bah! Doctor Goulliard from Lille. We supposed that he had died ten months ago; he must have arrived after our departure—but how? To the left there are academics from Italy and Switzerland, on this side the escapees from Amiens and Saint-Valery, the artists…the painter Nibot…hold on! Nibot? Why not? He has the gift of clearly remembering his dreams, which are vivid and colorful, worthy of a picturesque imagination. A good character too, esteemed by everyone. What he says will be taken seriously.

It's him, isn't it, Master? He's the one to whom you're instructing me to address myself?

He is sleeping peacefully, lying on his left side, in the gleam of a night-light. By virtue of a quasi-radioscopic lucidity, I can see the pineal gland within his skull, half-hidden between the cerebral hemispheres, which lie pale and flac-cid…

I brush it with a fluidic touch. It quivers and swells—but the sleeper does not wake up. He releases a sigh and stammers my name. O joy! He perceives my presence! Communication is established!

Mentally, I call out: "Nibot!"—and I see, by the mime displayed in his features, that he is avidly following the story of my adventures, and what I am telling him about the Terromartians.

"The swine will come, Nibot, my friend, in human guise—in a few hours. Warn the Abbé. No overt refusal. Ask for time to think. Better still—let them think that you will make a start by going to Genoa by helicopter. That might put them off the scent. In any event, you will have 24 hours, at least. Don't hesi-tate—flight is necessary, immediate flight outside Europe. The Magi's influence stops at the Atlantic. Once at sea, you will be safe—but until then, and as soon as you have left high altitude to penetrate the zone of the Perfume, you must not go to sleep, whatever you do! Engrave that in your memory, Nibot! Whoever falls asleep is lost, for sleep will deliver him to the Martian souls, and he will leave you immediately to rejoin his fellows. Stay awake, at any cost! Adieu…"

His forehead covered in sweat, Nibot stirs himself with a convulsive effort. He releases a cry of anguish, awakes with a start, sits up, and I see his eyes fix themselves upon me fearfully. For an instant, the dream is prolonged in reality, the mysterious lucidity of the hypnotic state allowing him to glimpse our astral form, whose dissolution is completed by a fuller awakening…

He rubs his eyes, turns a commutator, lighting up the room, and leaps out of bed, murmuring: "The Abbé…provided that he's still up…and that he doesn't think I'm rambling! That was a premonitory dream of the first order! My God! I'm still trembling." While pulling on his shoes he speaks at hazard into the room: "Thanks, Rudeaux!"

Perfect! There's no need for us to stay here, for the moment. The imminent arrival of young Moreau and his squadron will force the Abbé to make his deci-sion. For the moment, our duty calls us to the last of our civilized brothers who might be saved—in Edinburgh!

Edinburgh. At dawn, beside the Firth of Forth—whose green waters, devoid of any ships, extend to the sea—the old black city extends the ranks of its tall houses beneath the illusory safeguard of Castle Hill. Except for the new quarters in the west, which have been ravaged by fire, the ancient capital is still standing; this desert of houses, looted but apparently intact, and these streets and squares, from which not a flagstone is missing, give an impression of disaster more overwhelming that all the heaps of ruins we have already seen. It is as if human life has retreated from the planet...

But we have better things to do than glean picturesque impressions or philosophize as to the destiny of civilization. One of the last refuges exists within the city's perimeter. The University...

We eventually locate it, after some searching. Surrounded by parks and tennis-courts, its vast Gothic buildings ought to enclose the elite of the United Kingdom: a few 100 professors and scientists. But no! No one! It's entirely deserted and abandoned. We have arrived too late! They have already set out, on the road to perdition.

The general staff of the airborne squadron reckoned on "collecting" them, though. They cannot be far away; they have no helicopters—but as we explore the city's bounds, we see the daylight broadening, which is reducing our chances of intervention by the minute...

Above the docks, a brand new British flag is fluttering in the westerly breeze. A man comes out of the offices of Norddeutscher Lloyd, stretching his arms, then another. They are dressed in frock-coats and top hats, evidently academics. The fatter of the two gesticulates and points to the south, prompting his companion to scan the marine horizon of the Forth with the aid of a telescope. What are they waiting for?

As the other members of the colony emerge on to the quay, the sinister truth is revealed. The feverish gazes in those emaciated faces, the quivering hatred that agitates those bodies, the harsh and jerky accents of those voices...all-too-familiar symptoms, alas! There is no longer anyone here but Terromartians hoping for the arrival of their fellows. Hunger has sealed their fate. In order to distance them from the university, where they were offering too much resistance to the souls' assaults, a perfidious radio message told them that succulent foodstuffs were on the way—roast beef, pickles, sponge pudding, rhubarb tart—and the unfortunates came down to take delivery of them on the quay, where one night of somnolence in the atmosphere of the Perfume, attenuated though it is, has got the better of them.

Pity overwhelms us at this sight—pity mingled with horror; a complex sentiment strongly analogous to that awakened by the physical or moral decline of a relative. But the mix also contains a strong dose of hatred towards the Martians and the frustration of not having been able to deprive them of this prey...

Come on! It's done! The colony of Last Men that we are attempting to bring together will have to do without the academics of the United Kingdom; it

207

will have to do without those specimens of human wisdom that comprise dialecticians and theological hair-splitters!

Considering the Edinburgh episode closed, having cost us half a day, let us leave the banks of the Forth to return the summit of Mont Blanc.

VIII. The Flight to the Antipodes

The entire colony is assembled on the terrace of the Observatory, in broad daylight. Everyone is arguing animatedly, and fists are being brandished at the North-Western horizon, over which the Martian squadron has just vanished.

In truth, young Moreau had conducted himself marvelously. I could not have wished for better. He and his colleagues of the general, staff have behaved with perfect arrogance. Helmets on their heads and blaster in their fists, they have disembarked from the flagship-helicopter as if they were entering a conquered country, while the other seventeen helicopters hovered above the Observatory, ready to open fire on it. They have summoned the Abbé to take passage for their shore with his companions, to collaborate in works of public utility. They might just as well have made allusion to the true objective of that voyage and its terminus at the solenoid!

But the Abbé had had time to reflect on the painter's dream. He met the threat and imprecations of the Martians with the calm and dignified request for a delay of twenty-four hours to make his preparations—and the young admiral, who had expected overt resistance, had had to grant it to them. He had departed after announcing that the colony would be embarked on the following day, at the same time, of its own accord or by force.

Almost everyone can see the situation in its true light. Only a tiny minority of dyed-in-the-wool positivists are shrugging their shoulders and arguing against the evidence. Moreau has been recognized by several of his former comrades. The symptomatic appearance of the Terromartians has added the clearest possible confirmation to Nibot's story. The shaggies, in particular, excited horror, and these abject creatures appear to the Terrans to be a living example of the fate that the Martian souls had in store for them.

The Abbé's harangue concludes in favor of immediate flight. Unanimously, save for five votes, the abandonment of the station is agreed. No one is to carry any more than is strictly necessary. It is a heart-breaking business for everyone, but a matter of sacred duty to themselves and Humankind.

The Abbé goes back into his cupola one last time, embracing with a long glance the telescopes, spectroscopes and all the other instruments that have brought him the noblest joy of all. He wipes away a tear after caressing the ocular of the equatorial, faithful companion of his night-watches; then, resolutely, he chooses a few of the most precious papers from the heap of his manuscripts, slips them into his portfolio and goes out on to the terrace.

The 69 inhabitants of the Bunkers are there, ready to consummate the sacrifice. The women are in masculine clothing; everyone is wearing an overcoat and carrying an overnight bag, the only authorized item of luggage. For the last time, they take their places in the carriages of the funicular railway; for the last time they glance at the summit where they have lived for such a long time. Sobs mingle with the tinkle of bells as the convoy moves off, following the steep route that descends amid the snows and the glaciers to the inferior station of Chamonix.

An unforeseen hitch! The mechanics, the people who tend to the turbines and the manufacture of the Nutriment—20 people in all—immediately refuse to take part in the exodus. They have only seen Moreau's squadron from afar, and they are treating the Martian danger as a pure phantasmagoria. They are talking about resisting to the death and hiding in the depths of the Bunkers. The Abbé's authority and the fugitives' pleas have not convinced them all. A dozen are holding out; as time is pressing, the rest have to resign themselves to leaving them behind.

The defection of the aviators, two months ago, deprived the colony of its air-fleet: a cruel absence, in the present circumstances, in which speed is more important than anything else. How long will it take for these three ancient Alpine cars, into which everyone has piled, to make a journey from here to Bordeaux? It's a matter of life and death, for the magnetic effluvia of the Perfume will become manifest on the other side of Sallanches, and everyone has to understand that there must be no question of going to sleep before leaving the dangerous zone.

Everything goes well at first. The roads, left to their own devices for two years, are only slightly pitted here and there, but no one is worrying about a few bumps. The countryside goes by, in a solitude and absolute silence that gives it a prodigious majesty of history equal to that of the cities. Better than in their familiar refuge, floating above the clouds, the fugitives perceive that the reign of humankind has suffered a tragic and perhaps permanent eclipse, and that they are, in any case, its last survivors. Rain begins to fall after Valence, marking a further contribution to their dark mood, but at least it has the fortunate effect of hiding them from the gaze of Martian aviators and erasing the wheel-marks on the road.

A difficult crossing of the Cévennes; several broken bridges force long detours. The delays become worrying. It is dark when they reach the forests of the Cantal. They take the risk of lighting torches; the glare attracts animals, whose eyes gleam by the side of the road: foxes, wild boar and wolves, which bark, growl and howl in the darkness. The women release cries of fright, but the Abbé chides them gently; they ought to be thankful that they are thus protected against drowsiness!

That is, indeed, the real danger—and about 3 a.m., when the mountains are finally conquered and the convoy descends into the valley of the Dordogne, on an unexpectedly well-preserved road, the fugitives are anxious that somnolence is overtaking them—will they succumb to the assaults of the souls so close to home? Once again, though, the Abbé saves the situation; he intones one of those new ballads, which once helped weary soldiers keep in step; everyone takes it up in chorus, and this simple stratagem is enough to reawaken the most torpid....

The songs succeed one another indefatigably, in the black night, then in the dawn, then in broad daylight: the *Montagnards*, the *Petit Navire*, the *Madelon*—and the brightly colored autocars—marked "Route des Alpes" and "Grande-Chartreuse"—seem once more to be carrying a cargo of joyful tourists. What tourists! The Last Men, dispossessed of their planet, in flight through the infinite solitude, under the threat of the Martian souls and the helicopters that might fall upon them at any moment!

Libourne. The rain has stopped. Beautiful summer sunlight revives hope in their hearts, in spite of the desolation it illuminates. They will soon escape aboard a fishing-boat; they will reach America, then the South Seas, Tahiti or Samoa, and it will require the Devil's own luck for the Martians...

Bordeaux. The half-destroyed city is no more than an ossuary in which the crows are busy. Along the Garonne, packs of ferocious dogs are completing the pillage of the storehouses and the crates, sacks and bales that lie here and there, eviscerated. There are precious few ships on the river, all in a piteous condition, but downstream of the Quai de Bacalan there is a basin with its floodgates closed and intact, where two lovely submersible liners—the *Argonaut* and the *Nautilus*—are floating placidly, the latter ready to set sail!

In 50 minutes, the crew is constituted; the mechanics have got the surface engines going and are charging the accumulators for an eventual dive. Abbé Romeux, at his captain's post, gives the order: "Half-speed forward!" The hull vibrates in sympathy with the propellers, and the vessel passes through the lock-gates.

"Slow the port engine...more rapidly...full speed ahead!"

And the Last Men, leaning their elbows on the slender guard-rails on the back of the monstrous metallic cetacean, watch the gentle slopes of the hills on the two coasts of the Gironde, with their deserted vineyards whose harvests will never be used, fade into the distance beneath the radiant Sun.

At noon—exactly 24 hours after the departure from Mont Blanc—the *Nautilus* passes the Tour de Cordouan. The waves of harmful Perfume have ceased to be perceptible, and everyone is intoxicating themselves breathing the healthy and revivifying sea-breeze. Those most cruelly tormented by insomnia can grant themselves a reparative nap without fear, between the fine sheets of the luxury cabins.

For two days, we accompany the submersible, whose sharp nose-cone cleaves the green Atlantic swell indefatigably. Not a single alert has forced her to dive. There is not a Martian helicopter in view. The escape plan that I have suggested to Nibot is adopted; they are going to head for Panama, go through the canal and continue into the Pacific, with Tahiti as their destination—where the Martians might perhaps allow the colony of Last Men to live in peace.

But time exists for the disincarnate soul—or, rather, its elongation, at the whim of desire and impatience, which are submissive to even more fluctuations than those of vulgar mortals, whose organism tempers such impulses like a sort of unconscious regulator. The disincarnate soul seizes things by intuition, immediately—schematically, so to speak—while vulgar perception, before arriving at intimate consciousness, filters them through the inordinately complex network of nerves and cerebral connections making up the mundane sensorium, whose secondary vibrations are subject to a halo of harmonious resonances. For us, as pure spectators, the *Nautilus*'s crossing does not have the attraction of the thousand petty incidents of quotidian life, and its slowness and monotony exasperate us, haunted as we are with the obsessive idea that we have other duties to accomplish.

The works are making giant strides in the distant Martian city, where the Great Leader and his female companion are directing operations, incarnate in our bodies. Without fully admitting the full extent of the egotistical interest that the hope of soon being reintegrated into those bodies offers us, we delude ourselves with the generous illusion that, once we are disguised as these important individuals, it will be easy for us to intervene in the sidereal drama that has pitted the Titans of Mars against the children of the Earth. So, carried away by this secret desire, we let the last custodians of human civilization continue their exodus, and we return to Mars Central.

IX. The Titans

The Titans are celebrating this evening. The thousands of floodlights and searchlights that provide the city's customary illumination are augmented by the fantastic light of a giant torch, a worthy appendage to the Monument of the Shell. It is a rigid jet of white fire that rises into the night: an incandescent jet, which gushes forth with a formidable roar and falls back as an artificial rain into a basin, in which a sea of molten metal ripples before subsiding to smoothness. And all the people of Mars gathered around—all those well-nourished people, sure of their strength—acclaim the magnificent result of the new drilling operation, sent at Leduc's instigation more deeply than the first into the "igneous pocket" of the planet's ferruginous core. It is extracting more cubic meters per hour than any oil-well of yesteryear. Up above, in a helicopter illuminated by the fiery jet, which is slowly circling the dazzling stream, a Magus—supported by two assistants, for he seems ready to expire—is bestowing his tremulous blessing on the inexhaustible fountain of iron, which springs forth and falls back amid unanimous exultation.

"Countless cylinders!" trumpets the loudspeaker that is amplifying the weak and quavering voice of the Magus.

"Cylinders! All the cylinders!" bellows the enthusiastic crowd.

"Which will enable the sacred people of Mars to take a new step in the cycle of existences, and bring them nearer the supreme and endless Glory that awaits them in the resplendent bosom of Our Father the Sun. So must it be!"

"So must it be! To Venus! The Sun! The Sun!" howl various factions of the crowd, delirious with mysticism.

The Benediction of the Fire is concluded. The blare of sirens instructs the crowd to disperse and return to work. Ah, tonight will be full of joy and fervor! The glorious ceremony has caused recent setbacks to be forgotten—for three more Magi have succumbed to terrestrial diseases in the last few days, and it is the less afflicted of the two survivors of the sacred caste who has just allowed himself to be seen; the other, the Sovereign Pontiff Egregore XII, whose grandeur retains him in the Palace of Reincarnation, is on his deathbed, already discussing his impending funeral rites.

But what does it matter, now, if the passing of the Magi cuts short the emission of the Perfume and makes the recruitment of "volunteers" more difficult? So much the worse for those errant souls which have not yet had the chance or the skill to equip themselves with a body. Ferocious opportunists, the privileged individuals of Mars Central content themselves with regretting, hypocritically, the fate of the Faithful Dead who will not be taken forward. The success of the enterprise is already assured for the currently-alive. The exodus will have taken place before the Earth's orbit brings it close enough to Jupiter again for the Thunderbolt to reiterate its effects.

The exodus will have taken place, for there are sufficient numbers to do the work, and an abundance of metal.

Metal! That was a crucial shortage, until the moment when the new jet of "central fire" spurted into the air. The first well, whose yield was feeble and exploitation precarious, merely demonstrated that rendering the native metal usable for casting cylinders only required a refinement operation. The shortage was important, for the most perfect techniques of Martian steel-making and the most powerful furnaces would have been incapable of producing the thousands of tons of steel that the molds of future interplanetary vehicles would absorb from mineral ores.

Some already full and cooling down in clouds of acrid vapor, several 100 already hollowed out and provided with their feeding-grooves, and others at every intermediate stage of completion from the simple tracing of the rounded outlines of their mighty girth, the molds occupy a sandy plain 30 kilometers square, on the edge of the desert. Beneath the white glare of cold light projectors, it is the most active workplace in the entire city. Not that large numbers of workmen are occupied there! Manpower is scarce, and cannot be wasted, even for the task that constitutes the end-product and final goal of all the efforts of "Mars & Co." One Terromartian overseer and five or six shaggies are sufficient to work the tapping process—or, rather, to maintain surveillance over it, for the machines, powered by cables as thick as an arm, seem to be endowed with their own intelligence, such is the precision and regularity with which their seemingly-awkward and malformed mammoth limbs are functioning.

Borne on a circular base some five meters in diameter, solidly braced by eight concrete feet, a dozen ploughshares attack their individual sectors of the mold. The mold is hollowed out in a groove 60 centimeters wide, in sand that is hurled out of thick tubes to form artificial hills. A rudimentary lining, made of curved slabs of crystal, constitutes the rim of a sort of gigantic well. Lower down, to prevent the walls and the "soul" from crumbling as the ploughshares advance, the entire pit is filled with water, which is frozen by a network of tubes through with a powerful refrigerant circulates. The mold of sand, hollowed out with astonishing ease, is thus sustained like a block, until the moment when it is almost instantaneously filled by molten metal.[35]

---

[35] What Varlet is describing is a large-scale robotic production-line version of the "lost wax" method of bronze-casting used by sculptors, in which a desired shape is sustained in loose sand by a replica of the statue carved in wax, which is evaporated almost instantaneously when the molten metal is poured in, with no loss of form. As he goes on to explain, the "soul" (âme in French) is the sand the fills up the hollow structure that will be evaporated, thus forming the interior cavity of the bronze statuette—or, in this case, the steel spaceship.

Twenty of these machines are operating at the same time, in a line, and they have no sooner quit their row of molds than the cataracts of molten metal pour into them. Further away, the finished projectiles are artificially cooled. All the phases of the process thus proceed in sequence, so efficiently that, on the edge of the plain, other machines are already occupied in extracting the "soul" of sand that shapes the interior cavity of each cylinder.

The most advanced are being provided with their terminal nose-cones, and then being internally fitted-out. The wall of sand that encloses each shell is swept away, forming a sort of ditch in the middle of which it stands up, isolated, like the spike of some monstrous caltrop. Then the ditch is carefully shaped and its circular bank, which forms an angle of about 45 degrees with the horizontal, is decked out with silvered mirrors, as if to make the Sun's rays converge upon the shell at the highest point...

What is the significance of this curious arrangement? Where are the lifting and steering apparatus intended to draw these projectiles, 100 meters long and five in diameter, from their holes? Where are the wagons to receive them, the railways to transport them to the mouths of giant artillery-pieces? Where are the cannons themselves? There is no trace of them to be seen, or of the factories for manufacturing their explosives!

In that case, it cannot be the ballistic pressure of millions of cubic meters gas developed by the deflagration of explosive substances that will send these hundreds of shells hurtling into intersidereal space. The Martians must, therefore, have a means unknown to terrestrial science of lifting them off the ground to which their monstrous weight appears to anchor them. That is theoretically possible—but in that case, one ought to be able to see the future engines of that fantastic propulsion being built somewhere: giant catapults, I suppose; vast wheels whose accelerated rotation would generate the necessary millions of kilogram-meters to release shells tangentially from their periphery, when detached at the right moment, like a slingshot. Such playthings cannot be improvised in a matter of hours; they would be under construction, as would the motors designed to turn them—and they would need so many! They would need ten, or 20, and a factory of that sort would be clearly visible in the landscape visible from the summit of the Monument!

The *solar*? Yes, that enigmatic product appears to be necessary to the departure of the shells, and its name recurs frequently in the conversations of crews returning from work.

To begin with, though, the Terromartians' talk seems depressingly monotonous, whether they favor the Magi or Leduc. They merely repeat, in almost exactly the same words, the news broadcast every three hours by the official phonographs of the factories and phalansteries; according to these news broadcasts, the fabrication of *solar* is now guaranteed. The seasoning of political comment added by the "young-Martians" or "old-Martians" often escapes us, proffered as it is in a sour and harsh idiom in which we have a great deal of difficulty recognizing the ancient universal language, French, which is metamorphosing gradually and developing, among the managerial class and the shaggies, into two new and distinct dialects.

Besides, the problem of the shells' launch-mechanism cannot retain us indefinitely. If we are to recover our bodies in due course, and assume the personalities of the Great Leader and his female companion, it is necessary for us to study the population of the Martian city.

It differs from vulgar humankind much les than we thought at first. The ugliness of the common man, the ferocity of his appetites, the immensity of his stupidity, the obstinacy of his prejudices, are reproduced, multiplied tenfold, in the Terromartian, who does not correct that odious side in any instance by the sense of justice and eternity of which certain representatives of our species give evidence. And their physiognomies betray that absence at the first glance; the features of ex-Terrans are remodeled to some degree by the invading souls; they have forgotten how to smile, no longer knowing anything but bestial laughter, and, whether their appearance is human or simian, Martian faces can no longer express any but animal passions or the hideous ecstasy of their coarse mysticism.

I do not know whether the Magi possess some rudiments of a superior wisdom. No hint of that esoteric doctrine extends beyond the boundaries of their caste; only information adapted to their brutal egotism is transmitted to the common people. For the Martians, God is not a Universal Intelligence to be worshipped in a faithful and disinterested fashion. Their God is the vague master of the Sun, or rather the Sun itself, the final paradise of their successive existences. As for their faith in the immortality of the soul, that Vision, which human genius has clad in such noble forms, is no more than their obstinate passion to live, live, live, again and forever, in spite of death and beyond life. Their spiritualism is devoid of all nobility, and if they aspire to "salvation" it is not to affirm the reign of the spirit within the universe, but entirely to prolong the base enjoyments of their personal and collective egotism. Any means is considered appropriate, if they believe it capable of ensuring their "salvation," and the present enterprise, which has made Mars Central into a mesmerized formicary, clearly demonstrates that they do not hesitate even at criminality.

O wise people of Jupiter! Sublime paladins of truth and justice! How scornful you must be of these vile Titans, uncrushed by your Thunderbolt, and how generously you must hate them! What horror, what disgust, what revulsion must be inspired in you, if you can follow, with the aid of your televisors, not only the frightful ravages that they have wrought upon the Earth, and their preparations for aggression against unfortunate Venus, but every one of their actions, extending to the most banal of their gestures!

Even their nourishment symbolizes the grossness of their appetites. The Jovian Nutriment, of which they know the formula, might have been a precious resource in their situation. But no—rather than benefit from such economy of material provision and digestive labor, they prefer to cram their carnivorous stomachs!

An entire fleet of helicopters armed for hunting is occupied daily in collecting game—which has multiplied in a surprising manner since Humankind's dominion over the planet has come to an end. Every evening, cadavers are disembarked by the ton, immediately butchered by machines and deposited in refrigerated storehouses. They are of every sort, for everything is good eating for these gross Terromartians: elephants, giraffes, hippopotamuses, lions, gazelles, rhinoceroses, donkeys, zebras, jackals, hyenas, goats, sheep, camels, water-buffaloes—all the mammals in creation. Crocodiles are not disdained, nor boa constrictors; much smaller animals still make a notable contribution: cats, guinea-pigs, porcupines, jerboas, chameleons, lizards, rats, and even vipers! And the Magi have brought a sort of pink-haired dog in their shell, which multiplies with incredible rapidity, and whose fatter specimens are reserved for the leaders' table—as is another vile delicacy: fried scorpion. Only one animal, I believe, is spared by these unscrupulous guzzlers: the bat, because of the affinity of its appearance with that of the Magi.

As for beverages, the cellars of Rheims and Epernay, and the storehouses of Bordeaux, Béziers and Lunel, which the Hordes were unable to empty completely, are routinely plundered by the reprovisioning airbuses, so that tides of champagne, Médoc and all the fuller-bodied wines of the South wash down the gargantuan stews served in the Martian refectories.

Once, suppressing our nausea, we determined to watch a meal all the way to the end, and the spectacle of the cynical orgy that succeeded it was enough to make the most dedicated naturist blush.

Two months of such a regime, in the hot climate of Cairo, would be sufficient to ruin the most robust constitution. But the precautions taken against the heat at Mars Central rendered any hope of that sort vain, and permitted these lunatics to devote themselves to their debaucheries with impunity. All the places in the city—habitations, workshops, even hangars—were provided with cold radiators, which maintained the most favorable temperature for the conservation of the precious health of our invaders!

X. In the Great Leader's Skin

We have thus familiarized ourselves with the general aspects of Martian life, but before attempting the struggle that ought to put us in possession of our bodies, we must still study the Great Leader and his female companion; and if we want to play our roles well—to put ourselves in their skin—that study must be long and attentive. A week, if necessary, a fortnight, a month...

O fine resolutions of wisdom! O fragility, not of the flesh but of the human soul!

In the Palace of red glass, the private office of the Great Leader: opaline walls reflecting the harsh light; telephones, the horns of loudspeakers and the screens of periscopes; detailed maps of Mars Central and the plain of Cylinders, the latter numbered; a vast terrestrial planisphere, where miniature helicopters are moved telemechanically to replicate the progress of machines on missions; dials, commutators, bells, instruments of every sort...

The thief of my body, the Great Leader R'rdô [36] himself, is sitting at his work-desk, smoking a cigarette, gesturing with his little finger as I habitually do, frowning as he runs his eyes over a report.

It was Moreau's account of his adventure at Mont Blanc, where he expected, on his return from Edinburgh, to find the colony ready to embark with him. Instead of that, the Observatory bristling with machine-guns, the squadron greeted with continuous fire. One helicopter disabled, falling 200 meters and breaking up, along with its crew. A battle; the Observatory, bunkers and occupants pulverized by explosive charges...

Poor obstinate men of Chamonix! But their mad resistance has given rise to an error that is the salvation of the Last Men! That upstart Moreau imagines that he has destroyed the entire colony, and has no suspicion that Abbé Romeux and his 71 companions are, by now, beyond Panama. R'rdô naturally shares this illusion, and is enraged by such an inept way of conduction operations. I would never have believed that my vocal cords were capable of emitting the vituperations that he addresses, by telephone, to the Technical Director.

"I have you to thank for this, damn it, Leduc, for entrusting a mission of such importance to a mere errand-boy. It's your fault that brains like those of Romeux and the others at Mont Blanc have been destroyed instead of serving

---

[36] "R'rdô" is presumably a phonetic rendering of "Rudeaux" pronounced in a Martian accent. It is hard to understand why the Terromartians would retain their host bodies' names, even if one accepts that they find it convenient to speak French because that is the language to which their new brains are habituated. Their own names are, apparently, easy to render into human phonetics, as evidenced by the names of the last surviving Magi.

the Reincarnation! We won't find any more of that quality…when we're most in need of them!"

The situation between the two leaders is evidently tense. The altercation would go on, but the sound of a second telephone cuts it short, R'rdô puts it to his ear, starts and demands a repetition: "Hello? What? It's the Sovereign Pontiff who's dead?"

And he hangs up, murmuring: "That's all we need!" But the sight of a little wooden box on the table reassures him slightly. He opens it and examines its contents: a granular substance, the color of egg-yolk, which sparkles with a vaguely metallic sheen.

He presses a button. His companion comes in—his companion, in the stolen body of my beloved!

Like all the women of Mars Central—the simian females go naked—she wears masculine costume: a brick-red flying-suit with an overseer's cape and bicorn helmet. Nevertheless, our doubles are all too evidently husband and wife—they shake hands effusively, and the desire to be reintegrated into our bodies is sharpened by an avid jealousy.

"News, my dear!" R'rdô says, laconically. "Egregore XII is deceased, but"—he points to the box—"we've begun to manufacture *solar*, at last. The indispensable *geocoronium* has been recovered from the upper atmosphere."

A good Martian lady and loyal spouse (horror!), she throws her arms around the Great Leader's neck and cries: "That's adequate compensation for the old fellow's death! That brute Leduc will have to renounce his stupid tunnel project."

"Oh, his partisans no longer need a pretext; they still support him. With the last Magus gone, his ambition will have no bounds. He'll organize man-hunts to replace the Perfume. Loss of time, waste of effort…but who will oppose him henceforth?"

"You! You alone, among all the Terromartians, are qualified to succeed the Pontiff, in the absence of a true hereditary Magus. The majority of the leaders will support you. You have only to desire it, and within a month you'll be the sacred Emperor of the Martians!"

"And you the Empress!"

Eyes shining, face to face, they hold one another by the hands, breathlessly. In spite of ourselves, in spite of the hatred and the jealousy, the monstrous kinship that link us to these two beings causes us to participate in their intoxication. It is a whirlwind of contradictory sentiments that carries away our wise resolution to be patient. A vehement force of fury accumulates within us, more obsessive than the sanguine torrent and the thousand petty impressions of normal life that monopolize and distracting a portion of our agitation; it has no other possible outlet than the struggle for the re-conquest of our physical individuals. With very passing moment, our will, thus exasperated, becomes stronger and more imperious…

With a tortuous fixity of desire, we keep watch on the degree of resistance offered to us by their pineal glands, red and turgid with exasperated pressure. It is as if they suspect our presence, sensing the danger of dispossession; instead of going to bed they chatter and chatter, interminably, about their great future...

But our decision is irrevocable. The moment draws near. They're lying down. They're going to sleep. The red peas of their pineal glands are fading, becoming paler and paler...

Wait! Our couple breaks apart, and reach of our two wills gets ready for the desperate effort...

Sympathetic waves float around us; I vaguely perceive the distant assistance of the Venusian Master...

Raymonde has attacked first, for—victory!—the woman releases a faint cry; and there is the smile, the divine smile of my beloved, spreading across hr face! My turn! Quickly!

And I hurriedly introduce my will into my adversary's psychic fortress...

What's happening? Am I a fraction of a second to late? Has his companion's cry awakened the Great Leader? An unexpected resistance meets me; we are two souls, in the body where I thought myself the master...

Should I let go, to await a more favorable moment? No, oh, no! My beloved is reintegrated into her physical being, and I will not abandon her to my Martian rival, even for an hour! He does not wish to yield? Well, that's a pity—nor so I!

And Raymonde, her eyes wide with horror, watches the frightful internal struggle that shakes the body of the Great Leader as he and I dispute its possession, without daring to intervene—what could she do, in any case?

Seen from without, that struggle resembles a full-scale epileptic fit, a paroxysm of furious madness. Tugged back and forth by two rival wills, the limbs flail the air, the trunk twists, the eyes turn back, blood-stained foam flecks the howling mouth in which the teeth chatter randomly, biting the tongue...

Through the vicissitudes of the duel to the death in which or rival wills are engaged, I see the distraught Raymonde telephone for a doctor. The bedroom is soon invaded by a dozen overseers. They grab hold of the madman respectfully; he fights them with the superhuman strength of two present souls, but finally collapses, having been tied up, in response to an injection of morphine...

Unexpected assistance; it is salvation for me!

The numbing of the rival consciousness delivers me a body henceforth without resistance. My will installs itself within lovingly, sinks voluptuously into the depths of the brain, irradiates itself along the nerve fibers, checks the proper functioning of all the muscles with little twitches. I know that the other can no longer act against me, now, for the suppression of the Perfume deprives the Martian souls of all their power outside the Solenoids of Reincarnation—and no one will think for a single instant of putting the Great Leader R'rdô through them again because of the nervous fit that has just laud him low—a crisis of overwork, according to all the evidence.

Such, at least, is the diagnosis authoritatively pronounced by one of the overseers sitting beside my bed. "Don't worry, Madame," he replies to Raymonde's anxious interrogations. "Our revered Great Leader is out of danger. A few hours sleep, and there'll be no recurrence. The little incident will have no consequences; tomorrow, His Excellency will be able to resume work...carefully, though..."

Raymonde catches the slight smile with which I greet these words. She shivers with joy, takes my hand in hers, and—watched by her and the doctor—I finally let myself fall into a light sleep, firmly re-established in my body, enjoying the obscure sensation of my soul being weighted down by the dear burden of my limbs, entirely myself one more!

XI. The Ascension of Saint Egregore

What a joy it was, the following day, to find ourselves together again, triumphant accomplices, installed in place! What a delight I experienced in smoking my first cigarette of the day, while chatting to Raymonde and taking possession of my office!

A quantity of documents of every sort, on which I recognized the handwriting of *the other*—my own handwriting deformed by the Martian soul—was yet another source of pleasure, and reassured me slightly as to the consequences of our premature reincarnation. Thanks to the mania for taking notes transmitted by my body to the Great Leader, I would find what I needed in these manuscripts to document myself and replace the projected study of our characters.

Another discovery was less agreeable—that of "tenancy damage." Our bodies, having been in perfect condition two months before, when *the others* took possession, had been obliged to support the exigencies of tyrannical and unbridled souls, and we found them in a pitiful condition, aged by ten years. Raymonde was distressed by countless flaws inflicted upon her beauty, less by a real usury of the tissues, fortunately, than by a total neglect of the most natural concerns of cleanliness and hygiene. For my part, I saw myself condemned to wear a hideous collar-length beard; I had a stomach wrecked by the scandalous regime to which that brute R'rdô had subjected it; and a violent nervous tic agitated my lower left eyelid. Both our sets of vocal cords had been frayed by the abominable Terromartian accent—which we would nevertheless have to conserve, for fear of exciting suspicion, along with the new gestures and attitudes that the "regulation" of the usurping souls had inflicted on our limbs.

It was soon necessary for us to brave the presence of the senior staff. Raymonde, with a marvelous feminine intuition, allowed herself to be guided by the habits inculcated in her body, and played her character to perfection; the two or three lapses that she made were attributed to the upset she had suffered by virtue of my fit. Much less sure of myself, I offered the excuse of a violent headache and limited myself to listening, only replying in monosyllables.

The expedition of current affairs was, in any case, suspended; there was no longer any subject for discussion than the death of the Sovereign Pontiff Egregore XII—"Saint Egregore," as the leaders were now saying. Although it was a hard knock to the party of the Magi—our party—the national mourning could be exploited, and might even gain us adherents, provided that the funeral arrangements were sufficiently splendid.

They evidently had to take place the following day. Following the ancient custom, the mortal husk of the Magus was presently plunged in a galvanoplastic bath of gold chloride, being entirely coated with a thick layer of precious metal; transformed into a golden statue, it would be ready to enter eternity.

The opinion of the chiefs, however, was that a simple deposition of the statue inside the Monument would not be sufficient. The popular imagination must be struck by some new rite, the unprecedented splendor of which would add to the cyclopean pomp of the ceremony. As to its form—they had decided the matter between them—the chiefs asked me whether I would approve the canonization of Egregore being crowned by his *ascension*, in the presence of everyone.

"Certainly," I replied, without daring to say any more.

"And would Your Excellencies deign to administer the solemn unction yourselves, the one surviving Magus having agreed to cede you that privilege?"

"Willingly," said Raymonde, at the same time as me.

"It will reflect the greatest possible honor on to the Party...and on your two selves, Excellencies! There—your victory will henceforth be assured! The shaggies are sunk! A round of applause, gentlemen!"

And the triple-time applause of the chiefs gave us a foretaste of the anticipated popularity.

Raymonde and I spent the hours that passed before the ceremony turning the problem over and over. How could the Unction of the Magus—or, rather, his galvanoplastic statue—procure his final "ascension"?

We were no further advanced than we had been in the morning when a deputation of overseers came to find us, and took us—by helicopter, in spite of the short distance—to the first terrace of the monument.

Dazzled by the floodlights and dazed by the acclamations of the crowds swarming on the immense esplanade of the Pyramids, we were given little time to collect ourselves. Then the blinding beams of searchlights, aimed at us from all directions, prevented us from seeing anything beyond the scene in which we were acting, on the huge ledge caved into the flank of the mountain of light. On the summit of the mount—looming vertiginously, high above our heads—floated the Shell and the luminous Magus, whose arm had interrupted its gyratory movement to direct all gazes to the ceremony that was about to take placeAt an order from the surviving Magus—who was seated in an armchair, with his wings tremulously folded and his cephalic appendices sustained by protective steel wires—a kind of awning parted, like the entrance to a tent, and the defunct Pontiff appeared, cast in his gleaming carapace of galvanoplastic gold, with his arms and wings outspread and the rigid antennae standing up on his forehead in a superb gesture of boldness and defiance. The acclamations of the crowd were drowned out by the thunderous fanfare of the electric orchestra lodged inside the Monument and projecting its sonorous waves through the loudspeakers of enormous amplifiers distributed on the level of each terrace. Seven salvoes of heavy artillery set on the bank of the Nile accompanied the seven measures of a barbaric hymn.

Then, suddenly, there was a deep silence, and 300,000 pairs of eyes religious followed the rite of Supreme Unction. Twenty-one chiefs ranged on either side of the Pontiff knelt down while Raymonde and I came forward in response to a summons from the old Magus, into the dazzling glare of the floodlights.

"Take the sacred sprinklers," stammered the expiring voice.

Bewildered, but forcing ourselves to put on a brave face, we each took hold of a sort of thick paint-brush that was soaking in a bowl full of thick paste, the color of egg-yolk, with a metallic gleam. *Solar*! What were we supposed to do with it?

"On the head, the arms and the wings," breathed the ancient master of ceremonies.

And, with Raymonde standing to the left and me to the right, we conscientiously set about painting the upper parts of the statue.

That was what the crowd was waiting for, because its members burst into enthusiastic and frantic applause, interminably prolonged, while the orchestra in the Monument discreetly resumed the Canonization March.

Our role was complete, it seemed. Two chiefs came forward respectfully to take the sacred paint-brushes from our hands. As if in a nightmare we received the blessing of the old Magus, and the helicopter took us back to the Palace.

Alone! Alone, at last! One more hour in that atmosphere of mystic madness and we might have lost our minds! The memory of that crazy Unction and the fact that the noise of the celebration was continuing outside were already more than enough. All night long the redoubtable sonority of the Martian music continued to rage, along with the clamor of the crowd and the hymns howled by the megaphones in front of the galvanoplastic statue of the defunct Magus, the *solar* our unconscious hands had painted on to it glistening in the beams of the spotlights.

A dose of chloral finally put an end to our intellectual disturbance, and we obtained the rest necessary to face the second part of the funeral ceremony—the mysterious Ascension!

The radiant Egyptian Sun was already shining down on the 300,000 Martians on the Esplanade. Physically exhausted by the sleepless night, their barbaric souls were no longer good for anything but expressing the fury of their coarse mysticism, and the murmurous drone of their morning prayers rose up toward the Star towards which the arm of the titanic Magus dominating the Pyramid of Babel was once again pointing. On the first terrace, the folds of the tent had been closed, hiding the statue of Egregore from the gazes of the crowd, while the old Magus, slumped in his armchair, and the two neatly-aligned cohorts of leaders continued to look on.

The Sun had just reached the face of the Monument where the apotheosis was to be effectuated, when a fanfare burst out, brutally triumphant, reinforced by a battalion of "noise-makers" of every sort—hooters, rattles, cracklers, whistles, buzzers, gurglers—not to mention the artillery along the Nile and all the sirens in Mars Central. A dozen helicopters, made up as bats better to symbolize the pontifical ascension, and carrying the privileged spectators, including us—flew low over the Esplanade where the breathless crowd ducked.

All gazes were fixed on the level of the first terrace, on the hermetically-sealed awning. In a sudden silence, it collapsed all of a piece, and the statue of Egregore appeared. A stifled "ah!" escaped from 300,000 throats, immediately suppressed by religious respect and attentive anxiety. There was no longer any sound but the monotonous throbbing of rotor blades.

Then, struck by the full glare of the solar radiation, the dazzling statue appeared to quiver, to begin a musical vibration, on a note that was low at first, but then became increasingly shrill. The amplified voice of the Magus pronounced the final words: "Holy son of Egregores, rise up to the eternal glory and precede us into the bosom of the Beatitude!"

And the miracle was accomplished! Solicited by the irresistible attraction of the light acting on its sheath of *solar*, the statue left the ledge upon which it was resting, floated gently into the air, and rose up like a balloon towards the Sun, slowly at first but gradually accelerating in its flight.

It was crazy, contrary to all the laws of weight and gravitation. I refused to believed my eyes; the brute fact was there, however, and the delirious acclamations of the Martian multitude, along with the newly-unleashed fanfare of the electric orchestra, noise-makers, cannons and sirens, saluted that prodigious apotheosis—which no Roman emperor ever achieved when a living eagle was launched from his funeral pyre to symbolize his divinized soul! The mortal husk, the dazzling galvanoplastic effigy, of the Sovereign Pontiff of Mars, Egregrore XII himself, with wings deployed, rose up and continued to rise into the limpid azure sky of Egypt. He passed the summit of the cyclopean pyramid, from which the Titan's gesture indicated his route, moving ever more quickly, higher and higher, becoming tiny and eventually disappearing, absorbed into the dazzling radiation of the Sun. The crowd howled frenetically, to the orchestral strains of a triumphal hymn—which bore a strange resemblance, in our impious ears, to the chorus of an old popular song:

Bon voyage, Monsieur Dumollet, Prenez vos bottes....[37]

But a hurricane of mystical delirium was shaking the ranks of the Martians beneath us. Whipped up by the example of the apotheosis, their desire for the supreme solar paradise, which they would only reach themselves after two further avatars and unknown labors, burst forth in anguished moans: "The Sun! The Sun!"

Hypnotized by the blinding disk, they waved their arms, begging its paternal rays to carry them away too, to receive them as it had just done for Saint Egregore, in his glory! Nailed to the ground by weight, they wanted at least to draw nearer to him, to feel his burning kisses, to bathe in his paradisal effluvia. Jostling one another, crushing one another and trampling one another, a power-

---

[37] This is a popular French nursery rhyme.

ful surge of their serried ranks demolished the barriers, invaded the Monument's broad stairways and flooded the successive terraces. Within a few minutes, the Babelesque pyramid was garnished from top to bottom with a maddened swarm.

In broad daylight, on the Esplanade and on the seven terraces, all the Terromartians, in human and simian form, male and female, stripped off their clothes and stamped their feet in unison. The music was still playing. The artillery thundered. The sirens howled. The helicopters, intoxicated by the contagion, climbed vertically upwards with their rotor-blades going full tilt.

And while Egregore, anointed with *solar*, followed a continuously-accelerated course into the interplanetary void, 300,000 Martians celebrated his apotheosis, dancing in the nude in the ecstatic glory of the Sun.

Part One: Beneath the Imperial Mask

I. Facing the Martians!

Through the upper windows of the Red Palace; on the terraces of the Monument, where I presided, with the last old Magus, over religious ceremonies; on tours of inspection—several times a day, the Camp of the Cylinders extended before my eyes, with its humming machines, its enormous crucibles of liquid steel, the vapors of castings not yet cooled, its shells protruding from their sandy matrix or standing up right, finished, in the middle of their pits with sparkling walls.

No cannons, no munitions! The problem was resolved for me by the Ascension of Egregore. I knew as much about it as the Martians busy in the steelyard. And, doubtless like them, my imagination, vastly multiplying the few rows of finished shells, covered them with propulsive *solar* and saw them launched into space like the golden statue in serried battalions, one after another, at intervals of a few minutes, extending a chaplet of calamities, one bead at a time, ready to fall upon innocent Venus.

It was certainly necessary for me, in arriving at that vision, to overcome the repugnance of my reason, to vanquish inveterate mental habits, to cross out my memories of terrestrial physics. It was necessary for me, above all, to repeat on a smaller scale, but with my own hands, the experiment of apotheotic levitation: a simple matter, given that I had a wooden box full of *solar* manufactured in the workshops of Mars Central.

Alone with Raymonde, far from any indiscretion, I first exposed a pinch of the enigmatic substance on my palm. In daylight, the egg-yolk-yellow grains began to vibrate, seized by a turbulent sort of "Brownian motion," which tickled my skin. A ray of sunlight reached them, and they sprang instantaneously towards the star, like iron filings attracted by a magnet, and pattered against the window, to which they remained stuck with such force that I could not detach them.

Untiringly, I repeated the experiment in various forms. I smeared a concoction of gum Arabic and *solar* on to a heavy platinum paperweight, which I took in my pocket to the second terrace of the Monument. The metal mass was lifted like a feather and vanished into the heights of the atmosphere in two seconds.

My box of *solar* was not yet exhausted when I ceased to consider the heliophilic properties of the new compound—a product of Martian science—as a mechanical heresy. I was too familiar with the mathematical analysis to throw any part of the theory overboard, but I had acquired a material certainty that I shared with my entourage: in spite of their formidable mass, and solely by virtue of their sheaths of *solar,* the shells would be levitated towards the central star, then deviated in the direction of Venus by means of some unknown apparatus.

But this persuasion, this faith, which was accompanied in the Terromartians by a frenetic desire, awoke in me, by contrast—and in Raymonde, when she understood it—a veritable terror.

The duty that seemed to us to be light and easily accomplishable when the lure of our stolen bodies led us to assume the characters of the Great Leader and his female companion, increasingly appeared to us as a desperate and hopeless enterprise.

Previously, as disincarnate souls, it had been possible for us to protect the Last Men and guide them to their retreat. Now we were as powerless as the least of the shaggies to modify the trajectory of the cylinders, or to hasten or delay their departure—and that departure, whether it was more or less imminent, signified deliverance for Earth and ruination for Venus.

Emperor of the Martians! That prestigious title had contributed, without our being aware of it—along with the ravages of jealousy—to our premature reincarnation, while we shared the prideful intoxication of our "doubles." But would it be accompanied by effective power? At any rate, I did not possess it yet. The last Magus, almost forgotten by everyone, but alive nevertheless, remained between me and the title; by virtue of the death of his predecessor, he became the Sovereign Pontiff Egregore XIII.

Carried away by their political passion, the chiefs of my entourage had gone too far and added too much solemnity to the funeral of Egregore XII. That glorious and unusual Ascension had convinced the Martian people that the last of the Magi had risen up to the Heavens. The era of magical power seemed to be conclusively over; Egregore XIII was no more than a name, a time-server. In spite of that, he was unable, even if he wished it, invest anyone else with supreme power. Only the death of the last Pontiff would assure the Terromartian Great Leader the religious functions and the title of Emperor.

In effect, supreme authority was in abeyance, and the effective power belonged to the chief overseers. I soon began to suspect them of involvement with the Technical Director, whose occult projects had seduced them—although I did not discover that until later. What became apparent to me immediately was that I was a plaything in everyone's hands. At any rate, the difficulties of the adventure into which we had blindly thrown ourselves, prematurely, revealed themselves, one after another, to be much more disconcerting than we had estimated. They were of every sort, material and mental.

The deafening noise of machines, the unpleasant odors of the crowd and the indigestible food were a real and constant persecution, but there was hope that we might accustom ourselves to them, to some degree, and we would have given short shrift to those annoyances were it not for the greater anxieties that plunged us, from that first evening on, into a veritable distress.

The situation of a man who had been condemned, in another era, to live among the most barbarous tribes of central Africa, to share their life, their concepts, their aspirations, their joys and their troubles, was nothing by comparison with ours. The brutal mores and repulsive customs of the true Martian people of the factories and the steelyards would doubtless have inspired more disgust in us, and it would have been more painful to observe them in appearance, but at least horror would have preserved us from any possibility of contagion, and we would never have had to dread for a single instant that we might become like them in a fundamental sense. The milieu of the chiefs, which was ours, seemed much more dangerous to us, because it was more refined.

If I had only had my predecessor's notes to guide me in playing the role of Great Leader R'rdô, the task would have been beyond my capabilities. Fortunately, I still had the memories left in my cerebral circumvolutions by the Martian soul's sojourn, and I quickly became able to consult R'rdô's terrestrial memories without overmuch groping, albeit with many gaps.

As for Raymonde, the sagacity of her feminine intuition served her better than me in that respect, and she became the Great Leader's consort without further ado, to a degree that amazed me and made me anxious for the conservation of her human personality. She sometimes had occasion to warn me about faults presented by my discourse or my conduct, with respect to the viewpoint of our entourage, but I had no similar advice to give her. On the contrary, I had to make her party to my anxieties concerning the over-perfection of her simulation, anxiously pointing out turns of phrase—without mentioning the obligatory frightful accent—and Martian gestures that she employed even when we were alone.

Without our love, without our absolute union, these reciprocal and indispensable observations would quickly have degenerated into acrimony—and the slightest division between us might have been our ruination. We needed every minute of the few hours of each evening in which we had the liberty to converse without witnesses to check the progress of this slow Martianization, and maintain the worthiness of our souls for a human future.

We were alone—along against the whole Martian society! The least suspicion with regard to our real identities would have resulted in our being massacred pitilessly or, worse still, being delivered to the Solenoids of Reincarnation—but the thought of our distant friends on their way to Tahiti, and our sacred duty to the Earth, prevented us from losing our footing and plunging into despair.

In addition, the Venusian Master visited my dreams. He chided me gently for having neglected his counsels of prudence and assuming too soon roles for which we were not ready. He exhorted me to be patient, and promised me his aid when the moment came for decisive action. Almost every night, I saw him

seated before a sort of crystal egg, in which his supernaturally lucid gaze discovered scenes of Martian agitation in miniature, and made myself meeker and
more attentive while he imposed himself upon me. Every morning, I recounted
my vision to Raymonde, and that occult and distant sympathy was the greatest
comfort of our miserable gilded existence as spies and traitors for the cause of
good.

II. The Last Magus

I almost blush to admit—and this concession indicates better than all the rest what an empery the Martian atmosphere eventually exercised upon us—that the last Magus treated me with an affection that I was almost ready to return.

This illusory Pontiff, the last representative of the authentic Martians, remained a manifest religious authority to the common people, their race's supreme guide towards the solar paradise. Although Leduc and his shaggy followers had respected, to a considerable degree, the veto that his predecessor had imposed on the "Mechanist heresy," however, that party considered the last Magus as an anachronism. They regarded his prohibitions as null and void, attributing them to the opposing part of Old-Martians. For their part, the Old-Martians treated the "Son of the Bat" as a docile but cumbersome instrument.

At any rate, the old fellow was touched to find me asking for his advice and showing him an unexpected deference. My attentions were certainly not disinterested; I was, first and foremost, trying to obtain information from him that I dared not demand from my entourage. His mediocre knowledge of French, while importing a certain obscurity into his statements, seemed to me to be a useful veil for my ignorance of certain fundamental notions, and to authorize more direct questions by way of clarification.

It did not take me long, however, to recognize that I had before me, in the form of this "old wreck," an unusual intelligence, superior to all those I had previously seen incarnate in human form. In spite of his physique, hideous to our terrestrial conceptions, but in which the Martians saw the prototype and exemplification of Beauty—his membranous wings, his red-brown skin with a metallic sheen—old Egregore inspired a sincere respect in me. I hesitated to use any subterfuge with him other than the necessary dissimulation of my true personality, and I treated him as an equal. I had no need to simulate deferential attention. His gilded eyes, with vertical pupils like a cat's, sunk beneath the vast forehead with its luminous protuberances, shone with the full glare of genius, and I never tired of listening to him.

Beneath his awkward diction, warmed by an ardent fire, the little I knew of the Martian dogmas of transmigration was clarified by new light. The egotistical salvation pursued by the vulgar souls of the Terromartians became the noble aspiration of a race to attain its supreme destiny, in harmony with the evolution of worlds.

From their origins in the outer planets, incarnated for the first time on the frozen ground of Saturn—or Uranus, according to more ancient traditions—the presently-Martian souls had been subject ever since to the attraction of the Sun, forced to draw closer to its glorious fire. Liberated by the deaths of their initial envelopes, they had to pass on to the next planet inwards, to experience a new avatar there and earn the right to take another step on the triumphal Way. Jupiter, Mars, the Earth, Venus and Mercury were, therefore, their successive residences, and after that series of metempsychoses they would return to the flamboyant bosom of the original Star, there to know the unprecedented delights of fusion with the primordial All—Nirvana, as Earthly Buddhist doctrine expresses it.

For generations without number, the sublime pilgrimage had proceeded; millions and millions of souls had passed through the planetary sequence, cultivating en route the wisdom and the merits of which each one would make a gift to the Supreme Being, the Sun. And if things had followed their natural course, the souls would have continued, until the end of time, to undertake the long but facile voyage marked out by their ancestors, under the peaceful direction of the Magi....

But the Spirit of Darkness was watching. Bestowed on souls during each of their avatars in order to help them improve the adaptation of their planetary domiciles to their corporeal existence, Intelligence had become, by virtue of the Spirit's interventions, a two-edged sword. The animal instincts had monopolized its produce, exacted ever-more extensive services from it, and finally contrived to impose their domination upon it and draw it into wild adventures...

Intelligence fought back, and won—on Mars, at least—a temporary triumph. The wars of extermination to which people devoted themselves, by means of ever-more-advanced and murderous armaments, gave victory to the Sons of the Bat over the Sons of the Plesiosaur and Diploodocus. The Magi reigned alone, and for several centuries, Mechanization, under their guidance, was their humble servant, contributing to making the planet a pleasant abode for its passing guests.

Alas, old Egregore said—unconsciously parodying one of the fundamental laws of terrestrial paleontology—the perfection of a race does not long precede its irremediable decline. Material progress, especially, incorporates within itself an accelerating necessity that obliges it to surpass its normal and legitimate goals, exciting and corrupting the minds of its possessors and precipitating them towards their ruin...

The ambition of the "Mechanist" Martians increased inordinately. The planet became too narrow a field for their activity, multiplied tenfold, a hundred-fold by the vertiginous momentum of industry. They dreamed of formidable adventures, titanic conquests. They undertook to overturn the eternal laws that regulate the destinies of planetary souls. The slowness of usual transmigrations seemed derisory to them. Dragging their unanimously impatient adherents behind them, they resolved to storm the Heavens, skipping one of the links in the planetary chain by landing in their Martian bodies on the next planet: the Earth.

In the name of the outraged religion, the Pontiff of the time, Egregore II, anathematized their plans, whose frightful consequences he foresaw—but the people of Mars, blinded by their desire, rose up in the name of the divine Sun, and he had to give in, for fear of seeing the formidable engines of industry ravage the sacred soil of the planet. He consented to turn their blows against the brothers in Space.

Reluctantly, in order to avoid greater evils, the Magi had to associate themselves with the enterprise whose goal was the conquest of the Earth. After that, the series of catastrophes had unfolded, without remedy. The only concession they had been able to obtain was that the systematic bombardment of the Earth would consist of successive daily shells.

To begin with, I tried to get the old fellow to tell me what reasons could have been invoked for putting such a brake on the Mechanists' impatience, but I could not grasp his explanation. I simple had to admit that it was a matter of one of "those reasons which reason knows not" [38]—a religious motive analogous to the sabbatical prescriptions of Judaic law, or the Catholic observance of Friday...

The threats of Jupiter had provoked the most complete incredulity. The engineers denied that the sentence could be executed. The Magi thought it incompatible with the well-known wisdom of the Jovians. It had, in fact, been folly on the part of the latter to destroy the population of Mars, given that a considerable fraction of the inhabitants of Jupiter belonged to the race of Saturno-Martian souls, and that the successive avatars of their transmigration towards the Sun were supposed to follow an ideal sequence requiring the integrity of the planetary sequence. With Mars destroyed—or its inhabitants, and its soil deprived of all life—the souls originating from the outer planets would accumulate there without the slightest possibility of reincarnation, reduced to the miserable condition of souls in torment, until the distant day when the seeds of life scattered through infinite space would inseminate the sterilized globe anew and gradually produce organisms there sufficiently elevated to serve as temporary shelters for the pilgrims of the Sun.

While he explained the logic of the situation to me, the old Magus burst into desperately bitter laughter. "Justice!" he added. "The Jovians claimed to be serving Justice and Fraternity, while they swept the unfortunate planet of my ancestors clean with their thunderbolt! On the contrary, they were committing an unforgivable sin, in depriving the souls of two or three planets of their habitual

---

[38] This quotation is a partial rendering of the most famous aphorism contained in Blaise Pascal's *Pensées*, "le coeur a ses raisons que la raison ne connaît pas," traditionally rendered into English as "the heart has its reasons, of which reason knows not." Pascal probably intended it to mean that human beings have certain innate desires and appetites that are not the products of reason, although modern users often cite it as if it were a compliment to emotional intuition. Varlet cannot really have thought that it referred to seemingly-arbitrary impositions of religious doctrine, and seems to be using it to cover up his inability to think of a plausible explanation for the Magi's edict.

issue. Thanks to their intervention in this quarrel, in which the Earth alone was guilty of refusing us hospitality—and perhaps our Mechanists too, a little, of presumptuous hatred and pride—Saturn and Uranus, not to mention Jupiter itself, are henceforth deprived of their habitual communicative link with the solar paradise. Millions and millions of souls condemned to the Limbo of Martian Purgatory for an indefinite lapse of time!"

A profound emotion altered the quavering voice of the old Pontiff. I perceived, with astonishment, that he was the true defender of planetary Fraternity, and I measured the distance that separated his generous dogmas from the sinister application to which the religion of the vulgar Martians had put them...an inevitable schism, alas—similar on all planets—between the intuitions of Seers guided by the Universal Spirit and the trivial superstitions of peoples dragged down by their egotism and their vile material instincts!

Thunderstruck by Jupiter, Mars was no more than a globe of ashes and the souls of its inhabitants, surprised by the devastating scourge, had emigrated *en masse* to the Earth. A small percentage of those souls had been reincarnated. It was therefore important, above all else, that the Earth should live; it was vital that the human race survived, in order to furnish bodies, in due course, for all of the Martian souls. That is why, Egregore admitted to me, the Council of Magi had resolved to limit the influence of the Perfume to the Old World. That is why his predecessor had pronounced an anathema upon the Technical Director, because of his man-hunts on the American continent—which had been set aside as a "reservation" for humankind by the Magi. That is why it was necessary that the cylinders should take off as soon as possible, in order to avoid providing any pretext for a further Jovian intervention, and to spare the Earth the fate to which Mars had been subject.

"Ah," concluded the old Magus, "if suicide were not an outrage to God and Eternal Life, how infinitely preferable it would have been to realize the direct flight into the Sun that a few fanatical illuminates recommended!

"We would not have sinned involuntarily against sidereal Fraternity and induced Jupiter to commit its crime. We would not now be preparing, on a devastated planet, this new folly of an attack on Venus. We would not have furnished a pasture for those monsters, hatred and vengeance, which, immeasurably grown and fortified, have now reached the point of contemplating a sin equal to that of Jupiter, but more abominable still, since it has no justification: the destruction of the Earth! Yes, my friend, they're hiding it from you, but I know, personally, that these vile Mechanists, blinded by the delirium of the unlimited forces they have learned to manipulate, are thinking of applying them to this globe that supports us. Devoid of pity for the millions of souls that their flight aboard the cylinders will leave behind here, they not only want to capture every last Terran, but they intend to create an irremediable breach in the planetary chain. Jupiter has sterilized Mars for centuries? They will deprive the outer planets of their access route to the solar paradise forever—what does it matter to them that the souls of their brothers are caught up in the same catastrophe? *They will destroy the Earth!*"

But when he arrived at these invectives against Leduc and the Mechanists, old Egregore became incoherent. I could no longer extract any precise explanation from him. He mixed everything together: the Great Central Tunnel; the man-hunts and the new flying machines—*volvites*—designed for that purpose, and capable of flying speeds of 700 kilometers per hour; the daily excesses of the shaggies in respect of Terromartian women and the monstrous procreations resulting therefrom; the blasphemous priesthood instituted by the Technical Director in order to justify himself in the eyes of the people, against the reproaches of lukewarm religion; the superstitions introduced by these new priests, the *maki-mokokos*...

III. The Inauguration of the Drilling-Machine

They will destroy the Earth! These fateful words hammered within my skull; they vibrated within me, with the exact intonation that old Egregore had given them, and replied like an interior echo to the external braying of the loud-speakers announcing the results of the day's endeavors.

More than ever, I felt like a plaything in the hands of the chiefs. For two hours they had kept me in the Council Chamber directly above the fully-active Hall of Reincarnation, in order to persuade me of the necessity of an alliance with the Technical Director—"the Boss," as he was commonly known. All the shaggies, and an increasingly large proportion of the people were on his side, won over by his inexhaustible propagandists, the *maki-mokokos*. If we were not to find ourselves conclusively abandoned, a compromise was indispensable.

"Consent to everything," whispered Raymonde, enthroned beside me beneath the armchair in which the Sovereign Pontiff, with his wings folded and his eyes staring into space, maintained his indifference in these futile agitations. "Pretend to give in. The most important thing of all is to keep the semblance of authority attached to your title. Later, perhaps, we might find a way to avert the peril. Resistance can only ruin us and remove any chance of helping our friends on Earth and Venus."

Through the wide-open bay window, high in the bright blue Egyptian sky, at the very summit of the cyclopean Monument, I could see the Magus of the Shell extending his arm towards the Sun, and I could hear explosions of joy from the crowd massed in the Esplanade greeting every new concession wrung from my weakness.

"The Great Leader has given his approval to the clearance of America!" trumpeted the loudspeakers from the heights and base of the Monument. "Go and see the flying machines that will hunt the Terrans—the prodigious *volvites*! 700 kilometrers per hour…departure of the first official squadron in five minutes!"

"Hurrah for the Great Leader! Hurrah for the Boss!" howled the raucous throats of the Terromartians.

"Adoption of the Great Central Tunnel! Hurrah! Mars avenged on Jupiter! Blockade of souls in the outer planets! The Great Leader consents to inaugurate the works! He will go to the pithead of the Great Central Tunnel. Shaggies, Terromartians, workers not on shift, go and see the meeting of the Great Leader and the Technical Director! Three hundred helicopters at the disposition of travelers in airports B, C, D and F."

Supposedly to honor us, but actually in order to show off Leduc's triumph, my general staff and I made the journey—Raymonde was feeling ill and did not come—aboard a *volvite*. These machines, perfected and constructed in secret by

236

the Technical Director, were of an absolutely new type, marvelously adapted to their reconnaissance role and for the direct capture of human prey. Devoid of rotor-blades, shaped like an arrow and powered by atomic fission, they flew like a bullet, with the same characteristic speed and whistling sound. Their much-reduced fins made them almost invisible at a distance of a few kilometers, and it took a machine traveling at full speed less than two minutes from its appearance over the horizon to arrive directly above a determined point.

It was the first time that I had seen a *volvite* at close range, and the explanations the pilot gave me before departure plunged me into a painful reverie. Unfortunate Terrans of America and Oceania, dear Last Men, what will become of you? It was necessary for me to conceal this poignant emotion and to present a cheerful face to the chiefs sitting beside me in the narrow and uncomfortable cabin, while the sands of the Libyan desert fled beneath us—for the famous pithead opened forty minutes flight away from Mars Central, in the heart of the Sahara.

Conscious of his position as master of the moment, Leduc was waiting for us there confidently. The gross familiarity of his greeting—he received us with his pipe in his mouth and his hands in is pockets—was one more insult, which my associates swallowed with fixed smiles on their lips and I consumed in silence.

In any case, the surprise of seeing the guard of honor aligned in serried ranks around the Technical Director was sufficient was sufficient to cut off my speech. Quite different from the ordinary shaggies with whom we were in daily contact, 1000 monkeys [39] with long gripping tails, little larger than domestic cats and clad in thick fawn or silvery-grey fur, were standing proudly, grimacing and contorting their faces grotesquely beneath Magus-styled helmets.

"Ah, R'rdô, do you like my new recruits?" Leduc said, fixing me with the disturbing gaze that never failed to make me shiver every time we met—and he added, with a shrug, as if parenthetically: "You've changed a great deal, R'rdô, since your attack of epilepsy on the day Egregore died! Honestly, you're hardly recognizable! Patience, though!" Then, pointing to his monkeys, he said: "Maki-mokokos. All priests of the Sun, if you please. Technical ritual. Never let it be said that I lack religion...or altruism, eh! Here are souls provided with bodies! And it's only just begun. The forests of Madagascar and the East Indies are full of them. Oh, the lads are more skillful handymen than they look...and anyway,

---

[39] Varlet has been using the term "*singes*" (monkeys) to describe all the species Martianized as "*velus*" (shaggies), he found it necessary to use more specific references in his initial description of the specimens glimpsed by the narrator in the Hall of Reincarnation, and will find it necessary henceforth to make others. *Maki-mokoko* is a Madagascan native term for the ring-tailed lemur, but Varlet seems to use it rather indiscriminately to apply to all lemurs and some other small primates.

they take up so little room! We'll cram at least 4000 of them into a cylinder by piling them up a bit…ah, that'll stir things up on Venus!"

The maki-mokokos, immobilized in various attitudes, drank in his words. At the mention of Venus, their enthusiasm burst forth in shrill cries and excessive gestures. They extended their arms towards their chief, blowing kisses at him and capering on the spot, finishing up by babbling a sort of cantata: "Ha ha ha! Hurrah, Technical Director! He is the Great Martian, who will reincarnate us! Ha ha ha! Hurrah! Long live the Boss! He will lead us to Venus, the doorway to paradise! Blessed be he, the Great Martian who has saved us! We shall go to the Sun…to the Sun…to the Sun!" And, in a turbulent acrobatic rush, the monkey priests set about executing a series of perilous somersaults, which concluded in a pose of adoration, addressed as much to Leduc as to the Sun.

While this scene was in progress, the helicopters had begun to arrive. An increasingly dense crowd of Terromartians and shaggies was distributed on the slopes of dunes shaped into terraces, which a superficial vitrification had converted into a giant amphitheater. Its arena was nothing less than the mouth of the Great Central Tunnel.

The excavator, or, rather, the monstrous rock-drill destined to open this new shaft into the entrails of the globe, presented the appearance of a round platform supported at its periphery by seven feet comparable to those of the Eiffel Tower, pierced with a hole like that belonging to a skimmer—but a skimmer 200 meters in diameter, to which an entire series of transformers and auxiliary machines communicated the energy supplied by clumps of enormous cables: a skimmer as large as a city square, in which our official rostrum almost disappeared in the combined irradiations of the already-setting Sun and the metallic surface on which the maki-mokokos were agitating.

In a harsh and strident voice, amplified by the louspeakers for the benefit of the crowd, Leduc, proudly positioned in front of me and my general staff, began his discourse:

"Martians! The presence among us of R'rdô, our Great Leader and future Emperor, is sufficient justification in itself for my conduct and the fullest vindication of the Tunnel, whose excavation he will inaugurate with his own hand.

"However, as there are souls among us more timorous than truly religious, who still doubt the legitimacy of my designs, I would like to begin by defending myself against the reproaches addressed to me at the time when the late Pontiff Egregore XII—he reigns in the glory of the Sun!—misunderstood my intentions and believed that he detected a heresy therein.

"Martians! You know that the industrial production of *solar* is now an accomplished fact. The indispensable *geocoronium* has been discovered, in abundance, in the upper atmosphere. There is, in consequence, no more need to search for that substance in the depths of the terrestrial globe. That is understood—but that was only a secondary reason for the excavation of our Tunnel. There is another, much more serious and imperious reason, which every true

Martian soul...."—Leduc emphasized these words while taking a long look around, which appeared to pause insistently on me—"....*which every true Martian soul* will understand without difficulty and accept with enthusiasm: Vengeance! Sacred, just and legitimate Vengeance!

"Martians! A few months more, and your indefatigable labor will have completed the Cylinders that will transfer us to Venus and bring us swiftly closer to the solar paradise. The progress of that Mechanization so loudly decried by its retrograde blasphemers will spare us the uncertainties and trials of one avatar...and probably a second, if the feeble Venusians concede us the resources of their world, or if we win a victory over their feeble weapons.

"I have no need to tell you why it is necessary for us to make haste. The ruins of our dear planet, the scorched earth of our ancient fatherland, which the televisors show us every evening, are there to testify to the fate that is reserved for us if we delay long enough for vile Jupiter to recover its proximity to our present abode. We must, at all costs, decamp before the Jovian opposition.

"The so-called administrators of justice might use any means possible, even if we have gone, to renew their exploits—but they would evidently limit themselves to the destruction of Mars Central...a matter of ten minutes. The rest of the Earth would remain, offering, in the short term, a shelter for humans who have escaped our sweeps—and, in the longer term, a field of incarnation for the souls of the cruelest of our enemies. For it must be said: although the criminal folly of the Jovians has already been punished by the incineration of Mars itself, which has closed off access to the solar paradise to them and to the inhabitants of the outer planets, that prohibition is merely temporary. Sterilization is not annihilation, and life will flourish again on Mars sooner or later, offering our oppressors organisms that will reopen the sequence of avatars and open the way to the Earth for them.

"There it is, Martians—that which we cannot permit! Jupiter has shown us the way; we must follow it! We must create an irremediable breach in the planetary chain, conclusively blockading the outer souls on obese Jupiter—where they belong! We must not only *leave* but *destroy* the Earth!

"Destroy the Earth. Does that seem to you not to be easy?

"Well, it is—there's nothing simpler: by means of the Great Central Tunnel!

"Let us first set aside the objection that we have been anathematized by the late Pontiff, by reason of the waste of time. He feared—as you, perhaps, also do—that the supplementary labor would use up too much precious energy, which would be better employed at the Camp of the Cylinders.

"O ye Martians of little faith! You doubt Mechanization! The Mechanization that has furnished you so many irrefutable proofs of its limitless power! The Mechanization that has transported you as far as the Earth, in spite of your enemies, and will soon place Venus at your mercy!

"Be tranquil! Mechanization, the expansion of Intelligence, creates the instruments of its noble designs as and when they are needed. It draws them from inexhaustible Matter, multiplies them by formularistic application, at the pleasure of its desires. A few shaggies will suffice for the Tunnel drilling-operation. But we have too few, they say, to divert even a single shaggy from the factories of Mars Central? That is false! Those who say so are liars—or, like our late holy Pontiff, mistaken…and our ancient Pontiff who is still alive is stuck in fossilized prejudices in the face of Mechanization.

"I, the Technical Director of all the works in progress and to come—the Boss, as you call me—give you my word: there will be enough Cylinders! They may be a little cramped, but there will be enough for everyone, including our faithful maki-mokokos. And the Cylinders will leave in time! And if the molding and pouring slows down for two or three days because of the initiation of the excavation, you shall see it renewed with increased ardor as soon as the volvites return with their American recruits.

"I am multiplying projects, to be sure—but I am also multiplying the personnel. I am multiplying the volunteers and I am multiplying the machines. And the one that the honorable R'rdô will switch on in a moment, which is powered by atomic energy, finally put to industrial use, will excavate a Tunnel…*to the center of the Earth*! Look at this platform on which we are standing: you have the measure of its caliber before your eyes. Calculation has demonstrated that it is sufficient for a mine appropriate to the mass of the planet—a mine, I say, but a mine into which we will not have to introduce any explosive. That necessity is supplied in advance. The explosive is quite ready. It is Our Father the Sun who has providentially included it at the beginning of time, when He formed the planets from His sacred Substance! The explosive is there, beneath our feet. The central layers of the globe—like others whose depths are unconsolidated—encloses a mass of gas compressed to 1000 atmospheres, and reduced by that pressure to a quasi-solid state. Now, this magma of endothermic composites only requires, in order to dissociate itself with an abrupt release of heat, thus creating an explosion of incomparable violence, the introduction of a sufficient quantity of water. Well, we shall send that water down by means of the Tunnel. A profusion of water: a canal and an improvised sluice-gate will pour half the Atlantic Ocean into it, if necessary.

"All this, of course, will not function until the last cylinder is already en route for Venus, at a safe distance.

"And then, my friends—and THEN, Martians!—you shall see something out of the ordinary, I assure you: the accursed planet Earth exploding like a grenade, breaking into 1000 million fragments, pulverized, volatilized in the sidereal abyss! Finished, erased, cleared away. Nothing left in the orbit of the former Earth but a little meteoric dust, good for making falling stars. And who will be caught on the hop? The Jovians! Those holy fools, the Jovian 'administrators of justice.' Ah, if they're already biting their fingernails waiting for life to flourish again on Mars, they'll have to wait, then…for the Earth to reform—for its scattered particles to reaggregate, to offer a new abode for organisms and accommodation for the souls of the 'administrators of justice'!"

A cyclone of triumphant howls greeted these words. Drunk with hatred and vengeance, delirious, the Martians stamped their feet, and the maki-mokokos surrendered themselves to a riot of somersaults and joyful yelping. Ten minutes passed before the Technical Director was able to obtain silence and add: "Do you understand the reason for my Terran-hunts now? I don't want to blow them up along with the Earth without *utilizing* them!"

This time there was a hurricane of laughter—and no one asked what would become of the un-reincarnated Martian souls at the moment of the explosion.

As for me, I felt that I no longer had a drop of blood in my veins. Throughout Leduc's speech, I had made superhuman efforts to hide my distress from the orator, who appeared to examine the expression on my face curiously on several occasions. But when I had to follow the Technical Director on my own, and climb up with him into the observation-post where all the pit-head's controls were…when he placed my fingers on a lever saying, "The honor is yours, R'rdô—go ahead!"…I felt that I was about to faint, and darted a desperate glance around the terraces crammed with attentive Martians and at the enormous skimmer, free of occupants and ready to begin its sinister work.

"What is it? What's the matter with you, R'rdô?" growled Leduc's suspicious voice.

Three seconds of further hesitation and my career as Great Leader would have been irremediably compromised, along with all the possibilities that it reserved for me. For the sake of the Last Men, I had to commit that planetary murder!

I moved the lever in an arc over the marks of a graduated dial where blue sparks were scintillating; some lights came on and others were extinguished; the indicators of manometers moved, the needles beginning to turn vertiginously; transformers hummed; servomotors juddered—and with an enormous metallic brouhaha, punctuated by strident screeches, the entire drilling-machine was set in motion. It bit into the sand, which the holes of the "skimmer" threw out as it went towards an evacuation canal, where a deluge of water bore it away across the desert, as a river of mud.

The shaggy that was standing behind Leduc and me in the observation-post came forward to the control panel, and took possession of the levers. The regulated machines attained their maximum efficiency, and everything whirled, hummed, crashed, splashed and rushed in unison, with a formidable regularity.

In five minutes, the skimmer had disappeared beneath the seething sand, which visibly sank into a vast crater, whose walls, solidified by liquid hydrogen, hewed out the orifice of the Tunnel—of the Mine that would make a monster grenade out of the Earth, whose future annihilation the Martians in the amphitheater were cheering…

Open-mouthed and bewildered, I stared in turn at the abominable work that I had just set in motion, at the simian face of the shaggy monitoring his gauges, at the ironic and ferocious face of Leduc, and at the red and dismal Sun setting behind the horizon of the Sahara....

IV. Under the Orders of Mechanization

"Egregore XIII is dead!"

Such were the first words with which Raymonde greeted me, on the terrace of the Palace where the volvite deposited me on my return from that expedition.

Beneath our feet, the Martian inferno displayed its luminous panorama of floodlights and noisy factories, from the Camp of the Cylinders in the distance, dominated by the red geyser of "core iron," to the illuminated Monument where the Magus of the Shell was whitely silhouetted against the open sky.

"Egregore XIII is dead!" bellowed the city's loudspeakers, in their turn. "Tomorrow at midday: his funeral! And hallowed be his designated successor, R'rdô, Emperor of the Martians!"

It was necessary for us to endure the congratulations of the chiefs, even those of Leduc—yes, the Technical Director came in person to favor me with a vigorous handshake and these ambiguous words: "There'll be no more trouble now, R'rdô! You won't try to get in my way, like that old dodderer. We're old friends, aren't we?"

"What did he mean, beloved?" cried Raymonde, as soon as the door had closed behind our visitors. "Does he suspect...?"

"That the Emperor of the Martians is a human, willing to do anything to save the Earth and its last legitimate inhabitants? No, I don't think he's got that far. I have to make a confession to you: I've hidden it from you, thinking that my relationship with Leduc would always be vague and distant—but it turns out that this Martian Leduc has been R'rdô's political adversary for many years. I found proof of it in my papers, although the details were lacking, and I'll be taken unawares by any direct question relating to memories that he thinks we have in common. The way he looks at me is enough to tell me that my manner already seems suspicious to him."

"The fact of inhabiting a human body must excuse a good many anomalies, though."

"Wouldn't you recognize me, no matter how I were disguised, my dear? My personality must be one of those most familiar to the Martian Leduc—and that individual is threatening us with another danger even graver." And I told my companion the story of what I had seen and heard—and done—at the site of the Tunnel.

"The Earth?" she repeated, incredulously. "Blow up the Earth? But that's insane! Their insensate pride is blinding them. They'll never be able to do it."

"I fear that they will," I replied.

She lowered her head without asking me the reasons for my sad conviction, which was all too justified by the unlimited power of the machines whose dull rumbling and shaking was perceptible even in our apartment.

Once again, the duty to which we had sworn to dedicate our lives appeared to be a vast steep cliff, in which no hopeful ledge offered the slightest support to a climber. The cliff of our duty was becoming increasingly sheer and high—as was the impossibility of our task!

It was no longer a simple matter of saving one planet, but two: Venus, from invasion; Earth, from destruction! The problem of turning the Cylinders away from their goal—how?—was doubled by a new one: to prevent our world from being blasted apart along with the Last Men!

How could the mine be prevented from going off, even if it was of the "delayed action" type, set to explode after the Cylinders' departure? Once its mechanism was triggered, would I be able to stop it? In any case, as leader of the expedition, would I not be forced to depart aboard the imperial cylinder? If that particular cylinder was being steered automatically, I might, in theory, be able to deflect it away from Venus and send it plunging into the Sun with all its occupants—and myself. That cylinder alone! A futile gesture. Then again, might Raymonde, by some means or other, remain on Earth to take care of the mine? Impracticable, frightful...

Might it be possible, at least, to warn our friends? But how? And what could that handful of Last Men do against the Titans and their Machines? They had to remain hidden, for their own safety...

"Venus! Concern yourself with Venus first! Leave the Last Men until afterwards!" insinuated the voice of the Master-Initiate, that wordless voice, which obsessed my dreams every night. I had learned, even in a waking state, to distinguish vague and fragmentary intuitions within my own thoughts, in which I thought I recognized the appeals of our friends or the solicitations of Terran souls. While finding some comfort in the certainty that the Venusian Master had not abandoned me, however, I came close to rebellion on feeling myself subject, by way of his mediation, to the psychic pressure of an entire planet anguished by the threat of invasion. I considered it unnatural to be obliged to save these distant brothers, but not to be able to play the same role as the initiate with respect to terrestrial aspirations. Ah! The problem might be soluble, if all the scattered intelligence of my human brothers were to coalesce in a convergent beam focused on my soul, like that imposed on me by the occult power of Venus!

The Ascension of Egregore XIII, which took place the following day, partially reproduced that of his predecessor. As before, the Nile artillery thundered, the sirens howled, the Monument's orchestra unleashed all its brass and percussion, and 400,000 Terromartians and shaggies—augmented by the yelping battalion of maki-mokokos—shouted themselves hoarse singing the praises of the saintly Pontiff...but there was no naked orgy. When the golden statue was launched into sunlit splendor, to the accompaniment of the triumphal march— *Bonjour, Monsieur Dumollet!*—that brought the sacred occasion to an abrupt close. The helicopter that was carrying my general staff, Raymonde and me, which was made up to resemble a bat, descended majestically to deposit us on the second terrace, where the overseers, the maki-mokokos and the Technical Director were waiting for us.

"Here," a loudspeaker proclaimed in the silence, while the Magus of the Shell at the top of the Monument stopped indicating the Sun and pointed its fateful index-finger at me, "is our Emperor and Sovereign Pontiff henceforth. Like us, he is of the sad race of Terromartians. He is not an Egregore, but the last representative of that sacred dynasty, the defunct Magus—whose ideally pure form continued to remind us of the Beauty that once flourished on our beloved planet—has designated him as his successor. Egregore XIII has conferred his religious dignity and all his powers upon him; it is to R'rdô that the august task will fall of guiding us to the conquest of Venus, on the road of the Sun!"

The statement produced its extraordinary effect, and the fanaticism of the Martians burst forth in a storm of acclamation. An overseer advanced towards us, carrying sacred ornaments—but Leduc, with a decisive gesture, held him back. With an affected humility, well-calculated to make the glory of the ceremony reflect upon him and more clearly to affirm the nature of the alliance made between the religious and technical powers, he took possession of them, and dressed me in the imperial helmet and the artificial wings that I was the first to wear.

I understood in a flash what dependence would result from that coronation, but did not attempt to imitate Napoleon's gesture of snatching the diadem from Pius VII to put it on with his own hands. It was at Leduc's invitation that I conferred on Raymonde the insignia of her own power, equal to mine and, so to speak, doubling that authority in the eyes of the feminine fraction of the assembly.

The continuing acclamations rose up, followed by hymns accompanied by music, while I accomplished the first act of my pontificate, receiving the homage of two colleges of priests, one composed of chiefs, the other of maki-mokokos. I have to admit that the stink given off by the latter was almost intolerable, and that I promised myself never to attempt to usurp my Technical Director's guard of honor. The popular manifestations revived my courage, though, by proving to me that the authority of Egregore XIII lived on in my person, and that, even if the Great Leader R'rdô's role had been effaced, he would, as Emperor and Pontiff, become necessary to the government of the fierce and exacting mysticism of shaggies and Terromartians.

I feared, at first, that Leduc might make me into a kind of decorative idol, a Grand Lama, purely religious, through which he would dictate his orders, but he judged it more apt to "democratize"—as it used to be termed—my dignity and to accustom everyone to seeing me continually at his side, thus giving all his enterprises the irrefutable sanction of religion. It was even more convenient, from his point of view, that the public ceremonies of the solar cult had lost their initial frequency, because of the loss of time that they—and especially their consequent orgies—occasioned among the workers, and it suited him to take the troubled mysticism of the Martians in another direction. Without daring to infringe on religious functions that he felt it inappropriate to perform himself, he had already instituted the college of maki-mokokos. Almost incapable of any other mechanical occupation, these minuscule shaggies spent their days on the terraces of the Monument worshipping the Sun; their incessant prayers "gained merit" for their fellow citizens and thus brought some alleviation to their scruples. The Terromartians, however, like the shaggies, whose mystical needs were singularly developed, could only be satisfied by seeing the head of their religion—the Sovereign Pontiff and Emperor—involving himself in their laborious life and adding the encouragement of his presence to the Technical Director's tours of inspection.

Raymonde, for her part, had to respond to analogous solicitations. The absolute "feminism" practiced by the Martians on their native planet had been further reinforced, since their arrival on Earth, by the admission, in increasing numbers, of shaggies into the phalansteries of Mars Central. The uncontrolled appetites of the habitants of simian origin had, from the outset, caused acute problems for the good organization of the work, and it had been necessary, in order to obviate them, to group the Terromartians in separate units. The majority specialized in aviation, and when she was humbly implored to grant her patronage to the *Amazons of the Sphinx*, Raymonde thought it only politic to accept. Since then, for her as for me, everyday existence was a continual round of reviews, inspections and tours of every sort, to which we submitted by necessity at first, but also in the hope of solidifying our authority and discovering, somewhere or other, some means of coming to the aid of our friends on Venus or our Terran brothers—for the *Amazons of the Sphinx* carried out man-hunts, and their volvites were exploring America while waiting to go on to Oceania. I was hoping that an opportunity might arise to discover the secret of steering the Cylinders.

The necessity of keeping company with Leduc, however, inevitably sharpened my anxieties. He seemed to take a malicious pleasure in reminding me of details of our Martian past, and enjoyed my embarrassment when I eluded his questions by means of evasive answers. He never persisted, to begin with; it was all limited, for the time being, to a kind of game, like those that cats play with mice. Was his interest in these reminiscences only slight? Or was he secretly collecting material for a crushing indictment? A mystery. In any case, I took care only to be with him in the company of my associates. Quite happy to have conserved their privilege of a life of idleness and gluttony instead of being reduced to the status of mere workers by the death of Egregore XIII, the latter saw Leduc as their savior, and the true holder of power—as, indeed, he was, to a greater extent than me. They would have kissed his footprints. I abhorred their baseness, but their fawning had an invaluable effect: it flattered Leduc's gross vanity, and deflected his attention away from subjects more perilous to me.

The company of machines reassured me even more.

The animation of an airport, a glassworks or a machine-shop, the activity of a steelyard, the mere sight of a motor in rotation, produced in my enemy, as in all his peers, a strange fascination. The electrical wires, tubes and conductors of every sort, hollow and solid, whose inextricable network obstructed the sky, seemed to communicate something of their insensate energy to Leduc, as if by induction. The spirit of machines seemed to effervesce within him, contagiously, making him violent, haggard, agitated, trepidant, *automatic*. Drawn into the round of brutal forces, drowning his animality and intelligence within them, drunkenly, his eyes fixed and wild, forgetting everything else, he enjoyed their methodical rage, the forced turbulence of matter tamed by equations, and he only woke up from these dark Cabirian[40] ecstasies to absorb himself in the examination of some technical detail, muttering calculations, caressing the greased steel of a crank-shaft or scrutinizing the contours of a buzzing machine, with the solicitude of a father for his favorite child.

In this fashion, therefore, the central power stations and refrigeration plants, the glassworks, the abattoirs, the volvite factories, the airports, the generators, the radioactive batteries and workshops of every sort received my visits, as well as the port of Alexandria, the Camp of the Cylinders, the Equatorial Alternators at Khartoum and the Solar Accumulators at Aswan. Everywhere, the racket of metal, the hammerings and enraged drones of Machinery; everywhere, the avid ardor of furnaces and the blinding glare of floodlights; everywhere, the abominable stink of shaggies with simian bodies and quasi-human bodies, their eyes reflecting a sinister mixture of atrocious egotism, bestial passions and mysticism—and the rebellion of my nerves, which habit normally permitted me to conceal, but not to avoid, was redoubled by a horror that sometimes extended as far as terror, as the goals to which all these efforts were directed revealed themselves more clearly to my mind, or materialized before my eyes in the Cylinders lined up as far as the eye could see in their infernal dockyard—or, worse still, in the Tunnel, which was visibly deepening with a fantastic rapidity.

In the evening, after these mortal days—Raymonde had been subject to similar adventures among the *Amazons of the Sphinx*—we sometimes had to attend cinematic propaganda sessions on the balcony of the Red Palace, in company with the general staff. The apparatus was set up on the ancient pyramid of Cheops, and the screen extended between two terraces on the Monument. Captured by the televisor though the rare gaps in the clouds that shrouded the white plant, scenes of Venusian life—marvelous idylls of the Golden Age, unfolding amid landscapes of dream—drew nothing from the barbaric Martians of the Esplanade but cries of triumphant joy and anticipated triumph. Venus was nothing to them but a future field of carnage, and they rejoiced perversely in seeing its gentle inhabitants crowned with flowers, ready to bend their heads beneath the

---

[40] The Cabiri were a group of minor deities associated with Hephaestus, the metalworker of the Greek pantheon.

pitiless yoke of the invader. Hurrah! The way to the solar paradise was wide open!

But it was necessary to hurry! And the equatorial zone of Jupiter appeared on the screen: the formidable battery of Solar Accumulators capturing luminous-calorific energies, and, on the circular railway, the Projector that would transform those energies, on the day of the next opposition, into the jet of the annihilating Thunderbolt, if the Cylinders were not ready in time!

And the hatred, the cowardice, the lust for vengeance became delirious in the darkness, and the furious clamoring of Terromartian throats roe up from the Esplanade, mingled with the raucous yelps of shaggies and maki-mokokos—while Raymonde and I, leaning on the balcony of the Red Palace, lowered our heads, quivering, under the suspicious gaze of the Technical Director.

V. News From Panama

The American raids furnished an abundance of new recruits to the services of the Reincarnation, but the spectacle of the Hall had changed since the days of the Perfume. Only simian volunteers went to the Solenoids with confident expressions. The Martian souls had no need for any additive to dominate the feeble animal mentalities and expel them from their bodies. Because all species of monkeys—not just the anthropoid apes, as in the beginning—were admitted without distinction, the souls took full advantage of that license, and all the monkeys brought by the volvites were now, without exception, complete shaggies avid to receive the official stamp.

The Terrans went in a very different fashion. The atmosphere of the Perfume, whose occult properties had sufficed to slacken the spiritual bonds of the unfortunate humans, had earlier permitted the Martian souls to take possession without difficulty of all the survivors, black, yellow and white, of Africa, Asia and Europe. Since the passing of the sole custodians of the secret, the Magi, however, the Terrans no longer let themselves be vanquished as easily, and the majority of those who were now led into the hall still conserved their human mentality intact.

I witnessed horrible scenes on several occasions: unfortunates, captured by force and resistant to the last second, when the psychostatic currents of the solenoids left them at the mercy of souls competing for their prey of choice. A superb huge devil of a Canadian trapper, among others, left me the memory of his desperate struggle against two gigantic orangutans, and of his stentorian voice calling down the vengeance of Heaven upon his executioners...

Such occasions became increasingly rare, though. The Old World had been completely emptied since the reign of the Perfume, and the Terrans of the New World had, for the most part, taken refuge in the jungles of the equatorial rainforest, from which the volvites did not always succeed in extracting them.

Despite our repugnance and disgust, Raymonde and I did not miss any opportunity to cast our eyes over the hall on the days when the presence of humans was signaled in a convoy of "volunteers." We reviewed these unfortunates while affecting an idle curiosity, but were profoundly moved by pity, and the dread of discovering, among those hirsute and desperate faces, one that was familiar.

We had certainly told one another that, in all probability, our friends from Mont Blanc would have arrived safe and sound in Tahiti; that no danger threatened them there yet; that the raids might perhaps go no further than America—but presentiments of disaster wrung our hearts when we thought of them...

Among the numerous services accessory to the Reincarnation there was one, newly instituted, which excited our curiosity: the hypnotic school. The influence of the solenoid ensured each Martian soul a conclusive accommodation

249

in its host body—human or simian—and the re-education of actions operated for the most part, spontaneously. Sometimes, because the mechanism of language only existed in a rudimentary state in the cerebral lobes of monkeys, the Martian souls that had invested themselves with bodies of this sort experienced real difficulties in speaking. Baboons, among others, and spider monkeys and marmosets even more so, could only express themselves, after a month, in a frightful jargon that was difficult to recognize as the patois of shaggies, let alone as academic French. In order to overcome this lacuna—which the increasing profusion of "pithecoids" rendered more and more serious—a school of hypnotic instruction had been annexed to the Hall of Reincarnation, and, thanks to a method invented by Professor Landru and applied by his pupils to the neo-Martian monkeys, the latter were able to acquire, in seven or eight one-hour lessons, the means of expressing themselves intelligibly.

Two months in Mars Central and the daily company of shaggies had not sufficed to make us entirely accustomed to them. Their skill as mechanics did not surprise us overmuch, but hearing coherent speech emerging from their bestial mouths still caused us an insurmountable frisson, and a sort of unhealthy curiosity attracted us of the hypnotic school. One evening, I met Leduc there. Holding forth excitedly in the middle of a group of leaders, he called me over.

"Ha ha! R'rdô! Here's some news! That little bastard Moreau has had a finger stuck in his eye, after all! The Mont Blanc lot aren't all resting in the ruins of the bunkers! At least fifteen escaped, and took abrupt leave of our Admiral of the Air! Incredible, no? But true…this marmoset-shaggy has seen Abbé Romeux with his own eyes, in Panama!"

I felt myself go pale, and to hide my distress I leaned over the little animal, which was perched on a chair, huddled up in its fur, studying me with eyes as intelligent as those of the Martians surrounding us.

"Yes, I saw Abbé Romeux in Panama…Abé Romeux!" said the shrill nasal voice of the marmoset.

I stood up straight again, as if outraged by this diabolical denunciation. Raymonde, who had maintained her calm appearance, shook her head with well-feigned skepticism.

"And you're prepared to believe this beast, Leduc?"

"No more a beast than you or I, Excellency, He's passed through the solenoid. He's a Martian. But in addition to his psychic Martian memory, he's conserved his monkey memories in his monkey brain, of which we have given him the use…and the means of expressing the memories. Does that astonish you, R'rdô? But you know full well that all sensations remain stored in the memory, like a collection of photographic prints. Our will isn't always sufficient to extract them from their drawers, but hypnotism will do that…go on, brother shaggy, talk! And tell the truth—or it'll be detrimental to your matriculation!"

And the vile little animal, which I could cheerfully have strangled, spoke.

250

"When I be in the forest...I have found this body...not pretty, not strong, but nothing else.... O Majesty! Other souls say to me that you carry away to Venus with cylinders all good worshippers of the Sun, two-hands and four-hands alike. O Majesty! Souls they tell me the truth?"

Seeing me hesitate, Leduc said: "Yes, shaggy. But for that you would have come out of the solenoid electrocuted instead of Martianized. Go on."

"Then I follow footprints of brother-Martians, in forest, long time...I arrive at great River-of-two-Oceans, at the place where there be opened, four moons ago, by thunder-work of humans...."

"The Panama Canal," Leduc interjected. "The lock at Culebra was blown up."

"But all Martian brothers they be gone, before me arrive, with bird machines. Then me wait for other bird-machine to come. Stay two days, eat sugar-cane, worship Sun. Then a boat come far from North...big fishing-boat, with many two-hands on its back. I believe them Martian brothers, I show Sun to them, for them to take me away, for me not know how to talk then. But them two-hands not Martian brothers, them Terrans, them not worship Sun, not understand me. Then them see passage blocked and stop boat, and leader talk to them..."

"What was he called, their leader?" Leduc asked.

"Abbéromeux," said the marmoset, emphatically. "Ab-bé-Ro-meux! Him talk all alone to them, then them all together, long time. Then them get off boat, and boat sinks, see boat no more. Then them go forest, far south. But me stay river, me wait for Marian brothers come with bird-machine. Me worship Sun good, you make me four-hands just like two-hands, O Majesty?"

"Enough," Leduc cut in. Then he turned to me. "It's as clear as crystal. That damned Romeux had got away in a submersible and counted on passing through the canal—but he found it blocked, so he scuttled his boat to put us off the track. In fact, he and his pals are stuck in the vicinity of the canal with no other means of transport than their legs. Tell me, shaggy, how many are they, exactly? Did you count them?"

The marmoset rolled its eyes in embarrassment. "No, me not count—but them many. More than all in here." And it made a circular gesture with its pink-palmed hand to indicate the twenty or so monkeys—guenons and squirrel-monkeys—respectfully sitting on the other side of the room, holding their tails, in front of their hypnotist instructor, the seven or eight leaders, the two of us and Leduc himself.

The last-named emitted a sinister laugh. "That's all, good...Abbé Romeux, hey! Maybe the soul of an astronomer can jump aboard, in the solenoid! That doesn't depend on us though, but on chance, on some whim of a wandering soul! Our means are very imperfect—our spiritual methods aren't as highly developed as our mechanical ones, by a long chalk. It's the fault of the Magi, R'rdô! The Magi have always been laggards, behind the times. It doesn't matter, though. Romeux's brain will make a fine instrument for anyone other than a complete idiot. And the rest of the gang…adequate Terromartians. It's high time to readjust the proportions somewhat—we're overflowing with shaggies!

"But it's not settled yet; there's the matter of catching them. A spectacular hunt, the like of which hasn't been seen for a long time—an imperial hunt. Hee hee! If you weren't attached to Mars Central by definition, in tour capacity as Magus, R'rdô, I'd ask you to organize it. But for want of you, Her Excellency— Her Majesty the Empress, I mean—is made for the job, with her crew of Amazons…"

A refusal, or even a hesitation, on Raymonde's part was unthinkable. All eyes were fixed upon her, and it was with anguish in my heart that I heard her reply, in a voice in which only my vigilant affection was capable of discerning a disturbance: "Naturally, Leduc—I was about to suggest it."

VI. *Aboard the* Nautilus

You will recall that we left Abbé Romeux and his companions to continue their exodus to America aboard the submersible liner *Nautilus*, after two days of sailing.

No troublesome incident had occurred since the departure from Bordeaux. No suspect helicopter had been spotted by the lookout, and they had made steady progress in a west-south-westerly direction in a flat calm. Under the impulsion of her three propellers, powered by alcohol-fuelled turbines, the powerful steel hull clove the green crystalline waters of the Atlantic at twenty-five knots—46 kilometers an hour—and left behind a majestically straight wake in which seagulls played, excited by the sportive pursuit.

The Abbé had revealed himself at the outset to be as fine a mariner as he was an astronomer. The painter Nibot, who had sailed in his youth, served as his second officer; the former supervisors of the hydroelectric turbines on the Arve at Chamonix took charge of the engines. Everyone was a crewman of some sort, and the women donned stewardesses' aprons—so successfully that everything went as smoothly aboard the *Nautilus* as it had in the days when she transported rich passengers from Bordeaux to New York and *vice versa*. Everyone took turns to enjoy the best cabins and the luxurious drawing-rooms, and the bracing pleasures of idling on the deck.

Strange as it may seem, among people who had just escaped the most frightful dangers, good humor reigned and confidence increased with each passing day. The precipitate flight from Mont Blanc, the journey across deserted and ravaged France and the threat of Martian souls were all lost in the distance—the far distance, beyond the blue horizon, behind the immense expanse of ocean they had already crossed. The illusion of security returned to the exiles, and the future smiled at them again.

Even though they had found the ship's stores almost empty—the coal-bunkers, on the other hand, were full, as were the cisterns of fresh water—there was no fear of starvation because they had brought a sufficient supply of the Nutriment from Chamonix to support the seventy-one passengers for six months. In five days, at the most, they would be in Panama, and in Tahiti within a month, on the far side of the world, where there was a good chance that the Martians would not come to hunt them down.

Only the victims of sea-sickness—who were quite numerous, at first—saw the situation in tones of black, and had premonitions of catastrophe.

On the sixth day, a first warning lent support to the pessimists.

They were in view of the Bahamas, and the idlers on the deck, stretched out in deck-chairs, were examining the benevolent tropical landscapes through binoculars, when the lookout shouted: "A helicopter, to the North, heading straight for us!"

Fortunately for the exiles, who hurried inside as fast as they could, the volvites had not yet come into service, and the helicopter in question was scarcely capable of 150 kph. The *Nautilus* had time to fill her ballast-tanks and submerge without being seen.

The alert was thus without consequence—but it marked the beginning of tribulations that fate had thus far spared the fugitives—with the sole aim, one might have thought, of crushing them more completely. A sequence of misfortunes had begun.

First came the helicopters. Since leaving the Gulf Stream—for it had been necessary to go around the northern rim of the Sargasso Sea, whose tangled prairies of floating algae would have slowed them down too much—the *Nautilus* found herself, unknown to her commander, on one of the most frequently-followed routes used by Martian aircraft heading for Central America. The helicopters multiplied in a fashion that was terrifying and inexplicable to our friends. At certain times, the periscope could hardly be extended above the surface without a new flying machine forcing the vessel to dive precipitately. On one occasion, the hull was seen through the transparent water and a bomb was dropped, which obliged her to descend to a great depth and remain there until nightfall.

After that came the wind. One of the main advantages of submersible liners—the one that had caused them to be adopted by millionaire tourists and permitted companies to withstand the competition of the Transatlantic Tube—was sparing their passengers from the worst effects of sea-sickness by sailing for long periods at depths of 50 to 60 meters, at which the agitation of the superficial waves was virtually imperceptible, but the captain of the Nautilus could not risk traveling blind in these regions, where the charts warned of sandbanks and coral reefs. It was necessary to remain immobile for 48 hours, until the squall blew out, at a depth of thirty fathoms. The marvels of the abyssal world that they were then able to contemplate—luminous forests of polyps populated by cephalopods equipped with veritable searchlights and fishes whose flanks were equipped with rows of phosphorescent dots—were insufficient to calm the anxiety of the passengers, especially the female ones.

One might have thought that everyone had a presentiment of what was to follow: the damage, perhaps due to the inexperience of the engineers or a defect of the greasing, which caused the turbines to jam immediately after the coast of Haiti had been lost to sight and the eastern point of Jamaica doubled.

A heart-breaking disappointment! All the way to Panama, their course across the Gulf of Mexico was free of nautical dangers thereafter; they had hoped to pass through the canal, and escape the helicopters once and for all, in a day at the most—but there could be no question of going on solely powered by the accumulators, which would eventually have to be recharged. They had to make repairs, a soon as possible, and, given the nature of the damage—a "blade salad" in the main turbine—it would be best to head for the nearest port: Kingston.

The repairs took much longer than they had initially imagined. A month and a half was lost in numerous failed attempts on the part of the engineers, who could not find the necessary spares in the shops in the port, most of which had been destroyed by fire, and had in the end to resort to forging them themselves, at high risk of being detected.

Martian helicopters, in fact, passed by on a daily basis—not, fortunately, directly over Kingston, but a few kilometers out to sea. Nevertheless, it was necessary, after the first night to render the *Nautilus* invisible from above: to camouflage the dock where it rested with the aid of tarpaulins on which a vague representation of ruins was daubed—work that Nibot carried out in a few hours, aided by five or six other painters evacuated from Amiens and Saint-Valery.

It was not only danger from the air that the unfortunate exiles had to face, however. Scarcely were they installed under their tarpaulins, where the tropical Sun maintained the atmosphere of a Turkish bath all day long, when the Martian souls began to assail them. Those in Europe, which had tormented them from Sallanches to Bordeaux, were all too well aware of their powerlessness beyond the limits of the Perfume's reign, and they had left off after the embarkation aboard the *Nautilus*. The sea, empty then of all human activity, was hardly frequented by the wandering souls; they had scarcely been manifest since Bordeaux save for a few isolated nightmares, individual persecutions that were not difficult to repel. The souls of Jamaica were much more enterprising, because simian bodies, at that time, were only admitted to the honors of the solenoid after a rigorous selection process. The American monkeys, in particular, were mostly rejected—so they attempted the conquest of the refugees from Mont Blanc.

The engineers, fortified by their work against baneful suggestions, resisted well, but the forced idleness to which the other "castaways" were consigned might have been fatal, had it not been for the intervention of the Abbé. On the second night, three men and two women were invaded as they slept and woke up *possessed*, rolling their eyes wildly and clamoring raucously for the assistance of "their Martian brothers" and for "repatriation."

General consternation! What was to be done with these unfortunate fanatics, whose piercing cries might attract the next helicopter? Nibot and four veterans of the *Phalanx des 4-z'arts* tied them up and gagged them one after another. Doctor Goulliard was already talking about "communal safety" and insinuating that "before Pasteur's discovery people bitten by rabid dogs were stifled with pillows." The scientists nodded their heads approvingly...but Abbé Romeux stepped in.

"My friends," he said, "I have always respected your private opinions, and have never attempted to convert you to the true faith from which some among you have lapsed. I hope that they will do me the politeness today of letting me apply the remedy that the Catholic religion—to which I have the privilege of belonging—puts at our disposition in similar cases."

"Are you talking about exorcism, Monsieur l'Abbé?" asked Doctor Goulliard, during a pause interrupted by the stifled grunts of the possessed individuals. "My God, I wouldn't blame you in the least. I'm ready for anything, since I've been forced to admit the existence of the soul! However, exorcism is applicable to 'demons.' "

"When it was instituted, doctor, the Church could not foresee the Martian invasion!" said the Abbé.

He dressed in his ecclesiastical robes and, in the middle of a respectful and attentive circle, had the first possessed individual brought to him. It was Félix Delarue, a poet.

When the stole made contact with his hair, the possessed man, grinding his teeth, twisted his arms furiously. As he had lost his waistcoat and one of his short sleeves in the course of the fight, his biceps could be seen writhing beneath his skin "like a captive bat," as the painter Nibot told me later. His eyes avoided those of the priest and betrayed the anguish of the Martian soul, disconcerted by the ritual preparations, especially by the sort of magnetic chain formed by the audience.

"*Vade retro, Satanas*!" pronounced the Abbé, forcefully—and, under the inspiration of the moment, he added to the liturgical formula: "Depart, Martian spirit! Leave the body that you have stolen; restore it to its legitimate proprietor. Félix Delarue, I order you, in the name of the Lord and the living persons who surround me, to return to yourself!"

And the combination of human wills, united in an occult fashion by the Abbé and projected against the Martian, worked! The foreign soul weakened under the assault, and, with a despairing scream, the man fell back on to the ground. A few moments later, it was the real Félix Delarue who got up again, unsteadily, and threw himself effusively into the arms of his liberator, to the acclamation of the entire audience.

But the Abbé imposed silence on all manifestations of joy and gratitude. "You may thank God, my friends when we have vanquished the other demons…"

Half an hour later, not a single individual was any longer possessed; the five Terrans were victorious over their aggressors, and Doctor Goulliard himself came to render homage to the striking achievement of the Abbé, who wore his triumph with his habitual modesty and limited himself to replying to the congratulations: "You see, my friends, what a catastrophe the world might have avoided if there had only been more confidence at the outset in the aid of the Church! It is irreligion that has doomed the Earth!"

But the scientists, unconvinced, attributed the success of the exorcism to anything other than the words of the Latin liturgy. Whatever the reason, the

Martian souls considered it efficacious, admitted defeat, and did not renew their attempts upon the Mont Blanc exiles during the six weeks they remained in Kingston. They redirected their attention to the monkeys of the region and the rare humans who were still dragging out a miserable existence in the mountains of the interior—and their victory over the latter, in one case, subjected the passengers of the *Nautilus* to a frightful necessity.

This is how it came about.

On the evening of a day even more oppressive than usual, when helicopter alerts were so frequent that they hardly dared to light their muted lanterns in the shelter of the camouflaged tarpaulins—for the boat's interior was uninhabitable—the barking of dogs became audible in the distance, in the deserted ruins of the town, approaching rapidly. It was not the first attack of this sort, and the sentries were getting their blasters ready when the heard human calls for help, mingled with the voices of the dogs. In a fatal moment of thoughtlessness, pity over-rode prudence, and the Abbé himself ran outside shouting: "Over here!"

Twenty seconds later, two breathless individuals threw themselves under the tarpaulin, and the furious pack that was pursuing them was struck down, howling, by a salvo of blaster-fire.

The execution completed, everyone gathered round the escapees, who had been rendered into a pitiful state by the thorns of the tropic forest and the fangs of the dogs. What adventures had these dark-skinned "gauchos" with red shirts and leather trousers undergone before arriving here? To all questions however, they only replied with incoherent fragments of bad Spanish.

Professor Bianchini finally contrived to catch the word *Hermanos*. "Brothers," he repeated, darting a troubled glance around the assembly, whose faces were going pale. Then, in response to the gauchos, "*Si, siamos hermanos, todos hermanos...y hijos de la madre Tierra!*" he said: "Sons of Mother Earth? Oh no, they are not...not any more at least!"

The Martian souls inhabiting the bodies, having believed that they would encounter brothers from their planet here, recoiled at this revelation. The gauchos' eyes burned with infernal rage. "*Traidores!*" howled their raucous voices—and two unsheathed daggers were planted, one in Bianchini's breast and the other in the throat of his neighbor, a female painter named Bilitzka. Without the quick reaction of Doctor Goulliard, whose blaster decapitated the vile Martians with a double shot, Abbé Romeux would have been their third victim. Even so, he attempted to deflect the weapon.

"Don't kill them!" he cried, in the midst of the confused panic the drama had generated in its audience.

"Right, Abbé, you can look after them!" sniggered his savior, leaning over the wounded Terrans.

This adventure, which cost the lives of the two unfortunates, increased the impatience and general nervousness and caused the permanent abandonment of plans for settlement on Jamaica or nearby Haiti that the slowness of the repairs and the vicissitudes of the crossing had persuaded a few people to make. The mere possibility that other neo-Martians might discover the *Nautilus* before her departure and denounce her to the helicopters precluded any thought of staying longer than was strictly necessary.

It was with an inexpressible relief, therefore, that they finally re-embarked, at dusk, and felt the submersible vibrate once again under the impulsion of its turbines as it slid over the blue waves, quite ready to disappear beneath their blue veil. No helicopter searchlight came to add its threatening star to the marvelous constellations of the tropical night, however, and the Gulf of Mexico was crossed by night, at full speed, without incident.

When day dawned, the American coast was in sight, and at eight a.m. the *Nautilus* reduced her speed as she entered the Colon passage and proceeded along the inter-oceanic canal.

VII. The Massacre of the Amazons

The traces of the battles and the anarchist devastation that had bloodied America a year earlier appeared along with the city of Colon, a desert of ruins in which a few wary animals could be glimpsed. On the banks of the canal, along which the liner advanced more rapidly than the nautical regulations would have authorized, there was not a single building standing.

"Will we be able to get through the Culebra lock?" the pessimists wondered. "Provided that the opening mechanism is working—and that there's water in the upper reach!"

Alas, yes—there was, and plenty of it! But the lookout, on spotting the lock through his binoculars, could not retain a cry of despair. The lock-gates had been blown up and their debris, along with the quays that had collapsed into the lock, was blocking the canal with a formless barrage, over which the waters of the upper reach were pouring from a height of ten meters!

It was the end! They could go no further!

The *Nautilus* stopped.

Everyone, including the engineers, had come up on deck. They were looking back and forth, in bleak silence, from the fatal obstacle to the formidable walls of rock that encased them within the Culebra strait. From the top of one, on the right, a little monkey—a marmoset—was punctuating its capers with bizarre gestures. Nibot pointed it out to his companions, and forced himself to cheer them up with a remark that he thought witty: "There's one who won't denounce us to the Martians."

The ill-timed joke fell flat. At the mention of the word "Martians," the exiles shivered. The time when the helicopters usually arrived was drawing near.

"We have to turn back," suggested Doctor Goulliard, resolutely.

"Where to?" said the Abbé, softly, still holding on to the wheel.

Female voices protested "No, no! To Tahiti, no matter what!"

"Via Cape Horn, then? We'll never get there.

A general discussion started, watched over, as it were, by the monkey, whose minuscule silhouette was outlined against the blue sky.

Tahiti exercised a veritable fascination on all of them. Not only was it the goal adopted at the very beginning of the exodus, but there was every chance of finding the aviators of Chamonix and their "ladies" there. The rancor generated by their flight had dissipated a long time ago, and the deserters were no longer seen as anything but old acquaintances—the only other civilized people surviving on the face of the planet, an appropriate complement to the colony of Last Men.

The attraction of Tahiti, and the conviction they all held that the Martian danger ended with the Pacific coast, added to their perfectly natural reluctance to abandon the *Nautilus* and deliver themselves to the hazards of a desperate adventure—for it would be necessary to cross the isthmus on foot in the hope of discovering a ship capable of undertaking the voyage in the port of Panama.

"If there isn't one," cried Nibot, "then we'll have to go further, into Colombia, towards the equator...all the way to Patagonia if necessary—but, for God's sake, we can't stay here, exposed to the sight of helicopters without the option of diving."

On the commander's orders, they all equipped themselves as best they could for the expedition. The boxes of Nutriment were shared out, as were the blasters and their ammunition. Then, a few last turns of the propeller brought the Nautilus to a ruined stairway, and the seventy fugitives disembarked. Abbé Romeux was the last to leave the vessel, having opened the caps of the ballast-tanks. Slowly, the steel hull sank and disappeared into a whirlpool; when the surface had recovered its level, the enormous wreck became visible again, resting on the bed of the canal under two meters of water.

The Last Men, more deeply affected than they had been when abandoning the Bunkers, felt a wrench of separation, as if they had just broken the last link attaching them to the civilized world and their previous life.

They drew away from the canal and went into the forest, but they had no machetes; after an hour in the inextricable tangle of tropical vegetation had gained them a painful half-kilometer, they had to abandon the idea of heading straight for the Pacific coast following a compass bearing. The sad caravan retraced its steps and attempted to take an old roadway, which the lianas had not yet succeeded in blocking.

The Last Men marched beneath a dome of gigantic trees and arborescent ferns, from which bizarre parasitic plants hung down—orchids whose flowers were monstrous in both color and form. The high ceiling of foliage was impenetrable even to the rays of the mid-day Sun, but the heat was stifling and the humidity sickening. They walked for three days. Fear of the Martians gave way temporarily to a more immediate peril; in addition to the parrots, hummingbirds and monkeys, whose animation of the high branches was accompanied by chattering and deafening screeches, wild animals were abundant. It was necessary on numerous occasions to make use of blasters against jaguars, cougars, tiger-cats and snakes, and, by night, to surround their camp with a circle of fires, which attracted clouds of mosquitoes to the sleepers.

During the third day of the march, several women declared themselves incapable of going any further, and even the severe Doctor Goulliard judged it necessary to transport them on stretchers made from interwoven branches.

On the fourth morning, they emerged from the forest, and a unanimous cry of joy greeted the Pacific, displaying its lapis-lazuli sheet on the horizon. Closer at hand, the city of Panama sketched out its regular quadrilateral with the heaps of its ruins, and the sight of the port, surmounted by a confusion of masts, revived their hopes. There must surely be an entire ship among that crowd!

But all their searches were in vain. A folly of destruction had raged here too; dynamite had been placed inside all the large vessels; broken cylinders and twisted pistons were visible through enormous breaches in their shredded steel hulls. There was no longer anything afloat but humble sailing-boats—mere cockleshells that would capsize in the first squall in the open sea.

The Last Men were wandering sadly along the quay when the cry went up: "A helicopter!"

It was coming straight towards them at lightning speed: a volvite had discovered them. No matter—a gaping hangar was right beside them, ten paces away; they threw themselves into it.

With a gushing trail of fire, the unfamiliar flying machine—a cylindrical body tapered at the front, whose lack of rotor blades made it resemble a sort of stout javelin—set down horizontally on the quay. Immediately, like a jack-in-the-box, twenty Martians armed with blasters leapt out, with singularly high-pitched cries, and formed up like a firing-squad, in such a manner as to encircle the hangar. Only two pilots remained vaguely visible through the hyaline walls of the cockpit.

The besieged fugitives had no lingering doubts about the identity of their enemies. Those brick-red one-piece suits, each with a number displayed on the collar, those Valyrie helmets, those abrupt gestures and guttural voices—though shrill and feminine—had all been shown to them before, by Moreau's helicopters, at Mont Blanc. Martians! The Martians, of whose strength and perfidy they had formed a better impression since then.

At the first glimpse of those wild eyes, shining within the anonymous aviation masks, a wave of discouragement and despair ran through the ranks of the Last Men. They had an intuition of the power represented by these few individuals—the incalculable Martian power dominating the Earth. They were cruelly aware of their isolation. After them, no more fellows—no one at all. An Earth without Terrans. They had their backs, so to speak, to the void—the abyss into which all humankind had fallen before them, the nothingness that would breathe them in, into which they would disappear, along with the last hope of civilization, forever.

They were in the situation of criminals sensing, behind the gendarmes pursuing them, the millions of social beings interested in maintaining observance of the Law—but much worse, for criminals can, in theory, find accomplices or escape abroad. They were alone, all retreat cut off.

The very excess of the danger revived the defensive instincts of a cornered animal which charges head-first at its hunters, with the frantic courage of despair. Surrender? Never! They would fight to the death! Their assailants, armed, like them with blasters, were inferior in number, and the intoxication of catching up with their prey had made them forget the most elementary rules of strategy.

"A sortie!" Nibot proposed.

The Abbé squeezed his arm encouragingly. His eyes were sparkling. "Cut them off from the aircraft!" he said, tucking in his soutane in order to be better able to run. And he threw himself outside, followed by all his companions, not excepting the women. Disconcerted by this unexpected attack, the Martians hesitated momentarily before retreating toward the volvite, whose pilots called them back with hasty blasts of the siren—but it was already too late. The Abbé and his platoon hurled themselves into the Martians' path, and twenty-five blasters fired on them—while the women screamed, intoxicated by contagious heroism, and ten resolute men, led by Nibot, launched themselves forward in an assault on the cockpit.

The battle only lasted a few minutes. Caught between two fires, the Martians defended themselves fiercely, and seemed for a moment to be on the point of breaking through—but the volvite was taken, the two pilots bound and gagged, and Nibot, launching himself in support, rejoined the battle. The terrible blasters, with their *ffrrr...ffrrr...ffrrr...*, scarcely louder than a jet of soda-water, accomplished their sinister work from both sides. Thirty horribly charred and mutilated corpses littered the ground when the last of the assailants was no longer capable of doing any further harm.

The balance-sheet: Eight female prisoners—their sex had been established, dazedly—including the two pilots; 11 Martians and 22 Terrans dead, plus three slightly wounded....

The distant howl of a siren cut short the reflections of the Last Men, almost transforming the effervescence of the dearly-won victory into a disastrous panic. A wide-bellied transport helicopter, which had just witnessed the denouement of the affair, was arriving from the North-West! A second appeared on the horizon, drawn by its appeals! In five minutes, they would have an entire squadron on their backs! The distraught women wanted to run; the men reloaded their blasters somberly.

"Embark!" shouted the Abbé. "Everyone aboard! There's room—the prisoners too!" But all those captured on the battlefield had just been massacred by their guards; only the two captives in the volvite were left. By the time everyone had rushed aboard, piling at hazard into the hyaline cockpit, the first helicopter was no more than two or three kilometers away and had commenced firing. Nibot had untied and removed the gag from the Martian Pilot, who as still at the volvite's controls; he put the barrel of his blaster to her temple...

"Don't shoot, Nibot!" cried the pseudo-Martian, tearing her mask off with one hand, while the other seized the controls and engaged them. "I'm Raymonde Rudeaux! We're taking off! Hold tight!"

"You! Great God, Madame—save us!"

The volvite took off, amid a giant flood of artificial fire—staring at one another like cardboard figures, the fugitives were rooted to the spot by the stupefying revelation—and accelerated at full throttle, quickly leaving behind the helicopters, which soon disappeared over the horizon.

VIII. In the Works

Raymonde's departure to hunt the Last Men inevitably left me with cruel apprehensions. When I found myself on the platform of the airport, alone in the middle of the Terromartians of my entourage and the shaggies busy organizing further departures, I was tempted to recall the Amazon expedition by TSF. It was too late, though; we were both caught in the gears that were presently breaking my heart; it was necessary to go on to the end. Then I told myself— hardly able to believe it—that Raymonde's ingenuity and presence of mind might yet save our friends. I dared not ask myself, though, what would happen if the Amazons actually began to give chase; my best hope was that they had already left America and were sailing towards Tahiti.

Leduc extracted me brutally from my sad reflections.

"Well, R'rdô, shall we climb aboard. It's the turbines today!"

His voice had never seemed so harsh and vulgar, his tone so aggressive, the light in his eyes so disquieting—but I suddenly remembered that the Tunnel was causing him grave concern, and that a visit to the site was written into the day's program. Pulling myself together, I forced myself back into my false role as the Martian Great Leader...and my secret human duties.

It was on that very morning that I was to see a completed Cylinder for the first time, including the motive layer of *solar* and the giant hood that would shelter the whole structure from the Sun's rays until the last moment. If there were some interior steering equipment, it must be in place; I would see it, this time, and its sight would inspire me with the plans I had to make for the salvation of Venus.

We flew over the Martian City as usual, passing the roaring jet of the Central Fire, then the steelyard with the crucibles, and the Cylinders appeared, lined up as far as the eye could see in ranks of 20, looking more and more like caltrops as their reflective ditches were hollowed out around the partly-completed engines.

At the far end, the operations of molding, casting and hollowing out are proceeding methodically, but on the city side, the entire first row of Cylinders, hooded by their white tarpaulins, is gleaming in the sunlight, like tents lined up on the desert sands...

Each one is 60 meters high and fifteen in diameter, its interior divided into 25 stages for various purposes: storage-holds for mechanical equipment and chemical products necessary for the disembarkation; barrels of water, food-stocks—for the Martians cannot resign themselves to the Nutriment; barracks for shaggies, "cabins" for the general staff...

Most of the Cylinders will carry both Terromartians and shaggies—"It's safer that way" Leduc whispers to me. Why? I dare not ask him—50 or 60 of the former and 300 of the latter. A few cylinders are exclusively reserved for maki-mokokos, 4000 or 5000 in each. "They pack well," Leduc sniggers...

There are a full two million vehicles, in total, enough to contain the entire population of Mars Central, which has increased considerably since the exploitation of America had begun—and it is necessary to anticipate even more recruits!

This time, I have inspected everything, down to the smallest details—Leduc has remarked on my curiosity, sarcastically, as always—but there is no trace of steering equipment. Should I question him? But since R'rdô is presumed to know all that...

It will be necessary to examine the Great Leader's papers more attentively.

On the other hand, the control-room is here, where the apparatus will be mounted commanding the simultaneous withdrawal of all the hoods at the same time, for the departure, and the trigger that will set off the mine in the tunnel. Nothing is in place yet...but I wonder who will have the responsibility for working them. If it were me...!

That visit uses up the morning. The habitual turbulence of Mars Central. Nerves aggravated and tormented by noise, the odors, the odious proximity of machines, shaggies...and that of my fateful companion, the Technical Director...fortunately, other senior staff are also with us...hardly any time to think of Raymonde...she must already have reached he Antilles...

A meal in the staff dining-room—for I do not like to be alone...

These Martians eat with a vulgar sound of chewing, which provokes the same nervous irritation in me as listening to a dog gnawing a bone...and the food is desperately gastralgic, in spite of the champagne with which it is washed down: rump steak of sperm whale, this time, and a frightful dessert of weevils preserved in acetic acid!

An hour of siesta, exhausted by laborious digestion, in my air-conditioned apartment—then the new irruption of Leduc and the general staff...

A rapid glance at the *cracterite* factory installed the previous day: they wish to explain it to me...

Cracterite—the name acquires ten Rs in Leduc's pronunciation, and sinister overtones—is the explosive destined to charge the Mine...or, rather, its detonator: a shell, which will fall under its own weight, at the right moment, to the bottom of the 4,000-kilometer deep Central Tunnel. Shock and explosion cracking the thin solid layer reserved above the endothermic magma, which rises up in congruous quantity to encounter the Atlantic flood pouring in via the Canal. Meeting and intimate admixture of the two bodies transforms the Tunnel into a cartridge...

"And the Earth *cracks*...thanks to our *cracterite*," adds Leduc. But he does not have his usual air of triumph. He is too preoccupied with the Tunnel.

And we hurry through the factory visit: crushers, grinders and mixers of minerals that he does not deign to name for me...the final product is a green powder, which shaggies armed with wooden scoops transfer to an endless conveyor-belt before consigning it to railway wagons...

Forty minutes in a volvite over the desert...

The pithead of the Tunnel advertises its presence from afar with a monstrous emission of black smoke, which spreads out at an altitude of two kilometers into a prodigious parasol of volcanic eruption and resolves slowly, on contact with the air, into an impalpable dust, covering the surrounding region with a thick black snow...

What does this new aspect of the works signify? Has it hit some snag? Have they broken prematurely into some unknown reserve of subterranean fire?

I quiver with hope at the idea that the drilling of the well might be delayed, or halted...

Leduc, by contrast, becomes more cheerful. He rubs his hands.

"It's coming along, it's coming along!" he repeats. "Eight hours lost, that's all. We're still on schedule."

Between the airport and the pithead the spectacle becomes formidable. One might imagine that a steam engine, worthy of the Titans relegated by myth to the depths of Etna, is buried in the midst of the dunes, and that this is its chimney— 250 meters in diameter!—discharging that column of black smoke with a roar of infernal thunder.

The Titans who surround me—as audacious and powerful as those of old, in spite of their carnal envelopes, bimane or quadrumane—are delighted by the methodical cataclysm. The view is not yet sufficient. They want to study what they have unleashed at closer range. Following a sort of trench that shields us from the artificial squall and the airstream of the tornado, we reach the observation-post, in which a solitary Martian—a Chinaman with spectacles and a blue robe—is in charge of a collection of levers, gauges, pyrometers, manometers and so on, placidly directing the energies brought by enormous sheaves of cables from Aswan, Khartoum and radioactive generators.

The narrow crystal cage vibrates in the noisy gusts of wind that envelop it, as furious and continuous as a mistral storm. I expect to see it tear free from its concrete bed and fly away towards the tornado, which springs forth less than 100 meters away, rigid and almost solid by virtue of its speed, like a shaft of black marble.

The general staff snigger with pleasure; Leduc's nostrils dilate and he literally licks his lips as he listens to the engineer's report. Then he re-lights his eternal pipe and explains the situation to me.

"We can tell you now, R'rdô, and Your Holiness will loudspeaker it to the population this evening; it's been necessary to modify the drilling process. The drilling-machine you inaugurated—the Skimmer, which cleared its debris through a liquid channel—only got us down to 2652 meters. Beyond that, the rocks were too hard; the drill-bit broke and stuck fast. I've found a better way. Molecular disintegration at the point of attack—oh, very limited: that suffices to pulverize the minerals seized by the flood of radioactive particles and expelled in their whirlwind. Mean initial speed 350 meters a second. Spectacular 'draw' from the chimney, as you can see. We lost eight hours organizing the installation of new batteries in the Solar Accumulators, but we'll get them back by advancing at triple speed—and we're certain of getting all the way to the end, this time. Depth attained"—he pointed at a gauge—"2925 kilometers. In a week's time, we'll suspend the session for a few hours in order to go down and cast a glance over the interior of this old Earth. Then we'll finish throwing its entrails to the Sun!"

And on that note of vulgar buffoonery, the Technical Director unleashes a dprolonged burst of laughter. The staff were sharing his cheerfulness, and even the Martian servant has to let go of his levers momentarily to wipe the obscuring mist from his spectacle lenses.

A murderous desire, as violent as a stab of pain, wrenched my diaphragm. I put my hands in my pockets in order to clench my fists more easily, my fingernails drawing blood from my palms. I pressed my forehead against the hot crystal of the wall. How much pleasure…but there was nothing, nothing I could do—I could no more strangle these swine than uproot the observation-post and hurl it into that thundering tornado 100 meters in front of me. Impossible to halt the evisceration of my poor native planet. It must be endured it in silence, while observing, waiting and hoping that, in future…hope!

At 6 p.m. I disembarked from the volvite at the Red Palace, and chief A24—Nazir Bey, still wearing is fez, who had not accompanied us—came towards me. Turning his eyes away, he handed me a TSF message. News of Raymonde! I opened it avidly, overcome by the remorse of having forgotten her for several hours….

From Transport Helicopter RT28, Panama, 15:32.

Today at 14.:00, while flying over country 6 km north of Panama to embark shaggies, observed volvite AS1 (Amazons of the Sphinx) landing to port. Retained by difficulties of embarkation, impossible for us to help Amazons against Humans in time. Our helicopter too slow to catch Humans fleeing in captured volvite. Found cadavers, Humans and Amazons. Before dying, one Amazon declared that empress and pilot PA17 remained in volvite, abducted by Humans.

CRT281.

It was too much. I bowed my head beneath the sledgehammer blow, closing myself in with my distress, unable to respond. Besides, the technicians would have noticed. Successive telephoned calls inform me that a pursuit has been organized…that two volvites from the base in Mexico are en route…have caught sight of the fugitive and are giving chase…gaining on it…

Then the ringing eases off…nothing further received: the volvites have fallen silent. I stayed up all night waiting for the fatal news, in vain…despair, solitude. The cool evening air comes in through the open window, along with the immense rumor of the city, lit up by all its floodlights, while loudspeakers proclaim the imminent victory of the Martians from the height of the Monument of the Shell every quarter of an hour. In the intervals, bands of shaggies, obscenely drunk, howl on the Esplanade.

IX. In the Crater of Cotopaxi

The hull of the disquieting vehicle—a glass bolide, one might have thought—that cleft through the air 1000 meters above the ocean, with a jet of artificial fire spurting out, as if in anticipation of a final explosion, was built to accommodate twenty disciplined aviators. Twice that number of fugitive Terrans was crammed into it confusedly, still dazed by the battle and the escape. The volvite was hardly a suitable place for subsequent deliberations, or even coherent reflections.

The apparatus was much noisier than ordinary helicopters, in any case, and it was not until Raymonde had moderated its speed, the pursuers having disappeared, that it became possible to hear.

"Do you still want to go to Tahiti?" she asked.

"Yes," replied Nibot, who was sitting next to her. "Can't you take us there?"

"Unfortunately not. The volvites, not yet perfected, have a rather limited range. The one that's carrying you needs to change its activators in Mexico. The fuel we have left will scarcely take us 1000 kilometers."

There was an anguished silence, suddenly broken by the harsh voice of the second Amazon. She had surreptitiously worked free of her bonds and had taken advantage of the general inattention to get to the TSF apparatus.

"Ah, Terran wretches," she raged, gripping the manipulator. "You'll be taken this time...along with you, odious traitress—and your R'rdô..." But she had not finished giving the location when she was dragged away from the apparatus and tied up again.

Raymonde groaned. "I'd forgotten that woman—I'll never be able to see my husband again!" She briefly explained, in a halting voice, the role that she and I had undertaken to play among the Martians for the salvation of humankind.

"It's obvious," said the Abbé, "that this woman might ruin both of you..."

"She must die!" cried Nibot.

"What good would it do?" said Raymonde. The massacre of the Amazons is known; they'll know that I've consented to fly the volvite. I'm thoroughly compromised. The only way to take the responsibility away from my husband...alas, I can't ever go back to him—it's over! But I shall keep my promises, at least: I shall try to save you. Poor Léon! How anxious he must be!"

"We have to make a decision," Doctor Goulliard cut in. "We're squandering kilometers of flight..."

The only thing to do, since refueling at a Martian camp was unthinkable, was to go back to the coast and visit the equatorial ports, where they would eventually find a boat capable of taking them to Tahiti.

Since leaving Panama, Raymonde had been heading south-west; a 90-degree turn displayed the long snowy wall of the cordillera of the Andes on the horizon—but it also displayed two minuscule moving points low in the northern sky.

"They're following us!" the unfortunates lamented.

"Head for the mountains!" ordered the Abbé. "It's the only hope."

Raymonde steered to the south and opened the accelerator wide. The volvite roared and set off like a shell.

"756 kph," Nibot observed, terrified.

That speed was sustained for a few minutes. The enemies on the horizon lost ground. The mountains grew before their eyes. Several were crowned with volcanic smoke.

"Reference point: Cotopaxi," said the geographer Baumsen, pointing. He murmured details of the region—but the propulsive jet was losing its impetus. The accumulators were running out. The needle of the tachymeter descended from 700 to 650, then to 600. The Martian volvites were gaining again.

"We must get over that, though!" declare the Abbé, referring to a vast cliff towards which they were heading, as if to smash themselves against it.

A pass opened up on the snow-line, to the south of Cotopaxi. Raymonde steered towards it, demanding an ascension from the machine of which it was becoming less capable by the second...

They did not get over. There was a rattling sound, and the remaining propulsive force could only slow the fall, permitting an uncomfortable landing on a rocky platform, out of sight of the enemy.

Nibot was the first to leap down. "Blasters! Torches! All the levers and iron bars that are aboard—and quickly, quickly, over there!"

He pointed to a sort of gaping cavern whose floor descended gently into darkness.

"Is everyone here? Don't forget the prisoner! As for the volvite—four strong men!"

A precipice, at least 1000 meters deep, opened out on the edge of the terrace. The volvite was rolled into it, and its fall, awakening echoes, sent two gigantic condors—a male and a female—soaring aloft in large spirals, driven from their eyrie.

"That should put the Martians off the track. They'll spend a good hour searching for the pieces of our bodies down there. Forwards!" Nibot plunged into the vault as he gave the order, lighting his torch.

"Follow him," confirmed the Abbé. "It's the only thing we can do."

A few women were hesitant to go into the bowels of the volcano, but the icy air of the heights transported the distant blasts of the sirens on the Martian volvites, which were arriving thunderously; that decided them, and the little troop set off.

The opening was evidently that of an ancient crater; lava had hollowed out a passage there long ago, while Cotopaxi projected its igneous plume into the sky, as high as that of it rival Chimborazo. For the moment, though, its activity was dormant—except that dull rumbling sounds attested that a reawakening would occur one day or another. Near the entrance, stalactites produced by the infiltration of water suspended their alabaster draperies from the roof; the torch-light played with them capriciously. Lower down, the stalactites disappeared, and the tunnel's ceiling, like its walls and floor, was no more than volcanic rock: black basalt, whose large blocks, cut away by the cooling process, sounded hollow underfoot, like an iron floor succeeded by an even more sonorous phonolith. Then their footsteps became duller on an expanse of obsidian.

Monsieur Schwann, the professor of geology, was in Heaven, and had to be prevented from stopping every few minutes to stuff mineralogical specimens into his pockets. He muttered the names of sparkling crystals: agates, chrysoliths, amethysts, chalcedonies. He demanded that his companions admire pyrites, manganese ores, pitchblende, long shiny needles of antimony, blocks of quartz illuminated in all their facets like enormous diamonds....but no one was listening.

The tunnel, whose dimensions were nearly uniform—three or four meters high and as many broad—sloped downwards evenly, at an angle of fifteen or twenty degrees. No one was talking any longer; only the noise of footsteps echoed in the vaults. They went down mechanically, save for a halt of ten minutes, when Nibot lay down and put his ear to the ground. Then he got up and shook his head: the Martians were not coming yet.

"Damn it!" mumbled Doctor Goulliard, after an hour, wiping his forehead with a large blue-checkered handkerchief. "Where the Devil is he taking us? The centee of the Earth? I'm starting to melt!"

The fugitives had just emerged into a large cavern—a "bubble" in the Earth's crust—whose exceedingly high dome was lost in the darkness. One might have thought it a crossroads where the various chimneys of the volcano came together. The true crater opened in the middle of the grotto—a sheer gulf from which dull rumblings and the muffled sound of explosions emerged. The ground trembled underfoot like the lid of a saucepan. The heat was, indeed, intolerable.

"I'm looking for a way out," Nibot replied—for his companions, following Doctor Goulliard's example, were giving voice to their anxiety.

The painter set about making a tour of the cavern, examining each fissure attentively. The others, distressed, idled somnolently at the tunnel entrance. A few were talking about "going back." But Nibot, moistening his finger with saliva and raising it above his head, had come to a halt in front of a tortuous and irregular gallery, bristling with rocky protrusions, which was almost vertical.

"Here it is," he said.

A coolness was palpable at the end of his index finger, as if a slight air current were moving into the gallery. It had to communicate with the exterior.

"The question is, will it be practicable?"

At that moment, the geologist, who had been prowling around the central crater for several minutes, cried out: "An eruption!" And he pointed into the gulf.

Everyone came running.

Lava was rising up! Five or six meters below the ground-level of the crypt, a dark red liquid surface, like iron in a forge, was slowly oscillating, giving off a suffocating heat, groaning and rattling like a consumptive's chest. It moved from high to low, then from low to high, but each change of level brought it a little higher.

Mouths agape, hypnotized by that formidable threat, the Terrans were still staring when the Abbé, who had not left his listening-post, whispered: "The Martians!"

They were coming. From afar, perhaps several kilometers, the corridor, acting like an echo chamber, brought the faint but clear and characteristic sound of their march, with distant racket of their raucous voices.

Two women fainted. Others were weeping hesitantly. The bravest listened to Nibot giving his instructions.

"They've found a clue. They know that we're here. Good. What to do: first, decamp—and I've found a route, perhaps not very comfortable, but too bad! Second, slow them down, so that when they get here the eruption will stop them. How much time do we have, Monsieur Schwann?"

"In 20 minutes or half an hour, the lava will overflow."

"Let's say 20 minutes…to work, with the iron bars!"

The walls of the tunnel were volcanic tuff, cracked and friable. Twenty pairs of strong hands, stimulated by the danger, soon levered off enough rock to block the tunnel for an extent of several meters. A cat could not have got through.

"It'll take them a good half-hour to demolish that—longer if they haven't brought the necessary tools. By then, the crypt will sufficiently flooded with lava to make them recoil from the foot-bath. Let's go!"

They were just in time. The molten magma was coming over the lip of the enormous basin, and the air-temperature was rising rapidly. They had to follow the wall of the crypt to gain entry to the vertical tunnel.

"En route!"

The danger of "getting stuck" there lent wings to the heaviest. Even the ladies that had had to be revived from their faint scaled the "chimney" with the energy of desperation, with the aid of the projections of the rock and the support that the strongest and most skillful of their companions were ready to give them.

The howls of the Martians echoed, muffled by the barricade, mingling with the rumblings and detonations of the eruption.

"Where's the prisoner?" asked the Abbé.

"Left her in the crypt," replied Doctor Goulliard, who had been appointed as her guard. "Don't worry—I guarantee that she won't talk." The surgeon had, in fact, taken advantage of the confusion of the last minutes spent in the vault to disembarrass them of a dangerous enemy and himself of some "inconvenient luggage." He had sectioned her carotid artery with a thoroughly professional skill, and she had fallen without making a sound; no one had noticed. "The girl would have slowed us down," he concluded, by way of a funeral oration.

The Abbbé sighed, but said no more.

The inclination of the tunnel became less abrupt, and progress easier. The howls of the Martians became louder, thanks to the demolition of the barricade; then the discovery of the lake of lava filling the crypt changed them to screams of fear, which were soon lost in the distance by virtue of a precipitate retreat. Nothing more could be heard then but the subterranean flatulence of the eruption and the lapping of the lava against the walls of the crypt. Without the hot gusts that enveloped them, like the breath of a furnace, the Last Men would have called a halt, for they were saved now. So far as their enemies were concerned, the lava had, in fact, swallowed them up to the very last, along with the two Amazons—and this was obviously the news that The Martians hastened to transmit to Cairo, as soon as they were aboard the volvites.

While they climbed, the Terrans congratulated themselves on their deliverance. Nervous laughter mingled with the echoes of their footsteps and the sound of pebbles rolling down the slope of the corridor. Soon, a minuscule patch appeared before them. It grew into a fragment of blue framed by the orifice of the gallery. It was daylight—the blessed light of the Sun.

And continuing on their way, careless of the crevasses and the bocks of stone against which they stumbled, the Last Men hurled themselves tumultuously outside the mountain into the open air, dazzled by the splendor of the sky that they had not expected to see again.

Raymonde alone did not share in their delight, and maintained a bleak expression amid the cries of joy, embraces and prayers of thanks. Her brow furrowed, she wept silently, and her heart went out to me, whom she would never see again, and who would believe her dead along with the others…

X. The Banquet of the Sun

The mysteries of telepathy! The caprices of that mysterious force—the Yod of certain metaphysicians of the 19th century, which sometimes establishes between incarnate souls, between their brains, communications as clear, precise and detailed as TSF messages, and colored like a painting besides, like a scene from life!

Many times, in our past life, Raymonde and I had had the opportunity to experiment with this faculty: sentences commenced by one and finished by the other; premonitions of an unexpected return; perception at a distance of an action, a state of mind, or an adventure—but the majority of the messages in question were transmitted in banal circumstances, at no great distance.

I could not decided which of two events was the most grave, but I ought to record the singular fact the Raymonde's anguish during the Amazons' battle and her abduction did not give rise to any telepathic phenomenon between us. I had no suspicion of it until the moment when I read the report from the helicopter. By contrast, the escape from Cotopaxi was immediately revealed to me by that mysterious means.

It was 2 a.m. Stretched out in an armchair, I was waiting anxiously for news—I'm certain that I was not asleep—when the divination of a presence caused me to raise my head.

Raymonde! Raymonde, before me! Raymonde, whom I knew to be 10,000 kilometers away!

There was nothing nebulous or phantasmal about the apparition. Her leggings, torn and covered with black dust, her flying-jacket, which was in an even worse state, and her dented helmet, hardly able to restrain her disorderly hair, gave her a tangible three-dimensional quality of absolute reality. Projected by the lamp on my desk, her shadow extended obliquely over the giraffe-skin rug covering the glass floor. Raymonde! She smiled beneath her halo of volcanic ash, and her dear contralto voice filled me with an indescribable emotion.

"Don't be sad, beloved, I'm alive. I've escaped with our friends. Have confidence; we shall see one another again. My heart is with you." And, taking a flower from her belt, which she had recently picked—a huge lily with a scarlet corolla—she gave it a gracefully amorous kiss and threw it towards me…

I stood up, with an audible exclamation.

Raymonde had disappeared. I was alone: alone with the Andean flower with scarlet petals, which I picked up pensively, and from which I breathed in the intoxicating scent of vanilla.

But the ringing of bells, the noise of footsteps…I barely had time to make it vanish into my pocket. The inevitable Leduc, followed by my general staff, had come to bring me the news, with expressions of false pity.

273

"Condolences, R'rdô. Why, there's a funny smell in here! It reeks of perfume…oh, no one has telephoned the message yet? I thought you would be up to date. Well, the Humans went to ground on Cotopaxi, abandoning their stolen aircraft, and went deep into one of the volcano's craters. Our men followed them in—but an eruption occurred, and it's certain that the Humans have perished under the lava, their prisoners too. Condolences, R'rdô."

"Condolences, Majesty!" mumbled the leaders, in order of rank.

I had some trouble retaining my joy and simulating grief, in the face of such complete disrespect—and my hand, within my coat pocket, gently caressed the marvelous flower that testified to the salvation of my beloved.

"I presume," Leduc went on, "that you're going to cancel this evening's banquet?"

The banquet in honor of "the first 100,000 maki-mokoko priests of the Sun!" I had forgotten that I was to preside over it in my capacity as Sovereign Pontiff.

An impulse overtook me. The Venusian Master ordered me…ah yes, in my new situation, alone and without fear of exposing Raymonde to danger…to risk everything to gain everything, to take advantage of the opportunity. How, I don't know yet, but I shall find out! To shake the Mechanist tyranny…

And I raise my head, heroically.

"Festivals are few and far between at present; I don't want R'rdô's private mourning to prevent the Sovereign Pontiff giving the people the opportunity to hear the voice of our glorious Magi. The banquet will take place."

Leduc is astonished. "You're going to talk to them!"

"I shall try," I say, modestly.

The appointed setting for the ceremony that was to bring the entire unoccupied population of Mars Central together in a few hours was the construction-site of the Cylinders, The mounds of debris extracted from the molds had been formed into a superficially-vitrified amphitheater, from which the banquet's guests would be able to see the means of their future ascension lined up, extending into the infinite. All the apparatus of the feast—tables, benches, trays, plates, spoons, forks and so on—had been replicated thousands of times over, with a minimum of effort, thanks to impressions of moist sand, and several cubic meters of cast-iron appropriated from the fountain of core iron.

Formidable culinary preparations, in which I feigned interest while mulling over my idea, kept the shaggy cooks busy all day. Hippopotamuses boiled in their hide, elephants cooked whole in an autoclave, spit-roasted sharks, crocodile ragout, fricassees of vultures and boa constrictors, were set out on the tables, as far as the eye could see, as soon as the Sun set, alternating with fruits and vegetables of every kind, mainly intended for he simians: coconuts, bananas, dates, oranges, pineapples, lemons, guavas, carrots, potatoes, sugar-cane, and so on. To drink, enormous casks of red wine and white wine—especially champagne—dispatched their thirst-quenching floods to every table by means of branching conduits which provided a tap for each individual guest, who also had a big can of condensed milk at his disposal.

Terromartians and shaggies alike were sniggering as they took their places at this Pantagruelian feast. The guests of honor, the maki-mokokos, in the grip of their corporeal instincts, were gamboling gaily, grimacing as they saw themselves reflected in polished plates, spoons or goblets.

For the occasion, males and females were eating together. An even more lively hilarity was not long in developing once the first mouthfuls had been taken, in the glare of the recently-illuminated floodlights. At the imperial table, which overlooked the assembly, even the chiefs of the general staff promptly forsook the reserve that they believed they owed to my putative mourning, and set about guzzling and tippling shamelessly. I poured them floods of gin, kummel, whisky, cognac, chartreuse, Benedictine; I encouraged their coarse jokes. Leduc, belching and swearing immoderately all the while, declared me "a bloody smart fellow." With every glass emptied in my vicinity—needless to say, I had to imitate them—and every hiccup, I felt my plan ripening, and the moment drawing nearer.

The nights are cool in December, even at the latitude of Cairo. I am inclined to think that this circumstance—along with the metal seats, which had no cushions—must have contributed to giving birth, amid the Martians' Bacchic pandemonium, to the cry that propagated itself like a trail of gunpowder to become a sort of unanimous chant: "The Sun! The Sun!"

That is how I see it now, from a distance. At the time, though, it came as a revelation, a psychic trigger. "Eureka!" I proclaimed, thumping my fist on the table with all my strength.

Was I drunk? I don't know. In any case, I was resolved to undermine the authority of "the Boss," finally to use my prestige in a good cause: to hold that crowd of mystic brutes who saw me as a sort of sub-God in the palm of my hand—to be their Emperor in truth!

"Silence!" I roared into a megaphone, standing up in all my majesty.

They all fell silent, as if by enchantment.

Extemporizing eloquently, I proclaimed: "Martians! In the name of the Sun, the origin and end of our destiny, I, the humble successor of your Magi, the Sovereign Pontiff and Empreor of you all, Terromartians, shaggies and maki-mokokos, I tell you that we have taken a false path!" *General sensation.* "We are too timid!" *The chiefs exchange glances; Leduc's drink catches in his throat, almost choking him.* "Martians! What good does it do to destroy a step in the path of reincarnation, if we do not go on to the end—if we call a halt on such an open road!" *Brouhaha of astonishment. Stupor among the chiefs.* "The Sun, Martians! The Sun, distant paradise of our souls, must be the next paradise of our bodies! Yes, the Sun, not Venus! The Sun burns, you say? Only on the surface! Beneath that splendid ceiling...warm, maki-mokokos!...flamboyant, shaggies!...the paradise, Martians, promised by my infallible predecessors, the Magi, is lodged! And to arrive there without being roasted by its sublime rays...nothing is more simple...we shall pass...through the sunspots! Martians, straight to the Sun!"

Oh, I have struck a chord! The Sun! A magic word, charged with a magnetism accumulated over 1000 generations! The effect on which I was counting is produced, exceeding my hopes. The entire assembly rises up as a single Martian, repeating in an immense clamor: "The Sun! Hurrah! Yes, yes, we want the Sun!" And the frenetic repetition, in chorus. of "The Sun! The Sun! The Sun!" howled with all their might, rhythmically intoned by 500,000 drunken Martian madmen, precipitates a thunderous drum-roll of bare feet, hob-nailed boots, goblets, spoons and trays upon the metal tables: an indescribable din.

"Heresy!" cries Leduc, his eyes bulging and his face purple, apoplectic.

"Heresy!" repeat the shaggies faithful to "the Boss," the Mechanist part of their souls in revolt—for if they go straight to the Sun, it will be the end of Mechanization and their technical role.

A stir of hesitation among the rest...

Coincidence, miraculous for the Martians: a volvite, charged with distributing the dessert as a "surprise," releases upon the tables a continuous cataract of pumpkins, melons and gourds of every variety.

"The Sun! The Sun! The Sun is ours!" And everyone, hallucinated, takes possession of these thousands of solar symbols, juggling with them, clutching hem to their hearts kissing them, devouring them. A few maki-mokokos even throw them at Leduc, while bombarding the shaggies—who, unconvinced, gather together, surrounding their leader, protecting him...

And Leduc, his megaphone at full volume, launches this formidable challenge to the partisans of the Sun: "Piss off, then! You'll never get past me and my faithful shaggies!"

His gaze scans the ranks of the chiefs who are grouped around me, who have quickly judged the crushing force of my new stratagem. Four paces bring him face to face with me...I draw my blaster...but he only whispers a single word in my ear:

"Terran!"

But we are separated, dragged apart; the clamorous storm is redoubled: "The Sun! Hurrah! Long live the Emperor!" Melons, pumpkins and gourds fly from every direction. An irresistible ovation disperses my guard; I am subject to an avalanche of female maki-mokokos, who plaster me with 1000 kisses, winding their long gripping tails around my arms and legs...

A delirious battalion of Terromartians gets involved; I am grabbed, hoisted on to a bulwark of shoulders, and borne away in triumph over a vertiginous ocean of heads howling at the top of their voices: "The Sun! The Sun! The Sun is ours! Long live, live, li-i-i-ve the Emperor!"

....And without knowing how, I finally find myself back home, released from the nightmare that continues to fill the city with its insane clamor. In my office, strewn with hundreds of pumpkins and other solar *Cucurbitae*, brought with me by my frantic worshippers! Poor Raymonde! How she would have laughed if she were with me! Alas...!

It doesn't matter. I haven't wasted my day. The Venusian Master must be content with me!

XI. The Revolt of the "Pumpkins"

The howls of sirens and public loudspeakers woke me up, not without difficulty, from an opaque sleep. It was 3 p.m.!

I leapt out of bed and ran to the window. On the Esplanade, a few scattered Martians were still mechanically obeying the summons to the workshops—abandoned since the banquet—and lending their ears to the giant voice of the Monument of the Shell:

"Martians! Take care! There are false brothers and hidden enemies among us: Terrans! The Technical Director is aware of it. In consequence, for the sake of communal safety, he orders that a truce be called in religious quarrels, that the entire population of Mars Central, without any exception of origin, form, sex, *or even of rank*, must submit to a soul inspection by competent experts, and that everyone must pass through the solenoid again! Operations will commence today at 16:00 hours, with serial numbers beginning with Z. Alphabetical order will be followed!"

Despite the Sun's heat caressing my shoulders, I broke out in a cold sweat.

Infernal Leduc! He had found his response to my attack of the previous day. His hatred had heightened into divination; it had lifted my mask and recognized my true Human nature. To be sure, I now had three quarters of the people and all the overseers on my side, and a direct accusation would not have had the slightest chance of success. He had, therefore, adopted the only means of annihilating my power and having me condemned to death. If I refused to submit to this absolutely general inspection—and Landru, the chief examiner, was still one of the Boss's fanatical supporters—I would lose the confidence of the people and all authority over him at a stroke. I did not even have the resource of forbidding it in the name of religion. The idea that there might be Terrans hidden among them generated enormous emotion in the Martians.

A glance at the periscope screen showed me the streets of the city filling up with Terromartians, maki-mokokos and shaggies in a matter of minutes, marching confusedly to the Hall of Reincarnation. As the badge of their faith, the new sectarians of the Straight-to-the-Sun movement were wearing large slices of pumpkin, or even entire specimens of other Cucurbita, suspended on cords around their necks. They were exchanging challenging stares with the shaggies—but the quarrel was temporarily forgotten in the face of the public danger.

The crowd came out into the Esplanade of the Pyramids, which was gradually covered by its variegated fleece, and the bearers of the registration letter Z, contained by the barriers, marched bravely to the solenoid.

I turned around like a rat in a trap. My registration-of-honor was A. A telephone call told me that the chiefs were asking for an audience.

"I'll be with you in two minutes."

278

Seized by an inspiration, I went straight to the wall and found a dozen meters of flexible cable among the electric wires, which I disconnected from the apparatus in order to wind it around my body, underneath my cape. A Ruhmkorff coil and a small pocket accumulator completed the protective device, with the aid of which I hoped to neutralize the current of the fatal solenoid.

I had just finished sealing the contacts when a clamor went up. The crowd massed in the vicinity of the Hall of Reincarnation was crying out in protest and indignation, with increasing violence.

"Assassin! Treason! Vengeance!"

The Z series flooded back out of the doorways, gesticulating madly, and loudspeakers proclaimed the sinister news: as soon as they had been introduced into the solenoids, the first five "examinees" had dropped dead on the spot! [41] With one voice, the entire crowd accused the operator of having replaced the psychometric currents, on Leduc's secret orders, with an electrocuting voltage. The operator was torn into pieces. Landru and his acolytes barely escaped, protected by a battalion of shaggies, who beat a retreat through the exasperated crowd in a wedge-formation. The official loudspeakers replied to the accusations that the solenoid's victims must be the hidden Terrans, but in vain—the "pumpkins" were paying no attention.

Leaning on the balcony of the Red Palace with my senior staff, whom I had allowed in, I followed the progress of the riot with a mixture of joy and anxiety. By suppressing the examination, it had saved me from a danger that my improvised counter-solenoid might perhaps have been powerless to avert. But what consequences would follow from this popular ferment? Only non-commissioned officers and aircraft crews were armed with blasters, but there were the stores of weapons and explosives, and the carnage might commence at any moment!

The situation took shape. The howling of loudspeakers—some operated by the shaggies, others by the "pumpkins"—dominated the tumultuous clamors of the city and brought us scraps of news, confirmed by what we saw on the periscope screens. Leduc and his partisans had installed heir general quarters in the steelyards. They held control of the helicopters and the cylinders. The Terromartians had the volvites in their possession and the maki-mokokos had taken

---

[41] This remarkable circumstance is never explained, and the narrator does not find it sufficiently puzzling even to require any hypothetical speculation. We are subsequently informed that the solenoids have been put back into use, apparently functioning quite normally, but no attempt is made to reinstitute the examination program. The reader is free to wonder whether there might, indeed, have been more Terrans hiding among the Terromartians, and whether one of them might have been a more adventurous, enterprising and skillful saboteur than the remarkably passive and not-very-ingenious R'rdô. If so, the poor chap gets no reward at all for providing this invaluable *deus ex machina*.

possession of the explosives and the *cracterite* factory. They were threatening to blow everything up at the first hostile move—to which the shaggies responded that they would not dare, and that they, in their turn, would unleash the Jet of core-iron, which an improvised device would rapidly transform into a flame-lance...

However, neither of these boastful threats was followed through. The Martians, as they had already proved, were fundamentally cowardly, and neither party dared attack, fearful of reprisals. Shaggy-manned helicopters and "pumpkin"-manned volvites circled around, confronting one another incessantly, but it was all limited to salvoes of Homeric insults and blasters brandished at arm's length. In the Camp of the Cylinders, as in the cracterite factory, everyone lounged around filling their bellies, and finished up forgetting civil discord in the delights of idleness.

The sole result of a week of loud-mouthed rioting was, in sum, the stoppage of work on all sites save that of the Tunnel. The planetary perforation continued, obstinately and uninterruptedly, beyond the horizon, hurling into the sky its continuous tornado of volatilized slag, which fell back as black dust upon the surrounding country, now extending as far as Mars Central the kind of funereal shroud once imposed on coal-mining regions.

The hunting volvites similarly continued their customary flights to America, bringing back cargoes of "volunteers" every day, which accumulated in improvised holding-cells until the solenoids were returned to action.

Outside of these scattered activities, however, the strike was general, and if the Aswan accumulators had not been functioning automatically, even the lights would have failed.

The prospect of a battle seemed attractive to me at first. Since my propaganda had not been able to obtain the assent of the shaggies—without whom nothing could be done—and send all the Martians straight to the Sun together, the chance remained of seeing them destroy one another to the last one, thus purging the Earth of its invaders. That means was not repugnant to me. Had I been required to share their fate, I would have sacrificed my life willingly. It did not take me long, however, to understand that Martian cowardice set aside any hope of that sort. On the contrary, the stoppage of work, if it carried on, would become calamitous. If the cylinders were not ready, the Martians would remain on Earth for two more years...

Jupiter's Thunderbolt would surprise them there—but not, perhaps, without sweeping the surface of my unfortunate planet and reducing it, like Mars, to a ball of ash.

I would have been able to order a return to work; the partisans of the Sun, weary of ineffective bravado, would have obeyed me—but, as Leduc, "the Boss" had said, only too accurately, we would not have been able to get past him and his faithful shaggies, who had control not merely of the Cylinders but the power-supply—and they would never consent to an exodus direct to the Sun.

Never mind—I would find another way! For the moment, it was necessary to compromise—so I sent Nazir Bey to Leduc as an ambassador. The latter was not interested. He was too well aware of the strength of his position, and he made inadmissible demands. Out of rancor against the maki-mokokos—his creatures, which had left him for me at the Banquet and whose desertion had secured my success—he did not want to admit them aboard the Cylinders, and insisted as the first condition of peace that they should be abandoned on Earth.

Naturally, I refused. Any weakness on that point would have killed my popularity; I had to conserve that at all costs, for it was my sole safeguard against Leduc, and my very life depended on it.

The negotiations were suspended, but a muted unease was manifest among the popular masses. Both sides were subjected to propaganda, which recruited new adherents to each party—at the other's expense, of course. A baroque dance of change-your-partners took shape: some Terromartians who exposed themselves on the edge of the shaggy camp did not return; on the other hand, numerous shaggies mingled with the crowds on the Esplanade of the Pyramids, and did not take long to join in the solar hymn of the "pumpkins." Some of them even consented to operate the projection apparatus, and the cinema screen on the Monument began to parade the threat of the Jovian preparations before all our eyes again.

A "prodigy" then occurred which influenced opinion in the direction of peace: the Magus of the Shell, whose internal mechanism had not been properly oiled, ceased to direct its mobile arm in accordance with the Sun's apparent course; it stopped one morning, pointed towards the zenith, and all efforts to start it up again were in vain.

Even Leduc pretended to see this incident as an omen predicting catastrophe. He threw in the sponge and, on the morning of the seventh day, sent me a plenipotentiary charged with negotiating the terms of a definitive agreement between the two parties.

At the time, there was no one with me but a deputation of maki-mokokos, which had come to bring me their daily tribute of symbolic pumpkins, and I was hardly reassured when the envoy came in. It was the largest orangutan I had ever seen, at least two meters twenty in height, with jutting canines as long as a finger, and the physiognomy of a perfect brute. Clad only in his russet hide, he swelled up with pride within his aluminum collar—on which I read the serial number W2743—and stopped in front of me, supported by both hands on an enormous cudgel capable of decapitating all my trembling little maki-mokokos with a single circular sweep.

The sight of the horns and magical wings of my ceremonial dress, however, intimidated that Martian soul, and the formidable beast bowed and mumbled when I offered him a cigar. Then, in response to my invitation, he set down his club and took his place in an armchair—where he remained throughout the conference, sniffling with embarrassment and twiddling the thumbs of his feet.

I had prepared my speech. I began with a eulogy to Mechanists, whose constant efforts for the well-being of the colony merited general gratitude. Putting a brake on the solar impatience of my faithful followers and religious friends, I conceded to Leduc a halt on Venus, where his technical talents would have the leisure to exercise themselves in the conquest of that world. That conquest duly completed, everyone would then return to the cylinders, setting a course for Mercury or straight for the Sun, according to the circumstances.

W2743 declared my offer acceptable. There remained the delicate point of establishing whether everyone would be accommodated. Seven days of work lost signified at least 100 cylinders fewer than the anticipations of the plans. I replied, however, tit for tat, with a plan that avoided the difficulty in a manner as simple as it was elegant. A hundred cylinders fewer? No matter; we would make room in the others by leaving out the stocks of food judged necessary. No one would eat during the journey; everyone would sleep. A small proportion of "laughing gas"—nitrous oxide—released into the interior atmosphere of each cylinder by an improvised regulatory device would plunge all its occupants, Terromartians, shaggies and maki-mokokos alike, into a delightful sleep full of paradisal dreams...

This proposition seduced my plenipotentiary right away. He threw away his cigar, clapped his hands, pulled my arm from my sleeve with an ultra-vigorous handshake, and cried: "Agreed!"

And he added, as if it were Leduc himself speaking: "Ah, that'll stir things up a bit!"

The news of these preliminaries spread in a matter of minutes throughout Mars Central. The senior staff came to congratulate me on my moral victory, while the shaggies did the same for Leduc. A general amnesty for all abandonments of posts, depredations and acts of violence committed since the banquet was broadcast by the official loudspeakers, in the midst of unanimous joy. The shaggies de-fortified the Camp of the Cylinders and the helicopter airports; the "pumpkins" ceased mounting guard around the explosive dumps and the cracterite factory. The entire population came together and mingled on the Esplanade to watch the reconciliation of the two enemy leaders—the Boss and the Emperor—which took place on the second terrace of the Monument.

Leduc and I exchange a solemn handshake, while the solar hymn and the shaggy hymn are united in a charivaric cacophony. I meet the hateful stare that the other drills into me during the comedy.

Peace is fixed, to be sure, but warfare continues on the sly between the two of us! You know, Leduc, that I'm a Terran, you told me so, and you're more convinced of it than ever. Nevertheless, as you have no means of proving me guilty, you must keep your mouth shut. I have too many supporters, haven't I? Even the shaggies, now! It's just the two of us, hey? And, as you say: "that'll stir things up a bit."

"And now," Leduc said, over the loudspeaker, as if echoing my thought "everyone back to work!"

The sirens howled. Helicopters and volvites, cars, lorries and pedestrians sped towards the factories and steelyards. At 9 a.m., all the machines of Mars Central were humming at full tilt.

It was the Reincarnation service that had suffered most from the shutdown. A thousand recruits brought by the aerial transports were waiting, packed in special holding-cells, for the solenoids to be reactivated.

Pretending—for the benefit of the senior staff surrounding us—to bow very humbly before My Majesty, Leduc proposed that we start our official tour in the Hall. I consented.

What a sad surprise awaited me there, alas! Five-sixths of the postulants for Martianization were maki-mokokos, plus a few baboons, spider-monkeys and tamarins. This simian swarm filled the atmosphere beneath the glass ceiling with the reek of a badly-maintained menagerie, and I hastened past their ranks in a hurry to be done—but at the very back of the room, in front of the solenoids reserved for Terromartians, I saw some bound prisoners. With a painful presentiment, I headed toward them.

"And these," I asked, faking a detached manner. "Where have they come from?"

The individual in charge—a black gibbon with very long arms—grimaced amiably. "Tahiti, Majesty. Arrived yesterday."

I forced myself to remain impassive under Leduc's intent state. Guided by that name, however, I recognized among the wretched human wrecks heaped up between the barriers the deserters of Mont Blanc, the ex-aviators, Champoreau and Zanzi in particular. The latter was clutching his pet cat, Cognac, in his bound arms; the cat was mewling desperately.

"There you are, riff-raff!" sniggered Leduc. "I told you that I'd get my hands on you again, some day. You've had a lark, have you? Now it's time to stir things up a bit for your roll-call." As I made as if to draw away, he added: "Don't you want to wait a while, R'rdô, to watch these rogues pass through the solenoid?"

All the Martians of whatever sort, from the largest to the smallest, were very fond of such spectacles; my indifference would have attracted awkward comments, if not used against me by Leduc. So I stayed—and, cursing my weakness and evoking new execrations against the Marrtians, I saw each of the twenty-two Terrans buckled into an oblong basket with iron thread—a sort of creel—and submitted to the psychostatic currents. Their martyrdom was brief, though; the operation as quickly completed. Debilitated by long suffering, they put up hardly any resistance. Their human consciousness having faded away, they awoke again as Martians without further ado.

XII. Watch Out For the Bomb!

The telepathic vision of Raymonde, saved from the volcano, was not repeated, but I still had the precious "apport" that she had left me: the beautiful Andean flower with the scarlet petals.

When evening brought me solitude, after the agitation of my official life, and aggravated my crushing sensation of loneliness into the most frightful distress, I took that desiccated relic from my portfolio and extracted from the thought of my beloved the courage to go on living and to carry my superhuman duty through to the end.

I rejoiced in the stroke of luck that had prevented the Last Men from going to Tahiti, in pursuit of their original intention. She and they had thus escaped the frightful finale of the great hunt. I imagined her, in company with Abbé Romeux and the others, hiding on the slopes of the Cordillera, in some secure shelter from which she would not budge until the deliverance. The thought that she might be discovered there by the volvites sometimes threw me into fits of atrocious despair, during which the sight of a Martian face became intolerable to me. I shut myself up in my room, then and closed my door to all visitors, from the innocent and child-like maki-mokokos with their naïve presents of pumpkins to my devoted Nazir Bey—whom I could not forgive for having brought me, by way of consolation, a young and pretty Nubian girl.

In these hours of plenary distress, memories of our shared past reawakened with a tortuous vividness. Our days in Marseilles, in Amiens, at Mont Blanc, then our journey to Cairo, our disincarnation, our reign appeared to me as a paradise, uniformly haloed with the blissful glory of our cloudless union through the worst external catastrophes.

The desire to find my beloved again increased immeasurable, sweeping aside all other considerations, and I conceived the craziest plans to rejoin her, which seemed to me to be as simple and easy as things are in the exaltation of delirium or in opium dreams....to steal a volvite, corrupting its crew, who would follow me blindly, then go to join her and wait with her and the Last Men for the Martians to leave...

Immediately, though, I blushed at my cowardice. I remembered my promises: to save the Earth, to prevent the invasion of Venus. I stiffened my resolve. I climbed back from the depths of the abyss towards lucidity. I instructed myself to be grateful for the knowledge that Raymonde was safe, and rejoiced stoically in her absence, which would permit me to play the great game without any supplementary risk to her.

My first serious attempt to intervene dated from the Banquet. It had turned out that I could not succeed in convincing the mystic folly of all the Martians and sending them straight to the Sun; Leduc had blocked my plan. Very well—bbut he was not invincible. My next strike, better planned, would see to him.

but he was not invincible. My next strike, better planned, would see to him. What difference did it make that he more than suspected my secret Terran identity? It was sufficient that my moral authority over the great majority of the people tied his hands with respect to me. That was a result, and a valuable one.

They days went by, though, and I did not come up with any viable plan. The Cylinders were increasing in number, threatening Venus with invasion; the tunnel was getting deeper, threatening the Earth with destruction!

Destruction! And yet...I had absolute confidence, all too clearly justified by results, in Martian science and industry, but I could not quite persuade myself that the Tunnel-mine would have that frightful efficacy. I summoned my feeble knowledge of algebra and mechanics to my assistance to compare the mass of the Earth with the magnitude of the forces brought into play. Unless one supposed that the cracterite and the endothermic substances of the planetary depths had an inconceivable fracturing force...I doubted it. And when I saw Leduc wild-eyed, trepidant and incoherent, infected by the uncouth soul of Mechanization, I wondered whether that madman might not have overestimated the power of his formulas—I remembered the Tower of Babel—and prayed to God to confound the Titan's sacrilege.

A new manufacturing process had started: that of the penetrative shell designed to puncture the crust left intact at the bottom of the tunnel, thus letting out the central fire. At the same time, the wide-open sluice-gates would release the water from the reservoirs so as to fill the entire volume of the enormous well, transformed into a mine by the mixture and the instantly explosive combination of the two elements of liquid and fire. A spherical shell—a bomb, rather—200 meters in diameter, slightly less than that of the tunnel, to permit the air compressed by its free fall to escape around its perimeter: a bomb filled with the cracterite that was accumulating in silos, constructed in segments, transported one by one to the head of the Tunnel, where their assembly would take place as soon as the desired depth had been reached and the orifice disencumbered.

The drilling work was nearly finished. Thanks to the molecular disintegration process, a continuous progress of 1100 or 1200 meters per hour had been achieved during the last six months.

"Like cutting through butter!" cried Leduc, enthusiastically, as he followed the movement of the needle registering the regular descent of the drill-bit into the interior of the terrestrial mass.

About two cubic kilometers of volatilized slag fell back every day as impalpable dust over the whole of North Africa and the Mediterranean basin. In the immediate vicinity of the well, the fuliginous layer was several meters deep, transforming that part of the Sahara into a land of soot. Special machines were ceaselessly occupied in sweeping the observation-post and the hangars, and keeping the road clear. On several occasions the power-lines broke, as telegraph cables used to do beneath the weight of frost.

285

Out of all the work-sites, this was the one that exercised the greatest attraction on me. As a human, I anticipated apprehensively the day when the roaring whirlwind of microscopic material would cease to spring forth from the well, but the disinterested curiosity of the savant that I had once dreamed of being was stimulated by the idea that it would become possible on that day to descend into and explore the fantastic excavation. I thought about the geological discoveries that might be made there, and it irritated me to see the perfect indifference of the Martians in that regard.

Terrestrial science had, until the end, progressed in constant liaison with industrial applications—hand in hand, so to speak. Roadside ditches, quarries, wells and the galleries of mines had furnished their documents to geological science, whose lofty theories had then been applied to the tracking the course of subterranean seams. On Mars, this stage had been skipped. Mechanization had overtaken science and progressed with giant strides along the path of uniquely practical applications, multiplying creations as enormous and powerful as the "dinosaurs" of the primary epoch, but similarly monstrous and lacking a future. The tunnel's engineers, like everyone else in Mars Central, had never had the slightest desire to study the transected strata by taking samples therefrom. And if they talked about visiting its depths when the perforation was terminated, it was for routine technical reasons, to assure themselves of its verticality, and to see whether the vast hollow pocket encountered five kilometers down—when a serious incident had forced the work to be suspended for three days—presented any risk to the success of the enterprise.

Human explorations of the terrestrial crust had never exceeded a maximum depth of 3000 meters. When the drilling of the Tunnel was halted, it had attained 4000 *kilometers*, and that simple fact was sufficient to overturn all the notions of classical geology. It had been possible, thanks to preliminary soundings, to drill between two "igneous pockets"—the one that supplied steel to the Camp of the Cylinders and another to the west—and to descend almost as far as to make contact with the true nucleus of "central fire." Situated at a depth of 4000 kilometers, this occupied about a third of the terrestrial diameter—which is to say, much less than had been estimated by Terran geologists, who were almost all supporters of a uniform and very extended distribution of high-temperature matter. In addition to that cardinal fact, however—foreseen by a tiny minority of 19th and 20th century savants—what paleontological revelations might the tunnel offer me! The origin of life, perhaps: the hypothetical original beings, of which the poor preservation of "Archean" rocks—gneiss and mica-schists—no longer permitted the identification.

For two days after the conclusive arrest of the tornado, energetic ventilation had partly purified the Tunnel's atmosphere. The buttressed framework designed to suspend the monstrous penetrative shell above the orifice had already been put in place, and I imagined at first that Leduc and I would go down in a skip—but no cable could even sustain its own weight over such a extent, and the exploration had to be undertaken in a helicopter provided with a refrigeration chamber—for the pyrometers measured a temperature of 160 degrees at the bottom of the well.

There were three of us aboard the machine: a single shaggy pilot, myself and my enemy. Throughout the duration of the journey I did not take my finger off the trigger of my blaster, hidden under my cape and pointed at Leduc. One suspicious move, and that would have been the end of him—but he scarcely spared me a thought. The Mechanist ecstasy had gripped him, and he raptly contemplated the absolute verticality of the walls, striped by the illumination of our navigation lights, between which we were descending at a hectic speed, braked from time to time by a few turns of the rotor-blades.

I was bitterly disappointed, for, during these periods of deceleration, I saw that the rim of the formidable tube had been absolutely vitrified by the disintegration process, and that it presented a similar surface everywhere, save for changes of color revealing the layers of slate, basalt, porphyry and granite.

We paused for the first time at five kilometers to inspect the cavern that the Tunnel had encountered on its way. Spared by the vitrification, this lacuna, 100 meters high and not very deep towards the north and east, extended a gulf of darkness southwards and westwards, in which the beams of our searchlights were swallowed up. It was necessary to use the helicopter to explore it.

Suddenly, I had to bite my tongue until it bled in order not to cry out. On the floor of he grotto, harshly lit by the beam of cold light, was a fantastic landscape: an entire forest, complete with leaves; an immobile, petrified forest carried down as a whole into the entrails of the Earth with a "compartment" of former crust, after some cataclysm or other. And between the colorless, quasi-spectral branches, the forms of animals—three males and a female—were grouped around the remains of a fire. Animals? No—humans! Humans of the Tertiary period: the First Men!

"Look at that!" I could not help stammering, gripping Leduc's arm.

"What for? They're made of stone, R'rdô, unusable! Can't you se that?" And, as we finally came to the terminal wall of the cavern, he gave the shaggy an abrupt order to turn back. "A lacuna of no importance," he muttered. "No hindrance to the functioning of the Mine."

The spectral branches of the petrified forest closed upon the vision of the First Men grouped around the First Fire; the helicopter went back to the orifice of the second section of the Tunnel and plunged into it, vertiginously.

A dolorous emotion gripped me. I was no longer looking at anything. I could not tear my thoughts away from that prodigious memory: the distant ancestors of my species, briefly glimpsed, distorted by the hyaline thickness of the cockpit. Me, one of the last humans, confronted by my origin…the entire history of civilization thus reduced to its two extreme terms: anthropopithecoid savages and an heir to the progress won in the course of millennia…equally destined to perish in a few days with the maternal planet. O vanity of vanities…!

"Stop!" Leduc suddenly commanded. He pointed to the needle of a manometer whose progress he had been following with increasing preoccupation. "Eight atmospheres! That's bad. The walls of the cabin are warping. We can't go much further without being crushed flat, as if in a hydraulic press. Damn! I didn't think of that…we'll have to go back up."

That the best technician in Mars Central should overlook such a thing astonished me, but I saw it as a new symptom of the hypnotic reaction that the formidable workings of Martian industry exerted on their creators—as if the unknown forces extracted from matter and reduced to slavery were slyly taking their revenge, or as if the imminence of the exodus had saturated the atmosphere with a ferment of folly.

As soon we returned from that failed exploration, the assembly of the Bomb commenced. The several sections cast in the steelyard and brought to the vicinity of the Tunnel, were bolted together and welded into a whole. When the monstrous sphere was complete, chains with links as large as the body of an ox were passed through its ear-flaps, and it was guided towards the gaping opening.

And there is the bomb in place, ready to be charged. Suspended from the steel frame, it is balanced over the mouth of the tunnel like a monstrous spherical 400 cubic meter aerostat. But it is neither hydrogen nor helium gas that will fill it: it is the terrible cracterite, manufactured during the last six months and accumulated in the nearby silos, into which hundreds of thousands of tons of it have been poured. A suspension bridge, furnished with two railway tracks, has been established between the edge of the gulf and the upper orifice of the Bomb, and over this bridge, at great speed, file small wagons full of explosive, which succeed one another without pause and return empty to collect a new load. Untiringly, the wagons, empty their tons of cracterite into the mouth of the Bomb, to be carried into its depths by a spiral conveyor-belt.

Leduc smiles radiantly. Careless of danger, in the midst of his shaggies—although he has set aside his eternal pipe—he goes from the silos to the Bomb and from the Bomb to the silos along the suspension bridge, gauging the diminution of one and the replenishment of he other. He spends hours inside the Bomb, watching over the accumulation of the redoubtable substance. He invites me to accompany him, and, to prove to him that a Terran is as brave as he is, I accept. A wagon full of cracterite—a soft bed on which we sit in the Turkish fashion—carries us vertiginously over the suspension bridge; we leap on to the platform while out improvised chair turns upside-down and departs towards the silos, and a lift takes us down…

Inside the Bomb: an enormous, prodigious spectacle that no grotto, no "giants' hall," no Kentuckian "Mammoth cave" could ever equal! The beams of searchlights are dazzlingly reflected from the polished concavity of the sphere in which we are lost like ants in a pumpkin. Up above—high above—the orifice opens: an azure eye, into which the wagons, at ten second intervals, pour their tons of cracterite, which is transferred at the bottom of the spiral conveyor-belt, into other small wagons with rubber wheels. The bottom quarter of the sphere is already stuffed, and each new layer of explosive is carefully tamed by the pestles of a gang of shaggies. One might imagine that they were preparing an immense ballroom, with a floor of green cinders.

But what a dance! It would only take one spark...

And the temptation grips me to cause that spark—to strike my new Jean Bart lighter and to plunge its burning wick into the ground on which everyone is walking gingerly, barefoot. It would be instantaneous, without suffering. Poor Raymonde! The Tunnel useless henceforth, the Earth saved—perhaps?

Yes, but the Cylinders? I cannot. My hands are tied. So I come every day with Leduc—between visits to the Cylinders, of which only fifty remain to be completed—and I watch the charging progress stoically, and the filling of these great reservoirs, twice the size of the Pharaohs' ancient Lake Moeris...these reservoirs that will overflow into the Tunnel within ten minutes of their sluice-gates being opened...

The temptation took hold of me again, imperiously—and this time no logical argument militated against it—on the day of the final Banquet. A splendid occasion, not to say unique! The entire population of Mars Central, with the exception of a few shaggies detached to Aswan, Khartoum and Alexandria, and the crews of five or six hunting volvites—400,000 Terromartians and an equal number of maki-mokokos—came together to celebrate the completion of the Tunnel. The Bomb was charged, and primed, the reservoirs full, the apparatus for unlocking and opening the sluice-gates connected to the switches in the Cylinders' control-booth. If I were able to get away from the feast, to fly out there, to close the activating circuit...or, even better, act directly upon the conductive wires from here! It would mean the explosion of the Mine—perhaps the end of the Earth, if the floodgates opened simultaneously and Leduc's calculations were not mistaken—but also the total and definitive annihilation of the vile Martians, before the execution of their monstrous designs on Venus.

That result would be well worth the sacrifice of my life!

Alas, throughout the banquet and throughout the odious orgy that developed from kit consecutively, under the floodlights, until daybreak, the deadly Leduc did not leave my side, and lavished his seemingly-respectful attentions upon me—but what a diabolically ironic gleam there was in his green eye!

The wretch had guessed my intention!

Part Three: The Titans Take Off

I. The Cylinders' Steering-Mechanism

Why didn't I think of that? The Cylinders' steering-mechanism! It's child-ishly simple. It doesn't involve a motor, a brake, a tiller, or any kind of rudder—it's purely a matter of calculation and the exact timing of the departure. I've been racking my brains for ten months, devoting mental energy to the problem that could have been better spent, for instance, on figuring out how to contrive the failure of the Mine. Ten months ago, I had this piece of paper within arm's reach; it passed before my eyes, and I dismissed it as a theoretical calculation in astronomy, of no importance…oh, that habit R'rdô has of never putting titles in his private notes! Just like me, in the old days!

Here it is: using three constants, V being the gravitational attraction of Ve-nus, T the tangential velocity of the Earth at the latitude of Mars Central and Sg the acceleration due to the *solar*, and the variable *t*, which equals *time*, the series of equations is obtainable. Suffice it to say, though, that I have solved the puz-zle, whose decipherment took me long evenings—with not a single alegbra text-book to hand!

The trajectory of the Cylinders, on their departure from Earth, is not solely determined, as I thought at first, by the *solar* whose paradoxical properties made me forget everything else. The also participate in the tangential velocity of the rotation of the Earth, and that impulsion—nearly 400 meters per second at the latitude of Cairo, scarcely diminished by the passage through the atmosphere—will generate a certain angle of deviation. It is a matter of using that deviation, and combining it with the attraction of Venus, so that the Cylinders are captured in passing and land on the planet.

The attraction of Venus can only be effective in opposition to other forces, however, if it is exercised within a certain zone. If Venus is outside that zone when the Cylinders cross its orbit, it will be incapable of counterbalancing the enormous influence of the Sun. And this effective zone is narrow! A few min-utes could make the difference between the projectiles landing on Venus or grazing its atmosphere with too great a velocity and flying straight towards the central Star. The possible time of departure is on the tenth of May—the day after tomorrow—between 11:22 and 11:54 a.m. Any sooner or later, and the Sun is assured….

With what somber joy I completed that analysis! With what heroic intoxi-cation I glimpsed the means of affecting the course of the Cylinders by means of the devices in the control-booth!

290

Whatever the result of my intervention might be, the sacrifice of my life is made, and there is an element of Martian pitilessness in my resolution.

Raymonde? I don't say that I've grown used to her absence. No, I don't proffer that blasphemy. On the contrary, the purest part of her soul lives in me and my idealized memory of happy days—but in confrontation with the grandiose gesture to be accomplished, it is as if my egotistical personality has been resorbed into something vaster, into the consciousness of the Earth; even the joys of love, the highest of individual existence, seem paltry to me, seen from that heroic summit. Have they not been tasted already, in their plenitude? Have we not lived? What would a year, ten years, 20 years more bring to our sublime union? The re-attainment, on a few occasions, of the sublime level that we reached in the fullness of our strength and our trust? From then on…

Thus I exert myself to stoicism; I must harness all the energy of my soul, so that I experience the vibrant tension of the catapult that my will must become at the decisive moment, to project my life into a planetary holocaust.

The sly insinuations of the survival instinct strive in vain to reassure me, to persuade me that I still have a chance, that I can accomplish my duty in full and get out of it…I prefer not to lie to myself.

For certain technical reasons into whose details I have not enquired—difficulties of electrical isolation, I think—Leduc has terminated all the command-wires for the final hour in the control-booth, not in the interior of a cylinder. This does not mean that the operator charged with the maneuver will be condemned to remain on Earth after the departure of the trans-sidereal vehicles and to fall victim to the Tunnel. Once the mechanisms are activated, he will have twenty minutes to get into his cylinder and close the seal, having previously activated—in this order and at the requisite intervals—firstly, the parasol hoods; secondly, the bomb; and thirdly, the sluice-gates.

This supreme function thus involves nothing perilous, in principle—and it is me, the Sovereign Pontiff and Emperor of the Martians, who will be charged with launching my people towards the solar paradise, via Venus. This was officially announced to me today, at noon, at the banquet celebrating the completion of the last cylinder, by a deputation of overseers and shaggies, in the midst of unanimous applause.

Leduc said nothing. He could not protest, the honor being due to me—but all the evidence suggests that he has taken his precautions.

What precautions? If the famous "Terran" is, as I have every reason to believe, more than an improvised and meaningless insult, he must—never having taken notes himself—suppose that I am ignorant of what R'rdô knew. He must therefore presume that I shall trigger the Cylinders at the appointed hour—neither too early nor too late—but that I will deliberately leave the controls for the Bomb and the Tunnel untouched. In consequence, he will have taken care not to separate the one from the others, in order that the catastrophe will unfold automatically.

That seems to me to be the most probable means.

Should I attempt to verify the connections? What good would it do? I am too much the novice in these matters to contend with the tricks of the Technical Director: the control-booth is under observation, I would be seen handling the wires, and Leduc would be alerted...he would the have the material proof that he needs against me.

No. Nothing of that sort. My duty is to die with the Earth—but Venus will be saved.

Adieu, then! Thirty-one hours more!

II. The Penultimate Rotation

I would have liked to collect myself on the morning of the day when, for the last time since its origin, the Earth would execute a complete revolution on its axis. I would have liked to meditate upon the unprecedented adventure that was in preparation, to say farewell to humankind's past and the memories of my ephemeral being, which will be dispersed tomorrow in the gulf of sidereal space...but the means of reflection is lacking, with the tumultuous redoubling of the Martian orgy, which has not ceased all night to unfurl beneath the windows of the Red Palace...

For everything is ready. Since the evening of the day before yesterday. Nothing more to do; everyone is awaiting the departure—and that enforced idleness is becoming more and more irritating, as anxiety and excitement mount. The Monument orchestra—organs and electric brass instruments, noise-makers and sirens—alternates the tunes of "shaggy" and "pumpkin" hymns, whose choruses are repeated by the entire city, and which mingle on the Esplanade with wild dance tunes. The latter lead formidable sarabands, which terminate in confused scuffles in which simian males, pursuing and knocking down females of every sort, are abused in their turn by the Terromartians, amid the unbridled capers and delirious couplings of the maki-mokokos, whose shrill yelping dominates the paroxysms of exclamations emerging from every throat at once.

And the gluttonous revels mingle pell-mell with the dances and the drunken stupors. The refrigerated stores are pillaged and squandered; no one wants to leave anything behind on Mars Central's last day. Because it cannot be carried away, it is being absorbed; they are gorging themselves on foodstuffs. Mountains of fruit cascade underfoot, causing pedestrians to stumble. Whale-meat steaks and the carcasses of elephants are strewn on the pavements, picked to pieces at hazard as appetite allows. Barrels are rolled out, pierced and emptied straight down avid throats. Larger ones are stoved in and individuals bathe in them; maki-mokokos dive in with frog-like plops and drink as they swim, until they finish up floating, dead drunk, their bellies inflated like balloons—whereupon they are immediately ripped by 20 avid paws, thrown out of the vessel and replaced by others...

The chiefs of my general staff, accompanied by Leduc and his foremen, are coming to render me their customary homage. They seem to have departed already. I had almost got used to these hybrid beings, these monsters with foreign souls. I had adapted myself to them—just as they have partly adapted themselves to terrestrial life, subjugated by the influence of the milieu that created the races. At present, though, they are more distant from me and more odious than ever. They are Martians en route to the conquest of the Sun, and first of Venus, of whose devastation they are already dreaming.

Leduc and his foremen, most of all, are yawning, disorientated, as if prey to the stupefying vapors of nitrous oxide—the demoralization of workless technicians, of mechanized souls and brains of steel that no longer have anything to do but wait...

A loud clatter of scrap metal, followed by roars of demonic gaiety, resounds from outside. "Our faithful shaggies are having a good time!" says the Boss, guessing its source. And the north-western periscope screen shows us the tangled wreckage of locomotives and trains on the tracks at Alexandria station, which shaggy railway workers have launched against one another at top speed in order to watch the result.

Here and there, among the enormous rumor of the city, the sounds of broken glass, collapses and explosions are audible, still isolated and modest, but which are charging the atmosphere like a heady whirlwind of destruction. Evidently, all of this could be left as it is, since the Earth itself will be blown up—but no; that mass execution, which they will not witness, cannot satisfy the Martians. It is necessary that they exercise their methodical mania in detail. All this is no longer needed? Then all this must go!

And Leduc and his shaggy-chiefs watch, fascinated, the destructive work that is beginning on every side. They are dreaming of ways to make it technical and industrial, to conduct a general rehearsal of what will happen on Venus, just to pass the time. They cough, and wish to absent themselves, on the pretext of "surveillance." It is with regret that they first accompany me to the Hall of Reincarnation.

For the solenoids are still operating. Thanks to the elimination of the foodstocks, there are more places aboard the Cylinders than are needed and I have made a feigned concession to the charitable maki-mokokos, in order to disembarrass the Earth—in case it might be saved—of the greatest possible proportion of the errant souls that are fouling its atmosphere. For a week, the solenoids have been accepting small animals; it is anticipated that there will be an entire cylinder of rats and guinea-pigs, anesthetized by nitrous oxide and heaped up in regular layers to the thickness of each stage. Around the outskirts of the Hall, and in the Hall itself, there is a seething procession of rodents.

Just as, according to Diodorus, the gods of the Greek Olympus once took refuge in Egypt, fleeing the revolt of the Titans, hiding in the forms of the vilest animals, here, by a singular irony, the Titans are constrained in their turn—and in that same Egypt!—to put on disguises more abject still!

Yes, more abject, for the souls, panicked by the imminence of the exodus, are making frenetic attempts to be reincarnated. No more choice: anything that is alive is acceptable, including spiders, woodlice, millipedes, even flies! Even before the actual decree of tolerance, the attendants in charge of the solenoids were being harassed by an increasing invasion of insects. Now, there are swarms of Diptera buzzing in the Hall. When we leave, a veritable whirlwind of winged gratitude escorts us through the city to reach the Cylinders.

294

A few last helicopters and volvites, bringing back Martians on secondment elsewhere—in Khartoum, Aswan, Alexandria, America and at the Tunnel—are landing on the airfields. The return of these aircraft, whose service is no longer required, provides the shaggy avaiators with the opportunity for a new game. Helicopters and volvites, with no one aboard but with their accelerators full depressed, are launched vertically, their rotor blades whirling and their jets blasting until they are exhausted, forced to execute the most baroque acrobatics before disappearing, finally to crash down beyond the horizon.

They are not alone in the air, however, and other ascensions provoke the loud enthusiasm of the crowd. Like fairground balloons filled with hydrogen, animals—a cow, a hippopotamus, an elephant, several sheep—rise up, stiff-legged, heading straight for the Sun, indefinitely. To our amazement, various other objects begin to take the same route: tables, bottles, an empty pair of trousers, as if yanked from someone's feet...

"Ah, the clever lads!" cried Leduc. "What a good trick!" And he draws us, at the double, through an increasingly dense crowd, to the *solar* factory.

In front of the factory door, 200 or 300 shaggies are shouting and jostling one another around a vat half-full of the heliophilic substance, which is protected from the Sun's rays by a tarpaulin. They are using brushes to smear all the items of furniture and tools that come into their hands, and which other shaggies are hurriedly carrying away into the daylight, where they take flight.

"Boss! Boss!" yelp the improvised removal men. "It'll arrive on Venus, won't it? We'll get it back?"

But Leduc shrugs his shoulders. It's a nice idea to send the "whole bloody shop" by the same route, to conserve it along with the Cylinders, but if they have to recover up there everything that has been fabricated here, it's hardly worth the trouble of changing planets.

"No, shaggies! A clean slate! And everything starts again, at someone else's expense. You wouldn't want..."

Howls of fright, horror and surprise cut short his speech. A few paces away from us, a maki-mokoko, which has insinuated itself into the shaggy ranks and has been unwittingly spattered with *solar* by the dripping brushes, loses its footing, drawn by the luminous attraction.

"Help! Help!" chirps the unfortunate, kicking out, head down, two meters above the ground. Another maki-mokoko bounds forward and clutches its hands, retained in turn by two colleagues clinging to its legs, arms and tail—but the vertical force of the *solar* carries all four of the little animals, linked in a howling cluster, upwards, upwards...

An explosion of Homeric laughter greets their grotesquely desperate gestures, until their final disappearance into he dazzling sunlight—for the Martian is heartless; pity is foreign to his psychology, and the frightful fate of their brothers—asphyxiation, then freezing—evokes no such emotion in the audience.

"Take the Cylinders—it's safer!" Leduc sniggers. And we press on, without his giving a thought to the possibility of confiscating the shaggies' dangerous plaything.

But the squandering of the *cracterite*—several tons of which remain in the factory— calls for a semblance of caution, at least. A ration of 100 grams, with the means of making use of it, will be distributed to persons of good character, so that they might blow up a building or two.

And the explosions multiply, with the noise of falling masonry. Provided that the Cylinders, the Red Palace and the Monument are spared, free license to raze Mars Central to the ground is granted by the Technical Director to the Pilgrims of the Sun. He even encourages them, and equips them. Having arrived at the Well of Core-Iron—or, rather, on the edge of the enormous basin into which it falls back like a fountain of water—we see the shaggy steelworkers striving to capture the incandescent spray in order to transform it into an incendiary sprinkler. Leduc does not hold back, detaching two foremen to organize the work. A platinum tube, detachable extensions, isolating holders…after ten minutes, the apparatus functions as desired, projecting the liquid fire over a radius of 200 meters, at any desired angle. On contact with it, pavements and walls of crystal shatter, metals twist and melt, everything combustible ignites, and the rain of fluid iron, raining down on the smoking debris of the factories it has burned, sprinkles them and encrusts them with a carapace of rapidly-solidified smelter.

On every side, the triumphant clamor of the destructive folly is mingled with explosions and the sounds of collapse. Acrid smoke is billowing, filing the streets through which we beat a retreat to the Red Palace, where we end up taking refuge, while the methodical destruction is completed before our eyes.

The overseers watch sympathetically; Leduc and his foremen, overflowing with enthusiasm, applaud the spectacle…

The pyre of Sardanapalus! The burning of Persepolis by Alexander! The sack of Syracuse or Corinth, of Rome, of 1000 cities! The petrolization of Paris by the Commune! The bombardment and burning of anything at all by anyone at all! The destruction of Mars Central by the Martians! There is the ultimate result of the efforts of intelligence and industry, and of the civilization that hey have engendered!

At 5 p.m., even the Boss admits that it cannot continue and that it is time to pause for consideration. If we stick to the original plan, which was to embark everyone in the Cylinders two hours before departure, a good half of the Martians will remain on Earth, for they will be exhausted by their orgy long before morning and in no state to get out of bed. Where will they sleep, anyway? The phalansteries are no more than smoking ruins or cracterite-blasted debris. The majority of the streets are already impassable.

It is decided that all Terromartians, shaggies and maki-mokokos, without exception, will sleep aboard the Cylinders and not emerge again before the time of departure. As a further safety precaution, the nitrous oxide will be administered immediately.

For the last time, the Monument's sirens raise their familiar voice; the loudspeakers proclaim the final order to gather at the Camp of the Cylinders, where an immediate embarkation will commence…and I declare that latecomers will no longer be accepted after 9 p.m.

In one of the helicopters retained at the Red Palace, the general staff in its entirety is transported to its posts in order to supervise the operations.

Here are the Cylinders—or, rather, the hoods of white canvas protecting their *solar* cladding from the daylight. Ranged twenty abreast, these enormous tent-like entities are lined up in groups of five for kilometers. There are 2000 of them, and I know their capacity well enough to know that the entirety of the crowd that is beginning to arrive in innumerable processions will be accommodated here without difficulty.

Leduc and his shaggy chiefs get busy, regulating the assembly of the crews around the cylinders with the aid of loudspeakers. Everyone has been given an order number in advance, and a general rehearsal two days ago ensured the exactitude and precision of the maneuvers. In the glare of the floodlights, which light up in the dusk, Terromartians, shaggies and maki-mokokos—plus the last-minute reincarnates: rats, guinea-pigs and swarms of buzzing insects and scuttling spiders—gradually resolve their confusion and take their designated places…

Then comes the roll-call of identification-numbers by the crew-commanders and the rallying of stragglers by the sirens—and, as they disappear into the tents, the hurrying footsteps of the Pilgrims of the Sun begin to resound on the metal staircases of Cylinders.

For a full half-hour that dull rumble resonates incessantly, like subterranean thunder. It is succeeded by the clicking of steel—that's the covers of the "man-holes" closing and being solidly bolted into their impermeable mountings…

In the interior of each cylinder, the nitrous oxide gas is released and plunges to Martian into a blissful sleep, from which they will not wake up until they each Venus—they believe…

Only one cylinder is still open and free of occupants: that of the general staff. Indeed, Leduc and his three habitual acolytes, my overseers and I, are spending the night of Earth. Tomorrow morning, the rest will embark in their turn, except for me; I shall remain until the last moment to trigger the fatal mechanisms.

And, from the helicopter that takes us to the Red Palace, I direct a long look at the control-booth in which, tomorrow, the fate of two planets will be settled.

III. Go!

Leaning on the balcony of my apartment, I look out, alone before the starry night that is no longer veiled by the odious glare of Martian floodlights. Vast silence. Down there, behind Mars Central in ruins, the 2000 Cylinders are asleep under their hoods. No other sound than the distant call of a hyena or a jackal and, from time to time, the coarse snoring of Leduc or someone else, audible through an open window on the next floor down.

Bathed by the mildness of the Egyptian air, I contemplate the night—the Last Night! Tomorrow, the Tunnel and the Bomb, which are awaiting the spark of ignition, will have done their work, and it will all be over! In the roll-call of the worlds, which is deploying the jewels of its constellations before my eyes, the Earth will be absent.

The Earth subtracted...astronomers, revising the map of the Heavens, will notice that a star, formerly of the first magnitude, has totally disappeared, borne away by some mysterious catastrophe. Ah! If all the worlds in the Universe were moved to pity by the fate of the Earth! If infinity were to mourn the loss of the annihilated planet! But how many of our celestial brothers will do it the honor of wondering what has become of it?

The Earth...one of the smallest planets in the Solar System. It shines, blue and resplendent, in the sky of Mercury and Venus; it is visible from Mars; it is seen from Jupiter as a morning and evening star; but it is scarcely distinguishable from Saturn, lost in the Sun's glare as Mercury is for us, not a man in 1000 ever having seen it in his life. And beyond Saturn, from Uranus, Neptune and the Transneptunian planet—the Earth is invisible! Non-existent! Non-existent for the rest of the infinite Universe! Already, for the millions of planets gravitating around the innumerable suns of the Galaxy, and all the other galaxies in space, the Earth might as well not exist, and its disappearance will pass unperceived....

So what?

For the last time in my terrestrial life, I contemplate the starry night; I expand my mind: I embrace sidereal space—and a sublime pride brings me upright, thinking: "Man is naught but a reed, but he is a thinking reed..." And I substitute Pascal's text with this paraphrase: *The entire Universe may unite to destroy me, but I know it, and I contain the Universe!*

A sovereign peace, as vast as the Heavens with which I am communing, into which I am already plunged by my eternal thought, no more and no less than I shall be tomorrow—only my ephemeral existence, my avatar in this temporary body, with its joys and its sorrows, will vanish without return...

And almost unconsciously, my hand slowly takes out the Andean flower, the flower with scarlet petals...and I think of my beloved, over there, on the otherEarth, which separates us...and, on a sublime impulse, I give thanks to the death that will reunite us. Stronger than death, love will fuse our souls together, for ever this time, amid the ruins of the world!

I contemplate the night. Fortified against petty individual cares, my soul allows itself to be invaded by vast dreams, by grandiose scenes that resuscitate for me the destiny of the Earth. In the same way that a drowning man sees all his life flash before him in a few seconds, the Earth's past unfolds panoramically before me: I incarnate the supreme consciousness of the planet that is to die.

I see the Earth's entire past again...

First awakening to existence, an isolated vortex of cosmic matter drawn from the originating Sun—and gyrating in its orbit, in the estate of the minuscule Sun, for myriads of centuries. Then, in contact with the cold of Space, the surface gradually losing its heat, condensing the vaporized metals in formidable igneous floods which sketch out a pasty pellicle—a crust on which the waters rain down in their turn, in boiling oceans. In the bosom of primary seas, battered by storms, the rudimentary life of amorphous cells is born—aggregating little by little into complex creatures, rough-hewing flora and fauna: polyps, trilobites, ganoid fish. On the emerging continents, still hot, in the opaque steam-room vapor that the wan eye of an enormous Sun can scarcely penetrate, giant lycopods, calamites, Sigillaria, cycads and arborescent ferns emerge. In the marshy deltas of rivers their trunks pile up, preparing future coal-seams, in which spiders, myriapods and fantastic crustaceans are fossilized, and dragonflies with the wingspan of a crow...

And the centuries fly by; and on the beds of the seas, the future continents accumulate, a few millimeters per year, their layers of microscopic shellfish and madrepores...and here's the Secondary period: ammonites as large as chariot wheels, giant reptiles—brontosaurs, iguanodons, plesiosaurs, ichthyosaurs and the monstrous diplodocus, and the pterodactyls inaugurating the conquest of the air for the future birds. And the flora matures, flowers bloom, and the mammals of the Tertiary dethrone the reptiles: here is the paleotherium, the dinotherium, the machairodont, and the mastodons and mammoths—the mammals, extending their sequence as far as its coronation: Man, animal and naked at his emergence, but, Prometheus having stolen the sacred fire of Intelligence and universal Spirit distributed through Nature....

And civilizations are born, and evolve, from the humble nomad tribes of the Stone Age; fire is discovered, bronze, iron...and here is History: battles, heroism, ignominy, sainthood, science, ignorance, folly, wisdom; empire rise, crumble, replace one another: Chaldea, Babylon, Assyria, Egypt, Greece...and Rome, opening to a conquered world the hope of a peaceful evolution; and Christianity, undermining the gods of Olympus; and the inundation of Barbarism—the Middle Ages, the Eastern empire, the Arabs, and the West recovering the lost Tradition: Italy, France, Spain, England, Germany...and the Reformation; the 18th century, the new spirit of Revolution...the 19th and the 20th: Science triumphant, Industry progressing with giant strides, at an ever-accelerating, vertiginous pace—every advance of Intelligence monopolized by the Instincts and put in the service of Darkness—until the advent of interplanetary communication and the Catastrophe...

What would have happened, though, if Man had remained master of his planet? If he had followed the course of his evolution, free of Martian invaders? Would he have ended up by casting off atavistic retentions, to elevate himself to a state of superhumanity, more intelligent than instinctive? Or was he, having reached the terminus of his destiny, condemned to perish in one fashion or another, like any over-specialized species?

Old Homer's "rosy-fingered dawn" is, however, parting the veils of the night. The stars are dissolving in the expanding radiance of the Egyptian azure. In the east, Venus, a celestial diamond twinkling in the gathering light, is drowned by the fires of the Sun, rising—for the last time—on the Earth.

"Out of bed in there—get a move on!" Leduc shouts, jovially, knocking on the doors of the chiefs.

And the Red Palace fills with the sounds of brutal laughter; overseers and shaggies move from one room to another and, carried through the open windows, their voices echo in the distance on the Esplanade.

"A nice day for a trip!" jokes one.

"What about him—is he staying behind? Why aren't we taking him with us?" inquires Nazir Bey, pointing to the Magus of the Shell on top of the Monument, who is still broken down, his finger pointing to the zenith.

"The shell might come in handy, at any rate!"

"Forget these old things," Leduc puts in. "We'll do better on Venus!"

But this good humor is not sustained. The copious breakfast that they extract from cans of preserves and wash down with a flood of champagne weighs the Martians down. From 9 p.m. on, they talk about going to the Cylinders to cool down, for the heat is increasing here, and the distribution of refrigerant liquid has stopped since the destruction of the factory.

For his part, Leduc is afraid of missing the hour of departure; he consults his chronometer every few minutes.

I am on tenterhooks; what if they linger until the last minute, wanting to watch the manipulation of the switches? But I hide my impatience.

At 9:20 p.m., they decide.

"I could gladly go to sleep," declares Nazir Bey.

"With nitrous oxide," stresses another.

"That would be great!" hazards a third.

"Since there's nothing more to do here..." The Technical Director concludes.

During the entire flight aboard the helicopter, though, I feel his gaze weighing, intolerably upon the back of my neck.

I accompany them as far as the gangway that leads to the cylinder's "man-hole." One after the other, they bow to me and disappear into the gaping orifice.

"Pat attention, eh, R'rdô!" says Leduc, the last to remain. "No slip-up in the operation! See you later!"

He disappears in his turn, but without my hearing his footsteps on the iron staircase. He's probably watching me from a distance....

With an affected insouciance, I emerge from under the hood—which is reminiscent of a fairground circus—and head for the control-booth without looking back.

It is a small glass shelter, as big as an eel-fisher's hut, to the north-east of the plain of the Cylinders, overlooking the immense camp and the multitude of hoods shading the *solarized* domes. But I don't linger over that all-too-familiar spectacle. Here, inside, is the control-panel, which will only be used once: a thick crystal plate in which the switches are embedded. There are three of them. The one on the left—number three—delivers current to the dynamos activating the sluice-gates. The middle one—number two—lights the fuse that will pre-cipitate the Bomb. The one on the right—number one—simultaneously snatches away the tarpaulins and sets the Cylinders in flight.

My resolution is unbreakable. In five minutes—not in two hours, as would be required to send the cylinders to Venus—I shall close switch number one. If, however, I can avoid that activation bringing the two others into play....

And I examine the network of wires that is interwoven behind the control-panel, trying to trace the connections...

A slight scrape of a shoe on the doorstep...

I turn round...

Leduc!

He does not say anything. He comes towards me, a diabolical fixed smile on his lips. The barrel of his blaster protrudes from the pocket in which his right hand is buried.

"Ha ha! Are we taking a little lesson in applied electricity, R'rdô?"

But I don't wait for the murderous gesture that will inevitably follow this sarcastic remark. I have already leapt forward, a fraction of a second ahead of him. I have grabbed his throat in both hands, while my left leg squeezes his right side and paralyzes his hand. His recoil movement makes me lose my balance; I drag him down with me—with him underneath, fortunately. And I squeeze that throat, squeeze it frenetically; the larynx cracks in my clenched fingers. The nails of his left hand dig into my wrist. My leg is trapped underneath him, and I feel him spring back like an elastic mattress. He launches kicks in every direc-tion, and drags me little by little...towards the control panel!

Taking advantage of the fact that I have momentarily turned my head, he bites my ear. His teeth dig in. I struggle; I increase the force of my strangling grip. He lets go with a stifled roar. But I hear—horror!—the click of a switch depressed by his heel! Which one? My strength increases in my fists; in a sud-

301

den rage, I close my jaws on his nose, which happens to be within range, and I hold on hard with my teeth and my fists, indefinitely—with a mad desire to know which switch...

His groans grow feebler; his fingernails relax; the muscles of his body soften; one more twitch, a death-rattle...

It's over. His face scarlet, his eyes bulging, his tongue protruding and black, his limbs limp, he is no longer moving. He's dead. No matter; I take the blaster from his pocket and discharge it at his skull, which explodes with an atrocious odor of burned meat...

The control-panel! The Bomb switch is untouched! It's the one operating the sluice-gates that Leduc had activated! They're not closed. And, trembling with a hope that I am powerless to stem, I drive home the switch operating the hoods with all my strength. 9:45 p.m.! More than an hour and a half too soon! The Sun is a certainty!

By way of reaction, a nervous weakness overtakes me. I totter, dizzily, and am forced to lie down on the floor for a few minutes, side by side with the corpse, my head hidden in my folded arm, breathless, shaken by brief spasms that resemble sobs.

Blood runs freely from my torn ear and my lacerated wrist. Little by little, the buzzing of my arteries eases. I get hold of myself again on hearing a sound—the electric ventilator? Some clockwork mechanism?—which is coming from under the opaline floor-tiles. What is it? Oh yes, the delay-mechanism...the hoods...the sluice-gates...

I get up. I make an effort to disengage the contacts of switch number three. In vain-the current is already flowing. I abandon it. I'm afraid of activating number two. There's nothing more for me to do but wait.

Invaded by an icy cold, despite the stuffiness of this hothouse, irradiated by a Sun more than half-way to its zenith, I wait, I wait....

Distraught, I watch the white army of tents lineup indefinitely beneath the blue sky, in the ochreous frame of the naked desert.

Suddenly, the powerful throbbing of dynamos fills the Camp, and with a flapping of canvas like the unleashing of a great salvo of gunfire, with a dry clicking of metallic armatures, all together, the 2000 white hoods of the Camp of the Titans open up, falling to the ground—and like some magic trick, the 2000 visible nose-cones, fabulous sugar-loaves each painted "cadmium orange"—the propulsive bed of *solar*—and each surrounded by its sparkling bed of reflective mirrors...

I throw myself outside.

A vibration begins, a sonorous snore, as if an enormous organ were beginning to play a wild and prodigious tune, *crescendo* and *rinforzando*—the *solar* motivated by contact with the light. The Cylinders shudder, shiver, rise up from their holes simultaneously, exposing their entire height—a titanic array of blue-and-yellow skittles—and, suspended, freed from weight, leave the ground, climb, accelerate, on a note that is increasingly powerful and sharp, intolerable—a concert of 100,000 locomotives—and fly away, sparkling bolides amid the azure, in chorus….a tightly-knit swarm of glittering insects…finally to disappear, resorbed into the dazzling sunlight.

IV. The Night of Satan

The only movement I made in the course of the following two hours was to withdraw into the shadow of the control-booth. I waited, running my gaze over the empty mirror-sided ditches, and searching the sky instinctively for the Cylinders, as if they might return. Around me, an infinite silence. In the control-booth, flies were buzzing around the corpse. And I waited, my stomach churning with an animal anguish, waited for he explosion of the Bomb and the Tunnel— the annihilation of the Earth...

But the mechanisms had been stopped, their role accomplished: hoods removed, sluice-gates opened. That was all. The Bomb remained suspended above the flooded Tunnel, intact. A frightful threat for the future...

The future was a matter of indifference to me, though. While the understanding grew, little by little, that I was safe, the agonizing construction in my gut eased, and I was able to reflect.

The Martians gone, en route to the Sun; Venus saved; the Earth saved—I had yet to understand it fully; I did not feel any joy in the unexpected success, surpassing all my hopes. An enormous lassitude and an incomprehensible discouragement were weighing me down, at the idea that I was the only living human being on this side of the globe. To rejoin my beloved, out there, almost at the Antipodes, seemed to me to be a task beyond my compass...and the future of humankind to reorganize!

That crisis of mortal fatigue and fearful solitude revealed a part of my personality of which I had succeeded in remaining ignorant until then. I plunged into the secret abysses of my consciousness with horrified curiosity...

The Martians! Their collective atmosphere, coarse and odious, to which I had grown accustomed, was lacking! Something in me almost regretted not having gone with them. A sort of occult *martianization*, acquired by osmosis, had bound me to them! I regretted being, by definition, their enemy, instead of participating frankly in their power. Ah! Why was it that duty had force me to oppose their projects, to send them directly to the Sun, to obliterate the entire future of their civilization? It differed from terrestrial civilization? Even so, they too incarnated the universal Spirit! The esoteric ideal of their Magi was worth as much as the most noble thoughts of humankind! And as for the aspirations of the masses, the "well-being" pursued by us was clearly inferior to Martian "salvation"—and even to the frenzy for Mechanization, mad but disinterested!

With a burst of contrived laughter, I brought the examination of my conscience to an abrupt halt. Come on! I must be going mad, indulging myself in tranquil philosophizing when the situation required all my mental and physical energy—all that remained to me, after the exhausting emotions of recent days. A fit of nervous fatigue: nothing astonishing in being a little delirious.

Let's see—what is to be done? Depart for America? Yes, that's understood. But the Bomb? Is it solidly set in place above its hole? Shouldn't it be checked first? With due precautions, I ought to be able to cut the wires of the detonator, to take out the cartridge that threatens the security of the site. There would be nothing more to dread for the future of the Earth and humankind than the slow and gradual corrosion of rust…and by then, perhaps the cracterite will have been subject to the molecular disintegration common to all the unstable explosive derivatives of nitrogen. Or, better still, if all goes well, if the Last Men can reorganize themselves, the Bomb will have been disarmed and its charge rendered harmless.

The general staff's helicopter is here, on the Cylinders' airfield, 100 paces from the control-booth. The tanks are full. I know how to fly it. En route!

The familiar journey over the melancholy desert sparsely strewn with thorny bushes—cacti, aloes, nopals, Indian figs—seems inordinately long this time, for I have always undertaken it in a volvite. The Sun is brushing the horizon in front of me; this formidable day is about to end when I catch sight of the Tunnel. The immense reservoirs to the north, at the limit of vision, are empty; a miry crust of salt covers their bed. In the middle of the amphitheater of vitrified dunes, the Bomb, suspended from its double scaffold of steel, hangs over a circular lake 250 meters in diameter, whose waters are rippling placidly in a southern breeze, the wavelets tinted blood-red by the sunset.

Hovering, I hesitate to set down. An obscure fear holds me back, as if the danger were worse here, close to the center of the explosion—which would, however, destroy the whole Earth, if Leduc's calculations are correct.

I overcome this instinctive weakness. I get down on to the airfield, beside the observation-post.

Despite the falling dusk, the gusts of the sirocco render the atmosphere stifling. My muscles are tense, as if stretched to breaking-point, and my brain is seething. I sit down on the spot where I disembarked, on sand as warm as a beast's belly.

Beneath the darkening sky, etched in black upon the last glimmers of daylight, the enormous metal balloon attracts my gaze obsessively. What have I come to do here? I no longer know. A sticky torpor—which is not sleep—paralyzes my thoughts, grips me in a sort of lucid somnambulism. A world of ideas and memories stirs within me, but below the threshold of my consciousness; I only perceive them mentally as if, so to speak, from the corner of my eye. What monopolizes my attention is the prodigious convexity of that shiny globe, as stout as a telescopic planet—over which the Moon, which is rising behind me, imposes a hypnotic touch of light…

Suddenly, my hair stands on end. Leduc! Back there, in the Control-Booth of the Cylinders! What if he were not dead? What if he recovered consciousness? What if the supreme convulsion of his limbs were to strike the switch?

With a weary effort, I dispel the crazy imagination. He is definitely dead: his tongue is hanging out upon his beard, black and dribbling, and bluebottles are buzzing in his mouth.

But what about wild animals? If a jackal, for example, or a hyena got into the control-booth, and put its paw...

An icy chill, like the other, grips my guts. My throat is contracted, my respiration stertorous, my skull empty—and a sharp pain radiates around the back of my neck, as if someone has driven a nail into it.

A tragic atmosphere of imminent catastrophe. Ah! Who is that in front of me? The Magus? Egregore XIII? Those are certainly his pupils, vertical, like a cat's, but his phosphorescent horns are curved backwards, he is naked and hairy, and he is slowly stroking his thighs with his long monkey-tail...and his feet— goat's hooves! It's Satan! The classical Satan of witches and the Sabbat! But the longer I look at him, the more his features are modified, like "melting views," and I recognize, successively, Leduc, Schlemihl, Landru, Nazir Bey, all the Terromartians, one after the other, and the shaggies, and the maki-mokokos...

And while I attempt, distractedly, to seize these fugitive resemblances, to stop them in their flight, as if my life depended on it—they multiply and change. It is an accelerated exfoliation of 1000 superimposed masks. The voice of Satan-Fregoli [42] ridicules me, shriller than the cry of a seagull.

"Ha ha! You want to save humankind, little man, to contrive a philanthropy? Just a minute! I let you act with regard to the Cylinders, which will procure me a nice collection of souls, roasted to a turn—but that's enough. Parenthetically, I admire your ingenuity. Let's see—you seriously believe that your planet will profit greatly from having been delivered form the Martians, as you put it, in order that it can continue to waltz around its orbit, still carting around the animated mildew that you call civilized humanity? But you wretched little fellows have no need of Martians to devour one another—you carry that in yourselves. You're worse than Martians in the way you treat one another. *Homo homini Martianus!* [43] One knows one's classics! And it's unnecessary to add that the Martian in everyone is me. I pull the strings, and you dance, little chaps. There's not one of your inventions that I don't know how to use for he good

---

[42] Leopoldo Fregoli (1867-1936) was an Italian actor with a remarkable talent for mimicry and self-transformation, who became the archetypal "quick-change artist," touring Europe and America to show off his amazing versatility. Although Varlet could not have known it, Fregoli would later give his name to a "Fregoli delusion" identified by psychiatrists. Sufferers from the delusion become convinced that several different people are really a single individual, who keeps changing appearance; it is associated with paranoid feelings of persecution; this episode might qualify as the ultimate example of it.

[43] Satan is here adapting an aphorism from Plautus' *Asinaria, "Homo homini lupus,"* which suggests that man is a wolf to other men.

cause of your fraternity, my charming Cains! Not one! The most moral, the most sacred, those which you judge the most appropriate to safeguard peace and order on your mud-pill. Religion, damn it, the cult of the Other, of my successful colleague—God, to let the name slip—I've been able to make the prettiest pretext for squabbling...think of all the little chaps that other little chaps have killed, in the name of their God! From the gentle Hebrews running their sword-blades through all the enemies of Jehovah to the most modern battles, in which each side claims the All-Highest for itself, by way of the persecutions, crusades, inquisitions, terrors and religious wars of cults of every sort...God's will! Ha ha ha! Do you think so? It's ME who wills it! And you all march, all together, with such joy, dear little insects, Cains!"

As he spoke, my sinister interlocutor seemed to inflate, to grow. He looked down on me, his threatening form looming over me, and I was obliged to tilt my head back to see his face, with its inexhaustibly renewed features, standing out, lit by the Moon, against the convexity of the Bomb. My eyes were riveted to his, and in the bewilderment of my empty brain, his words awoke mighty echoes.

He continued: "But I'm straying from the point. I'm rambling. Every day, I become a little bit more aware of growing old. Let's get back to your plan to prevent this cracterite bonbon from going off. I'll tell you quite frankly that you can't, that you shouldn't, that you won't do anything at all...on the contrary!

"Does that astonish you? I'll explain.

"You must know that the totality of existing things is formed by the combinations of a number of atoms, which is very large, but limited—if not, everything would be full, wouldn't it? Now time, intrinsically, is not limited. It is infinite in both directions, past as well as future. Thus, the combinations of atoms that result in the present state of the universe have already had the time to repeat themselves and reproduce themselves, in exactly the same fashion. Everything has already existed in its present form; the same events have already taken place, in the same order.

"This series of identical repetitions is what one little chap, 24 centuries ago, called, in Greek, the Eternal Return...

"If I remind you of these notions of elementary philosophy, it's not to make a show of erudition; it's to come to this: that you, little chap, have already been in a situation *identical* to the present one, and that *you have already carried out the actions that you will inevitably carry out again.*

"You are sometimes astonished that certain little chaps are capable of predicting the future? Nothing more simple, every future also being the past: a past that, in return for a few formalities of red ink and parchment—a fountain-pen and vulgar paper, not even watermarked, is adequate nowadays—I shall be pleased to reveal to you...

"This is what you did...the other time—it was a few billion centuries ago. Listen carefully:

"When you found yourself, as now, in the presence of the Bomb, you understood how vain it would be to rejoin your colleagues on the other side of the world, to reorganize with them a civilization that would be perfectly derisory, since it would be beset by the continual apprehension that the suspended Bomb, after a few years, would annihilate it by virtue of its fall and subsequent explosion. You judged these efforts superfluous, for you as for the others, and you preferred to finish it immediately.

"How? That's child's play.

"See those two wires coming out of the observation-post and leading to the detonator on the scaffold. It's enough to scrape the insulation from each wire and bring the denuded portions into contact with one another. The current from the accumulators will flow immediately, causing a spark in the detonator, which will ignite the explosive, which will break the scaffold, which will release the Bomb—which will explode, and so on…

"Yes, that's what you did, what you *must* do, what you *will* do, little chap…

"Give me your hands; I'll guide them."

Then, fascinated by the eyes of the Satan-Fregoli, which were sparkling in a face as broad as the Bomb, towards which my eyes were raised, with my head tilted back, as if I were floating in an ocean of infernal ecstasy, agonized by horror, I submitted to the inevitable necessity. My will no longer existed. Drawn by an external and all-powerful force, my hands accomplished the actions indicated.

A spark sprang from the wires. I saw a luminous puff of smoke on the left arm of the scaffold, which broke off with a dry explosion…

In the place of the vanished Satan, I saw the Bomb detach itself and plunge into the water with a cataclysmic splash, which momentarily gave the Tunnel, in the moonlight, the appearance of a fantastic crystalline lace collar…abruptly overflowing as the monstrous balloon immediately sank. In a flash, I imagined its mad descent and the shock of the annihilating impact at the bottom.

A circular jet leapt up from the well: a foamy surge that reached me, bowled me over and carried me away, suffocating and blinded, in its tumultuous turbulence, all the way to the top of the vitrified dunes—where I lost consciousness.

V. The Hope of Humankind

When I came to, it was broad daylight. I was lying on my left side, and the Sun was roasting my wounded ear painfully. Two words were dancing in my clouded head like a chorus: "Little chaps...Little chaps..." And I suddenly remembered: the night, the sirocco, the fantastic apparition of Satan-Fregoli, his speech, my fatal action...

I opened my eyes with a start of alarm.

In the middle of the artificial lake, a metal convexity, the summit of a submerged dome, was bobbing on the glistening surface: the Bomb! It had not exploded, nor even reached the bottom of the shaft. Placidly buoyed up, it was floating, sustained by its charge of cracterite, less dense than water!

A great blast of hope, like the sounding of a clarion call, went through me and brought me to my feet. It was over, this time. Nothing more to dread for the Earth. The explosion of the bomb, if it were to happen some day, would only damage the top of the tunnel and its surroundings, a corner of Africa, even—but the rest of the world was safe.

My adventure left me with a considerable feeling of humiliation, though. Had I really seen Satan? Had the spirit of Evil become incarnate once more before me, as the anthropomorphic and theriomorphic gods once had in Classical times? But it was strongly reminiscent of a crisis of madness, especially if it really had been me who triggered the Bomb's fall!

Without daring to verify the condition of the conductive wires, I clung to the more reassuring hypothesis that the mechanism had been activated automatically, after a long delay, and that I had had a dream.[44]

At any rate, I was free of the spell by means of which the memory of the Martians had held me captive. My brain had recovered its lucidity and its vigor. With a shrug of the shoulders I rejected the poisoned sophistry that the Evil One had released into me. The idea of the suspended Bomb and the final annihilation of the Earth would have haunted the minds of men and paralyzed their efforts of

---

[44] The reader will doubtless realise, although the narrator does not, that there is a more likely hypothesis. The Martianized Leduc was most certainly killed in the control-booth, but that does not mean, given the story's central assumptions, that he was then impotent. His disincarnate spirit would surely have attempted to take advantage of the narrator's exhaustion and near-delirium to influence his subsequent actions vengefully. The face that "Satan" originally wore, as the process of hectic dissimulation began, was, of course, Leduc's, and the reader will recall that the spirit in question, when previously disincarnate, began to affect the behaviour of the real Sylvain Leduc some time before taking conclusive possession of his body.

recivilization? Not at all! They would have got used to it and would soon have given it no further thought. Does the certainty of death, inevitable for everyone, prevent one from living? History is there to show us that civilizations are equally ephemeral, but that each of them exerts itself nevertheless to make progress towards the apogee of perfection that does not long precede decadence and death.

While reasoning thus, I headed for the helicopter, which the nocturnal surge had lifted from the airfield and carried to the top of the dunes—without serious damage, fortunately. Darting a last glance toward the head of the Tunnel, I set a course for Alexandria, where I counted on finding fuel and food in the Martian establishments that the shaggies had not thought of destroying before going back to Mars Central.

To rejoin my beloved, to find the colony of the Last Men—that was, indeed, the idea blossoming within me, since I had overcome the quasi-delirious crisis of nervous exhaustion. Raymonde, my friends from Mont Blanc... I visualized them, hiding in some Andean crevasse, watching the sky in fear of volvites. I imagined their anxious anticipation, and their joy when they saw my liberating helicopter hovering above them. How would they know it was me, though? I had to make a flag.

I made one as soon as I arrived in Alexandria, with strips of blue, white and red cloth, which I stitched together unskillfully: the old flag of France would preside over the new destiny of the Earth.

As I had anticipated, the warehouses were intact, and I was able to replenish my food supplies, not without having to fight a veritable battle with blaster shots against the wild dogs and jackals that had already invaded them.

An hour later, with the food-stores well stocked and the tanks full, I took off again, determined to cross the distance that separated me from Quito in a single stage. Ten thousand kilometers, at a speed of 250 kph an hour, if all went well, would be a matter of 40 hours...

At high altitude, at top speed. The yellow desert, and yet more desert, speckled with rare green oases; to the north the distant crests of the Atlas Mountains. The noise of the machine kept me company; by their regularity, the throb of the turbines and rotor-blades, shearing the layers of air, hold my attention in the breathing-spaces between maneuvers. I forgot he absolute solitude of the world.

The Sun went down, directly in front of me, over the sea, as I passed the breakers of the African coast.

Then came the twilight, and the night; the Moon rose, filling the sky with its serenity, frosting the waves with silver gleams. Favored by an east wind, the helicopter makes progress with admirable regularity. An occasional glance at the compass and the altimeter, a twitch of the thumb on the levers—I had abundant leisure to take a light snack, and to indulge myself, during the hours of that nocturnal flight, in long reveries, lost between the majestic serenity of the ocean and that of the somber azure, its stars rarefied by the moonlight.

The next day's journey was more taxing. Easy as it was to maneuver the helicopter in the fine weather, it exacted a nervous tension, exhausting at length. The uninterrupted circle of the marine horizon exercised a dolorous fascination upon me. I ended up falling into a sort of somnambulistic daze, punctuated by total "absences," from which I awoke once or twice a few meters above the waves. I resigned myself, therefore, to landing that evening on the coast of Venezuela, in order to grant myself a little sleep.

It was impossible for me to sleep, though; in spite of the searchlights and navigation-lights, a horde of wild beasts besieged me with a concert of howls. At midnight, I judged that I was sufficiently rested to go on, by moonlight.

In truth, I don't know what prodigy effected my crossing of the South American continent; the 12 hours that went by before I arrived in sight of he Cordillera were, for me, more like the memory of a dream than an actual journey. I recall, to begin with, the somber procession of the equatorial jungle, cut here and there by pale and gleaming rivers, but after that, nothing but the sensation of trying to stay awake at the controls...then the snows of Chimborazo and Cotopaxi, shining against the sky...a detour northwards...and I started as if in response to an electric shock, and released a delirious cry of joy, when I discovered—overlooking the flat roofs, monuments and gardens of deserted Quito—a flag fluttering on the cupola of the observatory: the same French colors that I had deployed at the rear of he helicopter.

I sounded the siren as I descended. Some twenty people were moving on the ground, raising their arms; the sound of their voices reached me...

Eyes obscured by emotion, I set down. The cockpit door opened...and I found myself being hugged to Raymonde's bosom, covered in kisses, assailed by the anxious questions of the Last Men, who were pressing around us, with Abbé Romeux and Nibot at their head.

I had to tell the story of the Martians' departure—the reasons I had for believing that the Cylinders were on their way to the Sun and that the Earth was permanently liberated. I abstained, however, from making any mention of the Tunnel and the Bomb. There would be time, later, to open up to the Abbé and make my confession regarding my disturbing Satanic encounter.

The news of the Martian exodus was welcomed with all the joy imaginable. It was, however, not unexpected; if I found my friends in Quito, it was thanks to the suspicion of it that they had for a week. After their escape from the crater, in fact, they had hidden in a ravine on the north flank of Cotopaxi, whose eruption was limited to a placid lava-flow. Their supplies of the Nutriment had permitted them to spend several months there without venturing out and running the risk of being spotted by the daily volvites and helicopters. One day, they had stopped seeing them. The proximity of the Jovian opposition, and what they knew of the Martians' projects, led them suppose that the latter had quit the

Earth, and they had been sufficiently emboldened to go to Quito, there to install themselves in the buildings of the Observatory, to the great satisfaction of the Abbé.

That evening, while the Last Men were celebrating, now without constraint, in the open air on the illuminated terrace, their certain and conclusive deliverance, I wandered through the gardens embalmed with tropical perfumes with my sweet Raymonde leaning tenderly on my shoulder. I took the Andean flower from my portfolio, and presented it to her without saying anything. She released a cry of astonishment, for she had picked it after the flight from the crater, before falling asleep, exhausted but thinking about me. And it was marvelously heart-warming for both of us, when I told her about my vision, to understand the extent to which our union was perfect and intimate, since it had somehow transcended the distance! But the anguish and sadness of the separation had made us pay too dear for that proof, of which our true love had no need. Whatever happened now, we hoped with all our hearts never to be separated again and to confront the future that awaited us with the Last Men together.

What will that future hold? What role will Mechanization play in the new civilization that will emanate from our little group? Surely less than before the Martian catastrophe. It has shown us the dangers of excessive industrialism too clearly for us not to guarantee our children a future by a return to the simplicity of nature. In any case, even though we have had to abandon the entire apparatus of mechanization, one precious conquest remains to us: the formula for the Jovian Nutriment, which will remove the necessity of fighting against animal instincts.

Where shall we establish our colony, the future center of human expansion? Here or in Europe? The youngest and most adventurous among us are allowing themselves to be seduced by the beauty of the tropical sky, but the majority—which includes me, Raymonde and the Abbé—tend towards the second hypothesis. The charms of the gardens of Quito cannot make us forget the country of our birth. There is fine weather there too…

The Martians? We have just had news of them…for the last time. This morning—the 28th day after their departure—the Abbé, as is his habit, was making an observation of the Sun with the large telescope when he suddenly saw an exceedingly brilliant "flare" light up, in the very center of a sunspot: a phenomenon contrary to all the laws of astrophysics, and of which the only possible explanation is the arrival of an enormous bolide, or a group of bolides, in the inferior layers of the photosphere. The flare only lasted for a few seconds, but the Abbé remains convinced, as we all do, that he has just witnessed the sudden and simultaneous volatilization of 2000 Cylinders, with their cargo of Terromartians, shaggies and maki-mokokos, who have finally reached the destination of their pilgrimage: the solar paradise!

THE END

BLACK COAT PRESS

FICTION
Marcel Allain & Pierre Souvestre. *The Daughter of Fantômas*
Anicet-Bourgeois. *Rocambole*
Guy d'Armen. *Doc Ardan: The City of Gold and Lepers*
Aloysius Bertrand. *Gaspard de la Nuit*
Alexandre Bisson & Guillaume Livet. *Nick Carter vs. Fantômas*
Lucien Dabril. *Rocambole*
Victor Darlay & Henry de Gorsse. *Lupin vs. Holmes: The Stage Play*
C.I. Defontenay. *Star (Psi Cassiopeia)*
Charles Derennes: *The People of the Pole*
Alexandre Dumas. *The Return of Lord Ruthven*
Jean-Claude Dunyach. *The Night Orchid: Conan Doyle in Toulouse*
Paul Féval. *Anne of the Isles*
Paul Féval. *The Blackcoats: The Invisible Weapon*
Paul Féval. *The Blackcoats: The Parisian Jungle*
Paul Féval. *The Blackcoats: 'Salem Street*
Paul Féval. *Captain Phantom*
Paul Féval. *Gentlemen of the Night*
Paul Féval. *John Devil*
Paul Féval. *Knightshade*
Paul Féval. *Revenants*
Paul Féval. *Vampire City*
Paul Féval. *The Vampire Countess*
Paul Féval. *The Wandering Jew's Daughter*
Paul Féval, *fils*. *Felifax, The Tiger-Man*
Arnould Galopin. *Doctor Omega*
Victor Hugo, Paul Foucher & Paul Meurice. *The Hunchback of Notre-Dame*
Jean de La Hire. *The Nyctalope vs. Lucifer*
Jean de La Hire. *The Nyctalope on Mars*
Maurice Leblanc. *Lupin vs. Holmes: The Hollow Needle*
Maurice Leblanc. *Lupin vs. Holmes: The Blonde Phantom*
Gustave Le Rouge. *The Vampires of Mars*
Gaston Leroux. *The Phantom of the Opera*
Jean-Marc Lofficier. *The Katrina Protocol*
Jean-Marc & Randy Lofficier. *Edgar Allan Poe on Mars*
Jean-Marc & Randy Lofficier. *Robonocchio* (English-French / -Spanish)
J.-M. & R. Lofficier (eds.). *Tales of the Shadowmen 1: The Modern Babylon*
J.-M. & R. Lofficier (eds.). *Tales of the Shadowmen 2: Gentlemen of the Night*
J.-M. & R. Lofficier (eds.). *Tales of the Shadowmen 3: Danse Macabre*
J.-M. & R. Lofficier (eds.). *Tales of the Shadowmen 4: Lords of Terror*

Xavier Mauméjean. *The League of Heroes*
Frank J. Morlock. *Sherlock Holmes: The Grand Horizontals*
Charles Nodier. *Lord Ruthven the Vampire*
Charles Nodier, Antoine Beraud & Jean Toussaint Merle. *Frankenstein*
Henri de Parville. *An Inhabitant of Planet Mars*
John William Polidori. *Lord Ruthven the Vampire*
Pierre-Alexis Ponson du Terrail. *The Vampire and the Devil's Son*
Eugène Scribe. *Lord Ruthven the Vampire*
Brian Stableford. *The New Faust at the Tragicomique*
Brian Stableford. *The Stones of Camelot*
Brian Stableford. *The Wayward Muse*
Brian Stableford (ed.). *News from the Moon*
Villiers de l'Isle-Adam. *The Scaffold*
Villiers de l'Isle-Adam. *The Vampire Soul*
Philippe Ward. *Artahe: The Legacy of Jules de Grandin*
David White: *Fantômas in America*

NON FICTION
Stephen R. Bissette. *Blur I*
Stephen R. Bissette. *Green Mountain Cinema I*
J.-M. & R. Lofficier. *Shadowmen: Heroes and Villains of French Pulp Fiction*
J.-M. & R. Lofficier. *Shadowmen 2: Heroes and Villains of French Comics*
Randy Lofficier. *Over Here: An American Expat in the South of France*

SCRIPT LIBRARY
Mike Baron. *The Iron Triangle*
Emma Bull & Will Shetterly. *Nightspeeder*
Emma Bull & Will Shetterly. *War for the Oaks*
Gerry Conway & Roy Thomas. *Doc Dynamo*
Steve Englehart. *Majorca*
James Hudnall. *The Devastator*
Jean-Marc & Randy Lofficier. *Royal Flush*
Jean-Marc & Randy Lofficier & Marc Agapit. *Despair*
Andrew Paquette. *Peripheral Vision*
Roy Thomas, Janis Hendler & L. Sprague de Camp. *Rivers of Time*

www.ingramcontent.com/pod-product-compliance
Lightning Source LLC
Chambersburg PA
CBHW030341020726
47493CB00003B/629